PENGUIN

A GIRL AND

Usha K.R. has been writing fiction for _____ , beginning
with short fiction. Her short story 'Se_____ won the Katha
Award for short fiction in 1995. *Sojo___* , her first novel, was
published in 1998 and the second, *The Chosen,* in 2003. *A Girl and
a River* is her third novel. Usha lives and works in Bangalore.

PRAISE FOR THE AUTHOR

'What compels you to turn the pages is a fine eye for detail'—*The
Hindu*

'Usha K.R. is a miniaturist, and she shares the miniaturist's fierce
love of technical virtuosity and minute attention to detail'—*Indian
Review of Books*

'Usha's writing is intelligent—it is vigilant, prepared to defend the
story's flow . . . keeping in mind that the reader has certain rights
here too'—*Deccan Herald*

A Girl and a River

USHA K.R.

PENGUIN BOOKS

PENGUIN BOOKS

USA | Canada | UK | Ireland | Australia
New Zealand | India | South Africa | China

Penguin Books is part of the Penguin Random House group of companies
whose addresses can be found at global.penguinrandomhouse.com

Published by Penguin Random House India Pvt. Ltd
7th Floor, Infinity Tower C, DLF Cyber City,
Gurgaon 122 002, Haryana, India

Penguin
Random House
India

First published by Penguin Books India 2007

Copyright © K.R. Usha 2007

All rights reserved

10 9 8 7 6 5 4 3

This is a work of fiction. Names, characters, places and incidents are either the
product of the author's imagination or are used fictitiously, and any resemblance
to any actual person, living or dead, events or locales is entirely coincidental.

ISBN 9780143101239

Typeset in Sabon by InoSoft Systems, Noida
Printed at Repro Knowledgecast Limited, India

This book is sold subject to the condition that it shall not, by way of trade
or otherwise, be lent, resold, hired out, or otherwise circulated without the
publisher's prior consent in any form of binding or cover other than that in
which it is published and without a similar condition including this condition
being imposed on the subsequent purchaser.

www.penguin.co.in

In memory of my grandmother, S.R. Puttathayi

A PENGUIN BOOK

Part I
Distant Thunder

one

———

1987

We are driving down National Highway 4, my father and I, on the road that leads from Bangalore to Poona. But Poona is not our destination. We don't have to go that far. My father is not driving. We have hired a taxi, a trusty diesel Ambassador. My mother is not with us but there is nothing unusual about that; over the years, hers is an absence I have got used to.

We have cleared the city and have entered the suburbs. We are driving through Peenya Industrial Estate, home of motor winding works and credit cooperative banks. My father's factory which manufactures radiator caps for cars is here somewhere. This is the kind of place, I would imagine, where it is always noon and the sun relentless, where the roads are a pool of tar and the trees give no shade. Even as we escape the bounds of Sisyphean small-scale industry, we drive, quite incongruously, into the smell of fresh baking. It is the Mangharam biscuit factory—I think briefly of the pink wafers of my childhood, wrapped in waxy white corrugated paper, gifts from the infrequent visitors to my home—but soon the road reverts to the reassurance of petrol fumes.

As we travel on it, the highway acquires a Jekyll and Hyde predictability—shanties of shops and slush alternate with clean green space. The names of the towns and villages we go past tell of probable histories and lost geographies—some echo gods and kings and mythical beasts and some more banally, the district commissioners who had saved the village from the plague or built a dam; some are named after trees—now no longer there, streams—long dead, or hills—flattened for their granite; some fall musically upon the ear while others are descriptively matter-of-fact—my father's own cut-and-dry, two-syllabled town took its name from a fragrant backyard herb. But right now, for our beleaguered taxi, the towns and villages are bottlenecks on the highway, clusters of mechanic shops and tea-and-cigarette stalls and trucks parked too close to the road.

From time to time we come upon a stretch where the road seems to be holding on to a fast-fading memory of itself. Green fields stretch out on either side, their bounds marked by massive, knotted trees whose branches arch overhead, filtering the sky, harking back to the pre-reflector days, when the faded red-and-white stripes on the tree trunks were the only indicators the highway motorist had in the dark to mark the verge of the road. A train hoots and rattles in the distance and sends up a puff of smoke that uncurls in the sky; it suggests faraway lands and unknown destinations. There is not another human being in sight, except the moustachioed and turbaned man on the lone cement structure sheltering the tube well, his steady eyes affirming the miraculous powers of urea or phosphate.

'When did you come on this road last?' I ask my father. It's the first thing I've said to him since we left home.

He turns to me, startled. 'Oh! Long back. . .I've forgotten . . .several years possibly. . .I came last when there was a court case about the disputed land. . .'

I remember that. He lost the case.

We are going to a town about a hundred kilometres away, a small town where my father was born and where he grew up, to take a look at his ancestral home before it is demolished. I haven't seen the house before, and I know only as much of it and of his life as he lets slip now and then. My father isn't one for memories. I believe it is a healthy sign.

We have been talking about this trip for years, but this time

A Girl and a River

I booked the taxi and presented him with a fait accompli. Anything that varies from his routine is considered an unwelcome intrusion that he just waits to put off. It is not the onset of age; he has always been like that. I have lost count of the number of picnics we had planned when I was a child— the lunch all but packed into hampers and the newspapers that we were to spread on the grass all gathered—and had not gone on because my father would lose his mood that morning. Ours was a household regulated by the clock. Mealtimes were like running to catch an express train that stopped for just two minutes at the station.

At some propitious time, when his defences are down or when he is not so preoccupied, I have to tell my father that I will not be coming home again. I have applied for a post-doctoral research position in the university from where I graduated and from where I stand a very good chance of being accepted. I have also asked to be the citizen of my new home, the United States of America.

I doze off and wake up to the blast of an air horn. I have slept for almost an hour.

'This is it,' my father says.

We are in a crowded street. There are shops on both sides with railings on the footpath to hem the crowds in. A temple escapes on my right, its gopura crowded with brightly coloured humans and rakshasas and animals, ferocious enough to spring off the statuary—their beauty has always eluded me. But nothing can deter the cinema halls on my left, three in a row, their florid architecture outdone by the large pink-and-blue posters announcing the film, and cut outs of the film stars garlanded in faded marigolds.

My father sits back, stunned and then springs up in his seat.

'All this. . .all this,' he waves an agitated hand at the cut outs and cinema halls, 'used to be church property. It's all gone now. The Christians, they've betrayed this town'.

I hold myself in check. I've promised myself there will be no fights on this trip. After all it might be my last one.

I must remember my father belongs to a generation that expects a certain sense of morality, of honour, of nobility, of better behaviour from the Christians by virtue of their association with the British (my father even thinks Churchill is the greatest writer of English prose!). But not from the Americans; no, not them. They are the ones who bombed Hiroshima and Nagasaki.

So I just say mildly, 'They've done no worse than the others. Everybody is selling off their land these days.'

And while we are still bemused by the looming cut outs, somewhere on the opposite pavement the footwear and textiles part and we have left the road behind. We drive through an imposing gateway with no gates, on to a stretch of stony mud track, and when the track leads no further, we stop. The hum of the running engine fills the car.

There is nothing there, nothing but a looming emptiness, a huge hole in the air where the house should have been. The plinth is marked clearly in white with deep brown scars where the walls once stood. The driver switches off the engine, as if marking respect for the dead.

My father gets out of the car, stumbling over the stones, and I let him go alone. All that is left of the grand, beautiful, doomed house are the two magnificent trees by the crumbling compound wall, lush green matrons quietly savouring the memory of their fecundity, now that the flowering season is past. The copper pod is burnished against the sky and many monsoons must have watered the generous canopy of the rain tree.

'Krishnaiah Shetty had promised to wait for a bit before bringing it down. . .his family owes so much to us. . .' my father appeals.

But I cannot help him. The only responses I have are contrary. Once you sell your property, you lose all claims over it. Promises that are not on paper need not be honoured. He possibly still thinks of himself as a local grandee or a zamindar come home after long, to visit his dependants, and to find that the upstarts have gotten above themselves. I wish my mother was here. She would have matched his distress with the right noises, for she is a good wife who reflects all her husband's moods. (I have had to employ the most literary of retrieval devices to deal with her. The thought of it still makes me blush.)

I walk across the meaningless plinth tentatively. The house does not seem as large as I had imagined it to be. I stoop to pick up what looks like a tile made of mud with a rude floral design stamped on it. It does not tell me anything. Neither does the empty space. As with everything else I suppose I must return empty-handed.

'Which was your room?' I ask him, and then more boldly, 'And hers, which was hers?'

He turns round and stares at me. 'Room! What room?' he snorts. It is just not my day. 'We had no rooms, we didn't even have beds of our own. We just spread mattresses on the floor in the hall and slept on them.'

'Let's go!' he says abruptly, striding towards the car.

It was a mistake to have come, I can hear him think. It is best to let sleeping dogs lie.

He loosens his collar and inserts his folded handkerchief between the collar and the back of his neck and fans himself with his fingers. He shifts in his seat and flinches as the car hits a rut in the road. I look at his rheumy eyes, at the milky polyps glistening in their corners. I remind myself that he is sixty years old and that he has not worn particularly well.

At one time I carried a live coal in my heart. Now it has almost returned to normal, my heart that is—a muscle that receives impure blood and pumps it out pure. The years apart, the distance and a new life have taught me acceptance, if not understanding. The edge, the sharpness of immediacy is gone; the vinegar has receded from my tongue. I am ready to speculate on his compulsions, to look at things his way but I cannot undo what they have made of me. I cannot go back and smoothen out the wrinkled brow of my childhood. This is the first lap of my three-month stay and already I am irritated by the old unchanging things, fretting to get away. I would rather be elsewhere, getting on with my life and leave them to theirs. But there are things I must settle, gaps I must fill. Both for their sake and mine.

A Girl and a River

two

1933

It was eleven in the morning and she was not at school. Her brother, however, was. If this was not enough to induce that body-less feeling, that mildly euphoric state of disorientation, it must have been the heat. April *was* the hottest month and the town was situated on a flat, unrelieved plain. No hills or hillocks, no streams or rivulets, the soil a crumbly red. Once the natural ponds and lakes go, this town will be shut down, her mother said grimly each summer. The verandah where she stood was deep and safe, she knew, but one could well roast an urad dal papad on the bottom-most step where the awning of the portico ended.

Beyond the yellow blaze of the copper pod and the soporific hood of the rain tree was the road that ran all the way to the port of Honnavar; the road on which, if R.L. Stevenson and Shivarama Karanth were to be believed, she could 'run away to sea'. And on the other side of the highway to Honnavar lay the restful, tree-filled compound of the Methodist Mission. The only 'building' in evidence there, directly opposite, was a small white shed, which carried no legend but had a bird etched in blue on its cement head. Its closed shutter had tantalized her as long as she could remember. She had caught the shop open now for the first time and its magic was revealed to be just stacks of eggs on a counter and a bored-looking man in a white bush shirt fanning himself with a newspaper. To think that this was the source of her winter torments, the dreaded egg flip her mother made her drink in the morning because she was too thin. Past the egg shop, somewhere within the recesses of the vast garden was the carpentry workshop which had supplied all the furniture in their house, where her brother spent many an hour watching Mr Alpine examine each plank of wood for the perfection of its grains to fashion the massive rosewood dining table which was to be shipped in six parts to Buckingham Palace.

When the townspeople walked on the footpath in front of the gate, she imagined that they slowed down to tell themselves that this was the house of K. Mylaraiah, one of the most prominent lawyers in town, owner of lands, municipal councillor, sure to be nominated to the maharaja's legislative council, and in the reverential hush that followed they craned their necks, no doubt, to take a better look at the imposing house and the impeccable garden.

Behind her, the house stretched, a cool shell, thrumming to the beats of a long-practised routine. The comforting drone from her father's office told her that he had not yet left for the courts and his industrious clerk, Balarama, tuft protruding from his black cap, was still scratching away with his ferocious nib. If asked what lay in the sheaves of paper, wrapped in canvas across their midriff, neatly stacked on shelves with notations in an impeccable hand, she would say in her father's tone of conviction—British jurisprudence, the backbone of our legal system (despite what Gandhi says).

As soon as you entered the office what you first saw, was a cast-in-silver Ganda Bherunda with real rubies for eyes, displayed prominently in a locked glass case. The mythical twin-faced bird, held up by two elephants on either side, was the symbol of the state of Mysore and the ruling Wodeyars. This particularly fine handcrafted specimen had been presented to Mylaraiah in recognition of his services to the state. The district commissioner himself had come home to present the bird and drape a silken shawl round his shoulders, for however much he respected the maharaja, Mylaraiah would not go to the royal durbar and present himself as a supplicant.

Beyond the large hall with the veiny black floor and the high roof supported by wooden beams, where they rolled out their mattresses to sleep at night, the house hived off into two around the open courtyard. When it rained, it was difficult to get from the front of the house to the back through the courtyard. If you put your mind to it, it provided easy access to thieves, but thankfully nobody did.

On one side of the courtyard was the morning room, where her mother worked, where the light was the brightest and where the terracotta tiles crunched underfoot, however softly you trod. If she strained her ears she could hear the rattle of the charkha and the gentler wheeze of the takli—it was almost a religious duty with her grandmother and mother to spin their quota of thread on the wheel every morning, and send it at the end of the week to the Khadi Bhandar.

The living rooms were on the opposite side of the courtyard, all in a row. You walked past them and climbed down three steps from a low doorway to enter the coffee room. The morning's first cup of coffee or cocoa was to be had here. If the house had a lodestone, it was this room, to which all people gravitated naturally, whether it was coffee time or not, like water finding its level. Strangely, few entered the coffee room from the courtyard, preferring to enter from the living room, despite being knocked on the head by the inexplicable projection in the doorframe, and those who had grown into adulthood in the house were known to duck instinctively at doorways.

The territory beyond the coffee room was of little concern to Kaveri—the precincts of cooks and servants and the women of the household. Here were the kitchen and the puja room and an assortment of rooms to house the produce from her father's plentiful lands, which rolled in every few months in bullock carts. Even the coconuts had a room to themselves, where birds nested in the eaves; her brother had brought down a sparrow with his catapult once and the cook had never let him forget it, assuring him he would be reborn in a lowly hunting tribe in his next life.

Beyond the house proper were the cow sheds and the toilets and the acre of garden for coconut and mango trees and a small patch of corn, which fed the cows. Kaveri's grandmother usually pottered around this part of the house, when she was not shooting off letters to newspapers about cows. Bhagiratamma's fierce love of cows was not the only reason she hung around there. It was Kaveri who had made the connection and told her father about it and he had broken an important taboo by building a toilet inside the house, next to the living rooms, so that his mother-in-law would not be confined to the back quarters of the house.

She felt her toes grow warm and moist, and looked down.

'Zip,' she prodded him gently, 'Oi Zip, come let's walk to the gate to see if the tonga is coming. . .' But Zip wouldn't even twitch his whiskers at her.

She put on her shoes and started up the cobbled pathway by herself, squinting into the yellow haze. The day seemed to have completely forgotten that it had begun as a cool morning, that it had smelt not of the crisp dry lash of heat but of the soggy wetness of the just-washed stone steps and the elusive sap of the black seed pods of the rain tree, which her brother had bashed into a 'cork ball' on the verandah. She walked up to the gate and looked out, careful not to rest her chin on the bar. It was so hot that she could hear her bobbed hair singing about her ears and her legs, she was sure, were cooking under her long skirt. There was no one on the stone-metalled road other than a bullock cart at the far end. To her left stretched the road to Bellary, which was not her concern and to her right lay her school, the library, the cinema, the ice cream shop and Honnavar—all that mattered.

She felt a twinge in her left foot, bound in a length of mul from her mother's old sari—the result of an unusually energetic tussle with her brother that had earned her this holiday from school. Moreover, it had yielded an unexpected bonus. She would be the first to meet her uncle, her mother's cousin, who was promised that afternoon. As sure as the heat, summer brought its flow of visitors—cousins, aunts, uncles and assorted relatives. There would be picnics in mango orchards, by wayside streams; sitting on strange grass and eating off banana leaves. There would be pink ice candy from Glory Das's shop in a thermos flask. Her mother would take time off from her 'good works' and come out with them, her father too would sit with them and talk late into the night.

But right now Kaveri waited for her mother's cousin Shivaswamy, the superintending vet of the state stud farm and remount stables, whose voluminous coat pockets could yield anything from a cricket bat to a long playing record. When others visited, they brought with them merely the dust of their towns but Shivaswamy, he carried a prickling of daring and the whiff of experience beyond her imagination and her books. Both Kaveri and her brother Setu liked Shivaswamy, though they were aware that their father treated him with a certain amount of circumspection.

As for Setu, she had got even with him for drawing a moustache and fangs on her favourite calendar beauty. She had been diabolical, really. She had simply tweaked each 'va' into a 'pa' in his laboriously written composition, so that every 'kavi' read 'kapi'. Her brother's teacher, C.G.K. Sir, indulgent though he was in other ways, would simply not tolerate disrespect to hallowed cultural icons, and instead of 'the poet says' when he would read 'the monkey says', Setu would get it. She waited in sweet anticipation.

Setu set off that morning, frowning a little, wondering whether Chapdi Kal would be there and was relieved to find him swinging on the gate as usual, waiting for him. That was the pattern with Setu—easy anxiety and quick relief, and a perpetual doubting of certainties. Chapdi Kal had never disappointed him. He was there each morning by the time Setu came out, swinging the hinges off the gate undeterred by Timrayee's threats. Once he was leaning casually against the wall with a slender loris clinging to his neck—he had gone to the forest that morning to get it, he said, and now it would not let him go. As always, Setu felt a quick, keen surge of pride when he saw his friend. As rough hewn as his name, which meant 'stone slab' (it was only the school register that perversely identified him as Gangadharappa), he stood unshod and uncombed, his khaki shorts falling over his pitted knees. He was perhaps the only boy in school who had been kept back for three successive years in middle school, but one who would never submit to the humiliation of being escorted to school by a servant. Unlike his sister who had beaten Timrayee into staying a few paces behind her while she walked like a queen in front, Setu had to suffer his insolence; Timrayee insisted on holding his hand.

But once they crossed the main road and the band of the khaki clad began to swell, Timrayee was shaken off. A slight detour brought them into Electric Colony and a cluster of shops. At Anwar's, the straggling group came to order instinctively. Anwar's was perhaps the only one of its kind in the world—a cycle-repair-cum-sweetmeat shop. While no one could vouch for the cycles he repaired, Anwar was the undisputed king of komberghat. There was a quick counting of money, the clink of coins changing hands—sometimes, if they were short, the nearest head would get a clip on the ear—and each boy came away with a rustle of paper. A single komberghat—a sticky lemon-sized ball of jaggery and desiccated coconut—costing one paisa, could comfortably wad a boy's mouth for the whole morning and trickle slowly down his throat, and no one would be the wiser. If ever the authorities of the Government Boys' School had wondered about the exemplary ruliness of their pupils in the pre-lunch session, they would never attribute it to Anwar's komberghat. Anwar was not just a name, he was real flesh and blood. Once a year he moulted from his grease-stained shirt and became a tiger. He then led the Moharram procession, his bare torso ash'd and striped, his face hidden in a ferocious mask, dancing to the particularly disembowelling throb of the drum, as the procession made its way round the market square to cries of 'Ya Hasan! Ba Hussein!'

A darshan of the gods is a good way to begin the day. And if you can spot two in the space of five minutes, you can well believe that the world is an illusion. Even the prospect of school can sit on you as lightly as the body sits on the soul. Sometimes if the timing was right, they saw the Venkateshwara Company bus. A bus on the road was a rare sight, for there were only three in the whole town, and if they were lucky they could catch the bus going to Bellary in the morning. But there was more to it than the bus itself. And that morning, as they walked back from Electric Colony to the main road, thoughtful and silent—the daily komberghat ritual being more akin to pressing a bit of prasada reverentially to your eyes before putting it in your mouth rather than something as gross as 'eating'—and stood on the kerb, the large green Venkateshwara Company bus made its ponderous way down the road, its newly-washed windows dazzling in the sun. Sitting at the wheel ramrod straight, in dark glasses and pith hat, was the man who guided the destinies of many; the man who drove sixty five miles down the hot road into the wilderness.

'It's no joke, driving that heavy bus. First to Koratagere, then Madhugiri, Pavagada, Anantapur and finally to Bellary,' the seasoned Chapdi Kal had informed them. Setu, who had been to Bangalore just once as a baby, had felt the weight of his inexperience.

'His name,' Setu had imparted to his sister as a favour, 'is Jambaiah.' And she for once had said nothing but gazed respectfully after the bus.

They turned the corner and the moment of reckoning came—school was sighted. The day lapsed into another school day. They scuffed their way through 'Kayo Shri Gowri', the morning prayer and hoped that there would be something to mark the day, at least a tumbled inkpot. One didn't count the canings of course, for immediately after the prayer three boys, Chapdi Kal among them, were caned by the games teacher, this time for having bullied the district commissioner's son. With the district commissioner's son, their classmate, their relationship was on even keel—he was used to being teased and so long as they didn't touch him he kept quiet—he knew the hazards of being the son of the top government official in town and he also knew how to get even with the louts. Their real quarrel lay with the games teacher who was zealous in ingratiating himself with the 'authorities' in the hope of nebulous favours. The boys generally did not dislike any teacher on a permanent basis—their enmities were usually sharp and short-lived and rarely lingered longer than the sting of the cane, but with K.T. Sir, it was different. However, they had their own way of getting back at him. K.T. Sir had a secret, which he thought was well-guarded. K.T. Sir was afflicted with temperamental bowels and often the call came when he was on his way to school. Fortunately for him he lived near the lake, but unfortunately he'd find that just as he had finished washing, a stone would come skimming the surface of the water dunking once, twice and even thrice before falling with a mighty splash just *next* to him, wetting his dhoti completely.

'I'll see you at school, bastards!' he'd rise pendulously, shaking his fist at the shore.

And as he was fastidious, he'd go home and bathe once again, and come late to school.

The one teacher who roused grudging respect and managed to get anything across to his students was C.G.K. Sir. No one knew his real name; for generations of students he remained Chikka-Gidda-Kulla Sir, an appellation quite suited to his short and squat frame, if a little overwrought. C.G.K. Sir did not carry a cane, nor did he raise his voice. He taught Kannada and History and was never known to carry a text book to class; he knew the Kannada text by heart and as for History, he *acted* the lessons out. He was particularly good at battles and beheadings—the English uncharacteristically cutting off Charles's head, Marie Antoinette on the tumbrel, her golden locks being fingered with satisfaction as her head was tossed like a melon by the Parisian crowd, and Tsar Nicholas and his children being hunted down in their own palace. The distance from the door to the blackboard acquired the bleakness of the Russian winter through which Napoleon had retreated, one hand behind his back and the other inserted into the front of his coat, his head bowed against the icy wind—C.G.K. Sir's students often emerged from his classes as dazed as they did after two hours in the make-believe world of Shri Krishna cinema.

Causally, C.G.K. Sir tossed out bits of historical gossip. Cromwell's great grandson had come to India and become the governor of Bengal and that Sir Walter Scott's son—yes, the same Sir Walter Scott who had written *Ivanhoe*, the tenth standard text—had been a soldier in the East India Company and was buried in a churchyard in Bangalore. But when it came to the history of his own land, the state of Mysore, C.G.K. Sir became subdued and resorted to plain speaking. Histrionics required a certain amount of detachment, of disassociation from your subject matter. He found it difficult to romance something so close home. Sometimes he lapsed into silence and stared out of the window, as if what he saw was not the the broad sweep of the playground fringed by the magnificent ficus, the paddy field-edged highway leading to Koratagere, then Madhugiri, Pavagada, Anantapur and finally to Bellary, but the paradox of a drought-prone, famine-ridden land of rivers; a princely state within British India that still paid twelve lakh rupees every year as salt tax to the 'paramount power'. So much so that he often forgot that he was a government servant and was paid a salary directly from the maharaja's coffers.

They had a Kannada class with C.G.K. Sir after lunch, but that day just as he reached the door of their classroom, the peon came up to him and whispered in his ear, and C.G.K. Sir threw a rueful look at the district commissioner's son and went away.

'Ey Mukunda!' Chapdi Kal called out to the district commissioner's son, 'did you carry tales home about C.G.K. Sir as usual?'

Mukunda shook his head slightly from side to side, as if he were shivering, and tried to draw his neck into his shoulders. 'If you dare lay a finger on me. . .' he challenged shrilly.

'I wouldn't sully my hands!' Chapdi Kal drawled and Setu and the others sniggered.

Sometimes C.G.K. Sir brought the newspaper to class and read out snippets of news. The previous day, he had brought a whole sheaf of crudely printed pages to class, and read out a high-sounding, lengthy piece. It had ended with an innocuous reference to the maharaja distributing rock sugar to the people of Mysore, after which C.G.K. Sir had folded the pages deliberately and said, 'Of course, one cannot force comparisons between an English Charles or a French Louis XVI with our rulers, the House of the Wodeyars, our own Krishnarajendra. We are a model state and our kings are well loved. Moreover, we aren't even sovereign in the true sense of the word. Our state is a gift from the British. . ."His Highness" says proudly that he is part of the Imperial 26th British Cavalry, as his father was before him.'

C.G.K. Sir's views were common knowledge. Everyone knew that his sympathies lay not just with the Congress, but he was something much worse, he was a *Communist*—his house even had Russian books. It was said that he wrote trenchant articles criticizing the government in the newspapers under a pseudonym. So long as he did not air his views in school before his students, the authorities could ignore his political predilections, which were mere rumours as far as they were concerned. But once in a way C.G.K. Sir would get carried away and what with Mukunda in their class and his elder brother in the tenth, his 'incendiary' views would reach the ears of the district commissioner, and he was 'warned' from time to time by the authorities. Besides, criticism of the British they could be indulgent about, but when he targeted the maharaja, they had to be more vigilant.

The previous morning, C.G.K. Sir's manner had been deceptive enough and the class had not understood most of what he had read but Mukunda's eyes had narrowed purposefully behind his spectacles and despite Chapdi Kal's threats, the summons to C.G.K. Sir followed the very next day. Perhaps it was a sign of the watchfulness of the times or the attempts of the maharaja's government to intercept even the mild breeze of change that had reached this sleepy quarter of the state. In the post-lunch period of that uneventful day, when not even an inkpot had tumbled, C.G.K. Sir went off with the peon without entering the class, leaving the boys forlorn. Setu was lucky because the bomb ticking inside his satchel, his Kannada composition with all the va's changed into pa's, was not discovered.

'No C.G.K. Sir and only games after his class,' Chapdi Kal said. 'That coward Mukunda has run off, so we can't even tease him. But we could take the whole afternoon off. No one would find out.'

A half-holiday, unsought, came rarely. So much so that they had to bestir themselves to think of what to do. Cricket and football were out; if the principal found them playing when they were not scheduled to, he might send C.G.K. Sir back to class. The last time they had had such a holiday, more than a year ago, they had participated in a procession, part of the inner convoy ringing the famous muni who had his headquarters in their town. Once a year the muni came out of his self-imposed seclusion to shift from one matha to the other in different parts of the town, and to give darshan to his followers. The piety of those who went to receive his blessings was somewhat suspect as the muni, being a Digambara Jain, was always 'sky clothed', dressed just as when he had emerged from his mother's womb. Chapdi Kal and the others maintained that it was the kesari bhat that was given out as prasada in the matha once the procession was over, that made them go— it had so much ghee in it that it trailed down from their palms to their elbows in multiple rivulets.

'They are picking coconuts in my neighbour's compound and there's a kite's nest in one of the palms. We could watch,' one of the boys offered.

Picking coconuts was a skilled job; not everyone could climb a coconut tree. In Setu's house, the job was Timrayee's.

He would tie himself to the trunk of the palm, grip the trunk with both his feet and shin upwards like a frog, holding a machete between his teeth to hack at the tough fibres. Once at the top he would drop the coconuts one by one. It was quite a performance but not enough for a day like this.

But you don't understand, the boy insisted. There were seven trees in the yard next to his house and a Brahminy kite was nesting in one of the palms and would allow no intruders within the periphery of her vision. Every time the coconut picker started climbing and reached halfway up a palm, even if it was the tree farthest from her, the kite would sail towards him, without a flicker of her outstretched wings, making straight for his face. Twice that morning he had slipped and dangled at an awkward angle, his make-shift cloth strap just about holding; once he had dropped his machete, narrowly missing someone below. He had finally given up, promising to return in the afternoon. It would make a diverting spectacle. They could all cheer for the bird.

'No,' Chapdi Kal said, 'I know something better. They're picketing the shendi shop. It's the third day today. Let's go and watch.'

One of the boys sucked his breath in sharply as they all turned to stare at Chapdi Kal. To run off during school hours and participate in a 'nationalist demonstration'! They thrilled at the audacity of the suggestion.

'The bonfires are nothing compared to picketing,' Chapdi Kal said, 'Only, you must be ready to run.'

Perhaps it was the sense of danger, possibly even the sound of the word 'rusticated' ringing distantly in their ears that helped them make up their minds.

'Come on, I'll take you there and bring you back home,' Chapdi Kal urged, looking at Setu, who was the only one still looking doubtful. 'Okay, if you're scared. . .'

'I'll come with you,' Setu said immediately and to mark the momentousness of the occasion, he took off his shoes and put them in his armpit. Now, truly, he was like the rest of them.

Chapdi Kal led the way. They set off through Electric Colony and then came to the unfrequented parts of town—Pension Mohalla, Santepete, Aralipete—so far they had been just names to Setu. His ambit was the tamer quarter—the Mission compound, the town club where his parents played tennis, his mother's Samaja and the library. Occasionally, it included Shri Krishna cinema.

By the time they reached the market square they were hot and sweating. Three boys had dropped out. Never before had Setu walked so much, through such crowded streets, and that too without footwear.

As they paused for a minute in the square, Chapdi Kal turned to him and asked, 'Want to go back?'

Setu shook his head vigorously, sending the sweat flying. It was a strange ticklish new sensation, two streams of sweat trickling down the sides of his face. He wiped them off with his fingers at first and then, from time to time, used his sleeve just the way Chapdi Kal did. Chapdi Kal looked at him enquiringly and Setu smiled back.

The market square was the busiest part of town, always clogged with people and bullock carts. Here were the law courts, the district commissioner's office, the post office and the hospital, jostling with the fruit, vegetable and mandi merchants going about their business. Leading off from the market, but not quite off the square, the road dipped picturesquely and ran along the lake before joining the highway to Bellary. Right there, at the picturesque dip was the liquor shop, an innocuous thatch-roofed structure with two rough benches in front to seat its clientele. The liquor cart, mounted with wooden barrels covered with palmyra leaves, was a common sight on the streets (though you could smell it much before you saw it) and considered a good omen. Coming across the shendi cart accidentally meant that your transactions would go well, especially those of an auspicious nature. As the evening wore on, scenes of mild revelry could be witnessed outside the shop; loud raucous singing at worst or a misadventure in the nearby ditch, since the shop was located on a bank higher than the road. It was a spot generally avoided by 'women and children'.

Like an old hand, Chapdi Kal pushed his way through the crowd till they could get an unimpeded view. A group of young men, little more than boys, stood to one side of the shop next to the dip in the road so that the shop was perched above them. There were seven of them, their white dhotis or pyjama and jubba and white caps identifying them immediately as swayamsevaks, or Congress party volunteers. They had assembled in front of the shop as soon as it opened and by the time Chapdi Kal, Setu and the others arrived, the initial curious rush was over. The crowd had thinned, consisting now only of the regulars, the good-for-nothings who hung around the market place. The Congress boys were huddled together, and were beginning to droop. It was hotter now with the afternoon sun directly in their faces. The air carried the telltale sour, fermented smell and the flies hovering around could not be swished away for long. The sweat ran freely down Setu's forehead, but it no longer bothered him.

'That one there, right in front, he's C.G.K. Sir's son,' Chapdi Kal said.

'You mean that short chap with buck teeth, the last one who is facing us? I know him,' Setu whispered. 'He works for Nanjunda Kole advocate and comes to my father's office sometimes.'

'That's his uncle. He works in his office in the mornings, before college. I bet you didn't know that the K in C.G.K. Sir's name stands for Kole.'

There was no limit to Chapdi Kal's resourcefulness, thought Setu. He knew everything. His own first rank and the maths medal he won every year paled in comparison.

The owners of the shop, two of them, sat on the wooden bench outside the shop daring the boys in white to advance further. It was the third day of the protest and business had come to a standstill. Though the boys had just stood outside, sung songs and distributed pamphlets, none of the usual customers had had the courage to walk past them into the shop. The owners had lodged a complaint with the police.

'They take turns at it. There was a different lot in the morning,' someone said.

The picketing of a liquor shop was a rare event and the crowd really didn't know how seriously to take the thing. They were used to speeches in the maidan in the evenings, even the occasional bonfire of foreign cloth—people were free to burn their own clothes after all—but such forms of protest where the protesters were not demanding anything for themselves, only that others be denied what they wanted, was new. Moreover, the protesters here were very young and from 'decent' homes.

'*Listen, o brothers. . .*' the swayamsevaks struck up a song.

The owners had tried everything short of assaulting the protesters. They had tried appealing to the swayamsevaks to go home and when that failed, they had appealed to the crowd. The crowd, however, was fickle, sympathizing with the swayamsevaks one minute and heckling them the next. The owners had tried hiring their own crowd to out shout the swayamsevaks. They walked menacingly around them brandishing sticks but, since the boys were not on their property, there was only that far that they could go. The swayamsevaks carried on undeterred, saying that they would stand there till the shop was closed.

'Listen. . .' one of the owners, stood up from the bench and shouted, 'we're doing nothing wrong. . .this is a licensed shop . . .' he appealed to the crowd again.

'*Listen to the call of your conscience, listen to the beat of your heart. . .*' the boys sang.

'Look, you've made your speech, you've given out your pamphlets and sung your song. Now go.'

'*The women are weeping. . .the children are hungry. . .*' the song took a rousing turn.

The crowd shifted restlessly.

'Mere boys! Singing like women instead of going about their work. They say they're going to save the nation!'

Setu recognized the heckler with a start. 'I know him too.

It's Vyasa Rao, and he's a *gentleman*!' he whispered to Chapdi Kal.

It startled Setu to see people he knew out of the placid context of his daily life in the crowd. It surprised him that they had other identities, ones so completely different from what he was acquainted with. Until now, the buck-toothed swayamsevak had been the boy who carried messages from Advocate Kole to his father, the boy who waited on the verandah without knocking on the door or attracting any sort of attention, till one of the clerks came out to see what he wanted. As for Vyasa Rao, Setu was truly aghast to find him here, so much at ease with the riff-raff.

Vyasa Rao, distinctive in his closed-collar coat, long hair and red rimmed eyes, was an artist reduced to painting signs. He was the one who had painted Setu's father's name board— K. Mylaraiah, Advocate and Public Prosecutor—with eyes for full stops and commas. When Vyasa Rao had first approached her, Setu's mother had felt sorry for him and commissioned a 'temple tank scene'. He had taken an advance for the canvas and the 'special' paints and that was the last they'd seen of him, though he was profusely apologetic whenever he bumped into a member of the family.

'Look, horses! The mounted police are here!' Chapdi Kal said, spitting in excitement.

They heard the *thatack-thatack* of the hooves and saw sparks flying off the stone flints on the road as the horseshoes struck them. 'Hoi!' a voice commanded, 'Hoiiiiii!' and the crowd was pushed back. Setu staggered and almost fell, and when he recovered, he found that Chapdi Kal was not by his side.

He struggled, pushing blindly at the voluminous dhoti-clad waists that surrounded him, calling out his friend's name, when someone pulled at his hand. He was surprised to see Ramu, another of his classmates who had not been part of the original group that afternoon. Even as the two of them tried to make their way out, the pushing stopped, the crowd steadied and came together again, and miraculously Chapdi Kal was with them.

'Right, my sons, you're our guests, we must treat you well . . .' One of the owners hitched up his dhoti and tightened it round his waist. He now had the police on his side.

'Give them a drink. They've been standing all afternoon. They must be thirsty,' someone suggested.

'Yes, we must welcome them properly. Come boys, some panneer seve for our guests. Get out the silver sprinklers, let's anoint them with scented water.'

One of the men smashed a barrel open in a splendidly theatrical gesture and the owners began scooping out the contents of the barrel with coconut shells and flinging it at the boys. With the second barrel they grew impudent, climbed down the slope to where the boys were standing, and threw the stuff right into their faces. The swayamsevaks ducked, as if to ward off blows and wiped their faces, but did nothing else.

'Jokhe! Jokhe!' a policeman warned, bringing his horse up and the owners retreated.

An uneasy murmur ran through the crowd.

'They take it like wedding guests, with heads lowered the poor boys. . .from such traditional families, they wouldn't even know the smell of liquor. . .'

'They've been at it since morning, they just stand there soaking.'

One of the boys now seemed to be crying.

'Come, come, drink up your tears. . .'

'Mind you boys,' someone cackled, 'go home and wring out your clothes well.'

'Yes, you can get a whole barrel.'

'You can finally see what it tastes like.'

The crowd began to relax.

All of a sudden there was a stir and a murmur of excitement ran through the crowd. Yet another man in khadi arrived on the scene. He was older than the swayamsevaks and looked authoritative.

'It's Narayana Rao,' someone said.

'Long live Dandi Narayana Rao!' a voice called out weakly

from the back but there was no answering chorus.

Standing next to Setu, Ramu froze and Setu goosepimpled in sympathy.

'Ey Ramu, that's your father!' Chapdi Kal said unnecessarily. One of the owners brandished a coconut shell at him.

'Mahatma Gandhi ki jai!' the swayamsevaks shouted with a fresh burst of energy, now that their leader had arrived.

Narayana Rao's arrival seemed to incense the owners afresh and they greeted him with a new barrel. Stepping right up to him, despite the hovering policemen, they emptied the barrel over him. Narayana Rao was soaked to the skin, but like the boys he did nothing to resist, wiping his face instead. Then one of the men hoisted the empty barrel on to his shoulder and threw it at Narayana Rao, which he deflected with a neat flick of the elbow.

The crowd roared with approval.

'Gandhiji ki jai!' Narayana Rao pumped his fist in the air and the swayamsevaks echoed the slogan and the gesture, their voices ringing. The mounted policemen came closer.

In reply the owners rolled a barrel along the ground to dislodge the Gandhians. Since the shop was located on a slope and the boys stood on the road below, the barrel picked up speed even over the short distance and hurtled towards the swayamsevaks. Narayana Rao pushed the boys aside and stood directly in the path of the advancing missile. It hit him on the foot before rolling over and smashing into the ditch. The crowd surged forward, its more desperate members, Vyasa Rao included, running to stem the tragic waste.

'Back!' a policeman drove his horse into the crowd, 'get back all of you.' Setu was jostled again but this time they clung to each other, the three of them, and found themselves pushed right into the front, the hindquarters of a horse framing the scene for them. Even as the other policemen moved into their positions round the shop, a jeep drove up and a man in khaki, indisputably the highest authority in town, stepped out.

'The inspector general himself has come!' the murmur went.

'I know him,' Setu said, 'he plays tennis with my father.'

Even as Narayana Rao started limping towards the highest authority, things started happening. The swayamsevaks too started moving en masse towards the inspector general, and the policemen, in their zeal to forestall what they saw as a threatening gesture, swung towards them with lathis. Narayana Rao put his hands up to cover his face and ducked; the swinging lathi caught the swayamsevak behind him full on the face. As more policeman started closing in, Narayana Rao hobbled towards the inspector general's jeep and got in. 'You may arrest me but not the boys. Our movement will continue. We will not give up till this shop is closed down. Gandhiji ki jai!' he shouted before being driven away.

And then there was utter confusion. Ramu darted after the jeep, crying out for his father and was swallowed by the crowd. Abandoning the swayamsevaks, the policemen started for the crowd, swinging their lathis in the air. The horse standing right in front of Setu and Chapdi Kal turned round and prepared to charge. Chapdi Kal caught Setu by the hand and was out like a shot, the first to leave the crowd which would soon break up in chaos. Even when they reached the market square, they did not slow down, Chapdi Kal leading Setu through strange, labyrinthine streets till they were safe.

On the road that Setu lived, the road that led one way to Bellary and another to Honnavar, not a leaf stirred and not a man moved, except for the two boys. Setu leaned against the wall of his house and listened to his heart pounding in his ears. The two of them stood there awhile without speaking. Setu thought of the swayamsevak, the messenger boy whom he now identified as C.G.K. Sir's son, young, with just a hint of a moustache, who had borne the full fury of the lathi on his face when Narayana Rao had ducked. The boy's scream and the crunch of lathi on bone were almost simultaneous and Setu felt a churning in his stomach and the bile rise in his throat. But that and the chaos that followed had been an aberration; this was home, this was real.

'You will have to go back the way we came,' he said, timidly.

'That's all right. I'm used to it. I don't have to go far,' Chapdi Kal assured him.

'Ramu. . .?' Setu began hesitantly.

'He will have reached home too,' Chapdi Kal said, sounding less certain.

Both of them were silent, knowing that they must not mention C.G.K. Sir's son or even wonder how much damage the lathi had done.

'Why were the boys standing there and singing?'

'They are Congress people, Gandhi bhaktas. They want to burn foreign cloth and stop people from drinking. Only then will we become strong enough to send the British back.'

Something stirred in Setu's head, and a tentative connection was formed between the events of the evening, the charkha and the takli at home on which his mother and grandmother spun, and his mother haranguing her cousin about his drinking.

'Tell me, have you ever seen the British?'

'No, never.'

'Well, I know three English people—Dr King of the government hospital, who comes home and Mr Spencer and his wife from the Mission, but they're not the same as the British that C.G.K. Sir is always talking about.'

C.G.K. Sir's 'British', as Setu imagined them, were a formless but all powerful force, sometimes a phalanx of men and sometimes pure spirit, who could do what they wanted, be at different places at the same time, and control people's thoughts and actions whenever they chose; somewhat like God.

'And Ramu's father. . .' Setu could say no more, mystified by what he had seen of Ramu's father, radically different from his own and from his notion of fathers in general. 'Imagine Ramu darting after the jeep like that!'

'Well, naturally he'd run after the jeep. Wouldn't you do the same if your father was being taken away by the police? If your father fell into the fire wouldn't you save him?' asked Chapdi Kal heatedly, his sense of filial duty finely honed by the mythological films and melodramas he saw in the weekly theatre.

Setu said nothing for if any such circumstances arose, it would be his father who would be doing the taking away and the saving. He could never imagine it otherwise, but for the first time he sensed that the sins of fathers could well visit upon their sons.

When Setu entered quietly by the back door, it had turned dark.

'Where have you been?'

It was only his sister, lying in wait for him.

'Somewhere.'

'Where are your shoes?'

'Somewhere.'

She stared at him, at his new found cockiness. 'You'd better tell me. Or I'll tell them.'

'Tell. What do I care!'

He ran past her outstretched hand into the house. A few minutes later, when he had caught his breath, he remembered his shoes and his heart sank for they had been brand new; but right then he did not care. His sister's usual intimidating tactics seemed childish. He had, after all, now drunk the milk of a tigress. His shoes were there, somewhere among the splintered wooden barrels, the horse dung and the abandoned slippers of those who had run pell-mell, his first offering at the altar of adulthood.

In the days that followed, his pantheon of heroes would admit another. Other than Anwar, the komberghat-maker and Jambaiah, the Venkateshwara Company bus driver, Setu conceded that he wouldn't mind being yet another. All things considered, he wouldn't mind being Mohandas Karamchand Gandhi.

three

———

1933

That evening Shivaswamy asked for ice instead of hot water. It threw the servants into a tizzy. Timrayee ran off at once with the thermos, wondering whether he'd get any at that hour. The ice machine at Dorai's, it was believed, was a giant hen that would 'lay' its quota only at fixed hours. It was Morris Sr, a trader in assorted goods, who had first brought ice to the town one hot summer—a piece of the Wenham lakes that had travelled over two oceans in an American ship to land at Madras, and from there by rail to arrive here, wrapped in a piece of burlap. That had been more than fifty years ago. Morris Jr now owned the Mangalore tiles factory on the outskirts of the town, and ice was made right here in a clanking machine out of water from the local lake.

When Shivaswamy bellowed for hot water, the servants jumped to do his bidding with surprising alacrity, with excitement even, for it gave them a perverse thrill that this large, blustering man drank openly in a teetotalling household, behaved as if he owned the place and made the master of the house uncomfortable.

'Hot water!' was also the sign for the children to leave. He would then bring out his bottle of old Jamaican rum and sit talking to his cousin and her husband, drinking late into the night even after they had retired. For the daytime, he had a silver hip flask. 'Now, you two, turn the other way while I have a quick swig of my medicine,' he'd say solemnly. But this time Kaveri and Setu had clung to him even after he had sent for the ice. He had told them all the stories they wanted—as the Superintending Vet of the maharaja's stud farm, he had a fund of them—but he had not yet produced his mysterious 'gift', something that he never failed to do.

'How is Fernando?' Kaveri asked.

'And Chevalier?'

These were old friends whom they'd never seen but knew all about, descendants of the famous Pero Gomez, the first English stallion in the Mysore stables. Someone had tried to steal them once and Kaveri and Setu never tired of hearing about their uncle's overnight vigil in the stables and his hot pursuit of the intruders through the night. Yet another favourite story of his was how he had personally examined every single horse from his stables, before sending a hundred of them off to join the famous Lumsden's Horse in the Boer War. He had been all over the papers then, at his swaggering best, as Mylaraiah said.

And then, after all the preliminaries were over, he had asked them to close their eyes and dipped into his right hand pocket and brought out a *puppy*.

'You said you were bringing me a hound!' Setu said, looking at the scrawny creature, ribs showing, which struggled to stand on its feet.

'And a hound it is. What you see before you is the rarest or rare hounds—the Mysore hound—directly descended from a two thousand year old greyhound.'

For years, they knew, he had been trying to breed a local variety of the hound, and establish its pedigree with the Emperor's Kennel Club in Bangalore, who laughed at his claims.

Shivaswamy stood the puppy on the table, where it trembled pitifully, and pointed to its deep chest and arching stomach—all muscle and no flesh, a true yogi. He urged them to feel its legs, which looked like bent twigs, so powerful he claimed that when it ran it would look as if it were flying. In eight weeks' time it would turn so fast and frisky that their back garden wouldn't be enough to contain it. It had very little hair, so their mother would not object to having it indoors. Moreover, it was truly blue-blooded, mostly English greyhound with a bit of the African and the royal Egyptian thrown in. Legends of its bravery were legion. One of its kind was found mummified in King Tutankhamen's tomb. Having come into their country with Alexander the Great, it had travelled south and a local variety, bred some place in Bombay presidency, was known to have attacked a tiger and killed it.

Setu stared at the pup, which was now trying to crawl back into his uncle's pocket, and tried to summon the kind of reverence he knew it deserved.

'Well, a generous proportion of our local pie seems to have got mixed with the royal hound,' Mylaraiah said smiling.

'If Setu doesn't want him, I'll take him. He thinks it's a scrap of a dog with a small head and a big body,' Kaveri said saucily.

'Of course not, he's my dog,' Setu said at once, sweeping the pup off the table and cradling him in his arms. 'I'll call him Pat.'

Setu was not insensible to the honour that was being done to him—in fact he was surprised that Shivaswamy had tolerated their marked lack of enthusiasm for his precious Mysore hound. Man-and-dog legends about Shivaswamy abounded in the family circles.

'When you go hunting Setu, you can take him with you,' Shivaswamy said, apparently satisfied with Setu's show of affection. 'He'll save you from tigers and lions. Off with both of you now. I have important things to say to your parents.'

Once Bhagiratamma and the children had gone to bed, Shivaswamy settled down with his bucket of ice and bottle of rum for a long evening, hoping to provoke his cousin and her husband, especially her husband into a quarrel. That would happen when the conversation came round to what animated them the most—the state of the nation. When he was in a good mood, Shivaswamy could be quite entertaining for he was well travelled; he had met Gandhi and even heard Subhash

Bose speak. But Mylaraiah found it difficult to keep his temper with his wife's cousin. You mustn't take Shivaswamy seriously, Rukmini would say, what matters to him is the serve and volley of dialogue, he revels in repartee. In which case his heart doesn't lie in anything, Mylaraiah would retort, recognizing that he came out *stodgy* in comparison and resenting it.

'So Rukmini, I believe you're trying to ban the one pleasure in my life,' Shivaswamy began that evening. 'I hear Nani and his satyagrahis are picketing in earnest. I saw the mounted police charging away towards the market square today.'

Rukmini smiled back, ready to cross swords with him. All the sins of the Congress were usually laid at her door, and despite her distant sympathies for the party she was often called upon to 'explain' their activities. But hers was more an attraction for the personalities involved and her cousin often teased her about the torch she carried for the leading Congressmen, both national and local. The diwan, Mirza Ismail, too, was a favourite with her, for his sense of beauty, for his insistence as much on the aesthetic appeal of public structures as their utility. Mylaraiah was usually cornered into playing the conservative while Shivaswamy's own inclinations were fluid, depending upon the conversation. 'The chameleon', Mylaraiah had dubbed him. He was known to support the maharaja, Gandhi and the British vociferously—in the same breath.

'And why not?' Rukmini returned, 'I can't understand why men drink. What's the use? It ruins them, not to speak of their families.'

'Not just men, I've known some fine women who drink too. You should try it sometime. Then you'll know.'

For all your talk, Mylaraiah thought to himself, you wouldn't let your wife, fine woman that she is, drink anything stronger than kashaya, and you wouldn't even speak of such things in her presence. That he himself did not object to his wife sitting with the likes of Shivaswamy spoke a lot about his broad-mindedness, he felt. Only he wished Rukmini would appreciate it.

'My sympathies are with Narayana Rao and his boys,' Mylaraiah said, clearing his throat and preparing to get expansive, for this would be a long evening and he would have to defend his turf. 'Though what they're doing is not lawful, you know. There's no law against selling liquor, and that shop is licensed.'

'Ah Mylari, always the point of law with you. . .'

'Well, you can't deny it. Revenue from liquor has always been a major money earner for the state, we've fed fat on excise. And now it's not just lucrative but even respectable . . .companies like Parry's of Madras have invested in the business. Our Kanti's brother, retired from the state service, was the architect of the liquor policy. Didn't drink a drop himself but knew that manufacture and distribution had to be separated, and toddy shouldn't be mixed up with arrack. And just as he estimated, now the middlemen are gone and all dues are coming directly into the treasury. . .'

'So, just because it brings in money, is it fair to encourage people to drink poison?' Rukmini protested. 'Surely there are other. . .'

'Well, it's a business like any other. The government *owns* the groves on which dates for toddy are grown. There are farmers legitimately farming those lands. They earn their living by it. . .' If the legitimate systems were in place, Mylaraiah believed, all was well. 'And people like to drink, obviously,' he threw up his hands dismissively with the assurance of one who would never be prey to the weakness, 'I don't see how Narayana Rao or even Gandhi can change things overnight, especially when the maharaja's government doesn't particularly want to discourage it.'

'Yes, there's no point trying to do things for people's "own good", they never appreciate it. For once I agree with Mylari completely,' Shivaswamy said, pouring himself a generous measure out of his bottle. 'What a wonderful invention the thermos flask is, keeps hot things hot and cold things cold.'

'Picketing is very well, but it isn't enough—we at the Samaja know it,' Rukmini said triumphantly. 'Narayana Rao and his volunteers are very courageous, but we've organized women and students groups to go from village to village as part of the temperance programme. . .'

'Ah! Education and Idealism, the twin pillars that support our Rukmini!'

'As long as they stick to social reform I have no quarrel with them. . .' Mylaraiah cut in loudly, catching Rukmini's eye.

That Mylaraiah was uneasy about his wife's friendships with 'politically inclined' women was obvious, though he just stopped short of forbidding them. Whenever Umadevi, the local women's leader who was an active member of the Congress, and Rukmini would set off on a house-to-house 'consciousness raising' campaign or to collect money for a 'worthy cause', he would say nothing but pace up and down the garden till she returned. In fact, before Rukmini had agreed to become the secretary of the women's wing of the Khadi Association, they had had an argument about the propriety of it, whether it constituted a 'political' act on the part of a leading advocate and municipal councillor's wife to take up such a 'sensitive' position. Could it be construed as an anti-government act? It had taken all of Rukmini's tact to convince her husband that she wasn't breaking the law or jeopardizing his career by supporting khadi. Well, he had agreed, so long as she did not ask to join the Congress Party.

It was the Congress forays into politics that Mylaraiah had no patience with. He was all for temperance, Harijan upliftment; even the coarse, home-spun khadi, though unviable could, as Gandhi said, be a symbol of identity, something to knit people together, though it may not be an effective way to counter the Manchester dhoti. 'One paisa per day, that's all it gets the spinners,' he'd tell his wife and she'd retort, 'It's better than nothing, and incidentally, they make seven pice, not one.' If anything sent a chill up his spine, it was the term 'Swaraj', especially the way it was thumped out at every meeting in the market square. Every shamster and crook slipped into the cloak of patriotism when it suited him. The crowds were made up of riff-raff anyway, and one of the men who made the most impassioned speeches, 'a mere corner-shop grocer' was a known profiteer, who had suddenly grown rich after the war.

'And what do they expect to do after we drive the British out?' he had asked, the last time Shivaswamy had been there, and the papers had been full of the Round Table Conference. He had glared at the photograph which showed Gandhi, Churchill's seditious, half-naked fakir, flanked by the well-clad Indian delegation and 'that infernal woman' Sarojini Naidu, on the steps of St James' Palace in London. 'What a lot of noise they're making. Do they expect anything to come out of this? Does Gandhi seriously think that the British will allow us to rule ourselves? And can we, even if they did? How will he accommodate the princely states in his grand scheme? Two of those princes cannot sit together over a cup of coffee and have a conversation—provided their dietary rules permit them to sit at the same table—unless the viceroy is present to mediate.' We are twice insulated from self-rule, thank God, Mylaraiah would say—once by the British and once more by the maharaja.

'I don't understand you Mylari,' Shivaswamy smiled at him. 'On the one hand you tremble for the future, on the other you donate money to the Congresswallas. . .like the maharaja who goes out of his way to make Gandhi comfortable when he comes to Mysore, but arrests his followers when they burn foreign cloth and picket liquor shops. Hunting with the hounds and running with the hares. . .'

'It's one thing being hospitable and another doing the right thing when someone breaks the law. Gandhi is admirable. . . you can't deny that. . .as I said if only the Congress would stick to their constructive work programme. . .'

'Well Rukmini, the British have their own ways of cutting your Gandhi down to size. When he was in London for that fruitless Round Table Conference, they made him inspect their national Dairy Show and named the prize-winning goat "Mahatma Gandhi"!' Shivaswamy slapped his knee and laughed uproariously.

Finally, when the neck and shoulders of the dark, squat bottle were quite clear, Shivaswamy would come out with the most interesting bits of news and gossip.

'There's some talk of your hero—not your's Mylari, your's is right here in Bangalore we know, the good judge holding up the world, and I believe he's singing your praises—but your's Rukmini, is coming to our Mysore. . .'

Mylaraiah felt the blood rush to his face. The 'good judge', his supposed 'hero' to whom Shivaswamy's fruity, trouble-making tones were alluding was Darcy Riley, the chief justice of the high court, a Britisher. But he also knew the allusions his brother-in-law was making—to his complacent views, his refusal to look into the future, his need for a well-defined world preferably ruled by the British with the maharaja as their intermediary, his 'connivance' with the white man.

'I'm happy to be a pillar in a system run by people like Judge Riley,' Mylaraiah said stiffly, his lower lip jutting out, a sign Rukmini recognized, that he was hurt and would try to cover up by being ponderous. 'And there's no denying that whatever we have is thanks to them. Think of the chaos there'd be if we allowed our people to run things their way. Every man, right from the diwan to the petty clerk in the government office would be bringing his brother or his son in through the back door. . .We'd endlessly be salaaming worthless people even to get what was due to us.'

'Well, your Judge Riley may praise your opening statements but he will not help you with the Chikmagalur planters cases and with your aspirations in Bangalore. For that you need one of your own kind. If I were you I'd speak to our Vishwananth Rao. . .he's the district judge, tipped to be the next chief justice. . .could be of help. You can't be principled and ambitious at the same time, Mylari. You'll have to choose between the two.'

'Why do you take this Shivaswamy to heart?' Rukmini said hastily. 'You know he's only trying to provoke you.'

'Now Rukmini, I have news for you. I believe you may

actually get to see Gandhi in this town,' Shivaswamy said turning to his cousin.

'Well, he has to get out of Yervada jail first. He needs a rest after all his antics,' Mylaraiah said testily, and was immediately annoyed with himself for taking out his anger on Gandhi.

'I believe your Narayana Rao has a large hand in it. He's doing his best to see that Gandhi makes a stopover here.'

'Well, well, our Nani seems to have gone on to bigger things. . .no longer satisfied with organizing bonfires to burn the suits his father-in-law gifted him. He hasn't shown his face in court in a long time. The Congress seems to be the last resort for every brief less lawyer.' It was inexorable, the way Shivaswamy brought out the most uncharitable streak in him, making him take on all his wife's heroes—major and minor.

'Come, come Mylari,' Shivaswamy cackled, 'I myself don't care much for these Congress types but you cannot deny that Narayana Rao has made sacrifices. He has given himself completely to the work of the Congress. He could have had a comfortable life. . .a cosy practice like yours. . .instead he's taken on a thankless job. He has no future in the party—the Lingayats and the Gowdas would throw him out tomorrow if they could. His followers are so fickle, every time they have a difference of opinion, they walk out and start another Congress Party!'

'Look, there couldn't be a more sincere man, I agree,' Mylaraiah said, struggling to keep his voice even. 'If I give a generous donation to the Congress every year, it is because of Narayana Rao. The earlier committee head is still facing an enquiry for misappropriating funds. But I don't see how it's a sacrifice. Frankly, it's a little juvenile the way he chases his enthusiasms. "Dandi Narayana Rao" he calls himself, after having marched with Gandhi to Dandi and made salt there. If you ask me, each man must follow his vocation, do what he is supposed to, and what he does best. If he wanted to serve the nation so much he should have stayed back in his village and tilled his father's lands, there are drunkards to be reformed in the village too. He likes to do things with a flourish—the broad signature. And don't think he doesn't enjoy the power, the excitement, the accolades. I believe after 'Gandhiji ki jai!' the crowd chants, 'Narayana Rao ki jai!'

'He's a good leader then, if people chant his name,' Rukmini said, unable to restrain herself, 'and I can't see how it's not a sacrifice. Not just for him, but for his wife and family as well. I hear he's selling off his coconut groves to raise funds for his work.'

'Which is inconsiderate of him,' her husband snapped. 'Is it fair to his son for him to sell off his family property like that, I ask you! Has he consulted his brothers?'

'Which reminds me, I have to meet Narayana Rao before I go,' Shivaswamy said, suddenly businesslike.

'What for?'

'To buy those coconut groves, of course. They're on the land adjoining ours in Kanakanhalli and I know that he's in a hurry to sell.'

'Hitting a man when he's down?'

'Business is business. Never let an opportunity get past. If not me, someone else will buy it from him and at less, probably. You yourself just said that he was ambitious. If he wants to sustain his ambition, he must do what is necessary. Just as you must approach Justice Vishwanath Rao. . .When can I see him? Does he come at all to his chambers or will I have to go to his house?'

Both Rukmini and Mylaraiah ignored him and Shivaswamy had to repeat his question.

At that point a treble voice piped up from the hall. 'You can't meet him at all.'

'Who's that?'

'What Setu, not asleep as yet?'

'He's too excited to sleep. You know how the children are when you come.'

'Sitting up to listen to grown-up talk eh?'

'What do you mean, can't meet him?'

'Well,' Setu sat up, his excitement at being the bearer of

such vital news far outweighing the wisdom of letting it be known that he knew, 'he was taken away from the shendi shop today by the police. He's gone to jail.'

When Mylaraiah paused on the footpath to look up, he marvelled as much at the blue sky as the telegraph lines above with birds sitting on them like clothespins on a clothesline. That a device, which carried electrical impulses at sizzling speed, should be put to such benign incidental use amused him. The birds that perched on the lines would never know how they were being honoured or that, if it were not for the wonder of insulation, they were just a millimetre's thinness away from being charred to death. He was not surprised that some people thought them the work of the devil—his servant Timrayee would not touch the telegrams that came for him from his village. Well, Narayana Rao and his ilk had their work cut out, trying to educate the masses out of their ignorance.

Occasionally, when the blue sky and the crisp air beckoned, Mylaraiah dismissed his horse-drawn carriage and walked to work, his clerk trailing behind him with his files. On such mornings, he felt his blood was flowing more briskly, as if every keen impulse that had ever murmured in his veins had come to a head and was urging him along. This town was the world and this world was his home. But soon, his practical bent of mind insinuated itself, and then as a municipal councillor soon-to-be commissioner, he felt that it was his duty to survey the gutters, check the lamp posts, post boxes and other things. The orderliness of the networks pleased him—of roads and railways, dams and canals, munsiffs and amaldars, of courts and committees; he had an instinct for Cartesian control. Structures built with British technology and kept in order by the maharaja's civil servants trained on the British model. What was more, being enterprising, he had bought himself a share in the system. He too had a head for business, could sense his advantage and strike, and not in an underhand way like Shivaswamy. One of the decisions he flattered himself on was subscribing to the railway line from his town to Mysore and beyond, the money for which had been raised almost entirely from the funds of merchants, farmers and landlords like himself, from the districts through which the railway line would run. He had been the one, as member of the committee, to suggest that they import the pine sleepers from Europe for the railway line, instead of depleting their forests. Now every time he travelled by train, he almost felt that the he owned the landscape. Narayana Rao could picket liquor shops and hope that eventually it would throw off the foreign yoke, but he knew clearly, where his loyalties lay.

The maharaja, according to Mylaraiah, was a perfect product of their partnership with the British. In many ways he felt His Highness had the kind of balance in his personal qualities which he himself had. Krishnarajendra Wodeyar had a powerful forehand on the tennis courts, worked up a lather at polo, rode straight to the hounds, and loved his horses and dogs. He could sit at the same table with the king of England and use a knife and fork, play the violin like them and yet he was a Sanskrit pandit and reputedly, the first thing he did on waking each morning was bathe in the Kaveri. Moreover, it was not as if he and his advisers were blind to the writing on the wall. The very year he came to power, he had instituted a representative assembly, which rightly was an association of landowners and merchants—all tax paying men, and there were two women too—and a legislative council, to which Mylaraiah hoped to be nominated soon. Of course, things would take time. Right then the assembly was just an advisory body, which met once a year. It was also true that its members were more interested in their annual outing to Mysore from their villages, but people had to be trained to become responsible. Only then could dominion status under the protective umbrella of the British be considered. Independence right then would be like letting a whole lot of monkeys loose in a ripe mango orchard.

As Mylaraiah turned the corner, the government buildings came into sight and he stopped for a moment to look at the emblem on the flag hoisted above the district commissioner's office, noting with approval how smartly the pennant fluttered in the breeze. And in the fitness of things, in the inner enclave of the office, on the entrance wall hung the portraits of the maharaja and his father—grave, worthy men whose figured silk galebands sat perfectly on their shoulders, the little peacock feather that protruded from their diadems relieving the gravity of their expression. Some days back Mylaraiah's clerk had brought him a scurrilous pamphlet disguised as a newspaper— Mylaraiah usually did not bother with such gossip but this 'article' was being discussed in the lawyers' association as well. The article had suggested slyly that perhaps the Union Jack should fly alongside the Ganda Bherunda, and the viceroy's portrait be mounted alongside the maharaja's and his father's, for where would they be without the continuous kindness of the British.

There was a list of the various acts of kindness of the British to the House of Mysore, beginning with their deftness in getting rid of the upstarts Hyder and Tipu in the eighteenth century. The British had taken it upon themselves to deal with the adventurers Hyder Ali and his son Tipu who had usurped the throne from the legitimate rulers, the Wodeyars. Hyder had been a mere foot soldier in the Mysore army and unlike the Wodeyars had not been meek and compliant. Father and son had fought the British when the British had still been the East India Company. However, it was only a matter of time before the British took over. The historic siege of Seringapatam proved to be the final arbiter; Mysore was lost to the British— Tipu slain, betrayed by his own men, his body heaped casually among those of the soldiers who had borne the first onslaught of the invading British army. A hundred years after the siege, when Mysore was neatly parcelled and trussed up, the prince of Wales had visited the state and had wanted to be shown the exact place where the wall of the Seringapatam fort had been breached by 'our men' and sealed the fate of Mysore. From the ramparts of the disused fort, he had surveyed the Kaveri, which flowed past and pointed to the bamboo at the water's edge, whose roots had treacherously gained entry into the wall of the fort and had no doubt spread to its foundations. Nature too, the prince was supposed to have remarked, had willed a British victory.

With Tipu gone and nature on their side, the British had pretty much done what they wanted. In less than a hundred years, they had restored, removed and re-restored the Wodeyars to the throne of a truncated Mysore.

In the year 1868, there had been much joy in the kingdom of Mysore and quite a bit of the royal treasury had gone towards the purchase of rock sugar, which was freely distributed among the people. The pamphlet writer digressed here to recall that his grandmother's house too had received a lump of the rock sugar, which had been treated almost on par with the idols of the gods. His grandmother had kept it safe in a copper vessel sealed with a lid. After several years of ruling the state themselves, the British had installed the rightful ruler, the infant Chamaraja Wodeyar, in the palace that year. Quite literally, his majesty had needed the protection of his British masters. So great was the rejoicing at the palace that evening that Commissioner Bowring had to cock his hat over the boy king's face to protect him from the fusillade of flowers and the fountains of attar that his newly pledged subjects were showering on him. As a treat for the infant king, the chief commissioner took him to the Imperial assembly in Delhi when Queen Victoria was proclaimed Empress of India. Thirteen years later, when on coming of age the king had formally taken over the administration of the state, again everyone had marvelled at the good omen—a shower of rain just as the first royal durbar was about to begin! The state would receive a twenty-one gun salute at the Imperial durbar! Again, the maharaja would have the benefit of the 'advice' of a British resident and the 'assistance' of an English civil servant-secretary. It seemed to be in bad taste to mention that the annual subsidy to the British was raised by ten and a half lakh rupees, not counting the debt of eighty lakhs that already existed. In return for their many kindnesses, the maharaja had pledged his loyalty to Her Gracious Majesty the Empress of India—a woman who would not attend the Imperial assembly in her own honour in Delhi because she could not bear the thought of the heat and the insects.

At that point in its litany of British 'kindnesses' to the state of Mysore, the article had stopped, promising another instalment of the same. The author had called himself 'nobody' and there were rumours that he was a high schoolteacher. For a moment, Mylaraiah wondered whether Narayana Rao could have written the article, for this was just the sort of rhetorical, pointless and completely disproportionate exercise that he would indulge in, and Narayana Rao too made much of being a child of history, but then he dismissed the suspicion. Though Narayana Rao dwelt on the past, it was always with an eye to the future, and he was more interested in immediate gains. Such a recounting of facts and figures was suggestive of a teacher of history. At the thought of Narayana Rao, a forceful tide rose up in Mylaraiah's breast and he had to stop mid-stride, feel for an offending pebble on the footpath and kick it away. For Narayana Rao and he had a strange and long-standing kinship.

Both Mylaraiah and Narayana Rao came from the same village and belonged to the same sub-caste as well, their families having known each other for generations. One of the earliest memories Mylaraiah had was of travelling in a bullock cart, squashed between his mother and Narayana Rao's grandmother, on the way to the temple fair in the next village— the women and children of the two households had gone everywhere together. For years, Mylaraiah had escorted the younger Nani four miles each way to catch the bus to school in the next town, enduring him like a burr on his flanks for Narayana Rao was small, snivelling and always lagging behind. Even when he was quite grown up, his grandmother would hitch him on to her hip and feed him tuttus of mosaranna, standing in the porch for all to see. That was how Mylaraiah thought of him, a pair of skinny legs dangling from a girdle and a face with curd smeared all over it. No one had paid him much attention, he was one of a group of boys; no one really thought he'd amount to anything, either. But for all that he'd grown up to be a handsome lad and had gone on to study law from Bombay, just as Mylaraiah had from Mysore and after getting their degrees, they had apprenticed with the same lawyer in Mysore. Narayana Rao had returned from Bombay woollier than ever, and what was more, infected with the national cause. Though he had a good grasp over matters, during his entire apprenticeship, there was not a single case that Narayana Rao had seen through to the end, always tilting at windmills, more concerned with his vague notions of 'justice' rather than winning the case on hand. Or he would be ill, lying on his mattress in the corner of the hall that all the boys slept in. Finally, he had left in a huff over a minor matter, without completing his period of apprenticeship and set up a desultory practice by himself. No junior would stay with him for long and he did not have too many clients either. It was a good thing for Narayana Rao that the Congress had come along.

It would have been such a relief to him if all that he had felt for Narayana Rao was contempt. But from the tip of his discoloured toenail, to his pious tuft, Narayana Rao gave off an innocent, if tired, worthiness like a creature battered but whose demons had been eventually laid to rest, a man who had emerged from a trial by fire with his limbs scorched perhaps, but with a heart of shining gold. At the thought of Narayana Rao, slurry demons rose in Mylaraiah's gullet, like squirts of acid after a rich meal, hinting at the road not taken, at safe, cushy alternatives, at a less-than-full life.

Moreover, there was Rukmini's obvious admiration for the man. And the matter of the interchanged horoscopes, stupid and inconsequential now, but that too stuck to his mind like a burr, putting him sometimes into an annoyingly reflective frame of mind. Those many years back, as soon as the inauspicious month of Ashada was over, two proposals had arrived in the village simultaneously. Owing either to a rare oversight by the postal department or a quirk of fate, the two proposals had been interchanged, for the houses stood next to each other. The proposal that Rukmini's father had sent was actually meant for the tall and handsome Narayana Rao. The man Rukmini had ended up with was the short and dark Mylaraiah. By the time the lapse was discovered, it was too late; the respective parties had spoken to each other and agreed to the 'wrong' proposals. How did it matter really, for there was little to choose between two eight-year old girls belonging to the same community, brought up under almost identical circumstances, when the horoscopes matched. That lapse was immaterial now and didn't merit even a stray thought, but Mylaraiah could not help thinking sometimes, whether Rukmini ever speculated upon it.

This time, had it not been for his intervention, Narayana Rao and his boys would still have been in jail for picketing the liquor shop. He had taken up the case reluctantly, prodded by his senior colleague and Rukmini.

After his release from jail, Narayana Rao had come to see him. Which was surprising for in the normal course they rarely met; it was only when he wanted a donation that Narayana Rao would meet him. For they did not presume upon the familiarity of their youth; and familiarity it was, not friendship, for their paths had diverged too much for them to feel anything more than a general social kinship. This time, however, Mylaraiah had managed to get Narayana Rao and his boys' jail sentence commuted to a fine. A part of the hefty sum he had paid himself. Mylaraiah had guessed from Narayana Rao's awkward, tongue-tied overtures that he had come to thank him, though there had been nothing particularly respectful in his manner, for no doubt he thought Mylaraiah had only done what was his due.

Shivaswamy had snatched Narayana Rao first, as soon as he entered the compound, and had kept him talking by the gate till it was almost time for Mylaraiah to leave for his chambers. He never did find out whether Narayana Rao's coconut groves changed hands to enrich the Congress coffers, but after talking to Shivaswamy, Narayana Rao walked up into the verandah and into Mylaraiah's office.

As Mylaraiah had looked at the man across the table, unshaven and scruffy, in limp khadi, he had again felt the familiar impulse of anger and reluctant admiration towards him.

'And what will you do now Narayana Rao?' he had asked, a little brusquely.

'Why, get back into the fray of course,' Narayana Rao had said immediately, spreading his hands out in a helpless gesture, as if he was but a straw in the winds of fate, and that the nation, the state, the party and his boys, who waited outside the gate, were impatient for him to transact his business and get back to them, and of course, he did not expect Mylaraiah to understand his compulsions.

It was anger that spurted then, all admiration gone. No more, Mylaraiah had decided right then, would he come to Narayana Rao's rescue or to that of any Congressman, despite what Rukmini and the whole Bar Council said.

'Do you know what you are doing, where you are headed? You are setting an example to a lot of young men. Surely your approach can be less hysterical. . .'

'The decision was made for me long back,' Narayana Rao had looked at him deliberately, 'by an experience I cannot forget. . .'

And then, Narayana Rao had mentioned the amaldar of their village.

'Do you remember him?'

The amaldar was one of the most enduring images of Mylaraiah's childhood. He instantly recalled a distant cloud of dust advancing on the village path, which even as they watched, parted to reveal a blazing warrior on horseback, in khakis and sola topi, and flashing eyes that impaled the village shanbhogue and the patel and reduced them into genuflecting non-entities. The man would sit on a desk and chair set up under a tree, and as he went through the records, there would be a scramble to fan him and offer him food and drink. But he would eat and drink nothing and after bowing briefly to the village deity, he would ride off into another cloud of dust. Other than the sheer drama of the event what had impressed Mylaraiah was that the amaldar was powerful, he kept things in order and that he was a government official, and from there had begun his faith in all three. For Narayana Rao, who had cowered with terror at the thought of being trampled to death under the horse hooves, the man had been a rakshasa. And there was more.

'Do you remember a man who came with him sometimes, an Englishman?'

Mylaraiah had no memory of the Englishman but Narayana Rao could not forget him. One afternoon, the amaldar rode up to the village pond with the Englishman. A group of boys making their way home from school had been caught unawares. The others had fled as soon as they saw the horses advancing towards them, but Narayana Rao was left behind. The Englishman, as red as the amaldar's brown, had studied him carefully, prodding him a little here and there with his whip, while the amaldar stood and watched. He had flicked at the bare feet covered with mud, the thin shanks exposed under the drawn-up dhoti, traced the outline of each rib that stood clear under the mul jubba, and coiled the sacred thread that showed at the neck round the tip of his whip. He had contemplated the cluster of khadi threads for some time, before shaking it off. And then his whip had travelled up Narayana Rao's neck, up the swell of his freshly shaven head and had rested in a dry, abrasive clinch at the base of the tuft of hair that had been allowed to remain high up on the back of his head. He had lifted up the tuft questioningly and the amaldar's teeth had gleamed in reply.

At that time Narayana Rao had been happy to get away unscathed; it was only later, through his years at law college, and after reading Gandhi that he had understood the enormity of those few moments by the pond. Not a word had been said and nothing apparently had been done to him but an Englishman had been able to come up to him casually, inspect him as he would cattle or horseflesh that he intended to buy, and one of his own kind had joined the Englishman in the humiliation. The amaldar had been a Brahmin too and must have worn both a tuft and a sacred thread, at least at some time—and then the tragedy of his nation had become clear to him.

Mylaraiah had heard out Narayana Rao without interrupting, irritated by the long emotional tale, suspecting from Narayana Rao's practised air that this was not the first time he was relating the incident. To hold the entire English race hostage to the thoughtlessness of one Englishman and the entire Mysore Civil Service responsible for the arrogance of one lowly amaldar seemed ridiculous to him. Narayana Rao should have gone home and quietly cut the tuft off, which was what he himself and all right thinking men had done when they left the village. Why, he had taken off the sacred thread too. But Narayana Rao, despite his work among the harijans and his insistence that men of all castes should sit together and eat in his house, had clung to both his tuft and his thread.

'Well, Nani,' Mylaraiah had replied, 'let me tell you a story. It may not be as dramatic as yours but I want you to think about it. The other day I had an angry complainant. . .'

The man wanted to register a case against a policeman who had caught him while he was 'committing nuisance' against the wall of the district commissioner's office and had hauled him off to the police station. These 'civilizing' rules were new and had provoked a range of reactions—from bewilderment to indignation—from the public. The complainant had objected, not because he had been caught at a vulnerable moment but because the policeman, a Eurasian and therefore a *mlechcha*, had prodded him accidentally with his shoe while pulling him up from the ground by the collar. He was doubly polluted, he claimed—once by the touch of leather, the skin of a dead animal and the second time by the touch of an outcaste foreigner! Gandhi could fast himself senseless, Mylaraiah said, before he and his party could meld this vast, complex, ridiculous country without the glue of British intermediation.

If the many, disparate, tightly wound communities, cocooned in their unchanging ways, suspicious of each other and quick to take offence, were the bones in the spine of the country, the British to Mylaraiah were the gel-filled discs that separated the bones, defining them, giving them the space, the ease and the swing they required to live with each other. If the gel were to slip out of place, the body would be prostrate and aflame with pain; it was so easy for their dissensions to lose all sense of proportion. People could be strange; the most docile and compliant of them could go berserk if given half a chance.

Then Mylaraiah had stood up, knowing that there was nothing more that the two of them could say to each other. 'We cannot wish away our past, I know, but you cannot insist on looking at things through peepholes either. Here, I don't know if you've seen this,' he had handed the pamphlet with the scurrilous article to Narayana Rao, 'but it's just the kind of thing you'd appreciate. In fact I thought you had written it.'

Narayana Rao had barely glanced at the newspaper. 'Yes, I know that article. No, I didn't write it.' He had smiled slightly. 'A fine piece of work. It was written by a scholar. He is not part of the movement or the party but he is a strong believer in our ideals. He teaches our sons, by the way, lawyer Nanjunda Kole's brother, everyone calls him C.G.K. Sir.'

'Oh, Kole's brother? I know Nanjunda Kole very well. Pity his brother is so addled. Here is a man who still thinks Queen Victoria is the Empress of India. She's long been dead and he is still in her thrall. We have come a long way since then. Even your Gandhi refers to our maharaja as a rajrishi and the whole country thinks of us as a model state.' Mylaraiah had reached across, picked up Narayana Rao's unresisting hand that rested on the table and shaken it, so that he would get up and leave. 'And don't mistake me Nani, I'm with you when it comes to social upliftment. Only, don't be in such a hurry to drive the British away.'

Rukmini had come into the office room to find her husband working his arms into the sleeves of his black coat, frowning thoughtfully. 'There he goes, Rukmini,' he had pointed in the direction of the gate, 'the man in whose hands rests the fate of this town, if not the state and the nation, and in this man's . . .,' pointing to the pamphlet that Narayana Rao had refused to take with him, 'the fate of our son.'

'Never mind all that. Why had Narayana Rao come?'

'To thank me, I thought. But what I got was a history lesson instead. I was made to stand up on the bench. Your Nani will not let go of the past, Rukmini. He continues to suck on the piece of rock sugar distributed back in the 1880s when the maharaja's late father came to the throne, and it has turned bitter in his mouth. He also reminded me of our village amaldar's English friend who had apparently been rough with him long, long ago. He still feels the imprint of the cane that inspected his tuft when he was a boy.'

'Poor man, how he must have suffered. . .'

'Well, he's had a lifetime to get over it.'

'He looks so thin and ill. Must be his frequent trips to jail. No wonder his practice is doing badly.'

'Even otherwise he wouldn't have too many cases. He just can't apply himself to any job systematically. Can't survive without excitement. . .'

But Rukmini had just shrugged and gone inside And Mylaraiah had smiled ruefully at how determined she seemed to impute the best motives, even heroism, to Narayana Rao's human failings. Well, he said to himself, you could win the skirmish but the war would never be yours.

By the time Mylaraiah reached his office, the sun was up. His clerk had arrived ahead with the files in a tonga and his clients were already waiting for him. When Mylaraiah opened the first file and asked his clerk to summon the client into the room, thoughts of king, country, knave and wife had gone from his head. The only thing that mattered was the Modern Mills case.

four

1987

Before we return to Bangalore, we decide to visit a childhood friend. I am happy my father has acknowledged a childhood and at least one friend. And that he is allowing me to watch him skulk into his boyhood.

I am not enamoured of this town. It is too crowded and dusty, what charming buildings there might be have been elbowed out by small, mean structures. Everything is so chaotic, as if every man, woman and child and stray dog and cow, not to mention the cars and bicycles, have a mind of their own directly opposed to the other. We are driving on knuckly stone roads still waiting to be dressed with tar, which might never be. On one of the side roads, the squabbling new buildings stand aside for a moment, and in the middle of a large field, surprisingly unencroached upon, is a stately building of perfect proportions. The white paint is peeling and many of the windows hang from their hinges but nothing can take away from its gravity. It has the equanimity of a witness of history, of one who has lived through many happenings and taken every turn in his stride. With a solemn forefinger it bids you closer. This was my father's school.

'We used to play cricket on this field,' my father says. 'Mahatma Gandhi once gave a speech here.'

'When was that?'

'I don't remember. I was a boy then, about eight or nine,

or maybe younger. There was a very big crowd, one of the biggest ever, and a lot of dust. I think I got lost. . .We also hanged a cat here once.'

'What! Hanged a cat?'

I catch a strange look on his face, as if a forbidden thought had crossed his mind.

I smile to myself but keep quiet. I cannot imagine my father doing anything like that. Hanging a cat when he doesn't even hang out his wet towel after his bath! At one time, I would have been full of questions. But it is too late now for these things. This trip is not half as nostalgic or painful as I thought it would be. I have turned my face westward now. If my local Sam Spade comes up with something, it will help me bring things full circle.

We drive on the edge of a large green body. It is only after the smell seeps in that you realize it is a lake covered with weeds. The market square is so crowded and the lanes so narrow that at one point I suggest we abandon the car and walk. We are going to see Ramachandra Rao, retired head master of the Government Boys' School, who now runs the Citizen's Forum. My father is meeting him after almost forty years.

'His father used to be S. Narayana Rao, leading Congressman of this town and freedom fighter. Minister in the cabinet of the first state government after Independence, but could not handle the caste politics. Got a raw deal and eventually faded away. He got in for one term and I think he tried standing for elections again but lost his deposit. . .I cannot imagine why Ramu came back to this town. . .'

My father is getting positively garrulous now, after all these years. Memories lead to nostalgia and nostalgia is nothing but the dust of regret, he had told me once, and he believed in wiping his feet on the door mat before coming in.

'Narayana Rao had organized a bonfire of foreign clothes here in the market square and I remember throwing my shorts in, in a fit of patriotic fervour, and going home in my underpants. I got such a scolding from the cook.'

'The cook?'

'Oh yes. Achamma pretty much ran the household. We were answerable to her for all our minor omissions and commissions.'

My father uses some quaint expressions. Omissions and commissions, 'bounder' is another one. So and so is a bounder, he often says, but I can't figure out what the qualities of a bounder are—someone cheap and tawdry, I think.

We have stopped in the middle of what appears to be a wholesale market, judging from the vegetables and sacks that are piled into windowless sheds. Our car blocks the road. As I get out of the car, a bullock cart laden with sacks and coconuts jostles me. I see my father disappearing into one of the buildings—all the buildings on the road are uniformly dingy and one-storied—and I follow him quickly. A narrow flight of stairs with a wrought-iron banister leads to a corridor with several offices, each a single room. The double door has been newly painted in a greasy grey oil paint, so liberally, that the small board saying Citizen's Social Forum can barely be made out. The grey stone floor is cracked. From the high ceiling a fan is suspended, its pole and blades thick with cobwebs. In the far corner there is a stand with an earthen water jar, its mouth covered with an inverted plastic cup.

A man rises from behind the desk. He is small, bespectacled and is wearing a much-washed khadi kurta.

'Ramachandra. . .Ramu, it's me, Setumadhav Rao. . .'

'Oh Setu! After so many years! I got your message but I didn't think you would. . .'

They stand looking at each other across the desk. They don't embrace or even shake hands and of course, they completely ignore me. I'm sure my father has forgotten I'm there.

He walks up to the window and looks out. 'The lake, it's covered with water hyacinth.'

'Yes, it's a problem. I'm trying to do something about it.'

'And the town, unrecognizable. All the old landmarks gone, and every road. . .' he raises his hands.

I'm sure he does not mean it, but my father's manner seems to imply that it's Ramachandra's fault. Ramachandra just stands and shakes his head.

My father is looking round the room, studying the high ceiling and the fan. 'This used to be the Congress office, isn't it. . .'

'Yes, it moved out of here a long time back, right in the sixties. It's shifted near the bus stop now, much bigger place.'

'Your father. . .'

'No more. Passed away in 1964—a little after Nehru, actually. And your father? I heard. . .'

'He died a few years after we moved to Bangalore.'

Quits now. My father for yours.

They speak quickly, their responses coming a little too fast. They look at each other and look away, my father's eyes searching the room, till they come to settle again upon his friend with a hungry reluctance.

'You still live there. . .in the Agrahara block. . .'

'Yes, the old house. . .It's called Middle Class Colony now. I retired last year, took voluntary retirement. To think I was headmaster of the school. . .' They catch each other's eye and smile.

'Do you hear from the others? Chapdi Kal?'

'I lost touch with him after he left. I believe he is in Shimoga now. Shall I send for some coffee. . .' his eyes shift hesitantly in my direction, but he doesn't look at me.

'No, no, we don't have much time, must be going now. We want to get back before dark.'

The air, turgid with things unsaid, clears up for a bit, but they take one breath and it closes again.

'Your house. . .'

'That's what I came for actually. I don't know if you know, but I sold it to Krishnaiah Shetty, Anantaramu's son. Do you remember him? I came today to look at it. . .show it to my daughter,' he half gestures towards me, 'but he was in a hurry. Pulled it down already.'

'He'll probably build a cinema hall there.'

My father just looks out of the window moodily.

'And the Mission property? I saw cinema halls there too.'

'They're selling off the periphery but keeping the centre. Do you remember Alpine's son? He used to play cricket with us. He's gone off to Australia. And Morris, he sold his factory and went back to the US right in the sixties.'

'And you? Didn't you join the Congress party?'

'Oh no,' he laughs. 'My father's times were different. Moreover, I had a government job. Unlike C.G.K. Sir, do you remember, our Kannada teacher who used to train the Congress volunteers. Now I do some social work.'

'Of course, he used to quite scold the maharaja in class. . .is he still around?'

'Oh no, he passed away a long time back. Do you remember the student demonstrations that took place here, in '42 I think. . .Quit India. . .his son was shot. . .C.G.K. Sir himself was arrested. He died in jail. My father was with him.'

My ears prick up. This man has told me more about what I have been searching for in one sentence than what I have discovered in the space of half my life. Not a muscle moves in my father's face.

'The Congress is no longer what it used to be. . .'

As a schoolgirl, I remember living through an emergency declared by the prime minister—when the buses and trains were on time and so were the clerks in the post office, and all the opposition leaders were rounded up and jailed —but ten years later, when she was assassinated, I was at the University of Chicago. India was in the news then and I had to explain the politics of the country in a special classroom session. My father had sent me several newspaper clippings then, and quickly consumable capsules of information on the complexities of our society and our religions. I wonder how much sense it had made to my physics class, a group of people who are trained to order things schematically and to whom ambiguity and muddle-headedness were interchangeable.

'Those were the days. . .'

'I was telling her about the cat we hanged in the high

school field. She doesn't believe me. . .'

Ramachandra turns to look at me and stands staring. It is, I realize, to avoid looking at my father. 'It wasn't in the high school field, but your backyard,' he says shortly. 'And the cat . . .kitten was dead. . .one of O'Brien's kittens which he used to drown routinely. We strung it up on the mango tree.'

They stand in silence for some time. I listen to the noises from the street.

'Right I must be going. . .'

And then, *finally*, they shake hands and pat each on the shoulder for a bit. But the two bodies are not at rest.

'The next time, you must come home for a meal.' I cannot help but notice how relieved he sounds. 'My sister would want to meet you. She used to be the headmistress of the Mahila Samsthan in Bangalore, of course retired now. She lives with me.'

'Ah Kalyani, of course. How is she?' Without waiting for an answer my father adds, 'Tell her I asked after her.' Perhaps he is afraid that Ramachandra will ask after his sister in return.

I know he will not come back. There is a scrappy quality about the conversation and they are too awkward with each other. Too much water under the bridge. The past hangs too heavily here. I can feel its weight in the room, hanging from the ceiling like the disused fan, dusty with cobwebs.

'Is there anything to see in this place?'

Ramachandra starts at the sound of my voice. 'See? In this place?' He looks at my father doubtfully. 'Well, there is the Shri Rama temple. . .and the waterworks. . .and the Martyrs' Monument in the church square, if you can find it that is. Every year around Independence Day, they give it a facelift. The place is so crowded. Anyway, you have to drive past it on your way out.'

The Martyrs' Monument, of course. Quite by coincidence we stop across the road from the monument for petrol. I breast the traffic and enter a small park with dusty red crotons, dried-up grass and broken down cement seats. It is full of people and peanut vendors and all the seats are occupied. So is the grass. I walk to the structure in the middle of the park, enclosed by a freshly-painted grill. From the solid base of the cenotaph, pasted over with polished granite tiles, rises a pencil of cement. It doesn't go very high. The lettering on the plaque is hidden with weeds. The script in Kannada at the bottom is completely obscured, but the words in English on top are visible. 'In memory of the student martyrs who fell to bullets . . .1942' I decipher, after several attempts. No names are mentioned. Nothing to confirm my suspicion that I may know one of them. But even if any names were mentioned I would be none the wiser. I may have found another piece of the jigsaw but it is as inconsequential and isolated as this structure giving the finger to the sky. Already curious urchins have gathered round me. I leave before they can ask me for something.

When I go back to the car I ignore my father's impatient frown. I do not tell him either that that monument could be in memory of a man who could have changed his sister's destiny, a man whom he might have condemned to bullets, for he will deny all knowledge of it and anyway it doesn't matter now.

He hunches up in the corner of his seat and closes his eyes. I want to take his thickened fingers in mine and say something to comfort him, but there is nothing I can say; we have disappointed each other too long, too continuously for that. The ground that we share has turned barren now, not even the furry undergrowth of routine to mediate between us, as it does between him and my mother. Sometimes I think there is a layer of lard round our hearts, transparent but impenetrable, through which we can sense what the other feels but which will not permit an answering throb to go through; and finally, I presume that all feeling will die and we will only be left with the habit of it. He can see that, which my mother cannot poor thing, but there is nothing he will do. As always, he will do nothing, hoping to resolve things best by avoiding them. So be it.

When we enter the city I ask the taxi to drive on Lal Bagh

Road so that I can catch a glimpse of the old house. I always keep an eye out for it when I pass this way. This is the house my mother grew up in and was anxious to get out of, so anxious that she puts up with my father's abominable behaviour in gratitude for having taken her out of it. When I have been away, I have had the time to think of her life, of what it must have been to be brought up by a houseful of women who are indifferently affectionate to you, as they would be to a stray kitten, indulging it only when it amused them. I used to haunt these pavements at one time, when I was eighteen, on the pretext of jogging in Lal Bagh. The house looks shabbier than ever, just waiting to be pulled down. (If I were an American millionaire I would buy it for my mother and present her with the deeds on her birthday, tied in a red ribbon.) The painted windows of the office buildings next to it gleam white, like new dentures, waiting to test their strength on this hapless shell next door. I wonder how the women are doing and whether the garden still smells of a mix of drains and the champak—I have been inside just once, before I left the country. 'Before I left the country' has a nice, self-important ring to it, it tells me that I am an exile. But then, I have to acknowledge that this is my home, which is contrary to what I feel. I am trying to establish my home elsewhere, far away from all this. Well, there is no point in letting my mind wander, now that I've decided it doesn't matter. My father has not turned his head to look at the house, just as he did not get down to look at the Martyrs' Monument. I will tell them both when we reach home, when the three of us sit down together. Of course, they must come and visit me.

1933

Rukmini sat with her first cup of coffee in the verandah, in the ghostly dawn, listening to the birdsong. Though it was the cawing of crows that was the loudest, she preferred it to a silent, pitch-black beginning to her day. The hall was full, mattresses spread from wall to wall, full of sleeping children. She counted the visitors on her fingers—two of her husband's nephews; her sister-in-law who had begun to behave 'strangely' again and had been sent here to recuperate along with her three children; Bhagiratamma, her mother, who really didn't count as a visitor because this was one of her homes; her cousin Shivaswamy, who had gone to sleep in his cups; and a cousin of her husband's whom she'd not seen before and who would probably stay a long time. In summer, their house bustled like a market town. Even otherwise, they had a steady stream of visitors, but the traffic peaked between April and June. And Mylaraiah, her generous provider, made no distinction between his people and hers.

There were the many balancing acts that she had to perform. When Shivaswamy visited, she had to think of subtle ways of making it up to her husband. And there was the cook, Achamma, to be placated. When the press of visitors increased, Rukmini sent for extra help in the kitchen, usually a couple of burly male cooks from the local matha, to do the chopping and grinding and to serve the many batches that sat for lunch.

Achamma considered it a slur on her ability and hated the intruders in her kitchen, especially as they were men and they in turn refused to acknowledge her ownership of it, taking orders only from the 'ammavaru' of the house. For the past few years a certain Somappa had been a regular in the kitchen. Of kingly demeanour and courteous mien, Rukmini had taken to him immediately. Achamma claimed that he stole; that he made off with a good part of the vegetables he chopped every day, being partial to tender green cabbage. Though Rukmini did not say so to Achamma, she privately agreed. And what was more he did it brazenly, under her very nose, and she was helpless about it. When Rukmini sat in the courtyard with her afternoon tea, he would go past her in a stately glide, his hands folded decorously under his overgarment, no doubt to avoid swinging them past the lady of the house. He knew very well that she could not ask him why his stomach was bulging unnaturally, for that would amount to asking him to take off his angavastra and reveal his bare torso to her.

Achamma also claimed that the new servant who cooked meat for the dogs—this being a Brahmin household, meat was bought almost surreptitiously by a manservant whose duty was primarily that, and cooked in a pail in one corner of the vast compound—was eating up most of it, which was why the dogs whined most of the time these days and were so listless.

Each day was unpredictable, but she did not mind it really; it added an extra dimension to her; one more way to use her boundless energy. To the many gods and goddesses whose names she recited in the course of the morning's prayer—the gods of preservation and destruction, health, wealth and learning, she could well add Miss Butler's name, ordainer of discipline, organization and common sense. That she could manage a household as unwieldy and mushrooming as hers she attributed in good measure to her London Mission School grounding. Nothing could faze her now. At every crisis, she thought of a practical solution, prodded undoubtedly by the sense of calm, the quietude that the principal of her old school, Miss Butler, had possessed. The girls had worshipped the ground that lady had walked on, and along with her practical qualities, had hoped for some of her intimidating presence, her ability to simultaneously inspire them *and* show them their place. To Miss Butler also she owed her love of reading and her ability to sit still, qualities, she was happy to note, her daughter Kaveri had inherited. The process had begun when the Wesleyan Reverend Rice, headmaster of Garret's English School had taken her father under his wing, helped him through high school and gone on to find him his first job as an 'English writer' in the district commissioner's office at the then unimaginable sum of rupees ten a month. Once he had been given a leg up, he had risen, from clerk to jamedar and then amaldar, acquired lands, a wife and a family whom he brought up in the shade of the Protestant Mission, never once feeling a mismatch between their ways and his. If anything, they had cut and shaped him like a diamond, so that his natural light would shine. And it had been the same with his children.

The first crisis that Rukmini had dealt with as mistress of an independent household was when she was fifteen, five years into her marriage and yet to have children. Her husband had returned from a visit to his father's village, holding three of his younger sisters by the hand.

There had been an outbreak of plague in the village and his father had put up a camp to nurse the sick on his lands, personally supervising the arrangements. When the epidemic passed those who survived were sent home and the dead cremated. The camp was dismantled but soon, he himself had come down with bubonic plague, which swiftly turned pneumonic and before long, he had succumbed to it. Mylaraiah had had practically nothing to do with his father these last few years, since his father had taken on another 'wife' after his first wife, Mylaraiah's mother, had died. But he was his father's only son and had to perform the last rites. After the ceremonies were over, he had asked his three unmarried sisters, already showing signs of wear and tear, to collect their clothes and get ready. Mylaraiah had never believed, like his father, that his stepmother would be a mother to them.

'This is their home now. They are our first children,' he told his wife, and waited.

Rukmini, barely a few years older than the three tired, round-eyed girls who stood huddled around their brother, had looked at them and taken a deep breath.

'Yes of course!' she had said briskly. 'What they need is a good bath. I'll ask Ranga to get the wood fire going.'

That had set the tone of their marriage. Of the strengths and reserves he expected from her, the ability to read between the lines and the bounds she should not cross. When they were newly married and had set up home together, she had thought him quite stern. If she sang in the kitchen, laughed loudly, or even clapped her hands, he'd frown. Every morning, her husband would plait her long hair and set her a page to memorize from Palgrave's *Golden Treasury* before setting off on his cycle to the lawyer's office where he worked as an apprentice. After he left, she would cry for a bit, a little because she missed her mother, and a little because it would be evening till she saw him again, before getting into a panic about learning her poems or her tables for he took up her 'homework' religiously when he came back. However, she had acquitted herself well and had won his approval evening after evening, till all of Palgrave was done and she learnt to plait her own hair.

They were like paper kites in the sky, women, Rukmini thought. How high they flew and how long they stayed up depended on the slack they got from the men who flew them. Sometimes, they might not get off the ground at all.

The girls had grown up in the house, and she had looked upon them as her sisters. But when it came to whom they should marry and when, she had no part to play. When her husband had got them married off before they were even ten years old to two of his mother's brothers, she had protested. She herself had been married when she was ten but had not left her parental home till she had 'matured' at twelve. After her marriage, her father had wanted her to stop going to school, but she had fought. Miss Butler's influence had swung the balance. Rukmini continued at the London Mission School for two more years, till she completed middle school, faintly embarrassed by the thick gold chain that hung round her neck, which she hid by drawing the pallav of her sari round her shoulders.

'And if we have a daughter,' she had asked her husband, 'will you do the same? Get her married off so soon?'

'Of course not,' he had laughed. 'With my sisters, I have to do what my father would have done.'

At ten, as her father had bid her, she had walked seven times round the fire with an unsmiling stranger, a twenty-two year old law student from Bombay. Two years later, when he had completed his studies and set up as an apprentice, he had come to claim his bride and they had walked out together, man leading child by the hand. He had taken it upon himself to mould her into the kind of wife he wanted. I agree with Gandhi, he said, that women should not be restricted to child bearing and housekeeping. I cannot have an ignorant wife caught in the coils of domesticity. He had brought her books and insisted that she read the newspaper each day, had taken her with him to his club and taught her how to play tennis and encouraged her to go to the Samaja and 'get involved with the outside world'. Over the years, he had grown into the habit of talking to her about his work, even going over knotty points of law with her and over the years too, she had come to know him more fully than he would ever know her. She admired his discriminating mind, the diligent, methodical way he set about tackling a problem, his single-mindedness when he wanted something, like the way he was working right then towards the government advocate's post. Of her husband's many qualities she wished she had, it was his seeming ability to partition his mind into different compartments, dealing with several things, giving each the time and attention it deserved and then putting it out of his mind, not carrying the detritus of feeling and uncertainty as she did.

Of course, he had wanted her to show just as much initiative as was convenient to him. In ten years, she had become just the wife he had wanted. She knew that he wished her to curb her enthusiasm for her interests outside the house, of which he was not a part and of which he sometimes did not wholly approve, including the powerful forehand drive she had cultivated on the tennis court, while all the other ladies played a demure backhand.

The mind, she discovered, was a strange thing; you could not stop it from unfurling. For a while she had stepped tentatively, looking to him for guidance and approval at every step, and then had taken wing. The Samaja was her first arena outside home, and she had made it what it was. All its successful schemes—the bank for women, the health and hygiene programmes and even the Khadi group had been introduced and nurtured by her. All along she had had to mind the fragile feelings of the others, especially the older members—she had to defer continuously to Umadevi or make her feel that all the ideas had been hers in the first place, and the fact that her husband did not like the appearance of her success, her consequence. Left to herself, she could have done better, for the schemes, the organizing, the minute stock taking came naturally to her. You are a clever little thing, her friend Dr King had often remarked. With the right training, you could have gone places.

For all that, she didn't know a better man and couldn't think of a better husband than Mylaraiah. After all, all he asked for was the household not to be neglected, and that she should be mindful of his position. He was a man of sterling qualities—good, quiet qualities. He would not cause her a single day's worry, there would be no surprises, for theirs was a world of boundaries and limits. Only she wished both her children had not turned out dark and short-statured like him, neither was fair-complexioned like her, nor did they show any signs of growing taller. She had been married when she was ten, so there was no way of telling that in time, she would outgrow her husband.

The morning had not begun well for Kaveri. She had woken up late and had been the last in the queue for a bath. The wrong set of cousins had arrived first—her 'peculiar' aunt with her brood of whiny, snot-nosed children. Her other cousins, her father's youngest sister's children were still to come. There was just one week of school left before the holidays and she chafed to get over with it. She could not find the book she had been reading and was sure Setu had sneaked it off to read it first. The servant had ironed the wrong uniform. Today was Blue Birds' day, and as class leader, she had to set an example to the others. She had got used to Miss Lazarus complimenting her on her impeccable uniform and shoes, and had given the servant an earful, after making sure her father was not within earshot. She knew, she would be late today.

Even as she had begun her bath she could hear the purohit bleating out to the children to come for the mangalarati and prasada. On Friday mornings, in place of the simple puja she did each day, Rukmini got the purohit to do an elaborate one, with all the attendant ritual. Kaveri and Setu waited for the prasada they got at the end of the drawn-out affair. They loved the ceremony that went with it, the deep silver cups brimming with panchamruta, and such was Achamma's skill that she managed to turn the commonplace mix of milk, bananas, ghee, sugar and honey into food touched by the gods.

By the time Kaveri came out of her bath the mangalarati was over and so was most of the prasada.

'Is this all I get? A measly bit of watery milk with a discoloured banana-piece floating in it? And where's my silver cup?'

'Amma,' the purohit chided, 'aren't you going to do your puja first?'

She bent her head in shame and transferred her anger to the gods, tossing the akshate and the flowers, the vermilion and the turmeric in their direction with more force than she intended. Anyway, I was talking to Achamma, not you, she wanted to tell him.

'Shrihari. . .Shrihari. . .' he would not let it go at that and she felt her ears burn. 'The lack of piety in the young these days. . .'

To tell the truth, he was miffed by the lack of piety in the whole household, particularly the casual way in which they treated him. He had no complaints about the dakshina he received, in no other house was he rewarded more handsomely. Rukminiamma, he noted with satisfaction, did not enter the kitchen till she had bathed and her 'madi' sari hung out to dry on a pole indoors, quite separate from the rest of the washing. The master of the house too read his designated pages from the Bhagavad Gita, in Sanskrit, each morning. But there was something in the brisk nod that Mylaraiah gave him when he saw him, and the gentle-but-firm tone that Rukminiamma used while talking to him that suggested that he was the first among servants, and prayer one of the morning's ablutions.

Kaveri was still on the verandah struggling with her hair, her uniform unbuttoned and her shoes unbuckled, when she heard the welcome click of the gate and saw Dr King wheeling her bicycle in—which meant she would get a ride on the pillion till her school.

'Morning Blue Bird!'

'Good morning, Dr King,' Kaveri said awkwardly, watching her toss her sola topi on one of the cane chairs and shake her fair hair loose. The combination of her white skin, now flushed red in the sun, blue eyes and 'golden' hair, still tended to leave Kaveri tongue-tied.

'Dr King! You've come,' Rukmini cried with obvious relief from the doorway. 'She's been quite impossible today. . .'

Dr King's first name had been the matter of much speculation between Kaveri and her friend Kalyani. Kaveri was sure that the tantalizing 'M' that hovered respectfully behind the 'King' on the doctor's name plate stood for Marjorie, and not Margaret as Kalyani insisted. Her curls and blue eyes bespoke a Marjorie; Margaret would have had black straight hair and a grave manner. Her mother didn't know either, even though they went back a long way. The doctor had come home to deliver both Kaveri and Setu, and now would drop in obligingly, despite her hectic schedule, to look up any minor illness in the household.

Sometimes Dr King would come unannounced in the evenings after her day's rounds, and Rukmini and she would sit in the garden. The doctor would then light up the first of the evening's chain of Scissors cigarettes, fix it on to the long holder and start off.

'Mrs M, I thought I'd had it with that man,' she'd shake her head, and relate yet another skirmish she had had with an accounts superintendent who she insisted was refusing to give her funds for one of her schemes. 'I have a good mind to take him to the village—you know the one where my tyres always get punctured on the road—and leave him there, in a thatched hut, without water and electricity and with snakes for company.'

Rukmini would sit back and breathe deep of the faintly tobacco scented air, drinking in every single detail of the doctor's account. Sometimes she would ply her with questions— How did you know? What did you do then? What were the signs? Have you used the wonder drug penicillin? What truly interested her were the difficult cases, the ones apparently beyond hope, where every diagnosis had failed, till a fortuitous combination of common sense, presence of mind and luck provided the answer in a flash. In her dreams, Rukmini saw her own waiting room full of such patients—a case of snake bite where she had but seconds to administer the crucial phial, a forager in the forest gored by a bison, who waited patiently with his torn and bloodied limb wrapped in a towel while she saved the boy who had been bitten by the snake, a woman with a mysterious ailment who dwindled even as Rukmini's brain worked like lightning thinking of parallels—where had she encountered that peculiar pallor and shortness of breath before—there it was! Have you been eating peanuts, she would ask the woman triumphantly, knowing the answer even before the woman could nod weakly; and then she would laugh at herself for getting on like her children. Dr King's instruments, the stethoscope with the worn ear pieces, the gleaming forceps and syringes, she viewed wistfully and when the doctor sailed out of the gate on her bicycle, Rukmini felt that part of her was setting off to whatever village or hamlet that was scheduled for a visit that day.

Then there was the gossip. As the evening wore on and Dr King grew more relaxed, she'd start on an anecdote. 'Did I tell you, Mrs M, about the time I was summoned in the middle of the night to the Prince of Baroda's palace to attend to his Ranee. . .' she would say, her face already quivering with laughter. 'She turned out to be his dog.'

So she was with the Prince of Baroda before she joined the maharaja of Mysore, Rukmini would make a mental note, to fill up her trove of facts about Dr King—a game that she and her mother indulged in. It must be a man who caused her to leave, her mother said, she must have been crossed in love and you know what a big deal the parangis make out of love; Rukmini had laughed at her mother's prosaic mind. The two of them would talk till it grew quite dark and the only thing that could be seen was the glowing end of Dr. King's cigarette and the mosquitoes no longer let them sit outdoors.

Sometimes Rukmini marvelled that the person she should feel most kindred to, should be so removed from her —from a different country, a different race, a different life. They would always be 'Dr King' and 'Mrs M' to each other, and she would know nothing of the other's personal circumstances except for what she chose to reveal. From the little that they knew, Rukmini and her mother had conjectured freely about Dr King's family and fortunes. They knew she lived alone in the doctors' quarters attached to the government hospital and it was only of late that she had given up an itinerant career to settle down. Before setting up her separate wing for women and children, Dr King had been more of a wandering doctor, a familiar figure on her cycle in the nearby villages. Her father had come to India to seek his fortune and had found it as an apothecary in Her Majesty's Eleventh Bengal Regiment. He and his wife were buried in Calcutta's Park Street cemetery and every year Dr King made a trip to Calcutta to see her brother who was in the army and to visit her parents' grave. Occasionally she spoke of her two nieces.

'When I came back from University College, London,' Dr King said once, the only time she had made such a solemn and direct personal reference to herself, 'I knew the soft life wasn't for me—treating the ailments of the overeating and indulgent memsahibs of Calcutta or Madras, or even Bombay. And all the ceremony and the social set up. . .the first thing I did was to throw the Warrant of Precedence out of the window. I bought a bicycle instead and decided I would go where I want.'

It was this that appealed most to Rukmini—the romance of sailing halfway across the world and then setting off on a bicycle into the wilderness. It made her chafe sometimes, and she would be quick and impatient with her children for a while but then, before the slight feeling of regret could grow into real longing and then into discontent, it would die out, or drown in the hectic routine that claimed her. Or her eagle-eyed mother would jolt her out of it by listing their many relatives, women stunted by circumstance or by the sheer caprice of others, those who were not allowed to visit their parents, or had children every year till their wombs were worn out, or like her sister-in-law, driven to madness by indifference. Of course, Rukmini would have made a very good doctor, or lawyer, a good whatever-she-chose-to-put-her mind-to. Then, every time she waved the good doctor off down the driveway, watching her wobble away on the stony road she told herself that her daughter had her spirit, and she would make sure that she had the opportunity as well.

That morning, it was not just a routine duty visit to check her aunt's blood pressure and pulse rate that had brought her here, Kaveri knew, but the promise of Achamma's special summer curd-rice breakfast. The family found it amusing that the doctor liked the humble curd-rice so much, but Achamma could make even curd-rice taste like festival food. Of course, it was the incomparable maral-kanti rice, so named because the cooked grains resembled grains of luminous golden sand, grown in their fields, that Achamma cooked in a large pot and left to ferment overnight. The next morning she would turn the porridge-like mass over with a ladle, mix it with chunks of curd so thick that you could cut it with a knife, and serve it with dried-lime pickle.

'Now, you are truly one of us, Dr King,' Rukmini would tell her. 'You can't eat curd-rice and still be English.'

To which Dr King would reply, 'I have never felt any different from you, curd-rice or not. I cannot imagine feeling more at home anywhere else.'

There were other staples from Achamma's kitchen that Dr King enjoyed and whenever they were made, a 'chit' would be sent across to her and she would visit. Achamma would make her sit in the coffee room and serve her on a silver plate —a lady doctor who travelled all over the countryside on her bicycle saving lives, was worthy of such treatment.

But to Mrs Spencer, Rukmini's other English friend, wife of the missionary from across the street, a mere saver of souls, Achamma would not extend the same distinction. Mrs Spencer was served strictly on porcelain. Achamma did not care for bone china; it struck her as strange that this cold material should be considered the hallmark of elegance among the mlechchas but she was thankful for it as it saved the household from defilement; she made sure that the tea set was kept far away from her cooking vessels. Mylaraiah was the legal advisor to the Mission and the Spencers dropped in occasionally. While Mr Spencer spoke to Mylaraiah in the office, his wife would take tea in the garden. Mrs Spencer wore flowered dresses and straw hats and was closer to Rukmini's age than the older Dr King, but Rukmini's relationship with her was more formal. Kaveri had never seen them laughing together, as her mother and Dr King did. For Mrs Spencer, Rukmini brought out her best tea set, Huntley and Palmer's biscuits, and spoke of clematis and hollyhock. They had gardening in common and they both played tennis together—Mrs Spencer in a white skirt and Rukmini in her eight yard sari and canvas shoes. The two of them had introduced the annual flower show and the 'Garden of the Year' contest through the Samaja, which had caught the town's fancy.

A dedicated doctor and a missionary's wife would have had much in common, the least being that they were both English, Rukmini had thought bestowing on the English a homogeneity that they had bestowed on her kind. She was surprised that it was not so. Dr King also did not share Rukmini's enthusiasm for missionaries in general. 'I know your Mrs Spencer is a good soul and her embroidery and stitching classes are all very well. I will even go to her husband's church on Sunday mornings,' Dr King said, 'but Mrs M, spare me her chatter about little Dick and her efforts to grow violets here, in this red soil, or is it larkspurs? Why can't she stick to jasmine and have a bush full of flowers? There is no point trying to grow what is not suited to this place, and then moan that the plants keep dying.' So Rukmini kept her two English friends apart and she carefully trod the delicate balance between the two.

As the wife of a missionary, Mrs Spencer also spoke of her work among the people—the Mission was almost a hundred years old and other than the carpentry workshop, they ran a boys' orphanage, a girls' tailoring school and several model farms. Of her 'work', Rukmini thoroughly approved, but would never have dreamt of including herself among the 'people'. Even when Dr King told her amusing stories about the 'natives' she knew she was not one of them. Moreover, her childhood association with the Methodists had given her the comfort of being both—an honorary insider and a watchful outsider. She had drunk at that fount of Christian virtues—Miss Butler and the London Mission School—and imbibed their best, their discipline, their punctuality and dedication; also their ability to speak in low voices and close doors softly. In fact, in later years, when the possibility of their leaving became too strong to ignore, and the times too volatile for her liking, Rukmini would be heard remarking that she hoped the British would convert them all to Christianity before they left. That was not so much an assertion of her faith in the metaphysics or the spirit of the religion but in her belief in the essential immutability of things; that she belonged to a tradition that was truly eternal, and that the more things changed on the outside, the more they would remain the same on the inside.

When Mrs Spencer visited and sometimes even Dr King, both Bhagiratamma and Rukmini would be oddly watchful, particularly with Mrs Spencer, as if they had to be constantly on guard, like teenagers surreptitiously comparing heights and vital statistics. Anxious about whether they were coming up to measure on a purely imagined scale, where the advantage always lay with the other. Rukmini's conversations with Mrs Spencer sometimes seemed more like a pitting of wits, despite their impeccable grace and good manners, and she felt the weight of living up to standards set by those who had no knowledge of her life, except as a measure of what not to live by. They are the conquerors, her cousin Shivaswamy would say baldly, so they rule the roost. But it wasn't just that, Rukmini insisted. How many of their women would do the kind of work that Dr King was doing? Her own husband wouldn't let her travel from home and go to the neighbouring villages, and here was this woman setting off nonchalantly on a bicycle, halfway across the world from her home, to serve the sick. Eventually, it had to do with the spirit of adventure, of curiosity, of a certain intellectual discipline and rigour, which had led them to conquer the world and rule it at their own terms.

'Like I said,' Dr King was folding up her stethoscope and putting it into her bag, 'lots of rest and plenty of liquids—it will do her good to be with family. And you could order a good old vinaigrette from the Army and Navy Stores.'

'So, Blue Bird,' she said to Kaveri, 'ready for a ride to school?'

Kaveri smiled at her and waited, her hand poised on the pillion. But Dr King could not resist one last anecdote. 'Did I tell you that story about Lady Baden Powell, Mrs M? About her visit to Bombay?'

Lady Baden Powell, head of the Girl Guides movement, the counterpart to her husband's Boy Scouts, on a visit to a Bombay school, was supposed to address the junior wing of the Girl Guides, known as Brownies. Mindful of the colour and sensibilities of their Indian adherents, the Brownies had been rechristened Blue Birds in India. The good Lady, clearly a mass of good intentions and nerves, anxious to avoid any faux pas with the word 'brown', had burst out before a congregation of blue with—'Ah my little black birds!'

Both Dr King and Rukmini laughed. Kaveri could not see the joke and shuffled her feet impatiently.

'Don't,' her mother said, 'you'll scuff your toes. Goodbye, Dr King. I'll send word about how she is tomorrow.'

It wasn't the most comfortable feeling, being jolted on a sharply metalled road on a tiny seat with not enough cushioning, but the wind in her face and hair, warm though it was, made up for it. Dr King cycled past the post office and the public library, and people on the footpath stopped to look at them. Kaveri preened and sat up straight, awash with the sense of well being that comes from having eaten well— Achamma had made some more panchamruta for her after giving her a scolding for being cheeky with the purohit, from being well shod—she stuck out her feet and contemplated her shoes, satisfied that they were shining and that she was the only one in school to possess the buttoned up kind, made to order specially for her from Stein of Commercial Street, and from being well dressed—her blue uniform was not the standard thick poplin hand out, but made of a soft, caressing material, though she wished she had on one of her silk dresses from Green's. She wanted to stop one of the gawking passers-by and tell them that she had a flask of Ovaltine in her bag and a book that she loved, that the big house behind them was hers and what was more, it was the first in town to get electricity, and yes, this English doctor was her mother's friend.

Would you like to be a doctor like Dr King, her mother would ask as she oiled and combed her hair. If you are good and do well in school, you can go to the hospital in Vellore, or even Madras to study medicine, become the first doctor in the family. It was a happy thought but Kaveri would rather be Toad of Toad Hall and buy herself a bright red motor car. The appurtenances were in place; she already had a mansion, and servants and friends who were faithful in that they were dull and looked to her for excitement. What she would really like to do was write stories—stories about kings and battles, ships and pirates, even some faintly moralistic ones like the ones they had in school—Florence Nightingale, or King Bruce and the Spider, or Daniel and the Lions, or even Punyakoti the Cow from her Kannada text. Already she had reams and reams of paper, pulled out from her old exercise books and stitched together, full of the imaginary exploits of Peter and Jane. Peter swam seas, climbed mountains, hacked through jungles, jumped into burning houses to rescue children and chased thieves who were bent upon stealing unnamed 'treasures', while Jane was good and kind and loving. Stories about Jane had little lessons at the end like 'Don't be greedy' or 'Don't tell lies'. On the exhortation of Pushpa Miss, who happened to read one of her Peter and Jane stories, she had tried writing about Kamala and Timma, and had immediately been struck dumb. They were people like herself and she couldn't think of any 'stories' to tell about them. With Timma, there always seemed to be a drought, not enough rice and cattle dying in the fields, while Kamala brought in an ailing mother, an aunt who was recovering from childbirth and a husband who was being cruel to her in some unfathomable way—variations of the conversations that Kaveri had overheard between her mother and grandmother. The minute she wrote the names Peter or Jane on paper, it was as if her pencil took wing, her imagination was set free, and life was no longer a burden.

By the time she reached school, the bell had rung. She ran down the carriageway of the Empress Girls' School, built in the year of the golden jubilee of Queen Victoria, and the marble head of the queen curled its famous lip at her. She joined the flock of Blue Birds, and had to go to the very end of the row, not her usual place at the head of the line. Her leader's speech, prepared so carefully, remained thrust in the pocket of her dress. Somebody else was giving the speech, stumbling through unrehearsed sentences. And it was not Kalyani, her best friend and deputy.

'So ammavaru has finally arrived,' someone said behind her.

'Your perch has been taken, so stop fluttering, cropped crow. . .'

She turned round to glare at the offender but couldn't tell who it was. Her short hair and vermilion-less forehead were grist to the mill about her 'English' ways.

'Thinks she is a "parangi" just because she came riding on a cycle with one. . .'

There were two of them, Shanta and Nasreen Banu. 'Crow yourself!' she lunged, pulling hard at Shanta's handy plaits and kicking the other in the shin. 'Coward. . .afraid to show your face. . .better to ride on a cycle than to come in a covered cart like a sack of rice. . .'

Miss Lazarus clapped her hands. 'Blue Birds! Are you actually *fighting* in the back there?'

Once the speech was over, the games began but Kaveri could not see Kalyani anywhere. It was not like Kalyani to miss games. Finally she spotted her sitting on the cement platform on the flag square, in the shade of the Ganda Bherunda that fluttered above her head.

'I've been advised not to play for a few days. Complete rest. . .' she said mysteriously.

'Is it TB?' Kaveri asked hopefully, having just read a melodramatic story where the husband and wife had coughed to death, leaving their children destitute.

'No, Dr King has asked me to eat a lot of greens.'

'Oh greens!' Kaveri sniffed. She knew all about Dr King's greens. The doctor and Rukmini had devised a board game of snakes and ladders where every time you 'forgot to wash hands before meal' you slid down a snake and when you had 'two helpings of greens' you climbed all the way up on a ladder.

'No, really, she did. I have rice and soppina saaru in my dabba today.'

Kaveri looked at her with faint disgust, imagining the soppu slopping all over. No liquidy-stuff in my lunch box, she had decreed, no brown rivulets running down the sides of my dabba. Everyday she carried with her biscuits and two thick slices of sweet bread from Swami's bakery with a wad of homemade butter in between and sometimes, as a treat, a flask of Ovaltine—adding to the jibes about her 'English' affectations.

Kalyani's resolve was set. She wouldn't join even in the last game before they closed. Kaveri too was distracted and got out at dodge ball, when everyday she was the last in the ring. But before the class dispersed for lunch, harmony was restored. Everyone, Shanta and Nasreen Banu included, was sitting around her and listening to her Lady Baden Powell joke.

That night, when the servants had made their beds and they were preparing to sleep, Kaveri asked her grandmother a 'serious' question.

Usually, Kaveri's conversations with her grandmother were about who could throw an imaginary ball higher in the sky, she or her friends, which flower had the better smell, the rose or the something else or why the ash on an incense stick sometimes was a single long curl and sometimes scattered into powder. If she were reading a book, she would give her grandmother an impassioned account of every page. When Kaveri read a story, it was no longer make-believe, a figment of someone's imagination but a life that she appropriated. She lived it completely, extrapolating further on the situations, sharpening the characters, giving them an extra edge, something more than their creator had given them. If the book turned out to be a favourite, members of the family would be given parts and bits of dialogue. Right then of course, they sailed on the river with Rat and Mole and picnicked on cold tongue and pickled gherkin—'Cold tongue indeed!' Bhagiratamma had said when she had been given a piece of papaya instead, 'all I know of is sharp tongues!' It would be nice, her granddaughter would say dreamily, to live on a river, to which Bhagiratamma would reply, but you are one Kaveri, and a great river too.

It is all yours—the picnics, the quiet dips and gurgles in the valleys as well as the currents and the swift course and the falls through the hills. What do you want with a quiet, lapping river with toads and moles and rats when you can have the choicest crocodiles swimming in your waters and herds of elephants bathing on your banks?

'Ajji,' Kaveri said when the servants had gone, 'is it wrong to have "English" ways?'

'Nonsense!' Bhagiratamma said at once and Kaveri sighed with relief and shifted closer to her grandmother's comforting bulk. Bhagiratamma could always be counted upon to drive away your demons, however big or small. She was cut and dried about things, not like her mother who always prevaricated and gave a clever answer instead of coming to the point. 'We must take from others what is good about them but hold on to what is ours. No point clinging to our outdated customs or imitating others slavishly either. And what are these "English" ways?'

'Well, to cut your hair. . .and,' Kaveri cast about doubtfully for other such dubious ways, 'and to eat bread!'

Bhagiratamma burst out and then quickly smothered her laughter, remembering that people were sleeping around them. And then she coaxed the story out of Kaveri.

'Your friends are just jealous of you,' she shook her head. 'As for that Narayana Rao, I want to tell him that you can't walk in shoes of two different sizes. Can you imagine walking with one big shoe and one small, you'll start dragging your feet. Kole had better watch out. That son of his is up to no good. Those who start off picketing liquor shops may well end up patronizing them.'

Kaveri smiled, storing it up to throw at Shanta the next day, but would not let it go at that.

'Are the English better than we are?' she persisted.

Her grandmother looked thoughtful. 'Well, in some ways they are and in some ways they're not,' she said. 'They rule over us and they've given us good laws. . .but they don't really know us. And we have Gandhi.'

Coming from her grandmother, it was not a satisfying answer, so Kaveri reached for the book that lay next to the night lamp. She looked at the illustration on the cover—Toad strutting about in a yellow coat and a fat Mole lurking about in the weeds in tears. Well, if the English could have written this book, they couldn't be bad, she decided.

The day the schools closed for summer, Shivaswamy suggested a picnic. Before anybody could demur, the tongas were at the door, the cooks were ready with their cauldrons and supplies, and he was hurrying everybody up. This was what they liked about Shivaswamy. He took charge and got things done immediately, and though he could not be trusted in other matters, he knew how to take care of people. Everyone in the house was coming along, Shivaswamy said, except Mylaraiah who had to go to work. They were to go to a mango orchard that he owned by the river. It would be cool and the trees were laden with fruit. He has to inspect his orchard, make sure his watchmen are not stealing his mangoes, so he's taking you along, Mylaraiah told his wife sardonically. Killing two birds with one stone. We don't mind, Rukmini replied.

Bhagiratamma was not too keen on being jolted all the way in a tonga on an uneven road, but she had her reasons for going. For though it had been days since his arrival, she hadn't been able to speak to her nephew alone. The ride to the orchard would be the only private moments she would get with him, she knew, for the children took up all his time otherwise. Despite his mocking manner and affectations of contempt for the whole lot, Shivaswamy visited his relatives whenever he was in their parts and she depended on him for all the family news and gossip. Rukmini too had her reasons for going on the picnic. She hoped that at some point that morning, while the others were preoccupied, she could lead her cousin away and tell him she had thought carefully over both his proposals—and she had to do it when Mylaraiah was not around. Kaveri and Setu alone, it appeared, came with unmixed motives—they were glad school had closed.

It was a motley collection of guests and inmates that gathered in the verandah at five in the morning, before the sun rose and it grew too hot. Shivaswamy led in the first tonga, with Bhagiratamma alongside and all the supplies. Rukmini followed with Kaveri and Setu, her 'difficult' sister-in-law and her two children. In a bullock-cart behind the two tongas came the cauldrons, the servants, the dogs and two 'cousins' who were staying with them, and whose relationship to her husband Rukmini had not been able to figure out exactly.

'So Bhagirati,' Shivaswamy began disarmingly enough as they set off, 'how are your cows doing?'

Bhagiratamma's concern for cows was treated by the family with indulgence but she herself was passionate about it. She wrote letters, imperious in tone and full of bombast, to the Pinjrapole Society, to the newspapers, to Gandhi, to the maharaja, to anyone who would care to receive them, about the 'cow problem' and would pester her son-in-law's clerks to take her letters to the post office and get them franked. She had an opinion on everything—right from how much pasture land there should be in the state (she had arrived at one-sixth of the total land area, after much thought), how to conduct a cattle census and the proportion of pinjrapoles or refuges for cows that should exist given the number of cows in the land. Her good opinion of the Mysore maharaja rested solely on the care he gave to his cattle and the fact that he had established a model dairy farm in his land. And the Pinjrapole Society was constituted of good natured stoics surely, for no one else would tolerate the tone she took with them, on the strength of her 'generous' annual subscription towards the care of their old cattle.

Shivaswamy waited as his aunt described the health of her two beloved cows animatedly, and then slipped it in. 'You're still in your daughter's house, I see. No intentions of going home?'

'My son-in-law is a good man,' Bhagiratamma said simply, robbed of all her defences, 'He says I should consider this my home.'

However solicitous Shivaswamy may be, Bhagiratamma reminded herself, a conversation with him was like a boxing match. You always had to be on your guard and he knew your weakest spots. Usually, she gave as good as she got, but that day he had carried off the advantage early.

'Never mind your son-in-law,' Shivaswamy said, implying that he didn't necessarily consider Mylaraiah's hospitable qualities a virtue, 'what about your son?'

It had the desired effect. 'Ah my son!' Bhagiratamma rasped, winded partly by the movement of the tonga and partly by the thought of her son. It was a sore point with her that her son was so tardy in fetching her back from her visits to her daughter's house. Moreover, Mylaraiah would not send her home till he came to take her back,. Rukmini and Mylaraiah had often asked her to make this her home, but she wouldn't hear of it. Though she looked forward to her summer visits to her daughter's, her right place was in her son's home. This time six months had gone by and there hadn't been a word from him, except to tell her that his wife was ill or that he was too busy at the palace to take a few days off.

'He may be a daffedar in the maharaja's palace but once he comes home, he's a plain old "duffer". . .' Bhagiratamma bristled, too angry to notice her clever pun. 'Running in circles round his *maharani*. I haven't seen another man who's so scared of his wife. Oh the spinelessness of our men! Full of talk, such grand talk, but can do nothing! The house is falling on our heads, it leaks so much in the rains and all he asks us to do is wait. . .wait till the royal maistry comes to repair the roof. When he does come he assures us we'll have a house as splendid as the maharaja's palace.'

Bhagiratamma sighed and looked at her nephew. She had heard that he was given to sharp practices, and that he had made money in the Great War supplying cattle feed, but at least he was resourceful and got things done.

'The trouble with our Mysore men,' Bhagiratamma continued, unable to take her mind off the subject, 'is their indecision. And they make such a virtue of it. They confuse it with forbearance.'

'Not taking action is a course of action itself. . .'

'Don't quibble,' Bhagiratamma rapped her nephew sharply, 'you know what I mean. Others pay the price for it, never the men themselves. Well, you needn't worry,' she conceded. 'No one can accuse you of being indecisive. Your father came from a coastal village, so you carry the sea breeze and the nip of enterprise in your blood. . .' she tried to divert him, not wanting him to gossip about this when he next visited her son, for Shivaswamy was a great favourite with her daughter-in-law as well. 'How this tonga does rattle! I'm too old for such capers, I tell you. . .Did you see Raji when you were in Bangalore recently?'

Until they reached, the rest of their extended family was accounted for, ailment by ailment, travail by travail. . .and quarrels. Shivaswamy reported at least three quarrels in the family, one where blood had almost been shed, and Bhagiratamma was satisfied.

In the second tonga, Rukmini was preoccupied with how she was going to break the news to her cousin. As the tonga went past paddy fields and orchards, she wished she had taken her mother into confidence. The trouble was, her mother would have welcomed Shivaswamy's proposals, at least the one concerning Kaveri. To add to her discomfort, she was quite cramped in the tonga, the children were fidgeting about and her sister-in-law was shifting restlessly, digging her elbow into Rukmini's side. Every now and then her sister-in-law, who lived in the neighbouring town would feel 'low' and her husband would drop her off unceremoniously with their two children at Rukmini's place, saying—after all, if she can't rest in her brother's house where else can she? She had seemed normal enough in the morning and had climbed into the tonga willingly, but now she kept starting nervously every time the tonga jolted her. Her children, both girls, sat subdued by her side and it didn't help that both Setu and Kaveri were grinding their index fingers against their foreheads, making the 'screw loose' sign at them. Rukmini was forced to stop the tonga and send Setu off into the bullock cart at the back, from where he and his sister continued to talk in sign language.

Once they reached the orchard, she was glad they had come. For Shivaswamy's orchard made a picturesque sight, right by the river, the soil a rich red, the trees weighed down with fruit, their ripening tang filling the air. His watchmen hurried forward as soon as the tongas stopped, and in no time at all their mats were rolled out under the trees, commanding a view of the bend in the river. The cooks kindled a woodfire and set the cauldron to cook their breakfast, and Timrayee set down the harmonium that they had brought from home and Setu's mridanga next to it. Rukmini struck up a song, Bhagiratamma followed and soon Shivaswamy's off-key baritone was joining the chorus in the patriotic songs they sang. Kaveri was next, rendering quite faithfully, all the songs her teacher had taught her, with Setu accompanying her with more vigour than skill on the mridanga. Between them, they managed to divert the restless aunt enough to make her stop fidgeting, sit down on the mat and keep time to the music.

Once lunch was over, and the children had squished all the ripe mangoes they wanted, they wandered off with the dogs, Bhagiratamma settled down for a nap and Rukmini began racking her brains to see how she would broach the subject with Shivaswamy.

'How is she doing?' Shivaswamy asked, as they watched the tall, slim figure under the trees, pulling the branches down, holding a low hanging fruit to her face. 'You can't tell by looking at her that anything is wrong with her.'

'My sister-in-law? Quite unpredictable. . .' Rukmini sighed. 'I cannot believe this is the girl I brought up myself. . .' She had tried to prevent her sister-in-law's marriage to her uncle, her mother's brother. But Mylaraiah had insisted that both his sisters marry their uncles, so that they could be entrusted to 'known' men and their well-being would never be in doubt. 'And. . .well, it cannot be denied. . .there is a strong streak of ma—,' Rukmini hesitated, 'I mean melancholia in their family.'

'Melancholia is big word,' Shivaswamy said. 'I can tell that Dr King has been talking to you. Quite your mentor, isn't she?'

Rukmini frowned. 'Well, considering I haven't had any education so to speak of, except to rely on my common sense, I don't see why I shouldn't be guided by those who know better!' And who could know better, she seemed to imply, than an Englishwoman educated in England, and a doctor too. There were so many things that one accepted blindly in the name of tradition. If Dr King hadn't told her, she wouldn't have known about marriages between blood relatives and all the facts about them.

Then in a flash it occurred to Rukmini that she had found a way to refuse Shivaswamy's proposal and even make it sound reasonable. She braced herself and told her cousin she had nothing against his son Chamu, in fact he was an excellent catch and she envied the family that would get him eventually, but she did not approve of marriage between cousins, all that in-breeding, as Dr King had told her. Yes, they weren't first cousins, but still. Moreover, Kaveri was far too young and long engagements made no sense. In the same breath she rejected her cousin's second proposal that Setu be sent to a new residential school being opened by the maharaja, where he would be trained to be an engineer or for a career in the civil services. Her son was talented, she knew, in fact he never scored less than a hundred percent in maths each time, and it was kind of Shivaswamy to use his influence to get him into the exclusive school, but again, Setu was too young to leave home. Rukmini was glad to have got over with it when her husband was not there for he had been half-inclined towards both proposals. Though he did not think much of Shivaswamy, he was willing to slight his own disregard if things were ultimately to his advantage.

When Bhagiratamma roused herself from her fitful doze she found the air between the two cousins quite frosty, and so she told them about the ugly Sheshi whose uncle had been forced to marry her. The uncle had run away on the very day of the wedding, never to be heard of again. For four years Sheshi kept quiet and then one morning, in the wee hours, the household was woken up by what sounded like an animal in distress. Must be the cow in labour they thought hurrying out, and discovered that Sheshi had fallen into the well and was bellowing to be pulled out. She had changed her mind, she said, preferring to live half-a-life than end it in defiance. But to their question, how on earth did you climb into the well Sheshi, she made no answer.

They could not but laugh. Over by the river, the children played and their voices drifted over, Kaveri's high-pitched and teasing, followed by Setu's anxious, bargaining tone. The two had even managed to get their little cousins to run around, picking pebbles from the sand.

'I must say you've allowed Kaveri to grow up very naturally,' Shivaswamy admitted. 'They're both very lively and I've been happy to be with them. They're very close to each other, which is a good thing, considering there are only two of them.'

As always, Shivaswamy's compliments were double edged swords. So, she ignored the bit about the size of her family—Shivaswamy himself had six children—and said, 'Of course, the way they quarrel, one wouldn't think so. They are very fond of you Shivanna, you spoil them so. . .'

She said other things, mildly flattering to him and the air between them lay easy again. Rukmini breathed in relief. Her children were safe. Shivaswamy had not taken her refusal hard. Perhaps he had been expecting her reaction. Anyway, he appeared mollified enough to say that he would send her other proposals and horoscopes that came his way, and not of their cousins' children.

Further up, closer to the river, Kaveri and Setu and their cousins were playing with their dogs, in perfect amity, or so it seemed to those sitting under the trees. Kaveri seemed to be telling her brother and her cousins a story and from the rapt expression on their faces, it seemed to absorb them completely. They would have to be coaxed when it was time to leave.

Kaveri, in fact, was telling the others the story of the demoness who lived in the river and who came out each night to feast on the mangoes in the orchard. A woman with long hair and red eyes, who could live both on land and on water like a frog and was very good at maths because she kept exact count of the mangoes. That night when she came out, Kaveri told her open-mouthed audience, she would find the numbers depleted sharply and that would drive her mad with fury and she would come after them. So they had to appease her, Kaveri said, looking meaningfully at her brother.

Setu was quick to catch on. You must run up to the river, he told the elder girl, stand in it, say a prayer to the demoness, and run back before she could catch them.

'It's so easy. All you have to say is Rakshasi, Rakshasi, don't swallow me up!'

'And cup some of the water in your palm, spit into it and fling it over your right shoulder—'

'No, spit into it and swallow it—'

They grew bolder, seeing how frightened she was.

'If not remember she'll come out of the water at night and wrap herself round your neck. . .'

'Drink your blood. . .'

Their cousin, however, just stood still, holding her sister by the hand, grinding her heel into the ground, tears beginning to gather in her eyes.

'I'll give you a cocoa cap from my cocoa tin collection if you do it,' Setu relented, for he was kinder than his sister.

'Nothing doing!' Kaveri said, trying to tug both of them by the hand, 'and hurry up. The rakshasi can't wait all day. . .'

It was then that it happened. Even as the girls ran off in a sudden show of spirit, with Kaveri and Setu in pursuit, a figure in green streaked past them and plunged into the river.

'It's Amma!' one of the girls screamed.

There was a commotion under the trees as the servants shouted and the dogs barked at the same time and Shivaswamy tried to make himself heard above the din. Bhagiratamma stood up heavily, leaning on Rukmini and even before they could figure out what had happened, Kaveri had jumped into the water. Together, Kaveri and Setu dragged their aunt out and onto the bank where she collapsed.

'Kaveri! Setu! My children! Precious jewels! Blankets Timrayee!' Bhagiratamma shouted shakily as she reached out for them. 'Rukmini, look to that madwoman!'

'It doesn't matter,' Shivaswamy was saying testily, 'the river doesn't rise above the ankles here, and anyway its summer, and it's not even a river, just a stream. She's lucky she didn't cut herself on the rocks and stones.'

'Get a fire going!' Bhagiratamma continued shouting instructions as she stripped both Kaveri and Setu down. 'Now Kaveri,' she slapped her shoulder roughly, for Kaveri was in high spirits and was trying to peek at Setu, 'No flighty behaviour from *you*, now.'

By the time they had settled round the fire, their good humour had been restored. Shivaswamy made no more cracks about the water in the river not being enough to wet all their toes at once. Kaveri, snug in a blanket, hot cocoa in hand was being hailed as a heroine, and Setu, somewhat less lustily, as a hero. Only their aunt sat shivering by the fire, her lips red and chapped in her white face, her hair spread on her shoulders, her sari still wet. There was no blanket for her, and they were all sure she would dry off in no time in front of the fire. On the way back, she was packed off with her children into the first tonga, where Shivaswamy would keep an eye on her and Bhagiratamma and Rukmini came with Setu and Kaveri in the second one.

'You were very brave, Kaveri,' Rukmini, in an unusual demonstration of affection, cradled her daughter in her arms. 'And you too Setu.'

'Not Setu. He just stayed on the shore.'

'But I helped to get her out.'

'Both of you were brave.'

'Amma,' Kaveri nestled against her mother. 'Promise you will not put Setu into a hostel.' She whispered so that he would not hear. 'I heard you talking to Shivaswamy mama.'

'No,' her mother smiled. 'I won't.'

All said and done, the prospect of a house without Setu was too dire to imagine, for in truth, he was her first friend, her companion by instinct. For a moment, Kaveri had been so shaken by the thought of Setu being sent off that she had confessed to him about his mutilated Kannada composition and in return, her brother had generously said that he would not tell anybody he had seen her bum.

gandhi

When Mylaraiah came home for lunch, he found the courtyard full of women. Of course, the office bearers of the Samaja were meeting here today, as their premises were getting all spruced up for Gandhi's visit. Rukmini had managed a coup of sorts. She had wrested a half-hour slot from the Mahatma's tightly packed and jealously guarded itinerary to address the women separately. Narayana Rao had finally agreed to it. For he seemed to be taking a keen interest in the Samaja these days, which had got the women all hot and bothered. They had become *ambitious* about Gandhi. Rukmini, he knew, had driven herself to a fever pitch and had begun to feel that she carried every poor farmer on her shoulders and it was her duty to enlighten him about the benefits of spinning.

The Samaja was planning to present him with a report on their various activities *and* an independent purse for his Harijan Upliftment Fund. Umadevi and Rukmini had been collecting the money and people had been generous. Safe in the almirah, was a purse, fairly bulging and in a soft cloth bag were the pieces of the silver and gold jewellery that the two women had collected. Gandhi says they are just traps to collect dirt, your earrings and necklaces, Rukmini would tell the women she met. Sita wore no gold jewellery when she was in exile along with Rama. She wore only flowers.

Peering from the hallway, Mylaraiah recognized the khadi

regulars. Mangalabai and Sunandamma were there. Sumitrabai was the only one sitting on a chair on account of her bad back, and he wondered what Dr King, so loyal to her English tweeds, was doing here, till he realized she had been the initiator of the Samaja's programme on diet and hygiene. How she reconciled her admonitions on health to others with her own smoking, he did not know.

As he thumbed through the booklet on khadi that Rukmini had designed for the Khadi Bhandar, he was struck afresh at how good it was. She had put the booklet together after a lengthy correspondence and a visit to the state's khadi centre in Badanwal, near Nanjangud. 'Having spun the thread and given it a shining colour, weave it without knots and so guard the pathways, which the enlightened have chalked out'— Rukmini had begun with a quotation from the Rig Veda, a good way, he thought, of legitimizing the act of spinning. After the impressive beginning, she had gone on to trace how khadi had always featured in the lives of people. Apparently, according to tradition, the bridegroom's garment was always spun by the bride. Poetry had immortalized the hum of the spinning wheel and the beauty of the 'loaded distaff', Wordsworth had spoken of the wheel as a pious, virtuous thing, a friend of the poor. Doctors had commended the soothing effects of its rhythmic movements on the mentally ill. There were facts too, statistics and analysis. The place of khadi in the economy as a supplementary occupation for farmers was also discussed. She had quoted Gandhi at length on how khadi was a symbol of national identity and human dignity, of self-reliance and resistance to the British. 'Let the spinning wheel be your daily prayer,' the Mahatma had urged. There were neatly laid out tables in this section computing the production and sale of khadi in the state centres, the earnings of spinners, weavers, tailors, dyers, printers and washermen, even the amount of butter extracted from the cotton seed! The mysterious and often tiresome and frustrating processes of hand spinning and weaving were explained, right from the ginning of cotton, the staples of cotton meant for hand spinning, the spinning and carding of yarn, and how the threads were stretched lengthwise on the loom to form the warp and the weft came breadthwise to complete the process of weaving the yarn into cloth. The part that he liked best in the booklet was the 'handy tips' section illustrated by Rukmini herself, and as he flipped through the pages, he paused as always at the illustration of a woman sitting in a weaver bird's nest of thread—that was the tip on how to spin without getting the thread knotted. There were other tips and illustrations too—how to oil a charkha and stop it from rattling, how to make your own sliver and select a good carding bow, how to straighten a warped spindle, how to protect your thumb while spinning, and with each tip, the same woman, who bore a close resemblance to Rukmini herself, puzzled over an oil can, a broken thread, a recalcitrant charkha or sucked on her thumb, sore from plying the wheel.

When Setu and Kaveri sat down to 'practise sums' with Rukmini, it was to calculate how much time it would take three spinners to spin enough yarn for ten yards of cloth if they worked for four hours each day. Sometimes, complications such as a warped spindle or knotted yarn that had to be discarded, were thrown in. Setu was quick and would have the answer in no time while his sister struggled with the sum. But he would often ask, 'Why spin khadi yarn Amma, if it is so much trouble'. 'Because we can make our own cloth and we need not depend on cloth made in mills in England— stupid!' Kaveri would say. 'It gives us a sense of independence, of pride, of achievement, it gives us something to do with our hands,' Rukmini would explain. 'Do you know, your Kalyani and Ramu's father pays his party membership fees out of the sale of the thread he spins every day.' 'But Amma, my friend Pinjar Budda whose father is a weaver says khadi is more trouble than of use,' Setu would reply unconvinced.

Mylaraiah had to admit that he did not care much for khadi—it was too rough and even the smoothest weaves could not avoid the knots in the yarn, and the finer varieties wilted before the end of the day—and wore it only occasionally, more to please Rukmini. The booklet though was very cleverly and competently written, he had to concede. Rukmini had turned spinning into a romance, stressing on its irresistible combination of the spiritual and the practical. It could turn any sceptic into a spinner. He had heard that Narayana Rao could not stop singing praises of it and had recommended that it become part of the Mysore Government's manual on khadi.

It was from her mother that Rukmini got much of her doggedness, he felt. Bhagiratamma was there too, among the women, a fierce campaigner against cow slaughter. Right then she was in the throes of an earnest correspondence with William Smith, Head of the Imperial Dairy Farm in Mysore about the efficacy of *nux vomica* in the treatment of stomach ailments in cows. Our Amrit Mahal bullocks, like our men, have fought in Mesopotamia, she'd say proudly, and they were no less brave than the Mysore Lancers. Mylaraiah would often remark on her neglect of buffaloes—after all, the buffalo was the vahana of Lord Yama himself and all of them one day would be led upwards, holding the end of a buffalo's tail—and she would take it seriously, giving him reasons why buffaloes did not merit the same consideration as cows.

To Mylaraiah, his wife and mother-in-law's pursuits were more antics than activities. In a way, he saw in them a reflection of himself, of his tolerance and large heartedness. When he saw his wife sitting at her desk, in her typical 'thoughtful' pose and then heard the neat, brisk scratching of pen on paper, he allowed himself a moment's indulgence. This was the child he had nurtured, taught from the random books in his library, and groomed into womanhood with his conversation. She was now a credit to him. Of course, she would never be called upon to take any real decisions; she would always be insulated from the stuff of life. Sometimes, he thought, it was convenient not to be answerable to anyone or anything but your own conscience.

He stood in the hallway, listening for a few minutes and then turned to go into his office. He would have to wait long for his lunch that afternoon.

Any vestige of doubt in Rukmini's mind about her involvement with the 'cause' had vanished when she heard Narayana Rao speak. In the last few weeks, Narayana Rao had spent a lot of time at the Samaja, addressing their meetings. Gandhi was coming. They had to put their best foot forward. The Mahatma liked to see that the women were as involved as the men. So they had to work out a common agenda.

When he stood in front of them, tall, rangy, a little bent, deep shadows under his eyes, his hair overlong, more out of neglect than anything else—she was sure he never as much as looked into a mirror—his voice swelling, plangent and dramatic, and at times a husky intimate murmur, she had felt that he was speaking to her alone. A man like this, so transparent, as clear as running water, could undoubtedly sway crowds, not through the trickery of a demagogue, but by merely being who he was. For he seemed unafraid to speak his mind, to lay bare his vulnerability; if he contradicted himself in the course of his outpourings, if he pounded passionately at trivialities, if he stood revealed as impulsive and irrational, it made him more human, more endearing, for everyone knew that his dedication and commitment were total and unshakeable.

He had begun by thanking them for having had the courage to come out of their narrow, domestic confines, even if it was for a few hours a day, and work for their unfortunate sisters. He was sure that the natural qualities of women, their nobility, their application and dedication, their immense capacity for love, which were restricted to their families alone, if directed outward, could do wonders and transform society.

'You are Draupadis all, robust and independent,' he said bowing before them deeply, 'rather than delicate flowers like Sita. And it is not I who say it but Gandhi himself.'

He told them about the first time he had met Gandhi. His daughter had high fever and he had been given a case for the first time in his apprenticeship to handle all by himself. And then he had heard that Gandhi was coming to Belgaum. Overnight, he had made up his mind and taken the last bus out. He had arrived too late to hear Gandhi speak at the mammoth Congress meeting but he and a few others had caught up with him in the next village, where Gandhi had stopped briefly. How could he do justice to the small brown man dressed only in a dhoti and a towel on his head to keep off the sun? All he knew was that when Gandhi addressed the small gathering under the village banyan, he had felt as if he had been set on fire, even though Gandhi had said nothing incendiary; in fact, he had read it all before in Gandhi's writings and several times over. You have come because you are idealistic young men, you want to reach out and serve the poor, you want to cleanse what you see around you, but remember, the cleansing process must begin from within, Gandhi had said. You must be pure in body and spirit, as clean in habits as you are pure in mind before you reach out. You must live your ideals before you serve your community and finally join the larger struggle, the ultimate goal of Swaraj.

Narayana Rao had prostrated himself at Gandhi's feet and offered to serve him and go with him where he went, completely forgetting his wife and child back home. Gandhi had laughed and patted him on the back. 'Go, repeat the mantra of khadi as Prahalada did Vishnu's name. Spinning is a yajna that each of us must do for the poor. Go, induce your neighbour to spin for *daridra narayana*. To join the national cause begin by boycotting liquor and foreign cloth, and by spinning khadi.'

This applies as much to women as it does to men, Narayana Rao had told the Samaja. They may think that these were safe, easy commitments, but that was not so. Gandhiji himself had warned that women might find themselves in prison, may be insulted and suffer bodily injury. To suffer such insult and injury would be their pride.

'Tell us,' one of the women had asked, 'how it was the first time you went to jail.'

Narayana Rao had smiled. It was something he did not usually talk about, he said, but since he had been asked specifically, he would. He had been arrested for leading a group of satyagrahis to chop down the toddy-producing echali trees. He had gone, as Gandhi had said, without offering resistance, in perfect non-violence. He had carried with him his copy of the Gita in one hand and his takli in the other. My wife did not recognize me when I came back, he said, for we nearly starved for all of our three-month stay. The rice was nothing but stones, the sambar had small live animals floating in it and the vegetable was invariably rotting.

After listening to Narayana Rao, Rukmini had not dissolved into tears like many of the other women, but had carried home an enormous ache in her heart. To go to jail not knowing when he was coming back, indeed even if he would see his family again. She yearned, for such idealism, or foolhardiness as her husband called it. Fierce, if vague, notions of glory overwhelmed her—of plunging into the fray with a partner, buoyed by her dreams, seeking only the warmth of the spirit that fired her and knowing that it would tide over all difficulties. One afternoon, after he had addressed a general meeting of the Samaja, Narayana Rao stopped next to her and said, 'Will you do me a favour? Among your many talents I believe is a flair for writing. Could you compile a report on the activities of the Khadi Bhandar to present to the Mahatma when he comes? Of course you can have a whole section on the khadi wing of the Samaja.'

That night, as Rukmini lay by her husband's side, her mind travelled back fifteen years, to the horoscopes that had gone astray. She knew it was stupid and fruitless and she had pushed such thoughts out of her mind several times in these last few weeks, but again and again it came back to her that she and Narayana Rao were crossed by destiny. Thankfully, daylight and the physical presence of her husband brought sanity back.

In the days that followed, the wheel of Rukmini's charkha rotated faster and she spent most mornings on the khadi booklet, neglecting everything else. For this would be her personal offering to him and she had to produce a document that could not be bettered, and was worthy of him, a living testament to the ideals he lived by. She had to prove to him that in her own way, she was capable of the same dedication, an equal fervour, for in a way they were partners, weren't they? In the same heady burst, she had asked Narayana Rao to give the Samaja half an hour with Gandhi, exclusively, so that he could see the work they were doing for himself.

But right then in the courtyard, Rukmini was finding it difficult to translate the energy of the Samaja into collective action. The effects of Narayana Rao's talks to the Samaja seemed to have worn off far too soon. From a single body electrified with good intentions they seemed to have defused into a querulous, indistinguishably grey group in which women like herself and Umadevi flickered occasionally like fireflies.

Getting ready to greet the Mahatma was taking a lot of hard work and organizing. She ticked the items off her list as and when the committee decided on it. Mangalabai had taken charge of getting the dais erected and since her Hindi was the best, she would translate the report that Umadevi would read out. More then three hundred women were expected. Sumitrabai's volunteers would keep them in order—strictly no walking up to the dais to touch his feet. To avoid a rush, they had decided to make the collection beforehand and hand their purse over to him after presenting the report. It was decided that the Samaja would volunteer only one of their members to Gandhiji's welcome committee, since he was particular that a crowd of organizers should not travel with him or take him round. Here Rukmini had not stepped aside in favour of Umadevi as usual. This was not the time to hide her light under a bushel, for she would be sitting on the dais with none other than Gandhi and even her husband could not be impervious to that. After that even he could make no objections if she chose to enter the public life. Why, she might even be able to get him that post he was so keen on.

Dealing with people had been the most difficult part and Rukmini was amazed at the lack of common sense and the pettiness that she encountered. A simple thing like garlands, for instance. She had thought it self-evident that all garlands and buntings would be made of yarn and not jasmine, but she had had to fight to press the point home. Despite all the rehearsals and admonition, she knew that all the women would rush forward and flock round him like flies round a honey pot on that day.

'We have decided that Rukminiamma's daughter Kaveri will garland the Mahatma,' Umadevi said and if her voice was a little dry, Rukmini did not notice it.

That too had been hard won. Umadevi had wanted Narayana Rao's daughter Kalyani to garland him. Kaveri herself had been very difficult to persuade. I don't want to garland anybody. Besides, Anna does not like Gandhi, she had said. Rukmini had kept her patience and tried to explain to Kaveri that it was an honour which would not come her way again, and that her father had great respect for Gandhi, though he did not necessarily agree with his methods or his goals.

Another thing that bothered Rukmini was that Savitramma, Narayana Rao's wife had refused to be part of the programme. 'I just don't have the time,' she had said when Rukmini had visited her to try and persuade her to join. And looking at her shapeless form wrapped in a coarse khadi sari, much inferior to Rukmini's own elegant one of a finer count, her face flushed from working over a wood-fire stove, Rukmini had felt a little guilty.

Savitramma had steadily declined to join the Samaja, despite everybody's entreaties, including Umadevi's. Your husband is so broad minded, he urges women to come out of their houses and work for social causes, Umadevi had said. 'If both of us start serving society, what will happen to our home?' Savitramma had smiled. 'You know I just can't count on him, he's out of the house all the time, busy with his party activities, and when he does come home, it is always with a group of people. Sometimes I don't see him for days together, except when I serve him his meal. And you know our household, every meal has a different set of people sitting down to it, there are so many people coming and going. . .Of course, he never stops me but I can serve the nation best by serving him.'

The demands made on Savitramma, everybody knew, were

immense; for a woman without her willingness and her iron constitution, it would have been impossible. Like Rukmini's household, there was a stream of visitors from the village the boys they had undertaken to feed, and a host of other semi-dependents. The committee meetings of the Congress and all the discussions were held in their house and Narayana Rao would suddenly announce that a group of volunteers was coming from Dharwar or wherever and that they would be staying with them. Many of the senior leaders were old, of indifferent health or plain fastidious. The women always stayed in Savitramma's house. 'All of them, men and women, they won't dream of staying anywhere else and you know I can't bear to turn my kitchen over to cooks or get food from a hotel,' Savitramma had said and again Rukmini had flushed with embarrassment. 'And with Gandhiji coming, I can expect a full contingent from the party. I'll have so much to do—their food, you know the people from the north, Dharwar side, they have to have jowar rotis. . .to arrange for their baths I'll have to get the woodfire going really early. . .of course, they all help, good people. . .but you know how it is. Even when he was in jail, I couldn't go and see him. I just asked my brother-in-law to take the children. . .'

Moreover, Savitramma was deeply religious, observing all the routine fasts and ceremonies, undertaking several demanding ones voluntarily—many which Rukmini knew involved all-night pujas and cold water baths.

When the meeting broke up it was well past lunch time and Rukmini was happy with the outcome. Everything was arranged to the last detail and there had been no serious disagreements. If there had been a few sniggers in the back row she had ignored them. But when she made her way to the kitchen, she found that her husband had gone back to his chambers without his lunch.

It was implicit between Setu and his school friends that they would not visit each other at home. He may wait at the gate everyday, but Chapdi Kal knew better than to come in. He also knew that there was no question of Setu coming to his house in one of the back alleys of the market, where his father, a small merchant, traded. Sometimes, the boys played in the garden at the back of Setu's house with his dogs, but the servants were at liberty to shoo the boys off when they wanted, and some of the older ones like Timrayee would even box their ears. Apart from mere shyness, the boys understood instinctively that the bounds of natural ability ended where social hierarchy began. So Chapdi Kal was mindful of the honour being done to him and the risk Setu was taking in inviting him home. There was something that Chapdi Kal just had to see, Setu said. Of course, they would go in by the back door. The servants were all right, but they had to watch out for the cook. If she caught them, she would make them take a bath.

It was a visit that satisfied Chapdi Kal to the full. If, as their text book told them, the 'three sights' had brought Gautama Buddha closer to enlightenment, the sights in Setu's house, he would say, were no less revealing of the eternal mysteries.

At the back of the house after going through a maze of storerooms, they had come to the kitchen and on the floor of the kitchen, they had come across a huge man chopping what looked like a small round head on a wooden board. His fingers were blood stained.

'Don't be silly,' Setu whispered, 'that's a beetroot. The English doctor says it is very good for health. Our cook too used to refuse to touch it in the beginning.'

And in the next room, which Setu called the coffee room, was the English doctor in the flesh, sitting cross-legged on a chair, eating off a silver plate. The cook, the one they had to watch out for, was heaping a pile of fried sandige onto the doctor's plate. The few English men and women in the town were distant, hallowed figures to Chapdi Kal, best viewed from behind, and here was one, a doctor no less, eating majjige huli and aral sandige with her fingers, like everybody else.

'You should see her eat mosaranna. Just loves it,' Setu said. 'She's come to see my aunt, you know the one I told you about.'

Chapdi Kal was familiar with Setu's aunt. The previous summer Setu and the other boys had got into trouble for their games involving the aunt's six-month old baby. 'Rocking the baby', which was a competition to see who could rock the cradle fastest and highest came to an abrupt halt when the baby started choking and 'Where is the baby?', which had consisted of hiding the baby in ingenious places for the others to search, again had to be hastily terminated when Setu was caught trying to hide the bundle in the water tank.

This summer she had got better. Every day, Setu would come up with a new instalment of what his aunt did. Her performance by the river had been milked to the full. The milder diversions were her shrieks and groans and her constant licking of the lips, of which he did a good imitation. But she could quarrel spectacularly with the servants and had tried to run away twice already. She would lie in wait for Setu and accost him when he tried to sneak past her room. The past few days, she had kept asking him what he had done with her third trunk. She had tried different ways of getting the information out of him—one day she wheedled, the next, she was coy and the third, she demanded angrily that he return her property to her at once else she'd go to the police. Clearly, she thought she was travelling in a train and the others in the house were passengers travelling along with her. She would rock back and forth in her chair and say, 'I can see two of my trunks on the top berth, but where is the third? The one my brother gave me, olive green with locks on the sides and a catch that fits perfectly'.

'Go check with the ticket collector,' Setu would shout and run past her.

Kaveri had reported similar accostings, but her aunt, by some quirk of her disturbed mind, spoke to her in Hindi. 'Tell me girl,' she'd say peremptorily, 'can you understand the language people speak in these parts? I believe it's something called Kannad.'

Bhagiratamma said it was because she was prevented by her husband from writing the Hindi Visharad exam she had set her heart on. As for the trunk, it was explained away as the baggage of an unhappy home life.

That afternoon, Chapdi Kal had to admit she made a magnificent sight. Dressed in a red silk sari, her thick hair askew, she sat on her bed and fixed the boys with a vacant, glittering eye, all the brighter in her ashen face. She had just stared at them silently and then had let off a medium-level shriek and her head had fallen backwards like a stone, and hit the wooden frame of the bed with a crack. The two of them had fled before they could be blamed for it, stopping only when they reached the cowsheds at the back.

'That's a fine madwoman you have,' Chapdi Kal said enviously and Setu glowed with pride. 'Is that what you wanted to show me?'

'No,' Setu said mysteriously. 'But we must wait till there are no servants about.'

When the servants had gone, Setu led Chapdi Kal into one of the cowsheds.

'Here, look!'

'At what?' There was nothing in the cowshed, no cows; just two goats and a kid.

'These,' Setu said in a hushed whisper, 'are Gandhiji's goats. Do you remember C.G.K. Sir telling us Gandhiji did not drink cow's milk, only goat's milk? Well, that's why. And,' Setu savoured the next bit of information even more, 'do you know where they came from? From Anwar's house, yes Komberghat Anwar's house in Mohammedan Mohalla.'

Chapdi Kal looked at the goats, trying to work up the right mix of reverence and awe that they deserved. He knew that it was a rare privilege to be associated with not one but two hallowed entities, and he marvelled at the quirk of fate that had brought the two—Komberghat Anwar and Gandhiji—together. But the goats chewed on, regardless. The white one, the one with a beard, stood sleepily amidst its plentiful droppings, while the black one, the one with the silky coat, was sitting down, her teats splayed beneath her.

'When Gandhiji arrives tomorrow, Timrayee will milk them and take the milk to our school where Gandhiji is staying. After he leaves, the goats too will go back home. . .you can touch them if you like. They're quite tame. The kid was quite frisky in the morning. Here, feed the big one a carrot.' But the goats ignored them and soon the boys lost interest and went away to play with the dogs.

When Chapdi Kal left, with two tumblers of Achamma's excellent payasa sitting warmly in his stomach, he was quite replete. But, he had to admit that neither Gandhiji's goats, nor the Mysore hound were a patch on the madwoman.

Gandhi came in the first week of the new year and the day he arrived, there was panic in the house. To begin with the goats refused to cooperate and Timrayee had to be quite sharp with them. And then Achamma wondered whether the milk had to be boiled or sent fresh. Did one treat goat's milk the same as cow's milk? Should they send it as it was and would they boil it at the camp? The Congress volunteer who had been stationed in the verandah since the early hours of the morning did not know. Was it groundnuts soaked in milk or dates? Groundnuts, Rukmini said impatiently, she had clearly told Achamma to soak groundnuts in goat's milk. She had said dates, Achamma maintained. They soaked both afresh, just in case.

How, Achamma muttered under her breath, a man who didn't even dress properly—it was not as if he was the maharaja—could send the whole household spinning like a top, she could not understand. And what was wrong with cow's milk? They had been drinking it since Lord Krishna's time. It was all very well that he wanted to act like a poor man, but the poor would be only too happy to drink cow's milk if they could afford it. And groundnuts!

When everything looked set, Achamma, in her excitement,

dropped the thermos flask, the only one in the house. A new one could only be had from Bangalore. Now what were they to send the milk in?

'Rukmini, bring out the silver akshaya patre,' Bhagiratamma commanded.

'Send milk in a silver container to Gandhi?' Mylaraiah was aghast. 'Do you want my name to be mud in this town?'

Even as Achamma was washing out the remnants of cod liver oil from a black, large mouthed bottle, Mylaraiah hit upon an idea.

'Quick, get me a stool,' he said, as he took off his coat and then reached for the electric light in the passageway. He unscrewed the milky white dome shading the bulb and blew the dust off. 'Here Achamma, carry it with both hands and wash it well, and for heaven's sake, don't drop it.'

A lid was found to fit and the dome full of goat's milk was dispatched with Timrayee and the volunteer in a tonga.

A little later, at the head of the road on which the office was situated, the women of the Samaja waited for him, led by Rukmini and Umadevi. As soon as he arrived, the Mahatma would be brought by the Congress Welcoming Committee to the Samaja, his first stop, where after spending half an hour, he would proceed to the town hall, with Rukmini joining Narayana Rao and the other eminent people of the town in the escorts' party. They were there on the dot, and waited as the morning progressed from nine to ten o' clock and ten to eleven o' clock. But there was no sign of the Mahatma or Narayana Rao or anyone else, and the women waited in vain. Even their khadi garlands wilted and Kaveri flounced back home, refusing to wait anymore. When the Mahatma's entourage finally swept into town, it was almost noon, a good three hours behind schedule. The first item to be cancelled from his itinerary was the half-hour promised to the women's Samaja group—only nobody bothered to tell them that. It was almost time for lunch and the motor cars went on straight towards the town hall. Rukmini, was not in the escorts' party. The women, many of whom had come from the neighbouring villages and had waited for hours, continued to sit in the Samaja hall, hoping for a glimpse of him. Rukmini came home late in the afternoon with a headache and a fever, the first of her many mysterious bouts of illness. Waiting for the Mahatma on an empty stomach *and* maintaining order among a group of noisy women had proved too much for her. If there had been word from Narayana Rao, some explanation, she would have borne it better. It is only to be expected, Mylaraiah said, not without a touch of malice. He is far too busy and you don't really matter in his scheme of things.

'I have already seen him,' Setu announced when he came home in the afternoon, and lowering his voice he added, 'He was sleeping!' as if he had caught Gandhi out.

Setu's school declared a holiday since Gandhi and his entourage were to be accommodated in the school. But the boys had swaggered around all morning in the grounds in mufti—though they were not allowed into the classrooms; just by being present in school when they were not supposed to be made them feel they were thumbing their noses at it. In the afternoon, Ramu, to show off his privileges as Narayana Rao's son had made arrangements for his friends to peep at Gandhi. They had climbed onto a heap of rubble on the grounds next to the window to his room and peered in, each boy getting a maximum of two seconds. The Mahatma was taking a nap, fifteen minutes from 1.45 pm to 2 pm. When Setu's turn came, he saw a small, bald man asleep on the floor, slack jawed, his dentures waiting in a bowl beside his mat, next to his spectacles.

It was Bhagiratamma, Kaveri, Setu, the servants and a couple of unidentifiable relatives, who went to listen to Gandhi in the high school grounds in the evening.

'The crowd!' Bhagiratamma exclaimed when she came home after the meeting. 'I don't think I've seen so many people before. The whole high school field was full. Wait,' she fanned her face with the end of her sari, 'let me wash my feet first.'

'And so lively, I've rarely seen our people so avid. . .the

only time I've seen such fervour is at the local Maramma jatres and at the chariot festivals. They were behaving as if God himself had come down to earth. . .I can quite believe he can get them to do anything. . .but the dust! Kaveri was coughing all the time.'

'*In*! *In* to the bathroom! I've kept the water hot,' Achamma was urging Setu, 'Look at your *feet*.'

'What did he say?' Rukmini asked.

'There he was, perched on the platform high above the crowd, so small and frail, poor man. . .but his skin, Rukmini, even in the twilight it was shining like copper. . .what will we do after he goes?'

'Ayya, I didn't let any of them enter from the front door. Right from the back door to the bachalmane I keep saying, but they are too excited to listen to me. I've got cauldrons of hot water ready. . .God knows who all they have touched. . .'

'He spoke in Hindi, and Bhimappa, Nani's clerk, kept translating, but he wasn't quick enough, and moreover, we couldn't hear him clearly. . .'

'Well, *my friend* Ramu garlanded him and his father gave Gandhiji a purse full of money. . .'

'He's my friend Kalyani's father too, and she too was supposed to garland him. Actually I was, but I refused,' Kaveri cut in. 'Well, Kalyani's father gave Gandhiji a purse of one thousand rupees and you should have heard the crowd. . .like thunder.'

'What Setu! Still with your slippers on!' Achamma exclaimed, 'All *kinds* of people would have been there. . .'

'Achamma,' Mylaraiah said, 'the Mahatma is here especially to remind us about the brotherhood of man—he says that the arrogance of the upper castes and the way we treat the Harijans is what is weakening us. That is why the parangis find it so easy to rule over us.'

'I'm sure he never said anything about bringing in the dust of a thousand strangers into the house,' Achamma muttered mutinously.

'The Gita says you must treat other castes as you would

like to be treated yourself. . .'

'To each his own place, Ayya, and I would never refuse to wash my feet before entering anyone's house.'

'Wait, we haven't told you what happened after the speech,' Bhagiratamma said.

There had been a few anxious moments when the volunteers had moved between the rows, making collections and people had surged forward, anxious to put things into the collection bags. Bhagiratamma had caught the glint of coins, of silver plates and chambus, even the gleam of gold. For a few minutes, Bhagiratamma had been unable to see Setu in the crowd of arms extending towards the collection bag, but had then found him.

'Lawyer Nanjunda Kole's wife and her sister-in-law, Setu's C.G.K. Sir's wife, I saw them casually throw their gold bangles in. Nanjunda Kole's wife can easily afford another pair but that other woman, her husband is just a schoolteacher. I don't think she has another set to wear.'

It was only later in the night that Bhagiratamma noticed. Rukmini's diamond earrings, with eight perfectly cut stones that flashed blue in the night, stones hand picked by her husband for his daughter, were gone. But she did not say anything to Rukmini about it.

1987

I cannot claim to have had an unhappy childhood, I was often lonely and the house, very silent. It was the minding-its-own-business sort of silence that fills up large houses inhabited by small families. But sometimes the silence would turn slightly prickly and brooding, as if any minute things would change and people would show their true colours. Yet, they loved me, the two of them, of that I am certain now.

Father is a quiet man and he used to spend—still does—long hours away from home, presumably on work. He manages a factory which manufactures spare parts for the automobile industry, a factory that has been ailing for as long as I can remember. A cousin of his with whom I once got talking said something about his aborted career and family pressures weighing him down, but I don't know. My father has a look of baffled sincerity that men of slightly prognathous aspect, who are also bespectacled and balding, sometimes acquire. It comes naturally to him to vacillate; that is his excuse for not really trying, his way of anticipating disappointment—if this doesn't work out then the other alternative will do just as well. Left to himself, I suspect the only things he truly cares about are coffee and cricket. If we were to get down to particulars it would be the combination of Plantation A and Pea Berry from a certain coffee plantation in Chikmagalur in a 60:40 proportion, and the batting of G.R. Vishwanath. I would also admit to football. Once, to rile him, I said coffee used to be a cure for madness. Yes, he returned seriously, Mysore filter coffee could restore anyone's sanity.

Mother, too, is a peaceable body, but there is a grit-in-the-eye quality to her presence—as if she has lived all along with the discomfort caused by a small speck, an irritant that does not so much impair the vision as make you blink and your eyes water. The only time I've seen her forget herself is when she is in the garden. We have a large, well laid-out garden and she tends to it herself. Her pastimes are undemanding—gardening and embroidery—things that engage gently, things that fill your hands but not your mind, things that will not talk back to you, like reading or music.

Simple tasks, like answering a telephone make her nervous. I get the feeling that whenever she lifts the receiver, she expects a bomb to go off at the other end. In retrospect, I would say that she is also not very maternal. As a child, I was left almost completely to the care of servants. The only thing that seems to have given her pleasure was oiling and combing my hair (I, of course have short hair now, a man's crop). She would feel the bones of my head carefully and lovingly, like a blind person reading a text in Braille, and tell me how beautifully formed my head was. When I was young, I responded to her with the animal instinct of self-preservation, which makes you greedily suck at all things that sustain you. But when I grew older, I had no need of these services and I had to resist her attempts to bathe me long after it had grown to be an embarrassment. The trouble was she hadn't much conversation, wanting only to be reassured that my school was good, I was doing well in studies and my teachers were kind to me. She put a premium on kindness—Are your teachers kind to you? Of course, I would say, baffled, how could they be otherwise. They were kind to all of us in a uniformly indifferent way, they gave us extra blankets when it grew too cold in the hills and made sure we were dry in the rains. She revealed nothing about herself, my mother. Once I asked her about her school and she said it was an okay school round the corner, very near her house and yes, she had had friends but it had been a new set every year, she said in a matter-of-fact way, as if she had no further need of such things.

I cannot claim to have minded the way things were and ached for them to be different; some of my parents' insularity has rubbed off on me. I was brought up in the kind of comfort and security afforded by an old-Bangalore house—a large house painted in 'gopi' yellow, fronted by a closed, curved verandah, much like the side of a ship, a mirror-polished red oxide floor and windows with shutters opening inwards; a house with rattan and rosewood furniture and checked handloom bedspreads. I loved the house as a child and if I allow myself to admit it, I would say I still love it, in spite of everything. The house belongs to my mother, as I was told by that same cousin, and the information was supposed to mean something.

I studied in an exclusive residential school in Ooty, where I was sent when I was eight. That was the first time I suspected that there was a streak of wanton cruelty in their combined persona. It was not their sending me away to boarding school at such a tender age that I am talking about, but the way they did it. We drove up from Bangalore in a taxi—we were a very taxi family, we ordered one even to go shopping—and after a very hot drive it began to grow cooler and mother wrapped me up in a shawl. As the road began to curve steeply into hairpin bends, we had to keep stopping for her to be sick. It was dark and cold when we reached the huge stone building, which I thought was a fairy castle. It was, of course, my school. We spent that night in a cosy cottage with a fireplace and I was quite convinced that the cottage was to be our new home. They waved goodbye from the creeper-laden door the next morning but when I came back that evening, they were gone. I was led weeping into a large room full of beds lined side by side, like a hospital, and was sure they had been kidnapped, till the matron laughed at me and told me that they had gone home, and that she herself had seen them drive off quite happily. It took me days to recover from being abandoned like that and for some time I was sure I was an orphan, though my mother wrote soon after she went back. They must have thought that that way there would be no tears and tantrums or worse. But it was my first lesson in parental treachery, a lesson they were to reinforce in time.

But I recovered soon enough and I am told I showed signs of exemplary self-sufficiency, not asking to go home or see my parents. In other things too, I had none of that self-doubt that assailed so many of my classmates. Quite early, I knew what I wanted. Our library in school had large pictures of beautiful Gothic buildings, wood-panelled rooms full of books, and huge grounds lined with trees. When I sat in the library, the book in front of me unread, I would stare for hours at a particular picture of a milky sky, the ground covered with russet-coloured leaves and two girls sitting on a bench amidst those leaves, intent upon their books, not oblivious to the beauty of their surroundings as much as having absorbed it and become part of it. Even before I knew that these were posters advertising courses in foreign universities, I knew that was where I wanted to be. Right then I knew that I would, one day, refer to autumn as fall and I would see other shades of rust framing my window than the orange of the croton leaves that grew in pots in the garden at home. My plans took root throughout my schooling and college, which I sailed through, and for my research, I landed up like a homing pigeon one fall in the russet campus of the University of Chicago, in the physics department, one of the few to get a full scholarship in that year of 1982. I had picked the department with the largest number of Nobel laureates; things like that matter to me.

Once, when I was about twelve I think, my friend from school invited me home for the summer holidays. It was my first summer away from home—it was surprising how much I missed it and from the carefully casual expressions of my father and my mother, how much they had missed me. I did not spend another holiday away from home after that, but that's not the point. It was on that holiday that I learnt what a noise families made, how incessantly they talked and what a terrible thing it was for all your grandparents to be dead.

'Talk?' my father said carelessly, 'What do you want to talk about? You tell me. You talk.'

'Do you want new clothes?' my mother asked, looking frightened. 'Shall we go shopping in Commercial Street?' I could tell she was just waiting to get back to her compost heap in the backyard.

Rarely did we go out together, the three of us, Mother, Father and I. My parents didn't speak much and hardly to each other. My father's presence used to unsettle my mother, so much so that when she spoke she used her smile as a punctuation mark, a flexing of her lips when she paused in a sentence; she seemed not to know that it was a sign of happiness, an expression of pleasure, of joy. Mind you, he was always polite to her and had devised an over-civil form of address for her, only I suspect, to avoid calling her by name. As far as I can recall I was witness to just one 'scene'. My father used to come home in the afternoon for his lunch and a brief nap before going off to work again and returning late in the evening or at night.

We had just sat down to lunch.

'I don't remember,' my father said, pushing his plate aside and folding his hands across his chest, 'asking for a mouse in my saaru.' Only the muscle twitching under his right eye and the deliberation of his manner showed how angry he was.

It did look like a mouse, the clotted mass of tamarind pulp and curry leaves that sat upon his rice. My mother, all wrist and glass bangles, was in tears. Poor Mother, there was always something of the rustic in her, she hasn't too much finesse.

Father occasionally displays the flashes of arrogance of those habituated to plenty. When the land reforms came, sometime in the seventies, every single bit of the land his family had owned went to the tenant farmers who bought him out at very low prices. And fair enough; they were the tillers of the land after all. But he still has a certain largesse of manner which comes naturally to him, especially with the servants. They adore him; he is a good baksheesh giver. Once, when one of our infrequent visitors brought us jackfruit—ten yellow segments in a plastic bag—Father said something about cartfuls of jackfruit rotting in the storeroom at home, filling the whole house with its overripe smell till their nostrils and the very pores of their skin were clogged with it, and the boys having jackfruit ripping competitions—who could rip the biggest one open at the first attempt and throw it the farthest.

But at my eager, 'Tell me, tell me what else you did,' he would say 'Oh nothing,' as if what he had said was a slip of the tongue, an admission that he regretted already.

There *were* times when my parents went out together—it was to pay a visit to someone or someplace, I could tell. Right in the morning, when I drank my milk at the table, I could tell from the way my mother's shoulders were set that it was one of those days. Mother would lock herself up in her room—they have always had separate rooms—and Father would pace up and down in the garden, on the stairs and in the verandah and finally go into the room, and they would hold a fervid conversation in low voices. And finally he would lead her out, her face all blotchy, his, tired. When they returned, smelling strongly of floorwash, Mother would ask the servant if the water was hot and go immediately to take a bath and Father would sit still in his rattan chair facing the window and look out and smoke cigarettes till it grew dark, getting up only when the servant came in to switch on the lights.

There was a seesaw pattern to their relationship. Just as he was beginning to be civil to her and they would be listening to old film songs together in the evenings or going out for walks, the chill would set in and he would start ignoring her again—the pattern was connected to these visits they made together. He's had a tough life, my mother would tell her cousin whenever my father was surly in her presence.

He was not always like this, my father. I remember, as a little girl, on Sundays he would take me out in his Morris Minor to South Parade. One winter morning comes back to me with all the clarity of bright early-December sunlight. Maybe I remember it because I caught a glimpse, a faint glimmer of how things would have been if they had been otherwise. My father wore a checked coat and his cap sat at a jaunty angle on his head. He is a natty dresser, my father. That much I will say for him. We walked down South Parade to a field at the far end and sat in a pavilion watching a game of cricket. While I sat on a bench, my father went right up to the fringe of the green. 'Good shot!' he'd cry out, or 'Well played!' and once, 'Excellent line and length.'

So relaxed was he after the game that he hoisted me on his shoulders and basking in the admiring glances that we were getting, carried me all the way back to the car. We walked down the boulevard of South Parade and then stepped abruptly from the sunlit street into the darkened interiors of—a hotel! There were three aces on the door—the ace of hearts, spades and diamonds in red and black—and a uniformed doorman to open it for us. It took some time for the blackness to settle into grey shadows and then I saw the plush, satiny sofas, the tables covered in white cloths, the waiters in red hovering in readiness and I goosebumped all over in excitement and because of the air conditioning. One of the waiters pulled out a chair, hoisted me on to it and pushed it in till I was snug between the table and the chair, and smiled into my face, his moustaches dancing.

'Beer,' my father said, 'and a soda for the young lady.'

A band played in the background. I remember the soft but harsh crooning of the saxophone and the heartbeat of the drums. The waiter came back with a tall glass of orange pop on a tray and every time I bent to drink out of it, tiny bubbles, as effervescent as my happiness, exploded in my nose. And that was not all. The waiter came back and set down a creamy ceramic plate with a huge slab of ice cream in front of me. It was in three colours—white, pink and green with a sprinkling of small brown nuts, and a small spoon, smaller than a tea spoon, on the side. I had never eaten striped ice cream before. I still see the perfect granularity of its texture, like earth turned over with a plough, the white end just beginning to melt at the edges. The handsome waiter had smiled at me and said, 'Here, madam, just for you.'

Just then a woman wearing trousers and a blouse with full but transparent sleeves through which her arms glinted, stopped by my father's chair and said in a tone of mingled disbelief and pleasure, 'Setumadhav Rao! It can't be!'

'Hello Leela,' my father said calmly.

'So you still remember me. Weren't you supposed to be at Oxford?'

'That was a long time ago. Plans tend to change, you know. Here, meet my daughter.'

'Of course, your daughter. . .' She had stood looking uncertainly at both of us for a moment, trailing her nails across my cheek, flooding us with her perfume. That, I suppose, was my first encounter with glamour, with the feminine mystique. I was too young then to wonder how and when my father could have known such a woman, and now I am too indifferent to speculate.

But then the waiter came back and as my father turned to speak to him, her friends called from the table across the room.

'We must meet sometime,' she said and was gone.

Sometimes we would drive out of the city, turn on to a mud road and into a mofussil railway station, which had no name. There was just the one platform separated from the road by a fence made of black fish plates. The width of the platform scanned two stone benches and there was an old clock suspended from the iron scaffolding which held up the tin roof. We would sit on one of the benches and watch the single railway track in front of us, I do not remember ever seeing a train pass on the tracks or stop there. On the other bench sometimes, there would be a person or maybe two, carrying cloth bundles, who could have been vagrants or actual passengers. Nothing moved, not the stray dogs that slept on the platform, nor the flies in the tea stall and certainly not the masterful-looking clock. An old man in khaki shuffled past sometimes, carrying a green flag. He would salaam my father who would raise his pipe at him. We would sit there awhile in the silence, and while my father smoked his pipe

I would lick a pink candy floss clean to the stick and then wash my face in the tiled sink near the entrance before going home.

Few friends or relatives visited us. When they did, my father would bear off all 'his' people to the club. My mother had a cousin who called on her sometimes, a woman who had joined a religious sect called the Brahma Kumaris who were single and wore only white. For a woman who was supposed to have withdrawn from the world, she was quite sharp. Even as my mother hustled her upstairs to the balcony adjoining her room, she would stop on the landing and give me a measured look. Once she chucked me under the chin and said, 'She's beginning to look exactly like your mother, isn't she?' Then she hesitated and said with a sigh, or what I imagined to be one, 'How can she escape her genes, after all. . .' and my mother's answer to that was to urge her up the stairs faster.

Of my grandparents there was no obvious evidence—no garlanded sepia prints on the walls or the ubiquitous black and white studio prints framed on the dresser or in the showcase. Though the strangest of all was that there were no reminiscences. Neither my father nor my mother ever indulged in offhand remarks of the 'I remember the time my mother . . .' or 'When I was young. . .' kind. The only time my father formally recalled his parents was when he preformed their tithis year after year, assiduously. It was strange how on those two days the character of the house was completely transformed, making me suspect that another life lurked below the surface. The priests came early in the morning, my father bustled about dressed in a costume—a silk dhoti and angavastra, there were flowers and strong smells, and a delayed breakfast.

Once, when I was in high school, I got talking about family matters to that cousin of my father's, an old codger named Chamu, whose father I believe had been 'quite a rum bird', a vet at the state-run stud farm. Chamu himself is supposed to have thrown his drink in his English employer's face over a minor matter, I don't remember what, and walked out of his job. Probably the state of well-being induced by my father's best whisky had made him talkative that day.

'Ah yes, your family. . .' he stuck his lower lip out and nodded a few times. 'Tragic really, the combination of the two, the unfortunate affliction of nerves and the typical Old Mysore failings. . .Setu. . .well, things can be rough sometimes but you have to take it. . .your family, well they couldn't cope. . .your father did his best. . .'

I was alerted immediately. *Your family*, he said, not once but twice. I held back after that but I was clever about the rest.

'What,' I asked my father 'do you mean by Old Mysore?'

'The pre-Independence princely state of Mysore, ruled by the Wodeyars, distinct from the British-ruled presidencies like Bombay or Calcutta. The districts of Bangalore, Kolar, Tumkur, Mysore, Hassan, Kadur, Shimoga and Chitaldrug, and later, in 1956, it was expanded when districts from Bombay, Hyderabad, Madras and Coorg were added to it. It formed the kernel of present day Karnataka. . .'

'And what are the Old Mysore failings. . .' (The affliction of the nerves I disregarded.)

'Ah!' he smiled, realizing it was not factual information I was after. 'You could say, a certain lassitude, an inertia, a lack of striving, of ambition. Taking the safest way out. . .You could either call it an easy contentment or a bovine acceptance . . .yes, and a certain combination of obstinacy and pusillanimity, not being able to bite the bullet, to act when the chips are down. . .it's a hangover from the old days—a feudal disposition. Have you been talking to Chamu? Don't take him seriously. He thinks he's full of coastal sharpness, just because his father is from Mangalore. . .the bounder. . .'

Bounder. That was the first time I had heard anyone outside the dictionary use it. As also blackguard—*blagard*! Ablutions, that's another. Wherewithal, that's another. Duffer, yet another. My father had no idea how I hungered after them, these words he used, these tangential slivers that lodged themselves in my heart, from which I had to piece together a whole. It would take me such a long time to do it. Not to mention how exhausting the process would be.

My mother and I share a secret. She didn't ask me to keep it from my father but I knew I had to, instinctively. Some things you just know, even if you're only ten. Especially if you're ten years old. Like the rupee notes I'd see her slip into her cousin's hand from the kitchen mantelpiece when she thought no one was looking.

One summer morning when I was home the first year from school, and so had all my mother's attention, her cousin visited unexpectedly. I was experimenting with water colours, my paper and palette spread out on the dining table and my mother seated next to me, when we saw her cousin through the window, walking up the driveway. At first I thought it was my grandfather's tithi—I don't even know what he looked like for there isn't a single photo of him—for on the anniversary of his death my mother's cousin arrives early and furtively in the morning and secretes my mother away to an unknown place. Then Mother returns, quite wan and done in, late in the afternoon bracing herself for my father's coldness. But from the way my mother half-rose from her chair and drew her breath in sharply, I knew that this was an unscheduled visit and my mother was not prepared for it. She met her at the front door and instead of inviting her in, they both stepped out into the garden. Whatever it was that her cousin had come about, it made my mother lose what little presence of mind she had for they held their whispered, violently gesticulating conversation just outside the window, under the sweltering sun, forgetting to move into one of the many shady bowers and nooks that my mother herself had created in the garden.

When she came back inside my mother looked at me and said, 'I have to go out,' and it was a measure of her agitation that she used the same supplicating, tentative, ready-to-be-refused tone with me as she did with my father. It put the demon of mischief into my head.

'I want to come with you,' I said.

'No, you can't,' my mother said, her eyes widening, 'it isn't a place meant for children.'

'You mean, they don't allow children there,' her cousin said, stepping in and nudging my mother. But my mother's slip up had been enough to show me the way.

'I want to come,' I repeated.

'There are doctors there,' the cousin said threateningly— clearly she had had even less experience with children than my mother—'with huge injections,' she gestured from the middle of her forefinger to the inside of her elbow, 'and they'll poke you with it.'

'I *will* come with you,' I said, ignoring her and looking at my mother and to my own surprise, I began to cry.

Again, a whispered conversation and the cousin hissed, 'What rubbish, *I* can't go without you. Can't you. . .'

'No.'

'But. . .'

'All right,' my mother said, admitting defeat. 'What can I *do*,' she said to her cousin, 'I'm tired, I can't keep on like this, I hope it will all end soon. Let her come if she wants to. She can stay in the garden and you can wait with her. But,' she added raising her voice at me, 'you must hold my hand and not talk.'

'And no saying that you want to go home,' the cousin added for good measure.

Once we were in the autorickshaw, except for her hand holding mine tightly, she forgot about me, I knew.

'Where are we going?' I asked.

'What?' my mother said absently. 'Oh, to a hos. . .hot . . .' It emerged eventually as 'a hostel'. She could even have said, 'a hotel', I wasn't sure.

I remember stepping out of the auto into a big compound full of large, spreading rain trees. It was late summer and the pink, spiky, soft flowers had been shed and the ground was covered with their brown fuzz and the black seed pods. We crunched across a gravelly cement driveway but there, before we could enter the garden on the other side, I stopped. A section of the driveway was paved, not in cement or even tar but with metal rods, smooth and rounded, and I was sure my foot would slip and get caught between the rods.

'It's a cow trap,' my mother said impatiently, 'to prevent stray cows from wandering in.' But even as she said it, she and her cousin swung me across and I stepped into the garden on a high.

I still remember how the garden looked when we first entered, how commanding and symmetrical and beautiful it was, and how cool on that hot day. At the outer edge of the garden, all round its circumference, ran a 'lover's lane', a cobblestoned walkway with protecting slats of stone on top from which trailed a creeper with yellow flowers. I made for it at once, attracted by the flowers which hung down in bunches like yellow grapes. Throughout the lover's lane there were stone benches and people sat on them here and there with the desultory air of those whiling away their time, but they did not matter to me. I wouldn't have given them a second look. After walking through the lane once round, jumping up at intervals to see if I could pluck the flowers, I went into the garden proper. There were large trees here too, with gnarled trunks, their branches totally leafless, stretching out into the sky. They reminded me of the so many raised arms clamouring to answer the teacher's questions. There were shrubs between the trees, their leaves green and dusty, still to be shed, and multicoloured bougainvillea trailed everywhere.

Then I noticed the slide in one corner of the garden. It was a large cement slide painted brick red and there was a girl playing on it. But that didn't bother me for the provider of the slide had been generous, and though there was just a single flight of steps to climb up, it branched off on the top into three slides. They must have expected a lot of children. But of course, the other girl would insist on crowding me and waiting her turn at my slide. I brushed past her without looking at her and set off sailing down as majestically as I could on a pitted surface, and let out a sharp yelp as soon as my bare thighs touched the heated cement surface. That was what she must have been waiting for, for I heard her laugh and clap as soon as I yelped, her laugh a peal of pure joy with no trace of malice in it. Then when it was her turn she sat with her knees in the air and her feet flat on the cement face and came down, her thighs unscorched. After that, there was nothing to it but to share my slide with her and soon we were taking turns, in assembly line fashion. Her nose and her lips, I noticed, were large and her eyes small in a biggish face, and her limbs, though short enough to be manageable seemed to get in the way when she climbed or walked. She was my height and I presumed she was my age too. After some time she did not climb up the slide again and waited for me to come to her and we wandered off into the lover's lane. At the end of the lane we climbed up a little hillock of mud, stones and abandoned building material and there, without word or gesture, she led me through a broken-down tin door, into what must have once been a room, and sat down on the floor there as if that were her rightful place and I her guest. There were just four walls there with no roof, with termite's nests built high in the corners and grass growing from the huge seams in the floor; and then I saw on the floor, amidst the rough granite slabs, a toilet bowl with a pipal tree growing out of it. The bowl, still white, was full of mud and the pipal was a sapling, the leaves on top still a tender reticulate red, and there they stood, bowl and tree, more perfect than any of my mother's elaborate flower arrangements.

As easily as we had wandered in we wandered out and then I noticed the building. Along one side of the garden, almost hidden by it, was the grey stone building that had come into view when we drove in. The blocks of stone, perfectly cut, fitted neatly together, the cement ridges between them still visible in some places. There were large windows running along the sides of the building with smaller semicircular ones poised on top of each rectangle. The finish and regularity of the façade and its length combined to give it a certain gravity and stateliness, as if it were the house of a statesman or a place of refinement like a library with leather-bound books or a theatre for classical music.

It was only when they stirred that I noticed them. There were two men standing against one of the windows and one of them beckoned to us. It was difficult to make them out till they came very close to the window and practically flattened themselves against it, for the windows had an intricate arrangement of shutters and bars. Other than the normal vertical bars and wooden shutters the windows were fitted with close grills, so close that you could only just poke a finger out of it, as the men were doing, and over the grills yet another layer of geometrically patterned bars. My friend took no notice of the men who were wagging their fingers furiously through the mesh and making rude sounds but led me to an entrance at the side of the building from where we had a clear view. There were several such rooms running on all sides of an open quadrangle, only they were separated from it by a massive grill which ran from floor to ceiling. From the garden you could not tell that such a place existed just on its fringes or that it was so crowded, for the men could come out of their rooms into the corridor formed by the grill, but they could not go beyond. I could see many of them standing against the grill, holding on to it, and though they stood quite close they did not look at each other or even speak. The whole place in effect was a massive cage and the men swarmed it, like animals straining against its bars. They all wore a uniform of sorts, a white round necked tunic and high pyjamas with dangling drawstrings and they were all close-cropped. There were four men, different looking from the ones in white, who wore blue uniforms and carried stout sticks, and patrolled the cage hitting the bars now and then. At the opposite end from where we stood, there was an opening in the cage and from time to time one or some men in white would go out escorted by a man in blue and wait on a stool at the end of that section of the corridor. We saw a thin chap, so thin that his tunic was falling off his shoulders, shuffle out and sit on the stool. A woman in a bright red sari, whom I remembered from the colour of her sari as one of the many figures sitting on a bench in the lover's lane, tried to talk to him, at which he tried to bolt and was given a sharp crack with the stick by the man in blue, who shouted at him and brought him back into the cage. He came back meekly enough and went into his room, while the men around him jeered. Another group, holding hands but curiously unmindful of each other, locked in their own staring, stiffly shuffling worlds, was hustled out into the corridor by the men in blue to meet another crowd in mufti from the lover's lane.

All of a sudden, in the section of the corridor closest to where we were standing, I saw my mother. I was so surprised that it took me several seconds to recognize her. She was leading one of those creatures by the elbow, a woman with close-cropped grey hair and a white dress that came below the knees, quite similar to what my friend was wearing. The woman was lurching across the floor in a manner peculiar to the people here, barefoot and vacant eyed, staring ahead but not looking where she was going. She would surely have fallen if it had not been for the hefty woman who was holding her by her other elbow, as my mother had barely laid two fingers on the woman's elbow. They were out there in the corridor for a few seconds and then they turned into the room outside which we were standing and came close to the window. I saw the grey cement floor gleam for a moment when the door opened and the white frame of the metal bed onto which they hoisted her, I saw the dirt-blackened soles of her feet against the blue bedsheet, the cracked heels and the thick, curling toe-nails and then the hefty woman looked up and saw the two of us.

Even before I could turn to look at her, I heard my friend scream—more a howl of rage, which shook me up and left me deaf for a second. Two hefty women in blue saris had seized her by her arms and were bearing her off, kicking and screaming, while two heavyset men in blue shouted and made lunging motions at her with their lathis. Much to my amazement and satisfaction too, my friend did not go quietly and kicked the women quite a few times on their shins and even bit one of them on the knuckles, which made her let go but before my friend could run off they had caught her again, this time one of the men hoisting her up by the scruff of her neck.

'She always manages to run off, that one, don't know how she does it. . .'

My mother was standing beside me with her own hefty woman by her side. 'The amount of trouble she gives us. Her family has abandoned her, rarely comes to visit. And we're stuck with her. They may look as if they're wasting away, many of them, but you wouldn't believe the strength that they have. . .' she looked meaningfully at my mother who looked at the ground. 'Here, look at these bite marks, still not healed . . .' she held her forearm out to be inspected but my mother continued to look at the ground. 'Quite vicious they can be . . .I tell you, the things we have to do to fill our stomachs . . .our lives are in danger here.' My mother felt in her purse and took out a currency note, which she handed to the woman, still not looking at her.

My mother took my hand and I led her to the lover's lane, to the bench where her cousin sat dozing. 'Oh you're back,' the cousin said, yawning. 'She was playing and I nodded off. How was it?'

'They want us to take her away, no place they say. . .so many more urgent cases waiting. I can't imagine her at home,' my mother shuddered violently. 'I offered to pay more. . .' She looked at her cousin, waiting for her to say something.

'She is a gentle creature,' the cousin said at last, with a catch in her voice, 'always been. . .' She started to say something in an agitated way, but checked herself. 'What does he say, your husband?'

'He leaves it to me, as always. If you can manage her, he says.'

'Well,' the cousin said tartly, 'considering you manage everything, all the expenses from what she left you.'

Mother looked up sharply at her and she shut up.

In the auto, mother looked steadily into the distance. Once in a while she brushed away the loose strands of hair that escaped from her tight coil and got into her eyes, I thought.

It was only when we reached home that I recognized the smell. That place had smelt of the floorwash that my parents reeked of everytime they returned from their trips out together, and now I knew where it was that they went.

That night they had a long conversation, serious and surprisingly peaceful, which went on till late, so much so that my mother neglected my tuck box the next morning. She looked more puffy and distracted than usual and they went out of their way not to look each other in the eye. That morning I left for school. In the taxi Father sat in front, my mother and I at the back. As usual, when the car started winding up the hills, we had to keep stopping for her to be sick. I came back again only in winter and in the manner of most childhood memories where the least important details replace the big things or occlude them, I only remembered playing on the slide with my quiet friend and her being carried off screaming and kicking by the hefty women. At that time, I did not wonder what my mother was doing there and who that woman was whom she did not want to bring home. Funnily enough, as with memories, I have mixed up the woman on the bed with my friend on the slide and for a long time I thought, they were the same person. I went back there after ten years, armed with a yellowed receipt and a fresh green slip establishing me as kin, not to look for her for she was dead by then, but as always to find out more about myself, and as with everything I drew a blank. Maybe I had a faint hope that they would have made a mistake, or she would still be there chained to the white bed or to a drip hanging by the side of her bed, but she wasn't. The place was almost deserted. They had moved all the remaining tunic clad figures out somewhere else where their condition would be less conspicuous, for these are modern, humane times.

Part II
Reaping the Whirlwind

eight

_____

1934

Of Gandhi, it was said that he could stir up a whirlwind with a single breath. Once he moved on, those he left behind had to reap the whirlwind, so one supposed. While no one could claim winds of that magnitude in their small town, he certainly stirred up the dust in the alleys. In the Mylaraiah household alone, a mild Sirocco—of displacement and comprehension—sprang up; in the future, it was to yield a hot harvest.

At the Empress Girls' School, Miss Lazarus mentioned his visit in her morning address and at the Government Boys' High School, C.G.K. Sir went into ecstasies over 'our good fortune in seeing our leader in the flesh', throwing all caution defiantly to the winds. Even in the classrooms the students discussed the evening's meeting, which many of them had gone to. Kaveri was startled to find that the girls in class— ordinary girls—claimed Gandhi for their own. Given the fervent and familiar references to him in conversations at home, she had considered Gandhi some kind of home-grown pet. Between her family and the newspapers they subscribed to, she thought they owned Gandhi completely. But with Narayana Rao having been by Gandhi's side throughout his visit, part of the Mahatma's glory had spilled over on him, and what was more, his daughter Kalyani had begun to refer to Gandhi familiarly as 'thatha'. The girls pressed round her and Kaveri's descriptions of the glass dome full of goat's milk seemed not to matter a whit.

'If we are to become fit to rule ourselves, we must stand united,' Kalyani said softly, reflecting her father's serious tone. 'Which is why Gandhi thatha was here, to ask us to give up our notions of high caste and low caste and to give money to the poor.'

'My brother says,' Shanta began hotly—and Shanta had a twin claim on Gandhi—she was C.G.K. Sir's daughter and the sister of the swayamsevak who had earned a scarred forehead while demonstrating outside the liquor shop. He had also been right up front, controlling the crowds on the evening of Gandhi's visit. 'My brother says, there is no point asking people to give to the poor what they have in excess. Do you think the landlords will part with their lands on their own? Their wealth must be forcibly taken from them and redistributed. The crowd should have stormed the courts and the records office and seized the files. . .'

Kaveri recoiled with the instinct of a lawyer's daughter at the thought of records and files being destroyed. 'My father says,' she countered coldly, 'the minute the British leave the country, it will be the end. All our systems will collapse, the maharaja won't know what to do and we will all be at each others' throats. . .the poor will be worse off. . .'

'Only slaves suck up to their masters,' Shanta said knowingly, exchanging glances with Kalyani, 'and imitate their ways and manners.'

'My grandmother says, those who start off picketing liquor shops end up patronizing them!' Kaveri tossed her short hair to effect and walked off with a rival gang of girls.

The conversation was soon forgotten; they had repeated what they had heard their elders say. But that day if Kaveri came home feeling unsettled about the first-family status of the Mylaraiah household, Setu came home and announced self-importantly that he had joined a 'youth movement'. C.G.K. Sir was mobilizing a band of boys to volunteer at camps, to be the invisible working hands necessary for mammoth meetings and rallies to go off smoothly, to attend to the many delegates who would assemble. We get to wear a white cap, same as the grown-ups, Setu said.

There will be no holding back the rabble-rousers now, Mylaraiah said, clapping his hands wearily over his ears, or the fund of Gandhi-said-to-me stories. In this tide of new feeling, old slights were forgotten, snubs brushed aside. So, when Narayana Rao made a personal appeal to Umadevi and Rukmini, the Samaja was pressed into service once again to raise money for sewing machines and to devise schemes to train women in the villages to use them. We must not be petty, Umadevi urged Rukmini. So what if you didn't get to sit on the podium with Gandhi. These things happen. Our work must come first, not our egos. Rukmini had to step out of her cosy khadi confines, Umadevi decreed. She wanted Rukmini to travel with her to the outlying villages to talk about the Samaja's programmes, 'Just once a week, that's all. We need your organizing skills and your common sense, now when all our efforts are picking up momentum.' There was nothing 'political' about it, Umadevi reassured her, her husband could not possibly object. 'You can't wash your hands of us so easily, you know,' Umadevi said, 'even if you want to.'

It was an offer after Rukmini's own heart but she had become wary after the 'welcome committee' and 'escorts' party' debacle during Gandhi's visit, deciding that she was not suited to the hurly-burly of public life after all; Umadevi was more adept at it, though she may not be as capable. Moreover, her husband would not like it. Already he was angry with her for having given away her diamond earrings without asking him. But she had not apologized. They were hers, a gift from her father. She knew that he thought she had given them away to impress Narayana Rao, which angered her. To reduce her best impulses and her heartfelt causes to passing fancies, showed how little he thought of her. Again, if she had to do the things she wanted, she would have to be tactful, she would have to 'manage' things so that the house would not be neglected. Mylaraiah's career too was gravitating towards Bangalore and the high court. He had managed the plum catch, the cases concerning the European planters from Chikmagalur and there was another sensitive matter he was handling, the late Diwan Poornaiah's estate, which was a severely complicated case. Shivaswamy had got him an introduction to Vishwanath Rao, the district judge and that seemed to have eased matters in his favour.

There seemed to be no escaping the tide of nationalistic fervour. On his next visit, Shivaswamy claimed that he too, obliquely, had paid his own debt to the national movement. His son, the dashing and brilliant Srinivas, aka Chamu, one of the first metallurgists to emerge from Banaras Hindu University, had a much-envied job at the Kolar Gold Fields. That he had been hand-picked by *the* John Taylor of John Taylor and Sons, the engineering firm that was called in to mine the gold discovered at Kolar, had been much touted, as also that he hobnobbed with Englishmen as their equal. The story that was making the rounds was that Chamu had flung his glass of whisky in Lindsey Taylor's face—Lindsey being John Taylor's grandson—for having called a tardy waiter at the Kolar Gold Fields club a 'nigger'. It was said that Chamu had roared off into the night on his 3.5 HP Douglas motorcycle with opposed twin cylinders, and driven all the way to Bangalore. He was seen again only after six months, at the Ooty races, where he turned up to back his favourite horse. It was the kind of apocryphal story that always gets built around wastrels, Mylaraiah said, and acquires new heroic dimensions in the telling and retelling. Much like the exploits of Narayana Rao.

But few books of history or annals of accounts would ever recount how Gandhi's legacy, Narayana Rao's travails and the political fortunes of the Congress were played out in Mylaraiah's backyard.

Every time his father returned from a meeting or from jail, Ramu would bring armfuls of garlands and khadi buntings, and baskets of fruit for his friends. So long as Narayana Rao was in jail, there would be a steady stream of sweets. The one thing the jail manual allowed was for family members to meet the prisoners on 'festivals' and thanks to the generosity of the Panchanga, the traditional calendar, there was never a want of festivals and Savitramma would celebrate each one of them with the full complement of sweets. And whenever Savitramma sent a carrier to her husband, a bit of it would come their way as well. The previous year they had feasted on a variety of 'undes', as one of Narayana Rao's fellow prisoners, a famous Congress activist from Bellary, had a baby while in jail, and Savitramma had taken it upon herself to supply her with the nourishing diet prescribed for nursing mothers, which included a lot of sticky 'undes'.

And there were stories. Narayana Rao would come home and relate his experiences, quite dispassionately, to his family and fellow-Congressmen and Ramu would listen to him open-mouthed, and transmit his father's 'stories' to his friends, around which they would construct their games. Heads of ripe corn, row upon row, in Setu's backyard, usually suffered in imitation of the satyagrahis chopping down the toddy-producing eechali trees.

But this time Narayana Rao's trangressions were not his alone, he also bore the burden of Gandhi's visit and his sojourn in jail yielded the boys' best games—Prison Riot and Caning the Prisoners.

'I'll be a lifer,' Chapdi Kal said immediately.

'And I, a habitual offender.'

The prisoners in jail were divided into three categories. The satyagrahis were quite separate from the 'lifers' and the 'habitual offenders'. The latter were those who were repeatedly imprisoned for small offences, while the former were the big men, murderers at the very least. As they were political prisoners, the satyagrahis were housed in separate barracks and enjoyed privileges that the other two categories did not— the prison authorities were more circumspect in dealing with them.

It fell to the smallest and the irregulars to be the satyagrahis. In return for the free run of his compound, Setu was allowed to change sides at will and become whatever he wanted, which was what they all usually ended up doing. But none of the boys, not even Ramu, wanted to be a 'satyagrahi'. All that the satyagrahis got to do was walk in single file from their barracks to the superintendent's office, thump the jail manual and ask for plates or mugs or brass vessels, or clean latrines, and if those were not granted, go on hunger strike. Other than the histrionics involved in fainting from hunger, there was nothing exciting here. Lifers and habitual offenders could shout and scream and hurl stones or their plates and mugs at each other, and when one was reserve police, ah bliss! one could swing the lathi to the heart's content.

It was the superintendent who had breadth enough for a full scale theatrical performance. Apart from strutting up and down before the quaking prisoners, he got to address the satyagrahis as 'humbugs', and when really incensed, as 'scoundrels', 'fools' and 'rascals'. In truth, the superintendent reserved his venom especially for the satyagrahis as he held them responsible for all the trouble in his orderly jail, but he could not make free with them as he could with the others. It was they who had introduced the pernicious weapon of the hunger strike into the jail. The 'system' in the jail revolved around using the lifers to contain the habitual offenders—given the shortage of manpower, this was a system they had evolved and perfected and the smooth functioning of the jail depended on it. Having learnt of its efficacy from the satyagrahis, the lifers too went on a hunger strike to press their demands. The habitual offenders grew restive and there were 'minor incidents' in the barracks. The superintendent had to send for the reserve police to bolster the regular police force, which had grown nervous.

'I'll be the superintendent,' Chapdi Kal would say when the game had progressed far enough, 'and also the reserve police.'

When things came to a boil in the habitual offenders' barracks and the noise from there grew really deafening, the dreaded 'danger bell' in the tower rang—simulated by Setu ringing the brass bell that the priest used in the Friday morning pujas. The bell signalled a serious fight in the barracks or an escape attempt. This gave the reserve police license to swoop down on the barracks and thrash the habitual offenders and the lifers. At this point Chapdi Kal found his bastion stormed and all the boys switching from habitual offenders, lifers and satyagrahis to reserve police. Not only did this give the boys liberty to run amok in the corn field at the back but it also gave them the thrill of speaking in the pidgin Urdu which seemed to be the language of the police.

'Udhar kaun ki jaata, maaro!' they would shout with relish or, 'Saab ki paas galata karta! Mooh much!'

And finally, when order had been restored and the men herded back into their barracks, it was Chapdi Kal's sole moment of glory. He would become the superintendent, thin-lipped with fury, and order the shikadi to be brought out—this, the shikadi whipping formed the grand finale of the boys' game. The shikadi, a tall, heavy, three-legged stool, with a seat just broad enough for a man to stand on, would be brought out and placed in the centre of the quadrangle, in full view of the barracks. The men to be caned would be lined up outside the superintendent's office. One by one they would be stripped, made to bend over the seat of the shikadi, and lashed into place with a leather belt so that they could not move or struggle. The whole process was precise and methodical. The prison doctor would first examine the men and certify their soundness to be whipped. A thin film of ointment would first be used to anoint the chosen prisoner's bare buttocks, which would then be covered with a piece of muslin. The whip, as thick as a man's little finger, usually lay soaking in a small tub in the superintendent's office. The minimum was eight lashes and the superintendent was not known to go beyond thirty. Some men would break at the very first lash, some would start blubbering as the whip screamed through the air, while others like the legendary Kote Basappa from Chitradurga would shout 'Bharat mata ki jai!' or 'Gandhi Mahatma ki jai!' with every one of his lashes. The price of every lash was two paise and the man who administered the whipping seemed to believe in working hard for his money.

Since none of the boys was ready to be whipped, they had to make do with a log of wood but they did manage to get a good whistling whip. For the first few weeks the boys played the game with gusto, then one afternoon in the middle of a 'caning' session, Ramu looked at the much lacerated log and suddenly announced that he did not want to play the game anymore.

'In jail,' Ramu said in a small, high-pitched voice, 'they don't whip a log of wood. . .'

And the others sat round him, in a subdued circle of comprehension, their whips and iron rods of a second ago becoming twigs again.

Perhaps it was the subliminal effect of C.G.K. Sir's history classes, his son Shyam's Youth Movement and its lectures and drills in the field everyday or simply the fact that they had outgrown them, but the summer after Gandhi's visit saw the last of their prison games. They would not cane a satyagrahi again, even if he was a log of wood.

It was to these new winds of change that Setu owed his father's sudden affability, he knew.

Sometimes, but very rarely, when his father set off on a walk and he happened to spot Setu in the garden, he would ask him to come along.

'Want some hot peanuts?' he'd ask without a break in his stride and Setu, unable to believe his good fortune, would go running inside for his slippers.

That particular evening, his luck was so enormous that it almost brought on his stomach cramps. Even as they set off on the footpath, hand in hand, Setu was could feel his nervous joy turning into anxiety—that the walk would soon be over, the peanuts all eaten, the soda drunk, and his father would become remote and stern again. As soon as they turned left on the main road and walked alongside the Mission compound wall, Setu knew where they were headed. They would, as usual, buy their cone of peanuts and go into the railway station. There were two trains that passed through the station in the week, and neither of them was scheduled right then. But his father liked to sit on the wooden bench on the platform and watch the railway line. He would walk up and down the platform and watch the line disappearing into the distance on either side. And then would come a little speech, a soliloquy almost, on telegraph lines, the railways, the dams of Mysore, the feats of British engineering and systems—Setu had heard his father several times on these, his pet enthusiasms.

That evening Mylaraiah stopped often to examine and to admire, and to point out to Setu, to actually tell him things and ask him questions. Look at that post office building there Setu, a hundred years old and still strong—as if he needed to be physically reassured of the tangibility of his town, that things were still the same.

So charitable was Mylaraiah's disposition that evening that Setu actually summoned up the courage to ask whether they could go see a film. 'It's *Tarzan*. Running in Shri Krishna . . .'

'Why not,' Mylaraiah said, smiling.

When they came out of the railway station, his father hailed a tonga and as they clip-clopped towards Shri Krishna cinema, Setu could neither smell the grass-and-cowdung odour within the tonga nor feel the hard cane framework under the dirty coverlet, despite their being jolted quite briskly. And at the cinema, the manager himself came out and ushered them into the men's section, rapping out a sharp order to his boys to bring out the special seats. It was only after the film started that they realized that they were not watching *Tarzan* but the latest Kannada film, *Samsara Nauka*. Setu looked anxiously at his father, loathe to leave, and his father smiled at him and settled down in his seat to go to sleep while Setu was sucked into the travails of the young couple who had married against the wishes of their families. As always Setu found himself torn between the young man who underwent one hardship after another, and his family. Setu's instinct supported the grandfather, the figure of authority in the household who he knew must never be disobeyed and where all virtue and wisdom resided.

But these sentimental considerations were put aside when Dikki Madhav Rao, his favourite villain came on to the screen. For there was a series of sub plots that involved the unmasking of vice parading as virtue, which seemed to be a great hit with the audience. Dikki Madhav Rao, in the guise of a teacher had a young gullible widow in his clutches. The very first word he was urging her to write was 'prema' and everyone knew where that would lead. And then came the line that had become the catchphrase of the film, which everyone in school right from Chapdi Kal to Pinjar Budda would throw at the games master. One of the other villains, a minor sidekick called out to Dikki just as he was beginning to entice the young widow—'Ey Achari, Parama Chandali!' and the gallery roared in approval.

At this juncture Setu threw a surreptitious look at his father—even to him it seemed absurd that his father should be watching a film like this—Setu usually came with his sister, grandmother and Timrayee and together they all shed tears at the dramatic and vengeful situations that all the heroes and heroines seemed to be caught in. In fact he felt a little ashamed to be caught enjoying such a film by his father, but mercifully, Mylaraiah was fast asleep. At a critical point in the film, the Interval came, an attendant brought him an ice cream soda made and bottled by their own A.D. Swamy and Setu dislodged the marble stopper with a vigorous thump on its head, an act that gave him as much pleasure as drinking the soda. When Mylaraiah woke up he got up to leave. 'Enough,' he said, even as yet another convoluted turn in the young hero's life was unfolding, for the film was more than three hours long, a hundred and eighty-five minutes to be precise. Setu had had his fill and was ready to leave too.

'So, did you like it?' his father asked as they came out into the twilight.

Setu nodded groggily. The only other film he remembered having enjoyed so much was *Hatimtai*, which he had seen a long time back, a film where the handsome Hatim had had one fantastic adventure after another in pursuit of a beautiful maiden. That beautiful maidens were pursued by handsome men, that domestic travails were endless and the good were always punished before they were rewarded, were the three motifs of life Setu had come to understand. But the villains were always more impressive, more so the villains of theatre. Towering above all the villains of the screen as well as the theatre was Natabhayankara Gangadhara Rao of the Chamundeshwari Company of Mysore. He was known for his ferocious roars and Setu remembered screaming involuntarily when the man in his famous role as Duryodhana had bellowed at Arjuna.

They hailed a tonga on the way back and Setu tried to unravel the complicated threads of the plot and explain the film to his father.

'Through Santepete,' Mylaraiah told the tonga man, 'Anantharamaiah Shetty's shop. We'll stop a few minutes, his case is coming up soon.'

Anantharamiah Shetty's shop in Santepete was well known for the variety it held in the deceptively few shelves; whatever you asked for, his assistant would bring out from secret recesses and his shop was the closest to a Bangalore equivalent. Even the English crowd came here for their broderie anglaise and their paisley prints.

At Anantharamu's shop, they found the narrow entrance blocked by a group of boys. They were talking earnestly to the proprietor, who was trying to ignore them as best as he could, pinned to his seat by them.

'Greetings to the honourable Anantharamiah Shetty!' Mylaraiah said loudly and the boys turned round to look at him. 'What's happening?'

'These are your Narayana Rao's latest recruits,' Anantharamiah Shetty said with heavy irony. 'Want me to give up selling English cloth and sell only Indian made, preferably khadi.'

'Stop this and go home!' Mylaraiah said peremptorily to the boys. 'You are making a nuisance of yourselves. Anantharamiah will be forced to call the police!'

For a few seconds the boys stared at him and the one right in front was about to retort when another boy, who had recognized Mylaraiah, spoke first. 'Sir, we only want him to promise to stock khadi along with his other cloth and put part of the proceeds into a special Harijan Fund. It's for a good cause. All the other merchants have agreed.'

'You look familiar. Haven't I seen you somewhere. . .'

The boy hesitated. 'I have come to your office a few times . . .I'm advocate Kole's nephew and I work for him. . .' he admitted. 'But, we are just trying to request Anantaramaiah Sir peacefully, to convince him. . .'

'You can't arrive in a group and surround him like this and claim you are trying to convince him peacefully,' Mylaraiah snorted.

'All the others hide their bales of khadi under the counter the minute the khadiwalas leave. There is a khadi bhandar for it. Why do they trouble us? This is something new that they have started after Gandhi Mahatma's visit,' Shetty said angrily. 'All your Narayana Rao's doing. He sets people up and then goes off and hides in jail. . .the government's son-in-law. His Harijan Fund may be genuine but does he know how many people there are, going round, collecting money in the name of Harijans. This morning I had a couple of boys wanting a contribution for some other fund. It's nothing but extortion I tell you. In fact, I hear things got so bad that Narayana Rao had to go round in a tonga one day, with a loudspeaker in hand, saying he had nothing to do with all the spurious mohalla committees raising money in his name.'

'Look, you may think you're doing something heroic, but you are breaking the law; he isn't. If your leaders have put you up to this, they're irresponsible, they're letting you down. You look like students. Go back to your schools and colleges. Complete your studies and take up responsible jobs and do them well. You will serve your country better that way.'

The boys hesitated and Mylaraiah pressed his advantage home. 'If you carry on like this, you'll do worse and get into serious trouble. And if ever you stood before me in the dock and I were the judge, I'd sentence you without a qualm. No lawyer would choose to defend you. Go,' he said, 'go before you get into more trouble.'

'Sir,' the boy who had just identified himself as advocate Kole's nephew said, 'I would have no trouble standing up to any judge. I've stood up to lathi blows before. Do you see this scar on my forehead? But we'll go because you have asked us to.'

The boys left and the small crowd that had gathered outside the shop dispersed. Setu, who had been lurking in embarrassed silence behind a pillar came charging out.

'Do you know who that was? That was Shyam, C.G.K. Sir's son, leader of the Youth Movement!' He was fairly incoherent with excitement.

'Hmmm. . .' Mylaraiah said, 'and the famous C.G.K. Sir is the one who writes articles on yellow sheets of paper. . .his son seems no less.'

'They listened to you, Anna. You sent them away,' Setu almost sang.

'They were mere boys. . .untried,' Mylaraiah said.

'Could you have sent those boys to jail?'

'Of course, if I wanted to.'

'Then they would have gone with a bottle of water, a copy of their holy book and their takli to spin khadi. Nothing else. I believe that's what Gandhi says. They told us at the Youth Movement.'

'That's a lot of things to take to jail. . .And what's this Youth Movement about, let me hear.'

'I don't know, Anna. I've left the Youth Movement.'

'Indeed! And why did you leave?'

'I had a fight with Ramu. And I don't like sitting in the mud and listening to people talk. Both Chapdi kal and I have left. But Ramu is still there.'

'Setu, I want you to stay away from such "movements". Promise me that.'

'All right, Anna.' Setu was only too willing to comply.

'Until you fully understand what they mean. And for that

you have to grow up.'

'Anna, Ramu's father has been to jail. Chapdi Kal says C.G.K. Sir too could go to jail. You say that criminals go to jail. But everybody says they are good men. Are they good men? And Gandhi?' he added, now that he had his father's attention, 'And the maharaja?'

'So many questions, all at once,' Mylaraiah smiled. 'They are all good men, no doubt, but each thinks differently and that's where the trouble lies. Your Ramu's father and even your C.G.K. Sir are not criminals in that they haven't robbed or cheated anybody, but they spread the wrong ideas and they have broken the law, at least your Ramu's father has. And if you break the law, you get punished for it.'

'Why does Ramu's father want those shops closed? He was beaten by the police, or rather he ducked the lathis and let Shyam get hit. Chapdi Kal says that's cowardly. . .'

'He is a brave man. Sometimes we do things without meaning to. We mean not to be cowardly but our minds and bodies defeat us.'

Setu's fingers moved impatiently in Mylaraiah's hand. So much generosity he had not bargained for. He was hoping his father would make the usual slightly-slighting remarks about Narayana Rao.

'Ramu's father and Gandhi want to close down shops that sell liquor—you know Shivaswamy mama's bottle don't you—because it is bad for health and many men, quite a few of them poor, drink it in large quantities and this makes them ill and their families suffer too. It's true what they say, but you cannot go around forcibly closing shops which are running lawfully, you must let people decide for themselves what they want. If you want them to think differently you must educate them, teach them what is right and what is wrong, and then let them choose. So also people must be allowed to decide for themselves whether they want to wear khadi or mill cloth. Your Ramu's father and C.G.K. Sir and Gandhi want the British to leave the country and for us to rule ourselves, which they will, eventually. But before that we must learn how to rule ourselves. That's what the maharaja is doing. Fruits have to ripen slowly on trees, it takes time.'

'Listen Setu, Ramu's father is a friend of mine and I know your C.G.K. Sir's brother very well, he was my classmate. I admire their principles but not their actions. You cannot destroy the systems and the order that is there without replacing them with something better. There's nothing I consider worse than that. Remember Setu, each of us is meant to do what we must. I must go to the courts and argue my cases well and you and Kaveri must go to school every day and your mother must take care of the house and of us all. And it is the maharaja's business to govern his subjects. Once you grow up, your world will no longer be confined to your home and your school and your mother and me. Don't look so frightened, it's true, you will have to walk alone and then you will have ideas and opinions about things. There is always the danger that you may not understand everything completely, for a little knowledge, which is what those boys in Anantharamu's shop had, is a dangerous thing. If you remember then to do your duty by the rules, by the accepted ways, your confusion will be lessened. You will be pulled in different directions, but you must get your priorities right. And what does that mean? That means you must grade things in order of importance and give each of them the time and attention they deserve. . .We must think carefully before we act. . .not act on impulse. . .'

'Are you angry with me, Anna?'

Mylaraiah laughed. 'Of course not. So, do you still remember the story of that film? You had better recall it, to tell your sister and grandmother. Come now, don't look so solemn.'

Setu came home grave-eyed and feeling a little uncertain. The fact that his father had spoken to him non-stop on the way home both pleased and unnerved him. It meant that he had something on his mind. And he hoped fervently that whatever he did he would not displease his father. He would quell the warm feeling that rose in his breast when he heard C.G.K. Sir speak. No more Ramu either. He would throw

A Girl and a River   141

away the white uniform he had been given by the Youth
Movement immediately and grind the white cap into the dust.
His only regret was that the post-film events had so completely
eclipsed the film in his mind, that he couldn't recall a single
anecdote, not even his favourite Dikki Madhav Rao ones, to
relate to his grandmother and sister.

1934

Rukmini had followed the clamour the book had caused in the newspapers and had been curious about it. It was her cousin Shivaswamy who had brought the book for her from Calcutta, specially ordered, much before others even in Bangalore or Madras had read it or even heard of it. For days after that the handsome blue cloth-bound volume weighed Rukmini's wrists down but hardly left her hands. She would dart in and out of the morning room, assailing her mother and her husband, lowering her voice when the children were around, reading out choice bits that she had underlined, with comments in the margin when she could not contain herself—'*Ha*!', '*Indeed*!' and sometimes, quite plainly, '*All lies*!' Dr King borrowed it and looked thoughtful as she handed it back. Umadevi returned it in two days, saying it was too heavy to hold and moreover, her English would not last four hundred pages.

'What a title!' Rukmini exclaimed, 'so ironic—*Mother India*—so apt to rub our noses in with!'

Katherine Mayo, the author, it emerged, was an American journalist, by her own admission an ordinary American citizen, '. . .an agent of the British government sent to demoralize us', Rukmini said knocking her knuckles on the spine of the hardcover, as if it were Miss Mayo's head, who had travelled throughout the country a few years ago to tell the truth about it and make it known to her countrymen and women. During her extensive travels she had spoken to several people—to princes, commoners and officials, gone wherever she wanted—to hospitals and schools, the courts and the legislative assembly, and all she had found were an ignorant, poverty stricken, unsanitary, grotesque, ungodly and salacious people. Too deep and nuanced and numerous were the flaws in their condition, their character and their spirit, for them to be redeemed.

'Gandhi is right. It *is* a drain inspector's report, a "shilling shocker". But oh so clever, exactly as he says. Her facts may all be true but the whole is so untruthful.'

There was something in it for everybody—either to move them to fury or laughter. Rukmini would read out the right bits to the right people.

'All our problems arise, it seems because of our obsession with you-know-what, the preference of our men for child brides and our preoccupation with child bearing, more so among the Hindus,' she announced to the astonished Samaja women.

The 'obscene' nature of the linga and the mark of Vishnu on the forehead were the cause of much mirth.

'I wonder if Keshav Murthy, the purohit, knows what the conical stones that he so devoutly anoints each Monday morning, really are, poor man. . .' Rukmini giggled. 'What if we were to tell Balarama in the office that the long red-and-white naama that he paints on his forehead each morning after his bath, with such devotion. . .' here she paused for effect, 'is actually "a sign of the function of generation"!'

This had taken some explanation, but the ladies had found it so funny that Achamma had come from the kitchen to find out what the matter was.

For her mother, Rukmini reserved Katherine Mayo's account of Indian cruelty to their 'holy and hungry' cows and of the country being eaten by its own cattle. Like Indian men, Indian cows were thin and had low vitality, which gave them their hunted expression. The ignorant dairymen used the cruelest methods to increase the yield of milk.

'She does praise the experts of your Imperial Dairy Farm

for breeding cows that stand up well to our climate and produce a lot of milk but the next time you write to them, ask whether they really believe in disjointing the tails of their bullocks to make them go faster and whether they starve the bull calves to death,' Rukmini told her mother.

'Does she have nothing good to say at all, this woman?' Bhagiratamma wanted to know.

'Well she praises our state all right. She has a good word for the Wodeyars, of course, because they are guided by the British—we have electricity and parks and a Muslim diwan. . .'

The social aspect of Miss Mayo's work was of little interest to Mylaraiah. In any case Rukmini was too embarrassed to discuss the matter of the impotence of the Indian man or his penchant for child brides with her husband.

'Our greed for gold jewellery is what is draining our economy, she says, and as for the mills of Lancashire being run on Indian cotton, she says that's a myth. Indian cotton is short stapled and of poor quality—fit only for lamp wicks and cleaning cloth.'

'There's no denying our women's love of gold,' Mylaraiah snorted, 'but the whole world knows where our cotton is going. But Gandhi, what does she say about Gandhi, considering she met him?' he asked.

'Well, she says we have Gandhi; we also have tigers.' Rukmini shrugged. 'She sees him as an ineffectual man sitting at the spinning wheel. But despite herself she seems to respect him. Oh, and she thinks the British will never leave and even if they do, the Indian princes will keep their independence. And if the bedlam of our assembly sessions is anything to go by, we will never be fit for parliamentary debate. All that the opposition does is indulge in "sterile, obstructionist tactics".'

But once their displeasure over the book had been thoroughly vented, they settled down to face the facts squarely.

'Well Rukmini, there's no denying the truth of much of it,' Bhagiratamma said as Rukmini read out the introductory pages, describing Miss Mayo's visit to the Kali temple in Calcutta.

'Don't you remember Shivaswamy telling us about the bodies floating in the Ganga at Kashi and the way goats are sacrificed at the Kali temple—their heads just cut off, the carcasses heaped to the side and the rivers of blood. . .' Bhagiratamma shuddered.

A minor, but pleasing fallout of Katherine Mayo's book was that it had led Dr King to talk about herself in more detail in a few hours than she had done in the twelve years that Rukmini had known her. She opened up a surprising seam, when she spoke of how her mother had got a taste of the contrasts as soon as she landed in Calcutta, back in the 1880s.

Her mother had been part of the 'fishing fleet'—one among the women who sailed to India in the hope of finding a husband among the Englishmen posted in the country—the last of eight girls in a clergyman's family. With not much of an education or a future she had decided, after losing many a night's sleep over it, to marry her brother-in-law's friend, a doctor in the Indian army, whom she had not seen but with whom she had been corresponding for some time—Assistant Apothecary in Her Majesty's Eleventh Bengal Regiment.

Right from the beginning she had got into the spirit of the Indian adventure and when she had stepped off the P & O, she had the usual first-time-outer's souvenirs—a striped shawl from Simon Arzt's in Port Said, where the ship had made a stopover, and a soup plate hat inverted over her head. She had worn her oldest underwear on the journey and duly disposed of it through the porthole before disembarking, just as 'Going to India?' had advised.

'You cannot see Calcutta from the sea as soon as you land, as you can Bombay or Madras. You have to sail up a river from the sea. So she had to sail up the Hooghly, a hundred miles, to Calcutta where my father waited for her.' (That she was disappointed to find that he looked at least twenty years older than he claimed to be was something she confided only to her diary.)

The Hooghly, as she was to note in her diary, was a lovely,

placid river and she marvelled at the thicket of trees on either shore, with clearings in them that suddenly revealed mansions with graceful columned porticos and verandahs and high gateways, and their beautiful gardens rolling right down to the river. At a certain point, the river was crowded with masts of ships moored on either side, and she had particularly marked the Chinese merchant ships with arched masts and an eye painted on the side.

'And just as she was admiring the scenery she happened to look down and saw a blackened human head with a bit of shoulder still attached to it, floating up at her. She got such a shock, she says she almost jumped overboard! It was only later that she understood it was a partly cremated body.'

There were other instances that Rukmini recalled, anecdotes Dr King had told her about her early touring days in the villages, before she had settled into the local general hospital. She once spoke of a particularly harrowing case which the local dai had messed up by 'mucking around inside'. The baby had barely been delivered alive and Dr King had worked all night by the flickering light of a paraffin lamp, in a barn filled with sacks among which the rats roamed freely, their shadows cast in furry outlines on the wall. She had crouched on the floor on a piece of matting, which the cows had probably made free use of, and when she held out her hand for the knife to cut the umbilical cord, she had been handed a piece of broken glass. And when she was about to leave there had been a glass of sweet strong tea waiting, handed wordlessly to her by the same hand that had held out the bit of broken glass.

Dr King told a story well and Rukmini found herself laughing at her jokes and impersonations and agreeing with her assessment and judgment of things. But now, even as she chuckled over the intellectual Calcuttan with Dr King, reading out aloud—'bookstalls, where narrow-chested, near-sighted anemic Bengali students in native dress brood over fly-blown Russian pamphlets. . .'—she felt uneasy. Dr King and Mrs Spencer had read the book too and once the post mortem was done and the truth of things admitted, Rukmini waited for a placatory sign, for some attempt at locating the redeeming feature, at least a glossing over, which didn't come. She felt herself growing disappointed, and then angry. The next time Dr King cracked a joke about 'the natives' she found she could not laugh.

'Tell me,' she asked Mrs Spencer, when she could no longer contain herself, 'do you not get tired of doing good all the time. The burden of virtue must be very heavy. . .'

'Virtue, Mrs M, is its own reward. Besides, I am doing just what fulfils me the most, serving my fellow men.'

'But that comes from within you. Do you think you receive anything at all from them in return?'

When you set off in your straw hat, she wanted to ask Mrs Spencer, do you ever see the welcoming blue sky, feel the breeze in your face, the red earth that crumbles underfoot and the trusting smiles that take you to their heart as one of their own or do you see only souls that have to be reclaimed and bodies healed by *you*? Do you get anything at all in return, do you allow yourself to see it and receive it, for to set out just to give also means setting out to condescend, convinced of your own superiority. A Mrs Spencer may burn with it while with a Dr King, it had settled more calmly, more unobtrusively, into the blood in her veins.

'I look on everything as God's work, Mrs M, and if I have His grace, it is all I need.'

The mention of God shut Rukmini up immediately, and brought on the feeling of guilt and unworthiness that Mrs Spencer was so adept at inducing. It was one of the things she had to constantly guard against.

Rukmini did not dispute the truth of what Mrs Spencer said, it was just that she was weary of the unrelentingly sharp gaze that gave no quarter, that looked only to find fault, to correct and to save. Of course, their devotion and single-mindedness were splendid but still, she felt the burden of their favours and chafed against their power even as she succumbed to it and was grateful for it. She grew weary sometimes, of having to be ever vigilant, of having always to come off the better to prove an imaginary point. In the early days, still flushed with his contact with the Mission, her father would come home and harangue her mother about many of her innocuous religious practices—her insistence that the flowers from the garden be used only for worship and not be arranged in vases and put on the many tables and ledges in the house and her habit of washing everything and leaving sundry objects dripping wet all the time, and Bhagiratamma would say that the missionaries had given them a questioning mind but taken away from them their capacity for faith, the habit of prayer, for simple fulfilling ritual. They have made us sceptical about our ways, and left us with nothing. Thank God we aren't poor, Bhagiratamma would add, if not I can't think what a few grains of rice would have induced us into doing.

If Dr King felt a coolness in Rukmini's manner post Katherine Mayo, she kept away, while Mrs Spencer put down Rukmini's sudden flurry of volleys and drives on the tennis court, which trounced her, to a temporary lapse in Rukmini's otherwise faultless manners.

For Rukmini, the most telling passages in Katherine Mayo's book were those about the men she had seen and met. The bits that she had surreptitiously re-read were Miss Mayo's references to men, usually upper caste, in western dress and speaking faultless English, often scholarly or in positions of authority, who felt that marrying their daughters off as early as the age of nine or ten, was acceptable and even advisable. She could not help but reflect that she too had been married at ten to a man more than twice her age, and if her husband had his way, he would do the same by their daughter.

Rukmini would not have thought that the challenge would come so soon and so close to her heart. Even as Narayana Rao went on his whirlwind tours of taluks and villages, Kaveri came home one day and announced that his daughter Kalyani would not be coming to school anymore.

'She is getting married,' Kaveri said, and the announcement

had just the effect she intended.

'Getting married!' Bhagiratamma exclaimed, making her instinctive approval clear, and then adding with a guffaw, 'That Nani is a good one. Preaching the Purana to the whole world but not practising it in his own backyard.'

'It can't be true!' Rukmini said incredulously. 'If it is, then this marriage must be stopped!'

'Don't be silly, Rukmini. You can't stop a man from getting his daughter married. He is only doing his duty as prescribed by the shastras.'

'Narayana Rao cannot throw away everything he stands for!' Rukmini said, in genuine anguish.

'Who said he's throwing away anything he stands for. In fact, he believes more strongly than ever in his pet causes. Undoubtedly your Nani is a liberal man,' Mylaraiah smiled a silky smile, 'as you said, all hues of people come to his house and Savitramma cooks for all of them. He's willing even go to jail for khadi and temperance and Gandhi—but this cuts very close to the bone. You can change your ideas but you can't give up your customs. Remember, he still hangs on to this tuft and his thread. . .' Mylaraiah caressed the back of his own tuftless head.

Moreover, it turned out that Kalyani had already reached that much awaited and dreaded stage, puberty.

'Amma,' Kaveri asked, 'what is that?'

'Oh that!' Rukmini said shortly, 'You had better ask your grandmother.'

That night, as they settled down to sleep, Bhagiratamma saw her granddaughter's face puckering up in thought and forestalling her questions, she launched into a brisk explanation about the facts of 'puberty'.

'You mean,' Kaveri said incredulously when Bhagiratamma had finished, 'it will flow like that, like *urine?*' She used the English word in the hope of distancing herself from the whole thing as much as she could. So improbable did it sound that Kaveri was certain it would never happen to her. It must be an infection that silly girls caught, like the poor who caught

TB from living in congested places and spitting in the open. And trust Kalyani to go and catch it. 'That's why she has been acting so peculiar of late. . .refusing to play games and all that.'

'It happens to all women. Cows too. It's worse for them, they get it once in twenty-one days.' That had made Kaveri laugh, but of course Bhagiratamma would not be let off so easily.

'Is it a good thing or a bad thing?' her granddaughter asked, looking her in the eye.

'A good thing,' Bhagiratamma said with a straight face. 'It means you can get married and have children,' and wondered whether that was good enough.

Marriage, they had already gone over and Kaveri had come to understand that marriage was a natural state in the progression of one's life. You wake up, drink your cocoa, bathe, go to school, come back, play, do your lessons, and somewhere you slip in marriage. It was something that happened to everyone but you never took it personally.

'Just as you listen to your father now, you will listen to your husband,' Bhagiratamma said casually.

'And can I never come back home?'

'Of course not, you goose. You will have a brand new home as well, and more people to call family. Then you will have children and they will have children and you will all live together, like we do.'

Bhagiratamma usually did not allow her mind to dwell on the circumstances of her own married life. Dwelling on the past just made you more miserable, more dissatisfied with the present, which you hadn't the power to change. But if she were to give a 'brief sketch' of it, as Kaveri was asked to in her English and Kannada language texts, she would have summed it all up in a few phrases. Widowed early but all her daughters married before that thankfully; too many children lost in childbirth—all her sons taken except one; moving from one daughter's house to the other as her son would not offer her a home but would only tell her that she was welcome anytime. Nevertheless, she could not think of an alternative. A life without these constraints lay outside the power of her imagination. This was the way things were. Within these bounds one must not lose one's spark, the vital thing that made you more than animal.

Looking at her granddaughter's still-creased brow, she knew that she had not been wholly convincing with her answers. It tired her out now, trying to find honest but non-frightening answers for Kaveri's questions. Of course, Rukmini herself would not talk to her daughter about these things. Like money, she thought marriage was out of bounds for children. Such abstract topics of conversation were useless, she said, even for adults. There had to be a context to frame them. Well, Bhagiratamma wanted to tell her, your daughter may not be old enough to talk about marriage, but she is old enough to get married all right, at least your husband thinks so. Bhagiratamma also knew that while Rukmini stoutly hung on to her beliefs, she did not mind her mother talking to her daughter about 'these things', and even hoped that she would.

For a brief while, marriage became the standard insult between Kaveri and Setu. Amma, I can't stand it, he keeps hiding my book when I'm halfway through it. Let's get him married! Kaveri would say. Where is your sister? Rukmini would ask when she was in a hurry in the morning and Setu would shout gleefully, Gone to get married!

Bhagiratamma and Mylaraiah traded stories about Narayana Rao and his family. Narayana Rao's famous encounter with the Englishman made the rounds, Bhagiratamma quoted disapproving instances of his parents' unrelenting orthodoxy. She had had the misfortune to wait with them, on one occasion, to meet the Sringeri Swami, pontiff of the matha to which both their families were affiliated. The Swami had called Narayana Rao's parents to meet him immediately but had refused to see Bhagiratamma as she was not a traditional widow with a tonsured head. As if it made a difference, her hair was so thin and all grey anyway, Bhagiratamma said. Her son, then still a boy, too had been shooed away just as he had reached out with both hands for the prasada the Swami was holding out, as the man had spotted the leather belt holding up the child's dhoti. Bhagiratamma was sure Narayana Rao's parents had had a hand in it.

But once Bhagiratamma learnt that the groom's father was related to her and quite closely at that, she sang a different tune. Narayana Rao had done the right thing. Possibly, his parents had advised him. The groom was a law student, brilliant, people said, with wonderful prospects and his father, though a schoolteacher had plenty of lands and the family was well off. The wedding was to be in Nanjangud. No jewellery and certainly no dowry, Narayana Rao had said, no question of it.

It grew on Rukmini, with a palpable urgency, that if anyone had the power to stop Kalyani's marriage, it was she. She had heard that Savitramma was not very happy about the whole thing and surely, someone as enlightened as Narayana Rao could not be a willing party in getting his eleven-year-old daughter married. It must be his ferociously orthodox parents who had done it and he must have been too preoccupied with his work to pay much attention, she decided. For right then, Rukmini needed redemption. She had lost Dr King and her unshakable certainties to Katherine Mayo. Of course, they might meet again and giggle and gossip, but she could no longer escape the kind, practical, compassionate eye. They would continue to be friends, but she knew now that she had to count herself one among the 'natives', and that she would continuously speculate on Dr King's motives. As Narayana Rao said, there were subtle forces at play here. They, especially people like her husband, were willing agents of their own subjugation. Giving to their masters virtues that the masters themselves had not perceived, till they were willed into possessing them. Mylaraiah's much touted admiration of British systems was because they suited him, helped him keep his small world neat and orderly. At the same time, she was trying to take a more charitable view of Narayana Rao's 'large' vision, after he had so casually denied her and the Samaja their audience with Gandhi. What mattered of course, she argued with herself, was that he still considered them a vital wing of his social reconstruction programme. If the Samaja had been rejuvenated, if she had felt a new spring in her step, it was because of him. She had felt the tip of the Englishman's whip at the back of her own head and had sensed how it must have burnt its way into Narayana Rao's very being. It had transformed him into a man ready to forsake everything he had, family and fortune. Here was a man whose vision embraced the whole world, who did his duty truly without an eye to the fruits of his labour, for what did he possibly stand to gain but a life of hardship, even if it redeemed his soul. And somewhere in her heart was a small kindling of hope that he thought well of her; she did not mean to be presumptuous but she had a strong feeling that she had some influence with him. He had expressed admiration for her work; he must have guessed at the source of its inspiration.

She knew that she could not hope to speak to him alone, and was lucky to find both Savitramma and Narayana Rao at home, sitting together, poring over yellowing sheets of paper edged with haldi and kumkum, probably the horoscopes of the bride and the groom.

'I have come to talk to both of you,' Rukmini said, and Narayana Rao, who was preparing to go out of the room, returned.

They heard her out without interrupting, right through her impassioned plea for 'education' and her eloquent and informed argument against 'child marriage', to her triumphant clincher that surely such staunch Gandhians as the two of them knew that Mahatma Gandhi too was against it.

'Rukmini,' Savitramma said after she had finished, 'are you suggesting that we should call off our daughter's wedding?'

'No, I am just suggesting that you postpone it. Kalyani is too young. Surely, you can wait till she finishes school. Her mind and body must grow before she is burdened with domesticity. . .'

'And why should domesticity be a burden? It is what every woman aspires to, the most fulfilling thing in a girl's life. . .' Savitramma interrupted, and Rukmini fell back at the fury in her voice.

Recovering herself, Rukmini appealed to Narayana Rao. 'When you spoke to the Samaja,' she said, 'you said women must be strong oaks like Draupadi, not delicate flowers like Sita. . .that husbands and wives must be partners in nation building. . .'

It was only then that Rukmini realized that she had made a terrible mistake in coming. Narayana Rao had said nothing so far and was looking at her, not with reciprocal interest but in faint astonishment. Both husband and wife, she noticed, had remained standing, while she had been given the only chair in the room.

'Let me tell you something Rukmini,' Savitramma said. 'When I was eight years old, my mother woke me up from my sleep one morning and said we were going to the neighbouring village for a wedding. She dressed me in a silk langa as usual and made me wear gold bangles and a gold necklace. Then we sat in a bullock cart and trundled over to the next village. The wedding turned out to be my own. I have grown with the man I married, like Kalyani will, like you too have, no doubt. We are "partners" as you call it, in every respect. It is through him that I have become what I am; I support him in everything he does. . .' Savitramma pulled her limp pallu over her shoulders in a deliberately formal gesture, moving a fraction closer to Narayana Rao, and Rukmini knew that any misgivings that Savitramma may have had over her daughter's marriage had been resolved right then.

Narayana Rao interrupted his wife and spoke for the first time. 'Does your husband know that you have come here like this?' he said gently, as one would speak to a child that has run away from home and has to be coaxed back.

At that, Rukmini stood up and stumbled towards the door. 'Wait!' Savitramma said, suddenly apologetic. 'You have not had anything. . .let me give you haldi-kumkum at least. I know you meant well. The boy is related to you, from your mother's side. . .they are very good people, your mother herself said so. . .you must come for the wedding. . .'

But by then Rukmini had crossed the courtyard, climbed into the waiting tonga and ridden off.

She said nothing at home about the visit and if Mylaraiah noticed that his wife was unusually silent over the next few days and that she had abandoned her genteel writing pursuits for physically demanding tasks—she dusted the book cases and sorted out the books, bought bales and bales of cloth from Ananthramu's shop and ran up curtains for the whole house—he did not comment on it.

There was nothing, it dawned on Rukmini, that could be done. The Samaja too, she was appalled to find, did not think it a serious matter, not even Umadevi. It's their personal affair, we must not interfere, Umadevi said, sounding rather impatient. Narayana Rao is not an irresponsible man. He would have given it much thought. The Samaja has other, more important things to do.

The law too, apparently, could not interfere. The government, Mylaraiah informed his wife, almost with relish, hadn't ratified the minimum age for marriage for girls as twelve, even though the Assembly had passed the bill. Undue interference with the liberty of the subject, Diwan Mirza had said. Let us be practical, and check our ideals by actualities. You can't force reform down people's throats. Even the two women representatives in the Assembly had agreed with him. People had to be 'educated' out of their backward ways.

Over the next few weeks, putting matters of the heart behind, Rukmini applied her mind to the problem. For the first time she did not consult Dr King. Sitting with Umadevi, she worked on a petition to the Director of Public Instruction. They drafted a scheme by which girls could take the middle school exam after six years of schooling and not eight, since it seemed the rule that most of them would be married off by the time they were twelve years old. At least, this way, a man could marry a middle-school pass girl rather than one who had abruptly discontinued her schooling without a certificate to show for it and if he were broadminded, he would put her through school, or at least some years of it, till their first child was born. Mylaraiah, without a single aside on her 'defeat' or on the fact that Narayana Rao's name no longer crossed her lips, volunteered to carry their letter personally to the directorate on his next visit to Bangalore. One of the younger inspectors in the Directorate of Public Instruction was his friend Vishwanath Rao's son—the very same district judge who had been so helpful to him. What was more, this boy had a reputation for being dynamic and open to new ideas, though he was very young. Like his father, he was reputed to go far. To her astonishment, she actually received a reply from the Director of Public Instruction saying that her scheme had been appraised and something similar was already on the anvil. Well, Rukmini thought as she folded the letter and put it away, the next time her cousin Shivaswamy visited, she could rightfully claim to have assisted in policy making in the state!

t e n

1987

Houses are usually cluttered with memories, but ours had only shadows. There were few objects in it to recall associations or to spark off anecdotes. There were no photographs in the house, not even the mandatory wedding photograph, no memorabilia of any sort. As a child, Mother told me no stories; the written word has always been my best friend. Of the two mementos of his past that my father allows, one is the solid, silver-plated Ganda-Bherunda, which lives in the showcase, with its glittering red eyes. This mythical twin-faced bird is the crest of the royal family of Mysore and stands testimony to my grandfather's—my father's father's—excellent service to the Wodeyars. I know this much that he was a lawyer. The other one that my father tolerates is a takli, a small spinning wheel with a broken spindle that also graces the showcase. I believe his mother used to spin on it regularly. From his cousin Chamu's references to her, I know that she was an elegant woman, dressed in khadi. 'A very forward lady', he called her.

I am told my father nursed both his parents through their long illnesses and that he had to return abruptly from Calcutta where he was studying, to take care of his father. Sometimes, my father sings Bengali patriotic songs in his bath, loudly, with a lilt when it comes to the chorus. I find it difficult to connect this man who sings in his bath with the one who comes out of it. He seems happiest when he slips into the past, but it is a private country of which he is both monarch and subject. I cannot understand him, try as I will.

One summer, my holiday was rained out. It was raining in school, in the hills and I seemed to have carried the clouds home. Despite the gloom—which seemed to be deepened by the weak 40 watt electric bulbs—there was a hush in the house, not of anticipation but of relief. My mother seemed more cheerful, almost happy, but my father was visibly despondent. The whole of that year they had written few letters to me, they even made me stay in school for the shorter winter vacation—there were many classmates staying back, so I quite enjoyed myself, but unforgivably, the packages my mother sent me had smelt of floorwash.

The smell followed me, and when I came home, the house too smelt strongly and reminiscently of it. The guest bedroom had been thrown open to the sun. It was being fumigated. I learnt that it had been occupied for the past few months by my grandmother, and that she had died there. It was the first time that I had heard of her, my mother's mother, a woman I had never seen and would always associate with floorwash.

That summer we had many visitors and there were many conversations behind firmly closed doors. I could hear raised voices, and once, to my surprise, even my mother's. Cousin Chamu was in and out a lot, though from my father's manner, he did not seem very welcome. One evening I chanced upon him and my mother's nun-cousin deep in conversation in one of the bowers that my mother had so hopefully created in the garden. They stopped when they saw me and I still recall the heat of their resentful joint appraisal.

'So, they've managed it to their advantage, as always,' my mother's cousin said.

I just looked at them, knowing that no response was expected of me.

'Mothers and sisters are easy to deal with. They make no noise.'

'Your dowry's taken care of,' Chamu said to me in his

peculiarly grating voice, now sharpened by malice. 'You can marry a rich man.'

As it turned out, the money my grandmother left did not go towards my dowry but to send me abroad to an American university. It also saved my parents from selling off the house to Chamu, which may have explained his resentment. In her joy, my mother immediately got the house painted, which brightened it up—the red floor no longer seemed to drink up all the light, but though she constantly lit incense sticks in the guest room, she could not drive out the smell.

1934

'Don't you just love David Copperfield?' Kaveri leaned across the table to Ella and lowered her voice conspiratorially.

Her *Wind-in-the-Willows* days, the days of her babyhood, were behind her. Dickens and *David Copperfield* were Kaveri's latest passion. For a week now, she had lived in an aching haze of love for David Copperfield, feeling his curls between her fingers, and his suffering and fragility in the marrow of her bones. She had followed him word by word on his travails, begging him to be careful as she turned the page, importuning the fates to be kind to him, knowing all along that they would not. By an easy flight of the imagination, she altered her circumstances to suit his—a cruel stepfather whose duplicity could be spotted the moment he appeared on the page, but not, alas, by her who would be most affected by it, a beautiful but hopeless mother, incapable of taking care of herself, a batty aunt, a loyal servant, a friend whose weakness you could see but whom you couldn't help loving, the gross sufferings that awaited one of 'noble' birth—and felt it could well be her story. In fact, she would put David's suffering and nobility on par only with that of Punyakoti, the cow. The legendary Punyakoti was waylaid one evening by a tiger when she was making her way home from the forest. You are my evening meal, the tiger declared. Please, Punyakoti begged of the tiger, let me go home and suckle my calf which has been hungry all day and is waiting for me, and then I'll come back to you and you can eat me up. The tiger, who was quite a noble animal himself, let her go and true to her word, she returned after feeding her calf. So moved was the tiger by her integrity that he jumped off a cliff and killed himself.

'Ajji,' she asked her grandmother after her nightly feverish recitations of the story-so-far, 'is it possible? Can such things happen? To a boy of ten?'

'Is this the book you have been weeping over, *David Copperfield*?' Bhagiratmma turned the cherry leather-bound book over. In the past few days she had come across Kaveri huddled in a corner in the verandah, her face streaked and her eyelashes spiky, the book lying half in abandonment on her lap, as if she couldn't bear to continue reading it and yet could not let it go.

'No, tell me. Can it be true?'

'It is a story book,' her grandmother comforted her, 'and in a book, anything can happen. But don't worry. Things always turn out well in the end.'

Reassured that the world she lived in was a moral one, in which wrongs were righted, the evil punished and the good rewarded in the end, she read on with more ease. Not that it lessened the poignancy of each page; she still felt keenly everything that her hero was going through.

And here was the perfect opportunity to share her anguish and who better than an English girl who was surely born to such things. For weeks, she had waited in anticipation of Ella, Dr King's niece, hoping that she would not be too strange, that she could slip into easy familiarity with her like her mother had done with Dr King. In her more hopeful moments Kaveri felt that they would be best friends at first sight, they would connect in an unexplainable visceral way, as she could not with even Kalyani. They would understand each other's most secret thoughts, just like that. And so she repeated, though a little less confidently this time, 'David Copperfield. . .you know. . .don't you like Aunt Betsey's donkeys?'

But it was not to be. Ella had no idea who David Copperfield was, unless he was related to Lieutenant Copperfield of the Sixth Bengal European Regiment. She had never been to London and her own school was a splendid one in the hills of Darjeeling where she went each summer by toy train, and where she was treated very well.

'Oh, a book,' she shrugged. Well, she liked poems herself and could recite *The Wreck of the Steamship Puffin* fully. She had learnt it as a child and still knew it by heart but she hadn't the patience for books, she would rather play hockey.

The visit so far had not been a success. When Ella had finally arrived, Dr King had brought her over, said 'Estella, or Ella as we call her. . .Kaveri,' and gone off with Rukmini leaving the girls to their own devices, and Kaveri had found that she had to give Ella tea and entertain her all by herself. At first sight, she was not as intimidating as Kaveri had imagined, possibly because she didn't have light hair and blue eyes like Dr King. With her brown hair and brown eyes and normal frock with a Chinese collar, Kaveri felt that she was 'manageable'; even though Ella was taller, she could take her on.

In Ella's honour, the porcelain tea set—the same that was brought out for Mrs Spencer—was arranged on the table in the coffee room, the girls got cocoa to drink in the tea cups, and Achamma's gulpavate and chaklis were served in porcelain bowls. But unlike her aunt, Ella would not touch any of it. Lady Cannings she didn't mind, she said, she quite liked the coconut and sugar mix, and curry puffs which she had at the club when she went rowing with her sister. (Clearly, when it came to miscegenation, that was as far as she was willing to go.) But of Lady Cannings and curry puffs Kaveri was ignorant, and could offer her only bread and butter and cocoa—a choice of Von Hotten and Roundtree—the closest that came to 'English' food in her house. And no, it was not the season for strawberries here, nor had Kaveri tasted the Darjeeling orange— the only thing on offer was the humble Nanjangud plantain.

So, when Dr King and Rukmini came into the coffee room,

they saw the two girls at either end of the table, Ella working her way through thick slices of bread and butter washed down with cocoa.

'What's this?' Rukmini said, 'Take Ella for a walk, Kaveri. Show her the mango tree and all your knick-knacks.'

The walk was a little better. Though Ella would not climb the mango tree she peered into the hollow where they stored the salt-and-chilli powder mixture, and seemed satisfied with the Hindustan closet, gleaming white, which Kaveri led her to as if it were the royal throne. They might not have been able to come up with Lady Cannings and curry puffs, but the toilet arrangements in the house were not primitive, so Ella could be assured. Ella threw a few sticks for Pat and Zip to fetch and volunteered that she had had a pet parrot at school, which she had bought from a box-wala, but that it had soon died either from the cold or from being kept in a cage.

For the rest of the brief evening, till Dr King was ready to leave, they both sat in the wicker chairs on the verandah, legs dangling, and stared out into the garden, without saying a word. What use was an English girl, Kaveri thought, who did not read English books? Instinctively she knew that she could not boast about 'my English friend Ella' at school.

When Ella visited next, she had a little more conversation. By then Kaveri had discovered the reason for her petulance. Dr King, she learnt, had brought her away for she felt Ella was 'running quite wild' in her long winter vacation—from November to March—'too much walking on the promenade, shopping at Hogg's Market and too many Regimental balls and hanging around with her older sister and her beaus at the Great Eastern Hotel'. Within a week here, Ella had had enough of helping her aunt out in the Women and Children's Clinic in the evening and the morning visits to Mrs Spencer's embroidery and tailoring workshop. She had all but pronounced Aunt Mary (so it was plain Mary, Kaveri thought with regret, not Marjorie or even Margaret) a bore.

'My best friend Kalyani,' Kaveri tried, in a desperate bid to win Ella's heart, 'is getting married next week.'

'So will Lizzy, my sister, soon.' Ella returned.

After that there was no stopping Ella. Ella's elder sister Elizabeth, nineteen and a secretary in a shipping company in Calcutta, had a young man, a captain in the Royal Artillery and they were 'practically engaged'. Lizzy had already started ordering her trousseau, but of course they had to wait till he could afford to get married.

That was why Ella minded being away from home. She would miss the shops being all lit up for the Christmas season, the entertainments at the Club (this, Kaveri gathered was very different from the town club where her parents played tennis), the annual Treasure Hunt for which she was allowed. She would not see what her sister wore to the Regimental Club Ball, nor help with her clothes and shoes, and above all she'd miss the Governor's New Year's Ball. Had Kaveri even been to an entertainment at the Government House?

No, but she had been to see the Dussera procession at the Mysore Palace, Kaveri said stoutly, holding up for the pomp of the princely states against the grandeur of the Raj. The only balls Kaveri knew were from Cinderella.

Oh yes, Ella replied with a knowledgeable air, she knew all about the princely entertainments. She had spent a whole day at the palace of the Princess of Paraspur, a classmate, 'the only Indian in my class'. It had been quite boring for they had been shut up in a room all morning with a lot of solemn women servants who brought them endless glasses of sherbet and sprinkled them with attar of roses. In the evening they had sat behind a latticed screen in a huge hall with crimson and gold trimmings and seen the most amazing tricks being performed by a juggler and his pet monkey and finally, a group of gorgeously dressed women with pearls and emeralds worn in vast quantities wherever possible on the body, had danced to loud, wailing music. They had whirled and floated in their gauzy skirts and tight pants—Ella did a credible imitation—and one of them had balanced lighted lamps on her head and on her outstretched palms, exchanging them from hand to head so quickly that it was a wonder her hair did not catch fire.

Had Kaveri ever been to such a nautch?

Kaveri, who had begun to feel her inadequacy quite keenly, replied as nonchalantly as she could, that she had been to a play—either it was *Krishnaparijata* or *Sadarame* or was it *Bhukailasa*, she couldn't remember, in which a woman had danced on stage—actually it was a man dressed as a woman.

But it was the New Year's Ball, the one that she would be missing, that animated Ella the most.

The arrangements would begin days in advance, sorting out the guest lists and the menus and the flowers but the excitement really began when the reception tents began coming up on the lawns in the colour of the season—that year it would have been purple and pink—and the men started stringing up the coloured lights. There would be men polishing the wooden floor with wax and coconut husk and the whole room—at this point Ella closed her eyes and sniffed, nose in the air—would be redolent with the smell of fresh flowers and polishing wax. As Ella's mother worked in the governor's house, Ella was allowed to help with the flowers and the decorations on the morning of the grand ball. She would briskly tap-tap across the wooden floor all morning, delivering notes about the linen or the last minute changes in the menu. She would follow her mother as she placed the guest cards in the right places at the tables, ticking off names from the list of confirmed invitees, the two of them making their way carefully between the men polishing the ballroom floor. Till the last minute, there would be things going wrong because the stupidity of the hammals seemed to multiply at crucial times, and impending disasters would be averted in the nick of time, but come night, there would be no sign of the hectic morning.

There would be a band playing all night, led by Ella's father. . .

'Your father plays in a band and your mother is a. . .works in the governor's house?' Kaveri asked incredulously, imagining them to be the equivalent of Timrayee and Achamma. Wait till she told her grandmother about this.

'Oh yes,' Ella frowned, impatient at being interrupted, 'my mother is the assistant housekeeper at the governor's residence, I told you, and my father is the leader of the governor's band. You should see him, how splendid he looks in uniform. . .'

There he would be, the brass buttons on his uniform shining and his epaulettes standing stiffly, and the hall and the lawns would be full of ladies in gorgeous gowns and white gloves and glittering jewels and men in long coat-tails and crisp shirt fronts. They would all sit down at an enormous table with the governor, Sir John, at its head, and eat a never-ending meal of entrees and desserts—the bearers would bring in course after course—off silver plate, under the light of a hundred chandeliers. There would be much curtseying at the door and drinking of toasts to the King Emperor.

'And you,' Kaveri interrupted, 'where do you sit?'

At which Ella stopped and laughed heartily. Of course she wasn't allowed to attend the ball! Neither were her parents, technically. Both were on duty. She was supposed to be in bed, but she was allowed, as a special favour to watch from one of the ante rooms for a while. It was a native habit, her father said, to allow children to mix with adults and listen to their talk. The ball was meant only for 'fine ladies and gentlemen'; the only Indians allowed were princes and 'suchlike', just as in her class the only Indian girl was the Princess of Paraspur. And apparently, at the club, no Indians were allowed at all, princes or not.

'Well, in my house, there are places the English are not allowed either,' Kaveri said, by way of offering a fair deal. Much as Achamma admired Dr King, Kaveri knew she wouldn't dream of allowing her to enter her kitchen. And Rukmini would know better than to challenge her on it.

But Ella swept on, deaf to Kaveri, intent on the ball she would miss. That year, the ball would be really difficult to manage, Ella said, because the head housekeeper, to whom her mother reported had suddenly died in summer—she had gone to the hills as part of the governor's entourage, eaten too many pineapples there, so they heard, and was gone in the space of one afternoon. The new one didn't know a thing and Ella's mother had to do all the work. Her father too had lost his saxophonist, again to the heat, and a cellist to cholera, the list seemed endless. The climate here, it appeared, was unsuited to the English constitution, which was used to cooler temperatures and incessant rain.

'Then why do you stay? Why don't you go back?' Kaveri asked, moved by the quick depletion of Ella's father's band.

'My father says we have to stay and rule the country. What would the Indians do without us? They could never manage on their own.'

'Did you know Ajji,' Kaveri began tentatively that night to her grandmother, 'in Ella's school, there are no Indians except princesses and where Ella lives, there are places where the English do not allow us to enter. I told her,' Kaveri dangled her carrot, 'it was the same as them not being allowed to enter the kitchen in our house.'

'Well,' Bhagiratamma said thoughtfully, 'none of us would want to go to those places, to begin with. Tell me, would Dr King want to enter our kitchen or would you like to leave your nice school and go so far away to a boarding school. . .'

'Yes, but if I wanted to, would I be allowed?'

'People usually mix with their own kind. Even if they were allowed, they wouldn't like to go to places where they feel uncomfortable or be friends with people with whom they have nothing in common.'

How could the same family have produced a doctor and a *bandmaster*? It was simply inconceivable that the destinies of siblings could be so much at variance. It must have been a terrible disappointment to Dr King's parents, Bhagiratamma said to Rukmini who agreed with her, that their daughter turned out to be the doctor and their son the bandmaster, and one who seemed to have married beneath him. The English were strange they agreed; they might admire them but they would never fully understand them. Kaveri too, who was beginning to feel less and less satisfied with her grandmother's answers to her questions, could not connect Ella and her family, the Governor of Bengal who ate off gold plate and danced with fine ladies, with the British who ruled the 'natives', the makers of the laws which were held in neatly-tied files in her father's office room, the builders of railways and the conjurers of telegraph lines, and none of them, beyond doubt, could have written *David Copperfield*.

1934

Kalyani was to get married from her uncle's house in Nanjangud, the town famous for its temple and its small, sweet plantains. Her uncle, her mother's brother, was a prosperous lawyer and only too happy to open his large house for the celebrations. Since Rukmini refused to have anything to do with it as a matter of principle, Bhagiratamma decided to go with Kaveri, and Ella said she wanted to come too for she wanted to see an Indian wedding. Rukmini was hoping that Mylaraiah would refuse to let Kaveri go but Savitramma and Narayana Rao insisted. She was their Kalyani's closest friend, they would take good care of her.

It was not a large party that left from Narayana Rao's house—only about twenty people, Bhagiratamma, Kaveri and Ella included. Already, on the train, Kaveri began to feel strange for Kalyani, who had insisted that she come, would not talk to her and Ella was too busy looking out of the window. Kalyani sat sandwiched between her mother and grandmother, wearing a sari and feeling very important, refusing to return the faces that Kaveri pulled at her. Moreover, it was hot and other than wheezing ponderously, the train showed no sign of starting. Inside the compartment, the women kept fussing with their innumerable baskets and packages, which they made her count again and again.

Kaveri sat in her corner, rocking herself into a doze,

speculating idly on the prospect of matrimony. She could not quite believe that Kalyani, who sat right before her, her face hidden behind her mother's ample arm, and the almost-mythical Lizzy would be entering the same state soon. The way Ella described it, marriage was not the exalted, near-fatal thing her mother and grandmother made out to be; there was magic here, and mystery; a prince, a red dress and a glass slipper overturned at the head of a grand flight of stairs. But neither picture held true for Kalyani, who was just her friend behaving strangely. It was a temporary lapse and she would soon revert to normal.

The train set off. The pleas of the vendors were ignored. Narayana Rao made last minute enquiries after the ladies before going off to the next compartment where he was sitting with the men. Bhagiratamma pulled out a basket and started handing out bananas—a sign that the journey had truly begun. It was the periodic round of eats that pacified Kaveri on the journey, for Kalyani steadfastly looked at the floor of the compartment and Ella looked out of the window, not seeming to tire of the endless landscape or waving at the urchins who watched the train go by.

They reached Nanjangud at the end of the day, after changing trains twice, once at Bangalore and then at Mysore, and Kaveri was almost fast asleep when they were taken in a tonga to Kalyani's uncle's house where they were to stay for the next few days. Ella was to go to the guest house attached to the local hospital to stay with Dr Smith's friend. It felt strange to be without her mother but also oddly liberating. For three days Kaveri curled up on an unfamiliar mattress next to her grandmother, had coffee in the morning *and* in the evening—no milk, dusted her face liberally with talcum powder and borrowed a pair of dangling jhumkas to wear in her ears. Strands of jasmine hung down the back of her head, covering her short hair. Her mother would not have known her.

The morning of the wedding Kaveri stood with the other women at the gate of the house under the welcoming arch of mango leaves, armed with a sprinkler of scented water, ready to douse the guests when they arrived. Ella was given flowers, which she had to throw gently at the arriving group. The groom's party arrived to the blast of valagas and an elaborate arati. The women could not stare openly at him, so they watched his face reflected in the silver lamps and the red water of the arati, and the groom, a mere lad of seventeen who was studying in a college in Mysore, was quickly appraised and pronounced healthy although a little thin.

Then the rituals began. The groom pretended to have last minute misgivings and set off to become a sanyasi in Kashi, but was cajoled and escorted back under a stout black canvas umbrella to have his feet washed in a silver plate by Savitramma and Narayana Rao. Mollified, he returned to the mandap and Kalyani was led out by her uncle, dressed, much to Ella's disappointment in a plain white khadi sari. A mirror was brought out. The bride and the groom sat on a swing and looked at each other in the mirror.

There was a satisfied murmur from the crowd of matrons. 'This is the first time she is setting eyes on him,' Bhagiratamma said.

'First time she's setting eyes on him?' Ella echoed, bewildered. 'You mean they haven't seen each other before?' she whispered to Kaveri. 'Aren't they in love with each other?'

'You mean, like David and Dora?' Kaveri stammered. It took her a while to collect her wits for she was confused at this sudden untramelling of boundaries. Love between men and women was an emotion she had confined to the realm of her imagination, something she was perfectly comfortable confronting in the pages of a book, not any book but an English book, but not exposed like this in broad daylight. 'Of course not,' she said, with feeling.

'It's love at first sight, then.' Ella would not allow for a loveless marriage. 'Even Aunt Mary fell in love. . .What's that?' she asked, easily diverted. 'That pink thing round her forehead like a miner's lamp?'

'I don't know, ask my grandmother. What was that about Aunt Mary?'

'Shhh. . .it's supposed to be a secret. . .happened long back . . .she fell in love with an *Indian*. . .nobody talks about it now.'

A melodic blast from the valaga distracted them. They could not return to Aunt Mary. The tali was being tied. Kalyani's chin sank lower on her chest. The groom looked quite bewildered at the contrary instructions being issued to him on how to knot the tali thread. They were now man and wife.

'And now,' Kalyani's cousin, an older married girl, said, 'the fun and games begin. The next two days are the best.'

Kalyani and her boy-husband played 'house' with the black wooden dolls they were given—blessed symbols of marriage—under the guidance of a roomful of giggling women. There were mock fights and instantaneous resolutions between the two dolls, 'just as it will be between the two of them,' Bhagiratamma explained.

The women sang homely songs in which mothers-in-law and fathers-in-law and other relatives tried to make life difficult for the newly married couple, but they were advised to persevere till finally love and understanding won all. Kalyani had lifted her chin off her chest by now and was beginning to look around, sometimes even at her husband.

Then, with a clang of vessels the cooks came in to announce lunch or dinner or whatever meal it was—everyone had lost count in all the revelry. The fun and games continued well into the evening. What Kaveri liked best was the game in which the bride and the groom had to burst papads and rotis on each other's backs. If she had one like that, a fine urad-dal papad, so large and crisply fried, she would've thumped it to smithereens on his back, not patted it so half-heartedly like Kalyani was doing, and as for the fluffed out wheat-flour rotis, her's would've popped like a paper bag and nipped him sharply between the shoulder blades, she could assure. However, both Kalyani and this boy were shy and wouldn't enter into the spirit of things. Why, Kaveri thought, this was like Blue Birds, only the games were played indoors. If it was so much fun, she wouldn't mind getting married herself.

'This is not a proper wedding,' Ella complained, 'the bride and the groom haven't kissed yet.'

'Oh look,' Kaveri said, even as she pondered this bit of worldly wisdom, 'they're playing the war of the elephants—the rice elephant and the salt elephant!'

There were two elephants outlined in white on the floor, one filled with salt and the other with rice and Kalyani and the boy took turns standing next to each elephant and denouncing the other.

'Watch out,' the new husband cried with a confidence now given him by the gods themselves, 'I can wash your salt elephant away.'

'And I,' said Kalyani, finally with some show of spirit, 'will eat yours up. After all it's made of rice.'

And then it was Kalyani's turn to stand next to the rice elephant and wash out his salt elephant.

'Where are they going for their honeymoon?' Ella wanted to know.

'Honeymoon?' Again, Kaveri felt the tug of unchartered waters.

'They must ride off in a carriage with tin cans and other things tied to the back which will clatter, and go somewhere.'

'They might go to the temple. . .' Kaveri said doubtfully.

'Oh I don't mean that! Somewhere far off where they can be by themselves.'

Why on earth would they want to be by themselves, Kaveri wondered but knew better than to ask. The last thing Kalyani would want was to be closeted with a stranger when she had her family and friends and all the games here.

'Lizzy has already planned her honeymoon. She will go to Darjeeling, that's where my school is.'

'And what will Lizzy. . .people. . .do on this honeymoon?'

'Oh, stay in a nice hotel, go dancing and walking in the mall, hold hands. . .'

Meanwhile, the women had struck up a song, this time a love song.

'*Come let us play together, beloved,*' they sang, '*with this ball here, made of Suragi flowers,*' as the bride and the groom tossed a ball of white flowers, dipped in the red arati, at each other.

'*Come let us play together beloved. . .*' the chorus took it up. And before the song was over Kalyani's white sari was stained red with the red of the arati.

Then, there was a lull, as if a tide of sadness had overcome them all and the women grew suddenly subdued, so suddenly that a laugh from the back of the hall sounded embarrassingly high-pitched and a bit of conversation rang out of context.

That night, shifting on her mattress, next to her grandmother's gently snoring bulk, Kaveri contemplated the solitude of marriage, a new aspect that Ella had revealed. The thought of being alone with a strange man on a honeymoon caused her a vague sense of distress; yet she wondered what it would be like to hold hands with him. She held her palm up to her face and in the dark, saw her for-once ink stain-free fingers, and sensed the tingling in her warm palms. Then a flush mounted, from the base of her stomach upwards, through her neck, her lips, to her face and still tingling palms, and downwards, over her thighs to the ends of her toes. It had something to do with their bodies, she knew, a transaction of some sort, but when she thought of Kalyani wrapped like a bundle in her white khadi sari and the boy, with his stick-like legs, and shoulder blades so hollow and bony that you could easily hang two coats on them, she could not imagine what it could be. She wished her grandmother were awake so that she could talk to her, or that Setu were there so that she could have a fight with him and work off her uneasiness.

But by the next morning there was no room for dolefulness of any kind. It was time for the grand finale, when the new in-laws threw challenges and mock-insults at each other, all in rhyming verse and song, in which the bride's side was careful not to outdo the groom's. Ella too was so taken that she said not a thing the whole morning.

'*Don't worry*,' the bride's mother consoled her husband, '*we'll make do with eight Annas of gold*,' assuring him that their parsimony would get the better of the groom's people, '*we'll get it all with eight Annas of gold—the bangles, the necklace and the earrings, and have some left over for the nose ring as well. . .*'

Since Savitramma and Narayana Rao would not sing, the women sang on their behalf.

'*Don't worry*,' the bride's mother consoled her husband, '*we'll make do with four Annas of silver, and get it all—the chambu, the plate and the cups, and have some left over for the uddharane. . .*'

'Your uncle Shivaswamy,' Bhagiratamma said, 'is so clever, he can make up these songs on the spot, and really insulting ones at that.'

'*Don't worry*,' the bride's mother consoled her husband afresh, '*we'll make do with eight Annas of rice and get it all —vangi bhat, kesari bhat and bisi bele bhat, and still have some left over for the akshate. . .*'

And then it was all done and Kalyani, still in her white sari stained red with the arati, was led to the room that was earmarked as the groom's 'house'. She pushed the quarter measure of rice on the threshold with her right foot and walked in. She dipped her hands in the arati and left two red handprints on the wall, her unmistakable stamp on the new household, and wiped her hands on her mother-in-law's sari.

The women murmured approvingly. Kalyani's mother-in-law had worn a beautiful green silk sari, which was very generous of her, for that sari would have to be given to her daughter-in-law, and many women were known to wear their oldest saris, ostensibly not to get them stained with the arati, but in reality because they did not want to part with yet another 'good' sari to an untried daughter-in-law.

'Wipe well,' one of the women urged Kalyani, 'the two of you have far to go together.'

And there was further proof of generosity. When Kalyani searched in the Lakshmi chambu full of rice, she found not the usual eight anna bit, but a lovely coral pendant which made even Savitramma smile.

'Will they have a house of their own, a small one at least?' Ella whispered to Kaveri.

'You mean just the two of them?' Kaveri was perplexed that Ella should continue to harp on the subject. 'No, they'll live in his house.'

'With his parents and all? Surely they'll have a room to themselves.'

No, Kaveri said stoutly. They'd spread their mattresses in the hall and sleep like everybody else.

When her parents and the company of laughing women began to withdraw, Kalyani began to cry and Savitramma too hid her face in her pallav. The women struck up a song to tell them that this was the way of the world and they were not the first mother and daughter to be separated thus. Ella, Kaveri was surprised to find, was crying too.

There was one more thing left, Narayana Rao's sister-in-law reminded them. It was a family ritual and would not take much time—she knew that Kalyani's in-laws were in a hurry to go home with their new daughter-in-law and that Narayana Rao himself had a train to catch. There was a Congress working committee meeting that he had to attend the next day. The bride and the groom had to do a small puja at the temple and take a dip in the nearby river. The women would escort the newlyweds since the men had to attend to all the last minute arrangements, the tongas and the tickets.

The puja at the temple was done. The bell outside was rung and it resonated sharp and clear and pure, across the open courtyard and the space beyond. From the top of the steps they could see the Kapila river, diamonds of sunlight sparkling capriciously in her fluid trunk of translucent green, as she made her way downstream in a business-like way—I have fields to water and hydroelectricity to generate, she seemed to say, so what if I glint and leap about, I know I belong to the progressive state of Mysore.

They sat awhile on the steps and rested, now completely

relaxed—the wedding had been hard work and you could never ensure that things would go off smoothly. They knew they made a beautiful sight—women in silk in the mid-morning sunlight, filled with grace, content with having set a boat a sail on its journey, of having redeemed a promise to the gods. Surely, for hundreds of years people must have sat in the courtyard of the temple like this and given thanks, and felt the comfort of the granite-hewn steps beneath their feet; the bilva leaves and marigold flowers fallen on one side must have waited an eternity in the same spot, surely the tuft of grass sprouting in a crack in the barren rock face must have been there since time began, as also the split-tailed drongo that hovered over a mossy stone on the river bank. Temple, stone, tree and river; man and nature seemed to come together for an immensely still moment and strain towards a realm beyond, like the spire of the temple reaching to pierce the sky. They need not speak their hearts' desire, their hopes and their deepest fears, for even as they sat there, they felt a lessening of the load.

From the bottom-most step Kalyani dipped her feet daintily in the water and splashed some on her face—her bath was done—and stood back to make way for her husband. He stood in the water for a moment and then looked upstream. There was a broad ledge of stone that skirted the steps and the side of the river for some distance. A few feet from where they stood, the ledge widened invitingly into what could be a diving platform. It may have been the sun upon the waters or the natural playfulness of his still-seventeen years or the admiring eyes of so many women or he may have just felt he needed a bath. He shrugged his angavastra off and handed it over to his wife in a gesture of consummate husbandly authority. Then he climbed on to the ledge, his wet footprints clear on the dry granite down to the detail of the cushiony pads of his toes tailing off into tadpoles. For a moment his torso gleamed in the sun, the tender shoot of a banana plant, like something not quite of this earth, of base flesh, his sacred thread a heavenly girdle cleaving it cleanly into two. He put his hands

178 *A Girl and a River*

up, his shoulders dimpled as the shoulder blades moved with the athletic precision of well-oiled pistons, the tendons at his ankles tightened, and he dived into the water—and was gone.

1987

Every summer I came home from boarding school. My parents were glad to have me home, I could tell, but they did little to engage me except to see that I was always safe. Not that I needed engaging. I played with the servants, with whom I was imperious, and when I grew a little older, I got a bicycle and was allowed a territory of four streets behind and beyond the road on which I lived. Of course I went farther, up to Lal Bagh at first and soon the whole of south Bangalore was old ground for me. All these expeditions were solitary, for I had no friends; I simply didn't want any.

On one of my visits home, I discovered the attic. It wasn't an attic proper but a wedge-shaped room just above my mother's, with a ceiling that sloped dramatically from one end to the other, following the tiled roof of the house. There was a large window in the spine of the wedge which allowed light into the room during the day. There was nothing much of interest there, only my discarded rocking chair, old curtains which my mother could not bear to throw away and my father's official papers, copies of clauses of the Industrial Act and suchlike. But one summer, when I had grown tall enough to reach the cane hamper on the ledge and haul it down by its broken leather straps, I did so and opened its rusty clasp. The only thing it contained was a large white tin, the familiar Finlay's tea tin with its faint blue and pink markings on the outside—the Finlay's tea plantation had long closed down and we no longer drank Finlay's tea, in fact we hardly drank any tea, ours being a strictly filter coffee household. The box was not too heavy for my ten-year-old hands, and the lid, despite being shut for years, opened easily, no rust marks on the rim.

There were two books inside the tin, and a collection of soap wrappers, the same brand that sat in my soap dish downstairs, promising to keep my skin baby-soft forever as it seemed to have been promising since time began.

I opened the volume bound in cherry leather first, with gold lettering on the spine, a 1924 edition of *David Copperfield*. It had the owner's name inside. Despite being shut inside the tea tin, I couldn't imagine for how long, probably forty years or more, no silverfish lived among its pages and the book sat with such practised ease in my hands that it must have been much-read, and from the markings within, it must have been much-loved as well. I must confess to being a little shocked to see how heavily marked the book was, for I truly believed that books were an embodiment of the goddess Saraswati and must be treated with reverence. The pencil lines ran deep on successive pages of onion skin paper, and the comments in the margin were in a decidedly girlish hand—why, it could have been my own.

The other book interested me more at first, with its lurid cover on which a white woman in a décolleté gown cowered by a window while a dark-complexioned, bare-torsoed man leered at her through the bars. *Tales by the Hoogly* by Ella King. Charles Dickens I had heard of, but not Ella King. It was a paperback, already crumbly despite being only about fifteen years old, clearly not as well produced or printed as the other book. Nobody claimed ownership of it for there was no name inside.

I did not tell my parents about the books immediately, for they did not know of my daily sojourns in the attic which seemed to smack faintly of the illicit—looking at dead people's things is much like turning over their graves. I just came away from the attic each afternoon that summer with my fingers smelling faintly of Pears soap. I did not read the books immediately either, being just content to look at them and speculate on how they had got into the tea tin, for I am not much of a reader. Make-believe worlds have never interested me. I would rather play in the garden and the servants were only too happy to leave off whatever they were doing to join me in badminton, tennicoit or plain bat and ball. With time, I outgrew my childish games and started playing tennis at the club, coached by a true professional, encountering for the first time an opponent who was not happy to lose to me.

Before I left for school at the end of the vacation, I showed the two books, still unread, to my mother and father.

'Who is Kaveri?' I asked.

My father held the book by the spine and it nestled like an old friend in his palm. 'Oh this,' he smiled, '*Barkis is willing*. This is your grandmother's book. One of her favourites, I remember.'

I half turned to my mother but my father held the book away from her reach. 'Your mother would not know,' he said suddenly, his voice sounding raw, as if his throat had sloughed off its inner skin, 'she's practically illiterate, anyway. I don't know how these two books survived the white ants, in her care.' These sudden swings of temper and mood were part of my childhood; I took them in my stride as one does patches of eczema which flare up when unknown allergens chance to confluence.

I remember once my mother had appeared for lunch wearing a new pair of earrings, gold hoops with a little arch at the bottom through which a large pearl was strung. They were distinctly old fashioned, but my mother looked nice and girlish in them. Father noticed them immediately.

'What are you doing?' he asked incredulously. 'Go take them off.'

'They are mine, I have a perfect right to wear them,' she said with surprising show of spirit. 'They belonged to my mother.' But then it lasted for a very short while; she took them off and said in a subdued way that she was just checking to see how heavy they were and whether my tender ear lobes could support them yet. My tender ear lobes as yet unpierced, obviously couldn't, so they were put away and when the time came for me to formally wear earrings, I declared that they were far too much even if they had been my grandmother's, and I'd much rather wear something less obtrusive.

To the charge of illiteracy too, my mother said nothing. She just sat back in her chair and went on with her daisy stitch. I had always wondered why she put up with these irrational bursts of anger in an otherwise correct, in fact too-correct, and formal a relationship between them. But this was how it was between men and women, between mothers and fathers, I thought and knew right then that I would have none of it. All along I must have known, all along, even before what I came to consider my moment of truth, I must have known that this was a passing phase, that I was biding my time for a future elsewhere.

Why the Ella King book had survived, my father did not know. It had not been part of his library. In fact, he couldn't remember it at all.

By the time I finished reading both the books, I was almost through with high school. Charles Dickens was never a favourite. I found him sentimental and rambling. The only fiction I read now is crime fiction—I like guns and hard-boiled detectives. As I thumbed through *David Copperfield* every summer since my tenth year, I grew familiar with the book, with the texture of its leather binding and the rustle of its pages, till it came to sit as naturally in my hands as it had done in my father's. When you opened the book it automatically fell open at those pages which were underlined the most, possibly the most read. More than the story I looked for the notations in the margin my grandmother had made, and I smiled as I imagined her, a serious little girl, eyebrows drawn and tongue sticking out with the effort of writing, so taken up with the fortunes of an imaginary boy in a distant country. *Poor David*, she had said in one place, and in case the reader had not noticed, *David's mother is dead!* and *Steerforth is not a good boy!* There was even the desperate injunction on page 401—*Don't marry Dora!* —as if her exhortations in the margins would save him from the fate decided by his creator. The passages where young David suffered, his chops and his pudding eaten cleverly by the waiter at the inn on the way to London, his being humiliated and diddled in his new school, his toiling in the wine trade at the age of ten and his flight to Dover with his box being stolen by a common thief, were heavily underlined. The grown-up David seemed to have engaged her less; Uriah Heep and Micawber were unmarked.

At thirteen, I found the book with the lurid cover more interesting. It was a collection of 'Indian' tales, written in a heavy-handed style, mawkish, and the romance was of the bodice-ripping genre. There was one about a chaste English girl who studies to be a doctor and a handsome, swarthy 'Indian', an aide-de-camp to the maharaja of a princely state—they have a 'romantic entanglement', their child, which he doesn't know about, is still-born and she leaves him suddenly, to go as far away from him as possible. The last image was that of the dead child floating down the river in a basket with a lighted lamp to guide it. But the most preposterous of the tales was one called 'Bride-Widow', which featured at a breathless pace, a noisy wedding ceremony, cacophonous singing and blowing of 'native' trumpets, much spilling of symbolic blood and suggestive staining of clothes with yonis and lingas being brought in at least once on every page, and finally, a groom who gets washed away in the river as soon as the wedding is over. His bride is burnt on the pyre along with his body and the story ends with her clinging to his feet, until the smoke closes in on her and hides her from view.

There were two short anecdotes that I liked despite their hysterical plot and tone. One was about a soldier disabled in war, who lies on his bed all day in the hills, and is slowly driven out of his mind by the monotonous cry of the Brain Fever bird. And the other, rather ghoulish, was about refugees from Rangoon fleeing to Calcutta from the Japanese attack during the Second World War. Their progress up the historic

Burma Road was described very convincingly. They had set off along the Chindwin river, dressed in their best, clutching their plate and their pictures, and then up through Tamu or the 'Death Valley' by which time the jungle, the mountains and diaorrhea had begun to take their toll and they began to shed them all one by one, marking their exit through the woods with a litter of precious things, till at Palel, almost within sight of Imphal where help could well be at hand, they fell down dead and then a host of butterflies—large, colourful and lovely, fluttered down and settled silently on the not-fully-dead bodies.

This book, published in 1955 by a little known London publisher, had no name or message inscribed in it. My father did not know who Ella King was and why the book had been preserved. About the author, the book said that she had been born and brought up in Calcutta and had returned to her 'native English soil' after India became independent. I cannot tell how far such a book or such writing skills would have taken the writer but the book kept me rivetted through my thirteenth summer. (I used the Pears soap wrappers that I found in the Finlay's tea tin as bookmarks.)

Quite by chance, I found the letter. It was among the soap wrappers, the same colour, scented now and without an envelope. It was written in purple ink and the handwriting was so small and crabby that I couldn't read it. Moreover the ink had run in several places. It began with 'My' so I could tell that it was a letter but 'My' was not followed with a 'dear', and it had neither the addressee's name nor the writer's. A letter that ignored the basic rules of letter writing that even I, a ten-year old knew and which hadn't the decency to possess an envelope was not worth bothering about, I thought then, and lost interest in it. As I rifled through the soap wrappers for other keepsakes I found a fragment of a picture—of a masked woman holding a whip above her head—the picture had been torn across the middle so that just one masked eye, a bit of white thigh and the whip-wielding hand flung above her head were left. It seemed to belong more with Ella King's book than with David Copperfield, so I inserted it into *Tales by the Hoogly* to use it as a bookmark.

I knew instinctively that I had to keep quiet about my find. In a few years' time I would know the letter by heart and unmask the woman in the torn picture, just as I would be able to reel off the annotations in the margins of *David Copperfield*. Many fruitless hours would go in speculation and detection. Two books and a letter. In time, they would not just intrigue me but become quite an obsession, the cause of much heart ache. But of course, at ten I had no way of telling that.

Part III
The War and After

1938

The war came to them in its own time, gradually working its way off the inch tall newspaper headlines and settling into the alleyways of their small town. There was talk of mobilizing troops from Mysore; time again, Mylaraiah thought, for Shivaswamy to get rich. Then the trucks began to appear, the convoy of green army trucks rolling in stately stealth on the newly asphalted highway, on their way to or from Poona. Soon the rationing would follow, as it had twenty years ago during the First World War, all supplies being diverted to the army. Of course, Mylaraiah's and Rukmini's household would run as it always had since their fields grew everything they needed—they even had their own castor oil press in the backyard. As it had been during the previous war, in the evenings, people queued up at the back of the house and Mylaraiah's clerk distributed grain and oil from the store. This time the district commissioner's office had announced a system of coupons for cloth and petrol, and Mylaraiah knew that it was only a matter of time before the coupons started changing hands not for goods but for money. Those who argued most vociferously that the British must go would be the ones doing it too.

The white boat cap and the khaddar dhoti-kurta of the Congressmen were becoming noticeable in the market square these days, and it was not surprising, for the Congress had got a firm foothold in the state now, having subsumed the local parties in its fold. Narayana Rao, good man, was the district head of the newly fortified Congress and a member of the state-wide Congress Committee. Actually, things couldn't have been better for Mylaraiah either, right then, for he had been nominated to the maharaja's legislative council and his appointment as government advocate was almost confirmed.

'Have you ordered the robes for the ceremony?' one of the lawyers asked him half-seriously.

'Hope we'll get an invitation to the grand durbar.'

'I believe you are handing out your local briefs to your juniors. What have you decided about the Modern Mills case? Have you allotted it to anyone? You know I've been following that case with interest. . .'

Had it not been for the war, Mylaraiah was sure he would have been instituted as government advocate by now. Thanks to Vishwanath Rao, he had already fixed up a house in Bangalore. It was a little more than what he would have liked to pay and he still had to find the money, but it was in one of the most coveted areas of the city. He was also disconcerted to find that the valuation for his lands was so much at odds with what he had imagined was their true worth, but this was not the time to look into such things. Setu's school too had been settled, and Kaveri of course, would be married off soon. It would do Rukmini a world of good too, for she was becoming morose of late, ever since her mother died. As soon as the war was over, they would move and things would change. Of course, they would retain this house too, for it was his ancestral home, built by his father.

For Rukmini, the war was just one in a series of events. If she were to mark the one from which things began to spiral out of control, she would say it was Kalyani's wedding, four years back; on her Richter's scale, it was the epicentre of a quake that set off many unlikely tremors. It festered in her mind, like an internal injury to a vital organ, unseen and unapprehended, but which bled quietly inside, sapping her of her vitality, her health. Perhaps the connections were all in her imagination, but she could not shake off the feeling of sadness and exhaustion that invaded her and the house.

It had first taken its toll on her mother, for Bhagiratamma had returned from Nanjangud a bent old woman.

'Rukmini,' she said as soon as she came home, 'it is just a matter of time, I know. Send for my jewellery. I want to give you what I have put aside for Kaveri.'

While she still could, Bhagiratamma went one day, leaning heavily on Achamma's arm for Rukmini had proclaimed with a vehemence that seemed strange to Bhagiratamma that she would not cross their threshold again, and spoke to Savitramma and Narayana Rao. Get Kalyani back, she told them, many families have done that. Or at least persuade her in-laws to enrol her in a school.

'She can come home now, can't she,' Kaveri had said, 'and join our class again. She hasn't missed much.'

And Rukmini's heart had caught as she watched her daughter sitting by the window, shoulders squared to do battle, as if it were all a matter of sorting out the practicalities of schools and readmission. Quite unlike herself, she had whispered a quick prayer for her daughter's well being, for her high spirits to be tempered into a natural docility, and then scolded herself for her stupidity. She should not forget how resilient children could be, she had told herself, and Kaveri was but a child. In fact, on coming back home Kaveri had given her brother a graphic description of Kalyani's husband being eaten by a crocodile—a huge beast that had jumped out of the water, snapped him up and carried him off, his legs kicking in the serrated clamp of its jaws. She had repeated the story to her friends and as she continued to embellish and fine-tune the image through retellings, she came to believe it completely.

'Kalyani has a new home now, and new people,' Mylaraiah had answered his daughter seriously.

Rukmini had frowned at her husband, at the note of finality in his voice, as if his statement brooked no argument, as if it were a law of nature and not a man-made stricture.

'Our Kaveri thinks it's as simple as going to her house and

fetching her back in a tonga,' Bhagiratamma had sensed a breach and stepped in.

'I know you have to travel by train first,' Kaveri had said impatiently. 'When I get married, I'll catch a tonga and come home whenever I want.'

Her father and grandmother had laughed. But not Rukmini. Kaveri had said, when I get married, a change from her usual, I'll *never* get married.

'. . .Kalyani's people, Narayana Rao's sambandhis seem to be good people.'

'Oh yes, the father is the headmaster of the government boys' school. . .'

'But the mother, what about the mother?' Rukmini's dictum was, when marrying the son, look at the mother, for she will be the root of all his faults.

'Well, she allowed Kalyani to wipe her dirty arati-stained hands all over her new sari,' Kaveri had said triumphantly.

'Shhh. . .don't butt in when grown-ups are talking. . .'

'Our Kaveri is a clever one, she may be a tomboy but she notices everything. . .' Bhagiratamma's voice had quavered as she pulled Kaveri on to her lap.

Bhagiratamma slipped away one night, without bothering anybody, her conversation with her granddaughter about the ramifications of married girls 'coming back home' incomplete. The final straw had been her son's refusal to come and fetch her even when she had sent word for him, saying she was ill and would like to die at home. She had gone inveighing against the wickedness of subtle, underhand women like her daughter-in-law—give her a woman who hitched up her sari and brawled like a fisherwoman any day—and the culpability of spineless men. Better to do wrong, she said, than to do nothing, than to build an anthill of routine around yourself and hope that keeping yourself occupied from morning till night will make the things you didn't want to confront, disappear.

Rukmini grieved quietly. The house and its relentless routine claimed her, it did not give her time to brood but she found herself feeling more and more dispirited. One morning, a few months after her mother's death, she discovered a whole shock of silver at the back of her head, which had escaped her notice, and she was barely thirty-five! Her husband put it down to the strain she had been facing of late, she would recover soon. Rukmini went about her chores, outwardly calm and orderly as always, issuing instructions to the servants and working out the Samaja accounts, and stopped from time to time, feeling for the phantom limb by her side, the absence of which she felt as painfully as if it had been amputated. She had lost an ally, her sounding board, her intermediary not just between herself and the world but between her home and herself too. You should have waited, she complained to her absent mother, you should have hung on for Kaveri, for you were her friend and I can only be her mother.

The copper pod at the end of the compound blazed into life in April and May, and in June, with the rains, the pods turned a quiet brown. Rukmini walked under its shade and that of the generous rain tree once in the morning and once in the evening; she was too tired to go to the club and play tennis any more. She had even detached herself from the day-to-day work of the Samaja, though Umadevi would not hear of her quitting. She could not work up much enthusiasm for spinning either, though she sat at the charkha quite religiously. That year she gave the annual Ramanavami harikatha by the famous Panneerbai of Madras a miss, an event which was almost a pilgrimage for her and which she had not missed in years.

'Rukmini,' Mylaraiah said to her gently, 'what is this? Shivaswamy tells me he has written to you suggesting possible houses in Bangalore and bridegrooms, but you haven't written back. She must be really ill, he says, if she's left the house-hunting to you.'

Rukmini made no reply. She did not tell her husband that in the same letter, Shivaswamy had made a pointed reference to Mylaraiah's 'dealings' with Vishwanath Rao. She did not ask him why the seedy lawyer Bhat, known to be a broker in the shadiest of deals was visiting his chambers these days; she did not even ask him why they were short of so many sacks of rice that year. As for his appointment, which everyone considered a done thing, she would believe it only when she saw the government order, complete with the Ganda Bherunda seal on it.

'I have been thinking. . .anyway, Achamma and Timrayee are going to remain here. I will continue to stay here with the children. We'll see how it goes with you in Bangalore and then shift. . .'

'The house in Bangalore I will take care of,' Mylaraiah said, 'and yes, we can even shift in stages, but what about the proposal? Shivaswamy said he suggested a Bangalore boy and got no response from you.'

'A proposal?' Rukmini looked up. 'But she hasn't even completed her Intermediate. . .'

'I'm surprised at you Rukmini!' Mylaraiah was less gentle this time. 'Your elder sister started looking for grooms for her daughter when the girl was twelve—but of course, I forgot, you are "progressive". Does that mean you have to shirk your responsibilities? Today she's sixteen, tomorrow, before you know it, she'll be twenty.'

Rukmini sat back in her chair and shut her eyes wearily. 'We must talk to Kaveri first,' she said, her eyes still closed.

'What is there to talk about? She knows very well. Girls sense these things. We are her parents. We know what is best for her. You may want her to heal the sick and the poor like Dr King, but Kaveri herself shows no particular inclination in that direction. And it's not as if she's shining in her studies. Her school-leaving results were disappointing—don't deny it— and there's no sign that her Intermediate results will be better. And how can they be when she sits around reading story books all the time!'

'She needs to be guided,' Rukmini said 'She may want to be a teacher. She's good at languages.'

'She also says she'd like to act on stage. Remember, when the Gubbi Company was in town, we couldn't stop her from singing and dancing and "acting" round the house.'

'If she wants to go to the university, she could stay with my brother.'

'Why are we just bandying words like this? Your brother could barely tolerate having his own mother in the house. You don't even get along with your sister-in-law. Do you seriously think our daughter can stay in that household? And what is this talking-to-her nonsense? We must just tell her and be done with it.'

There was no point in asking her anything, he said, as she did not know her own mind. No girl of seventeen brought up the way Kaveri had been, would. The most demanding decision she had taken so far was to choose the colour of her sari.

And then Rukmini said something which made Mylaraiah lose his temper.

'Even Kalyani,' Rukmini said, 'is being put through her BA in Mysore by her in-laws.'

'You want to compare our daughter with the unfortunate Kalyani,' Mylaraiah said coldly, 'and that too to disadvantage! And after her BA, what? Will you find your daughter a nice widower to marry? No one else will be ready to marry her then. You really are peculiar. Other women would be hounding their relatives, especially their husbands by now, scouring the countryside for grooms, matching horoscopes, setting up meetings, but not you. You think your daughter is still a baby. Perhaps it is you who should go to Mysore to do your BA.'

Mylaraiah gathered himself with an effort and sat down in front of her, forcing her to look at him.

'Am I an unreasonable man?' he asked

'No,' Rukmini replied. Like all benevolent patriarchs he was the soul of reason so long as his word was not questioned. But that did not count as being unreasonable.

'Am I a bad husband or father?'

'The best,' Rukmini replied, looking down, feeling the heat rise in her cheeks. 'And if Kaveri could be as fortunate as I am I would wish for nothing more. . .' she said in perfect truth.

'Have I not taken care of you well? Have I not provided

for all your wants?'

Rukmini looked at him reproachfully for asking her such a thing at all. He would have wrapped her in an old mul sari and put her away at the bottom of the chest of drawers if he could; she was precious enough for that. It was that that she did not wish upon her daughter, while wishing her the love of a good man.

'You are making it so difficult for me, don't you see. . .It is not easy for me either. And things are getting so uncertain these days, it is better we absolve ourselves of our responsibilities. . .' There was something in his voice that made Rukmini look up and in that moment she read in his face and tone a premonition.

Rukmini had strange dreams of late, dreams that woke her up in the middle of the night, dreams of which she had no recollection, but which left her uneasy. One night she dreamt of her children—the ones she had lost before Kaveri and Setu were born. She saw their small faces clearly, eyes open, resting in their graves, watching as the earth was spaded on to them. After that, she decided to stave off sleep as long as she could, and would sit in the moonlit courtyard or stand by the window watching the glistening leaves. Sometimes she would stand for hours by their bedside and watch them sleep—Setu and Kaveri—these are your children, she would tell herself, watch over them well.

Of her son she was sure; he was still her own, her baby, transparent and totally amenable to her control. He would work hard at what he was good, like his father, not allowing himself to get distracted. His father had great ambitions for him. That he would study maths in Presidency College in Calcutta, like his uncle before him, and then, given his natural proficiency in the subject, a degree from Cambridge, like Ramanujan himself. Yet it was Kaveri, less ambitious but more lively, who could well slip through her fingers. She was growing up so fast, with each passing day she seemed to be moving towards the edge of the circumference of Rukmini's ambit; Rukmini feared that soon she would escape it altogether and then would float free, light but directionless, vulnerable to being buffetted about.

If you find the world at odds with yourself, if you think the fault lies outside, look within yourself, Gandhi had said. In all probability, the dissonance was within you and you were projecting it outside. It was not just her home, her body and her mind, but the world outside too seemed to have become a strange place, with new ways of working that she could not quite understand or keep pace with.

I am losing my grip, I had better watch out, she told herself, when she stared stupidly at the dabba of Mysore Pak, still fragrant and hot from the stove, that came from Narayana Rao's house. It was Savitramma, of course, marking her husband's appointment to the highest Congress post in the district, and Rukmini wondered whether a similar reciprocal gesture was expected from her, to mark her husband's successes.

'Savitramma may have been a little hasty with the Mysore Pak,' Mylaraiah remarked. 'The talk is that Narayana Rao may make way for a much junior party-man, a Harijan. The others in the party have challenged him, considering what a champion of the oppressed he makes himself out to be.

Mylaraiah's own foray into 'politics' brought him little joy. 'Rukmini,' he said when he came home after a meeting of the legislative council, his smart gold-edged turban wilting on his head, his excitement over his nomination already worn off, 'today in the first joint session of the two houses, the Congress members in the assembly actually walked out when the session was in progress. . .and the noise they make! A far cry from the Westminster model, I tell you. I think his days are numbered.'

'Whose? Narayana Rao's?'

'Oh no, not Narayana Rao's. He and the Congress will grow from strength to strength. Our future lies in their hands. I mean the maharaja, if the mood of the assembly is anything to go by. He will have to go or at least concede a truly representative assembly, not just the noise-making, demurring body that it is.'

'The maharaja is like a woman,' Rukmini mused. 'Just as a woman is safe as long as she stays within the bounds set for her by her father or her husband, His Highness too is assured of his throne so long as he has the protection of the British.'

Mylaraiah's anxiety about the world at large translated into fresh strictures at home, a tighter curfew. Setu and Kaveri were to come home straight from school, especially Kaveri who would be escorted everywhere by Timrayee. Teach her to walk with her head bowed, Mylaraiah said in some irritation to Rukmini, she cannot consider the street an extension of her home. And see that she keeps her shoulders covered. In matters of propriety, he seemed to imply, Rukmini should have taught her daughter better.

fifteen

1939

When Kaveri had just turned fourteen, one morning in her bath she felt herself and her fingers came away wet and dark and she knew that puberty had caught up with her. Her mother gave her a lecture on diet and hygiene and showed her how the strips of cloth from her old mul saris had to be washed and dried away from sight of the world. A glass of milk and four almonds were placed on the coffee room table every night for her. And yes, she was no longer to fight with Setu, or climb the mango tree in the back yard.

It scared her in the beginning, it made her feel as if she were in the first stages of a wasting disease, till she got used to the routine. So this, she understood, was the key to womanhood; this bore, this nuisance, this ever-damp piece of cloth wedged between her legs. There seemed little connection between the explanation Dr King her given her, complete with charts of the human body, the uterus and the ovaries spread out like the canna flower in her mother's garden, and the indignity she was subjected to every month. No wonder her mother was so grave about it. She wished her grandmother were there, to lighten the load, for them to laugh over it and put it in its place as it deserved to be. All the women in the world aren't fools and they aren't weeping either, her grandmother would have told her. So, just get on with it. She remembered the time some years ago when she had come out of her bath and got into a panic.

'Ajji!' she had pleaded, 'I can hear an ocean roaring in my ear! When I walk it thuds against my head!' And without looking up her grandmother had said, 'Did you wash your hair? Water must have got into your ears then. It'll come out on its own, don't worry.' And sure enough, in the middle of the maths class, a warm trickle had emerged from her right ear and she heard the ocean no more. To tell the truth, sometimes she found her mother's 'high-mindedness' a little tiring. At night, when she drank her medicinal glass of milk and in the mornings, while she submitted herself to her mother's ministrations with the coconut oil and the comb, Rukmini would try to talk to her about school and college and the books she was reading, but she usually ended up giving instructions.

But there were some compensations. She got her first sari, a pumalo-green silk, all the way from Bangalore, from Kapurchand in Chikpet, for which her mother paid all of five rupees!

'Oh my!' her father teased, 'don't tell me this is our Kaveri. I thought it was back-street Sarojamma come to invite us for her son's namkarna.'

'I won't talk to you,' her brother sulked, 'you look like somebody else.'

'Ayya, it's time to look for a suitable groom for our Kaveramma,' Achamma said.

Kaveri tossed her head and pretended not to care, but in truth she loved the feel of the soft folds of silk around her ankles, and its breathless sussuration when she walked. If her manner had a new composure, it reflected nothing of the excitement she felt; perhaps it could be put down to the cotton bodice, cut out and stitched by her mother, which sat snugly, like a secret beneath her blouse. She looked at the two slim gold bangles that she now wore and noticed how fragile her wrists were, and the heavy hoop earrings, brought out from her grandmother's hoard, set off a rush of tenderness for her ear lobes; her whole being seemed centered in the hollow between her new breasts where the pendant of her gold chain nestled. Rukmini saw the soft glint in her daughter's eye, as if surprised by its new-found beauty and wished her mother were there.

Wash well, Rukmini had told her, dry your clothes in the sun, not in the shade, in the far corner of the yard behind the screen of bushes. But she had not told her the other things. That her feet would not tread quite so heavily and that she would not look everyone in the eye anymore, and that her mind would wander. She did not mind the castor oil and soapnut powder routine now, for it would help her hair grow— she longed for a plait like Shanta's, and she even rubbed her face surreptitiously with turmeric before her bath—to stop any hair from growing on her face, as Achamma had whispered to her. Her sandalwood book marks and the wrapper of her Pears soap she put between her clothes, so that the perfume would linger. And when Setu burst in to announce that Dr Murty was driving on the main road in his Ford V8 with *eight cylinders*, she waved a languid hand at him and continued to read her book.

School—the all-girls' Empress High School—gave way to the co-ed Intermediate College, and Kaveri found herself one of the two girls in a class of eighty. Her school-leaving results had disappointed her mother, she knew, but she couldn't summon an interest in maths and science; give her a novel, a 'story book' as her father called it, any day. However, she had done quite well in the languages. What would she do after Intermediate? She wished her mother would not keep asking because she did not know. Right then she was considering the possibilities of each day as it rose before her and doing the most with it. With her now best-friend Shanta, the only other girl in the class, she had learnt to enjoy theatre and music. There was one glittering season of the theatre when Gubbi Veeranna's troupe put up their stock favourites, and she had seen all their plays. T.P. Kailasam visited and sang on stage and the whole town was agog for his parodies. All day Kaveri hummed *Nam Tippar-halli balu doora*, Kailasam's take off on

It's a long way to Tipperary. All of Dickens she had finished by the first year of college, *The Three Musketeers*, and by far her favourite now was *The Scarlet Pimpernel*.

When it came to theatre and books, she found it all—intrigue and mystery, romance and glory but when she looked around her, she was disappointed by how little there was on offer. No one to take her by the hand. All ready and primed, what she needed was a touch of the wand to bring her to life. She did not feel as much at ease in her college as she had done at school. Perhaps because she and Shanta were the only girls in class. The boys in her class were shy, and there was no question of her talking to them. Shanta and she sat alone on a bench meant for four, right in front of the class and the bench behind them was usually empty, even when the rest of the class was crowded and the boys sat six to a bench. When the Kannada master wanted to punish one of the boys, he'd make him sit in the empty bench behind them and once, for a grave misdemeanour, he had made a boy sit *alongside* Kaveri and Shanta. The boy had not come to college for days after that.

At home there was talk of marriage. Her uncle Shivaswamy came with proposals from eligible boys and at night she could hear her parents discussing the various prospects. When her mother asked, Kaveri would you like to get married, she said nothing. On the one hand she wanted her life to continue forever like this, in this pleasant stream of outings and conversations, but on the other, she knew she was ready for more, for a different kind of life, only she did not know what it was. When she listened to her uncle's descriptions of the 'boys' who seemed to be only waiting for her answer, and looked at their photographs where they stared back at her, some smooth, some innocent, some self-assured and some plain bad-looking, she saw, reflected in them, proof of her own desirability. She played a little game with herself, reconstructing briefly a future with each of them as she imagined it would be—an engineer's wife in Calcutta, a lecturer's wife in Bangalore, a lawyer's wife in Shimoga—and found all the prospects equally pleasing, depending of course, on how personable the man in the photograph was. It was at such times that she missed her grandmother. This one, she would have said whimsically, this one looks as if he'd be kind to animals, marry him.

Then there was Shanta's brother, who was a journalist in Bombay. It was only now, after so many years of knowing Shanta that her brother had been given a name. So far, he had been 'Shanta's brother' or 'that Kole boy' or 'C.G.K. Sir's son'. She had been in middle school and he must have been in Intermediate College, when he had earned a brief notoriety in town for picketing liquor shops. He had voluntarily lost a year of Intermediate when he had become a member of the Sevadal and had joined their alcohol-and-untouchability awareness campaign. He had come to be known then as 'Junior Narayana Rao' for he was a regular at Narayana Rao's speeches and marches and ran a local newspaper, a two-page newsletter for students where he wrote on political events and social issues in a fire-and-brimstone manner. Unlike Narayana Rao, he was short and bespectacled but an unfortunate speech impediment made public speaking impossible, so he reserved his ardent opinions for his writing. One of his articles, 'How long will we be slaves?'—Kaveri remembered it from its provocative title and the sensation it had caused—had caught the attention of the district commissioner and Shanta's father, in his avatar as C.G.K. Sir no stranger to the district commissioner himself thanks to his son Mukunda's bulletins about his history teacher, had been summoned.

They heard little of him when he was away at college in Bombay till he came back with 'Gandhi is not the way forward', which was featured prominently in *Vishwakarnataka*. Subhash Chandra Bose was the man of the hour, he said. In their small town, where championing Gandhi was the mark of a revolutionary, it created quite a stir. Bose was a distant star, a chimera, the stuff of newspaper sensationalism and legend; at least Gandhi Mahatma was real, he had spoken in the high school field and there was a maidan named after him. And here was their own C.G.K. Sir's son saying that the Gandhian methods of non-violent non-cooperation would not work and that the British had to be resisted with violence and if need be, the maharaja as well.

Kaveri had first noticed him the other evening when she and Setu had accompanied their mother to the waterworks. The waterworks was at the edge of the town, a huge windswept space with two large, high tanks at one end, with pipes leading from them, much like grotesque giants trying to fend the wind off. The town was justifiably proud of its waterworks, one of the first water treatment plants of its kind, the envy of many bigger, more prosperous towns in the state. The waterworks was enclosed within a compound wall and treated as sacred but in the evenings, the gates were opened to the people. Perhaps it was the direction in which the place was located and the height, but the wind whipped up your hair and clothes as you walked on the bund that was built round the ground, which was quite refreshing. Of late, this had become Rukmini's favourite evening's outing. She liked to walk for a bit on the bund and then sit quietly and listen to the whistling wind.

One evening there were about twenty young men in white in the bowl of the waterworks, whom Setu identified immediately as the boys from the 'Youth Movement'. They watched them from the bund and listened to the faint melodic sounds that floated up to them. The boys seemed to be practising a song. One of the boys provided the lead and was followed by a lusty chorus—*we will not rest, we will not rest*.

'They will not rest till they have done what?' Kaveri asked.

'Freed the country from the British, what else,' Setu replied scornfully.

'Who is that, the main singer?'

'That's C.G.K. Sir's son Shyam, your Shanta's brother,' Setu's tone was non-committal but his eyes were watchful.

'So, that's Shanta's famous brother. Hadn't he gone off to Bombay, or was it Calcutta, to study?'

'He's returned now. To start a newspaper and to train the boys again.'

'He sings very well.'

'You should have seen how Anna scared him off once, from Anantaramu's shop. They were trying to bully Shetty.'

'I *still* think he sings very well.'

'What are they doing here?'

'They must have just finished their meeting. The song always comes at the end.'

'What do they do in their meetings? You used to go to them didn't you, Setu?'

'That was a long time back, and I just went once or twice,' Setu shook it off as one would a youthful indiscretion. 'It's a complete waste of time. I remember he tried to teach us all to clean toilets, and many boys ran off then. I believe now he makes bombs in secret. Right in a house in the Agrahara Colony. It's no laughing matter,' Setu said angrily to his sister, 'It's true. He's a dangerous fellow, Shyam.'

Kaveri was smiling at him, her eyes bright. 'He seems really talented. . .he can clean toilets, make bombs, sing, and look now, he's playing cricket!'

The singers had disbanded and most of them had gone. A few were still there, hitting a ball around with a bat, looking absurd in their white pyjamas and caps.

'He's good, he was on the Intermediate College team. . .' Setu admitted grudgingly as he watched Shyam give the ball what seemed like a gentle pat but which sent the other boys scampering across the ground after it.

'Why do you say it's a waste of time?'

'Anna says all these people—the Youth Movement, even Ramu's father and C.G.K. Sir, they are destructive. They just make us feel dissatisfied with what we have but they can give us nothing instead.'

'Poor Setu! Anna's parrot!'

Before Setu could retort, they saw the Youth Brigade coming their way, their game over. While Kaveri stared after them boldly, Setu avoided looking at them and in an attempt to appear insolent, dangled his feet over the sides of the stone bench and swung his legs rapidly. Kaveri looked at her brother's averted face and noticed for the first time the soft downy black above his upper lip and a purple pimple on his smooth cheek from which sprouted two black strands of hair. She knew better now than to tease him about it.

'Why don't you join them?' she said, for she could sense that he was torn between his attraction for the boys in white for they were young and vigorous after all, and the counter weight of his natural abhorrence for immoderation combined with their father's strictures.

'I play in school, after classes, in the field—not with this lot. That Shyam. . .I hate him.'

Kaveri smiled to hear her brother use so strong a word but said nothing.

The next time Kaveri heard of Shyam, he was being discussed as a possible invitee to one of the Samaja meetings. After a fiercely divided discussion (in which Rukmini did not participate), the Samaja invited him to address their next gathering. It proved to be their most successful evening yet. The hall was thronged with people. Many young men had gate-crashed and had been allowed to stand at the back. Kaveri came late and sat discreetly somewhere in the middle of the hall, while Shanta and her mother occupied the privileged seats in front. Though it was a little difficult to see him from where she was sitting, she could hear him clearly; he seemed to have got over his speech impediment.

'I am glad to see so many young women and men here today, for you are the future of this nation, you will shape its destiny,' he began and was immediately greeted with loud cheers from the young men at the back.

People get the kind of rulers they deserve, he continued, and an apathetic, comfort-loving people would get the worst sort; they would find the ground shifting like a tectonic block from beneath their feet. This time the young men at the back were silent.

'Our young men are emasculated and our young women, too timid. We have lost the vital spirit of youth, too fond of our food and drink, our unhampered routines, our clothes and

A   Girl   and   a   River

jewellery, our meaningless entertainments, so much so that we want others to rule us, to think for us, to tell us which is our right hand and which is our left. . .we don't even mind being slaves so long as we are not disturbed from our state of rest.'

They sat back and listened to his mild scolding turn into a taunt and then almost a call to arms. Then just as the Samaja women were beginning to look alarmed, he cracked a joke, told them how anxiously he had practised his speech all morning till his mother had told him he wasn't going for a swayamvara, he needn't be so nervous; he digressed, he even recited a snatch of poetry, and protest as poetry and song, the Samaja women were comfortable with—poetry and song gave everything an unquestionable legitimacy.

'Do you want the fragrance of the full-blown rose?' he quoted from his hero Bose, and here Shanta's brother's lisp returned.

'Do you want the fragrance of the full-blown rose?
If so you must, accept the thorns.
Do you want the sweetness of the smiling dawn?
If so you must, live through the dark hours of the night.
Do you want the joy of liberty and the solace of freedom?
If so you must, pay the price.
And the price of liberty is suffering and sacrifice.'

Kaveri had come out of a sense of loyalty to Shanta, expecting another evening of mild entertainment, and more to observe Shanta's brother than to listen to him. And she had to admit that her interest had been aroused since the day at the waterworks when Setu had attributed such perversely varied skills to him—singer, cricketer, toilet-cleaner and bomb-maker. And now, she felt that all his sharpest observations were being directed at her. When he came to the bit about women being consumed by their clothes and jewellery, she squirmed; she had worn her best sari, a silk, for the occasion and all her new jewellery. She was stung by his insinuation that she was vain and that her interest in the world ended at her own doorstep. After his speech, which was wildly applauded, she wanted to ask him questions but he was so mobbed by the young men that she could speak neither to him nor to Shanta. On her way back she swung between anger and admiration but by the time she reached home, she had to admit that she was impressed, even though he was only Shanta's brother.

After that, at college she paid attention to Shanta's 'my brother' stories and tried to find out more about him without seeming curious. It was in Bombay that he had gone to the university and not Calcutta as everyone said—Shanta's stories had now begun to acquire an 'everyone' or 'people' angle as well—and he worked for an English newspaper in Bombay.

'Who is this Shyam that our Kaveri is always quoting?' Mylaraiah asked Rukmini.

'The Kole boy—Nanjunda Kole's nephew, Setu's C.G.K. Sir's son. This boy used to be Advocate Kole's apprentice, he used to come with messages from Kole's office at one time. He had planned to study law but his mother tells me he abandoned his studies half-way in Bombay and decided to become a journalist.'

'Trust Kaveri to fall in with the Swadeshi lot. Narayana Rao's daughter first and now C.G.K. Sir's daughter.'

'Well, they are her classmates. Kalyani was, till she got married and Shanta is the only girl in her class now. Anyway, Setu has forsworn their sons. He will have nothing to do with Ramu or with Shyam and the Youth Movement,' Rukmini said. 'He believes they are both "disruptive elements".'

'And so they are,' Mylaraiah said approvingly. 'But girls are not so bad. Shanta is the docile girl who walks to college with Kaveri, isn't she?'

Rukmini smiled. Her husband's first yardstick for judging a girl was how biddable she was.

'I have nothing against Kole's family, just as I have nothing against Narayana Rao, even though I disagree with them. They are eminently respectable. So long as she stays clear of their ideas.'

'The boy's speech at the Samaja was a grand success, so they tell me. It isn't just Kaveri. Since then even Umadevi has begun to sing his praises.'

'Wasn't he Narayana Rao's shishya. I remember he used to be part of the picketing and protest brigade.'

'Shanta says he's organized many student protests in Bombay. Even here, when he was in Intermediate he was arrested once.' Kaveri rushed out onto the verandah, her comb tangled in her hair.

'They should have kept him in jail and not let him out,' Setu said.

'And the penal fines almost cleaned his father out,' Mylaraiah snorted. 'He had a tough time keeping him out of jail. I remember he borrowed money too.'

'In Bombay he was beaten up by a policeman and I believe a bullet narrowly missed him,' Kaveri said, deaf to their taunts. 'Here too, he was hit with a lathi when he was still a student. He has a scar on his forehead. . .when he frowned, it looked like a perfect star.'

'All his brains seem to have leaked out through the star-shaped hole. . .' Setu baited his sister.

'So, he has already become the stuff of local legend,' Mylaraiah said dryly.

'He's the one who wrote that article quoting Bose, calling Gandhi a useless piece of furniture. . .no longer useful,' Rukmini reminded him.

'Oh! I'm sure he's surprised to see how Gandhi has suddenly sprung back to life, the grand old sofa brought back into service. Churchill called Bose a lunatic.'

'Churchill also called Gandhi a naked fakir,' Kaveri returned spiritedly.

'So somebody's been reading the newspaper closely, I see.'

'You told me that yourself, Anna, I didn't read it anywhere.'

The next time she went to Shanta's house, she was careful to wear only khadi, but she couldn't resist picking one of the finer saris; she kept her gold bangles on, if not, the eagle-eyed Shanta would notice and tease her. But he wasn't there. One evening, when she was rushing out of Shanta's house with

Timrayee prowling impatiently at the gate, she came face to face with him in the doorway and turned speechless. She had thought of so many different things to say to him, but now they were all lost. Even as she noticed how compellingly his eyes held hers through the thick lenses, she had to fight a tiny squiggle of disappointment that they were level with hers; he must be about the same height as she was. But perhaps it helped her find her tongue.

'I wanted to say. . .' she stammered, 'after your talk at the Samaja that day. . .Shanta may have told you. . .' Where was Shanta? Never around when she was needed most. 'My sari may be silk but it's Mysore silk. . .' she said abruptly, 'and the gold from my bangles is from Kolar. It's pure swadeshi.'

He smiled at her outburst. 'Well, I hope I haven't caused you to change from silk to khadi,' he gestured towards her sari. 'I'm no votary of khadi, not anymore. Not at all practical to wear and makes no economic sense. I don't know how we expected to demoralize the British with it. Make sure you don't get wet in the rain,' he said mock seriously, 'the thing will become so heavy that you won't be able to stand up.'

She stared at him, trying to think of an appropriate retort for she was sure he was laughing at her. He caught her eye and smiled a sudden gap-toothed smile, and she could not but smile back. Shanta came in with coffee and they both sat down in the verandah. He followed, and sat down at the desk in the verandah, for the house was small and they had turned the open verandah into a study-cum-drawing room, humming under his breath. While Shanta and she had coffee in steel tumblers, he had tea in a cup and saucer with biscuits on the side. As they watched he poured his tea into his saucer and started drinking out of it, dipping his biscuits into the hollow.

'Is that how you drink tea?' She could not stop herself. 'I mean,' she tried to make amends, 'don't you drink coffee like us?'

'Both tea and the way I drink it is a Bombay habit,' he said, continuing to drink out of his saucer.

'Bombay, I believe changes people. My uncle says so. . .'

Bombay people, he said, were without pretensions. They were not afraid to show themselves to be what they were, and they were vigorous and straightforward. It was the sea, he said. It sweeps lethargy away and fills you with energy. And if you lived near the beach as he had, the sound of the waves was with you all the while, setting your spirits humming. He had learnt music in Bombay, amidst attending college, organizing and attending meetings and writing for the newspaper. Classical music it was and from none other than Dinanath Pandit himself, who had told him he had a future as a classical musician if only he were not so distracted.

'You sing very well,' Kaveri said generously. 'I heard you at the waterworks the other day, with the Youth Movement boys. . .'

'If you keep making the boys march all the time or lecture to them about swadeshi and Swaraj, they're sure to turn British sympathizers. So we sing songs. . .play kabaddi, even cricket. In Bombay, all of us would go and see films together sometimes.'

'Films? Charlie Chaplin?' Here was a name that would not make her look as provincial as she was feeling.

He waved Charlie Chaplin aside carelessly. In Bombay, he had learnt Hindi. He had learnt Hindi, not to follow the Mahatma's speeches so much as to understand Hindi films. *Devdas* and Kundan Lal Saigal were his favourite, which no doubt she had not heard of. The film had taken Bombay by storm. And how that man could sing. He began humming again but the sound of Timrayee banging on the gate broke through.

'The next time you come to the waterworks, you can watch us fly kites,' he called out after her. 'That's another thing we learnt to do very well on the beach in Bombay.'

Timrayee grumbled all the way back about how late it was getting and how ayya would be sure to scold him, all because of her, but she took no notice of him. The evening breeze helped cool her inflamed cheeks and she played their conversation over and over again in her mind. She thought of the sweep of his not-unattractive, spatulate hands as they had gestured towards her, saw his gap-toothed smile and heard the laugh rumble in his throat. She basked in it till she sighted the familiar gate posts. For once she was unhappy to have reached home so soon.

Shanta would tell her about the terrible arguments there had been at home despite her father's nationalist leanings. C.G.K. Sir was a votary of Gandhi, of passive resistance, a prayer and petition man, a social reconstructionist. He did not hold even with Narayana Rao's forcible picketing. He did not hold with his son's call to arms at the slightest provocation, a product of the distempered Bengal–Bose school of resistance. But in Shyam's mind it was very simple. People must work for the kind of community and nation they want and they must be ready to risk everything for it. He had never held with working from within the system to change things and he had often urged his father to give up his job just as Narayana Rao had given up his practice. In fact, he had been sent away to his uncle's in Bombay because he was becoming too conspicuous in their small town. C.G.K. Sir had hoped that the anonymity and even the lure of Bombay would temper his zeal and that his activism would take on the *seva* avatar; but if anything it had thrown him among more like-minded people and given him direction. Three years into the law course and he decided he had had enough. There wasn't time for an elaborate and indulgent studentship when there was so much to be done. He had joined a newspaper, for as a journalist he could best feel the pulse of his times and his articles were considered very provocative; they had just stopped short of challenging the section on sedition in the Press Act. And now he was back. To serve his hometown, he said, by starting the right kind of newspaper and continuing with the Youth Movement where he had left off.

Shanta also kept her informed about his comings and goings. Today he has left for Bombay, she would say, having progressed from 'my brother' to 'he'. She implied that he was involved in activities of a mysterious and secretive nature on which the

A Girl and a River

future of the country depended. 'He has refused to see Gandhi, says he will meet him only when he does something worthwhile.'

Once again they met unexpectedly, this time when Shanta and she were on their way to college. He stopped to talk to his sister and looked appraisingly at the books Kaveri was carrying.

'Shanta tells me you read a lot.'

So Shanta had been talking to him about her. She glanced quickly at Shanta, who looked impassive.

'*The Scarlet Pimpernel*!' he stared at the jacket, astounded. 'What kind of book is this? What! An English aristocrat who rescues French aristocrats from the French people?' He stood on the footpath and laughed, rocking squatly on his heels. 'Being read by an Indian girl who would rather wear silk but wears khadi.'

Before Kaveri could retort Shanta had grabbed her elbow. 'We've reached. Come on, we can't stand on the footpath and talk forever. . .'

Their exchanges were always short. Shanta was forever cutting them off. But Kaveri would carry the resonances of the last conversation till they met next. She had also begun to feel that she was now on a different footing with Shanta. It was barely noticeable but she could tell that Shanta was beginning to condescend to her.

A few days later Shanta handed over a khaki-green hard-bound volume to her. '*Mein Kampf*. . .My Battle. . .Adolf Hitler?' Kaveri ran her fingers over the red lettering and the red swastika separating the title from the author's name. He had asked Shanta to pass on a message as well. Read about real people in the real world, men who are poised to change the course of history, not make-believe tales of fops who did trivial things.

'How can you get so immersed in cooked-up tales of fictitious people? How can you remove yourself from the real world so easily?' he asked her at their next accidental meeting. Sometimes, when he was in town, he would walk Shanta up to college and then carry on to the newspaper office, and they would walk part of the distance together.

'On the contrary, it is the real world created differently. And people are the same everywhere. The things that happen to them in books, their thoughts, their feelings, everything seems so much more enjoyable and more real too because you are sitting in a chair and reading about them and they are the ones getting wet in the rain and having problems and. . .' she stopped, for she had been about to say 'falling in love'.

'That's escapism. . .'

'No, it's another way of getting to know the world and yourself. You see films don't you. . .'

He stood on the footpath, rocking on his heels—she had come to recognize his characteristic stance—looking at her speculatively. 'You have a keen mind. . .' he began. 'And you have such a sound grasp of language. Would you go through our articles and correct them? Some of our writers have such important things to say but they say them so poorly. . .so many mistakes in language and grammar. . .And I'm sure it would do you good too.'

'I must ask my father,' Kaveri said.

'Ask your father? For such a simple thing. . .you a modern miss who can even take on Hitler. . .' he mocked.

Kaveri turned on her heel and walked off. But she sent word with Shanta that she was ready to take up her brother's offer; only, she would not come to the newspaper office, the articles would have to be sent home to her.

Soon, Shyam's newspaper became the new entertainment for the family. While the news reports were patchy, depending on what correspondents he had managed to muster, the editorials, written by various 'eminent' personalities varied widely in tone, style and content. At night, Kaveri would read out the choice passages—sentimental, sententious and poorly written—and Mylaraiah remarked that Kole's son did not have to go all the way to Bombay to learn how to gather trash like this. Sometimes, Rukmini would find Kaveri quite absorbed in what she was reading, and those were invariably articles that

Shyam himself wrote. 'Did you know Amma,' Kaveri would call out, 'the number of people who died in the famine, the year Queen Victoria's durbar was held in Delhi?' or 'If all the money we spent on the Dasara celebrations could be directed elsewhere, do you know how many more schools we could have?' Some of Shyam's articles were eye openers for Rukmini herself. Forcefully written, if a little over-wrought, they brought home the facts well; the mere titles were illuminative. 'How the Manchester Mill ruined the Indian Weaver', 'The Sponge that sucks from the Ganga and swells the Thames', 'Why are we Plagued by Famine?' We must accept the facts of history and move on, Mylaraiah would say as usual. Far from being the cause, the British benifice—their railways and irrigation systems—has helped relieve our natural conditions. And in any case, machines of iron will replace our tools of wood. Look at the motor car. A time will come when we will say goodbye to the tonga, though you cannot imagine it right now.

As the war progressed, opinion in the coffee houses was evenly divided over the maharaja's support for it. The newspapers recounted the number of martyrs from the Mysore Cavalry in the first great war and the fact that Mysore had contributed fifty lakh rupees to it even as the state recovered from a famine. All India Radio broadcast the progress of the war regularly and one day they thrilled to the sound of Churchill's voice. Churchill! Mylaraiah's hero and by default Setu's too—announcing that his aim was victory at all costs but he had nothing to offer but blood, toil, tears and sweat. All India Radio played the speech over and over again till the brandy and cigar growl rang familiarly in their ears. Often, by twiddling the knobs of the radio in the opposite direction they would catch one of Radio Berlin's broadcasts—what Mylaraiah dismissed as 'German propaganda'—on which a clipped British accent detailed the number of British ships sunk and assured the world that Britain was on the edge of collapse.

Every morning there was a tussle for the newspaper between Kaveri and Setu after their father had finished with it, to read the latest bulletin from the war front. At that time, in a journalistic 'coup', the first of its kind, one of the newspapers—the one in Bombay that Shyam wrote for—produced Gandhi's undelivered letter to Hitler, where Gandhi had apologized for his 'impertinence' in writing to Hitler and called him 'the one person in the world who can prevent a war which may reduce humanity to the savage state'. The British government had impounded the letter and secreted it in their files before it could do any damage. For months, the letter was discussed all over town. The local newspapers commented on it at length. If only he had been allowed to send it, the local Congress loyalists said, Mahatma Gandhi might have stopped the Second World War!

They discussed Gandhi's letter and the war as they strolled in the waterworks, Rukmini, Kaveri and Setu.

'Britain will win the war!' Setu said.

Kaveri agreed with the coffee house verdict. 'No, Germany will,' she said.

'Anna says if Hitler wins the war, the British will be sent packing, and then this country has had it!' Setu said.

'Shanta's brother says given Germany's airpower, there's no way Germany cannot win.'

'Shanta's brother's parrot!'

And before the argument could develop into a fight, they spotted the man in question himself, in the bowl of the waterworks, playing cricket with his boys.

'There he is, Amma,' Kaveri said excitedly, 'That's Shanta's brother, Shyam. You remember the article we were reading yesterday, "Why are we Plagued by Famine", you liked it too. . .'

'He must be really stupid to continue playing in this wind. It's so strong in the pitch that it might quite blow the ball away,' Setu said in the scornful manner that he acquired whenever he spoke of the Youth Movement.

Almost as if they had heard Setu, the boys in the middle

wrapped up their game and started dispersing. Shyam walked in their direction, stopped by and first said namaskara to Rukmini, before turning to talk to Kaveri and Setu. He exchanged a few pleasantries with them, folded his hands in Rukmini's direction again, and went off.

'Today, they didn't sing. Too windy, he said.'

'How dare he come over and talk to us so. . . so boldly!' Setu fumed.

Rukmini too was struck by his poise, his confidence. Few boys his age would have acknowledged a female acquaintance in public, leave alone salute her mother.

'Why not!' Kaveri said. 'It's only polite to greet people you know, of course such things wouldn't count with your country bumpkin friends. What's his name, Chapdi Kal, aha!'

Rukmini said something suitably soothing and non-committal to stop them from fighting, and then she looked at both of them. Kaveri's eyes lingered after Shyam, and so did Setu's, their expressions quite dissimilar and far from childlike. Oh no, she thought in a quick burst of panic, the Kole boy would not do at all. Apart from the fact that her husband would come down on Kaveri and herself like thunder, she herself did not want it. She did not wish for her daughter a future like Savitramma's. She could imagine how their life would progress—he marching ahead with bright-eyed fervour either from pinnacle to pinnacle or from jail to jail, while his wife and brood of children—for few men would give up on that—stumbled after him as best as they could. And unlike Narayana Rao, Kole had no lands to sustain his ideals with, he was a poor man.

'Kaveri,' Rukmini said and Kaveri was surprised by the tone of reproof in her mother's voice. 'Your Intermediate will be over next year. You must think of what you want next. Your father is quite determined to get you married before we shift to Bangalore you know. Have you thought about it? Those photographs that Shivaswamy has sent, and which you keep looking at. . .it isn't a game.'

'And you, Amma. What do you think?'

'Amma thinks the same as Anna, what else!' Setu interrupted tartly.

They ignored him. 'I would have liked you to do medicine, but that is not to be.'

'I will do my BA perhaps. . .'

'*Perhaps* it would be best if you got married!' Rukmini was really angry.

'Every one of those photographs looks better than goggle-eyed shorty there,' Setu did a perfect imitation of Shyam's expression and Kaveri burst into laughter.

'You should see the way he slurps tea from his saucer. Like a cat!' Kaveri gurgled.

For the moment, Rukmini was relieved. She had presumed prematurely upon her daughter's affection for that young man. But these were fleeting anxieties and in many ways, inconsequential. What Rukmini wanted was to get to the heart of the matter, if only she knew how to do it without making heavy weather of it, for then she would embarrass both of them. There were so many things she wanted to tell her daughter, so many things she could not explain to herself completely, thoughts that even as they passed through her mind, seemed ponderous and clumsy. These were things that had to be slipped in, in between snatches of laughter but she could not strike the same pitch of intimacy with her daughter as her mother had done. So when she asked her daughter whether she would not like to be like Dr King, riding around merrily on her bicycle, she could sense her daughter's bewilderment and despaired of ever making sense to her. I do not want you, Rukmini wanted to tell her daughter, to be hemmed in by motherhood and domesticity before you have had a chance to know your mind; I do not want you to be led into womanhood by the hand, on a straight and narrow path, under the umbrella of a husband's care, for it will mean that you cannot step out of its shade, however benign. You should not end up like a perfumed flower on the lapel of your husband's handsome coat, happy only to obey every command. At the same time, beware of men who ride on their ideals for you will never matter in their scheme of things, they will let you down when you are counting on them. Unless. . .unless both of you march in step, to the sound of the same drummer, unless the ideal matters to both of you equally, unless you have the determination and he the courage to be yoked like a pair of oxen, ploughing the field together. I want for you a full life but for that you have to want it first yourself, and you will have to prove your mettle. But how was she to tell her daughter these things without frightening her? She longed so much for her mother's methods, her imagination, her lightness of touch. Of late, to tell the truth, she lacked the will as well. Like Setu, she wished Kaveri was adept at reading between the lines. The trouble with Kaveri was that she flitted too much. Perhaps she would ask Dr King to talk to her.

1940

Dr King arrived unexpectedly and in a fluster one evening, nursing her grazed knees and elbows. She had fallen off her bicycle but seemed more dazed than hurt. She had been making her way from the hospital to the Women and Children's clinic on the other side of the Bellary Road, as she had done each evening these past ten years or so, when her path had been blocked by a gang of khadi-clad college boys. The incident had not robbed Dr King of any of her self possession; she seemed more annoyed with herself for not having manouvered her cycle past them skilfully.

Achamma and Timrayee flapped around her ineffectually, till Rukmini carried in a basin of boiling water herself and dismissed them with a sharp word.

'They wanted to plant a flag on the handlebars of my bicycle,' Dr King said, wincing as she cleaned her own cuts with tincture of iodine, 'Their flag, not the maharaja's and I wouldn't let them. No, it's nothing serious, just a superficial graze,' she assured Rukmini. 'It was more a show of bravado than anything else, they didn't frighten me.'

'I'll talk to the district commissioner about it, and Narayana Rao too. It's absolutely irresponsible of him to let his boys loose like that. If anything, things will get worse,' Mylaraiah said grimly.

Dr King's injuries, which were minor, were attended to,

and soon she was sitting comfortably cross-legged, drinking some of Achamma's excellent coffee from a silver tumbler and as a concession, she was allowed to light up a cigarette in the coffee room.

'And to think,' Dr King said, 'that the man in Rothney Castle, Alan Hume, whom the whole of Simla considered an oddity, was responsible for starting the Congress Party.' Dr King was her usual self, unable to resist telling a story, the more bizarre the better.

People in Calcutta used to laugh at him, him and his grand passions and his grand house. Alan Octavian Hume, the retired English bureaucrat had dabbled in succession in ornithology, mysticism and politics, giving to each his fullest and most passionate attention in turn. His house used to be full of stuffed birds at one time, all of which he shipped off to London when he took up with the Theosophists. There was talk of mystical séances and other goings-on with Madam Blavatsky their founder, reputed to be a Russian spy. Madam Blavatsky's seances in Alan Hume's house were a byword. She wrote letters—in English and on pink letter paper—to her two Buddhist 'mahatmas' who in turn conveyed those letters to the realms beyond. The letters were transported between Simla and an unknown cleft in the mountains in Tibet where the 'mahatmas' lived, part of the way by the postal department and then by astral osmosis. All this, Hume believed implicitly. According to witnesses, Madame Blavatsky had on occasion demonstrated her psychic powers. She had once 'discovered' lost jewellery in Rothney Castle in the course of a séance, leading her mesmerised audience, herself in a trance with her eyes closed, from the dark room in which contact was first made with the 'spirits', to the garden and had asked her hosts to dig under a certain bush. Of course the precious brooch had been right there, and so forceful was her personality and so excitingly self-deluding the whole caper of communicating with mystic realms, that nobody in Simla doubted her or openly suggested that she had used her hypnotic powers to mesmerize her hostess into planting the brooch under the bush in the first place.

'The Theosophists moved on from Simla to Madras,' Dr King paused to sip her coffee, 'and Alan Octavian Hume moved on to found the Indian National Congress. People presumed it would be yet another "tamasher", which would quietly lose steam in a couple of years, and he would move on to another fad. And look what it's become in fifty years! I'm sure Hume didn't intend your Gandhi to come along and *seize* the Congress by the scruff of its neck. . .' the veins in her neck stood out and her hand clenched into a fist, 'and use it against us. . .'

'You cannot say he *seized* it. . .' Kaveri's impassioned voice rang out from the doorway and they turned to look at her. 'It is only natural that we will take what belongs to us. Our systems may have been given by *you*, but one day *we* will run them.'

'Kaveri!' Rukmini said, surprised as much by Kaveri's argument as by the forthrightness of her manner.

But Dr King did not think anything was amiss. 'Hello Blue Bird,' she said easily, 'I wouldn't have recognized you. How much you have grown and how graceful you look in a sari! How old are you now. . .let me think. . .I remember you were born right here, there in that room. . .and a difficult time you gave us too. . .'

'Sixteen, Dr King' Kaveri said, in a small voice.

'Sixteen! I don't think I can take you riding on my pillion any more.'

Kaveri smiled at her, and looked shamefaced, ashamed as much by her outburst as by the memory of riding pillion with Dr King to school; at one time she had thought no honour could be greater that that!

'How is Ella?'

'Well. She sends greetings. I don't see what you wanted me to talk to her about, Mrs M,' DrKing added in an undertone to Rukmini, 'here is a young lady who seems to know her own mind.'

'Well, Hume started the Congress in good faith,' Mylaraiah

said, struggling to return to his regular, measured tone, giving his daughter a searing look, 'but and I doubt if he ever wanted it to come to this. At their first meeting of the Congress, the delegates actually swore an oath of loyalty to the Queen Empress.'

'Well, the Congress is loyal no longer. I remember when I picked myself off the ground, after those boys had knocked me down,' Dr King heaved on her cigarette holder, 'one of those boys said, "soon, you will have to go too".'

'Not you, but the British government. The Congress wants self-rule,' Rukmini said placatingly.

'I have lived here all my life, Mrs M,' Dr King said, as if it had just struck her, 'I was born here and I can't imagine living anywhere else. My brother says he will go back if we lose the War and concede the Empire, but I can't think of it.' Dr King put her tumbler down sharply, and then sighed and sat back in her chair.

They remained silent for a while, Rukmini and Mylaraiah leaning against the counter, Kaveri hovering by the door and Dr King contemplating the plug of ash that had collected on her cigarette. Kaveri caught her mother's eye and held her tongue. Things would become uncertain for everybody, she had wanted to add, but more so for people like Dr King, who would have to switch sides from ruler to subject. She was a good soul, but as Shyam said, people like her were representations of the anachronism the British had become, at their best, well meaning.

'Your nationalist sentiments do you credit,' Mylaraiah said to Kaveri as soon as Dr King had left. He spoke to her in English, for matters of such gravity had to be addressed in a formal tongue. 'They are the fashion now. But you would do well to refrain from airing your half-baked and borrowed ideas in public, where you will shame us and yourself. Keep them confined to your debating club. You are not at liberty to be rude to our friends. You will write a note to Dr King apologising for your bad manners.'

'It's those Koles,' Mylaraiah said to his wife. 'That fellow who writes the most unbalanced and illogical nonsense in that rag of his, and his sister. Rukmini, I hope Kaveri hasn't been frequenting their house. They are together in college, that's enough. Not that I have anything against Kole's family, they are entitled to their views, but a girl like Kaveri, whose head is full of fanciful notions can easily be led astray. She can stop that newspaper business too. . .waste of time. And I hope you have written to your sister-in-law about following up that Mysore proposal. She finishes her Intermediate next year. Old enough.'

1940

Setu slept alone in the large hall, on the single piece of bedding that was rolled out for him. When the occasional male visitor arrived, another mattress would be brought out, but their numbers were dwindling now that it was known that the family was in transit. His sister slept in their mother's room now, after her mysterious transformation from long skirts to that damning garment, the sari. It was a strange garment, the sari, badge of comfort-giving motherly and grandmotherly laps, distinct from the equally voluminous dhoti—you would never dream of resting your head on a dhoti-clad lap for what use is a man's sinewy and muscled thigh for a head that seeks to lie down. And what a miracle-performing garment the sari was. It could put a ten-year old girl who had just now been grinding your face in the dust, beyond reach, almost as if she had become a member of a different species altogether. Not that his sister was ten years old, but she certainly could grind a boy's face in the dust if she wanted to. He remembered the whispered conversations she and his grandmother would have at night, on the far side of the hall. He would catch a word or two, sometimes whole snatches of it, and often he too would join the feast of nightly whispers. He would fall asleep each night to the music of his sister's teasing. Now, all that was gone. The nature of their sparring too had changed. Earlier, it had been an elaborate Machiavellian strategy, complete with a master plan and emergency short-term tactics, one waiting for the other's move before planning the counter-move. It had always been in deadly earnest. They went all out, testing the limits, devising new ways of outdoing each other, but they were always equals and together, they would take on anybody. But now she seemed always in a hurry, impatient, looking more to kill the conversation than finishing him off. It was almost as if she could no longer take him seriously as they no longer shared the common ground.

The other day she was putting up a picture on her cupboard. His sister had always put up pictures on her cupboard but this one was different. It was the picture of a masked woman showing off her fat thighs in a short black dress, holding a whip above her head. It had been an honourable if unwritten rule between them that anything she put up on her cupboard, he would deface. That could provide fodder for weeks of warfare, of a pitting of wits. Pictures of butterflies, blonde babies and flowers one could mutilate. The blonde baby could acquire a moustache, the butterfly could be made famously cock-eyed and flowers could sprout jagged teeth. But what could one do with a picture like this, already shamed and defaced?

'Hunterwali?' he read the lettering on top of the picture aloud. 'Who is this?'

'A hunter is a whip, and this is the woman with the whip so, Hunterwali, in Hindi,' his sister had explained with exaggerated patience. 'It's a Hindi film in which the heroine rides a horse, beats up men. She is bad to the rich and good to the poor.'

'How do you know? Have you seen it?' His heart pounded for fear of confirmation that she had seen such a film without him, and worse, before he had.

'No, it has been shown only in Bombay. Sh. . .Shanta told me about it.'

He peered at the poster, at the words someone had written in ink on the clear space at the bottom. 'If you are fond of rescuers in disguise, here is one better than the Scarlet

Pimpernel. One of our own!'

'What does that mean?'

'Oh nothing,' she shrugged her shoulders, bringing the conversation to an end.

It was that Shyam, he knew, who had turned his sister's head. As for the poster, he did the only thing he could. He tore it down the middle and left it there, on the cupboard. He waited all evening for her to start a fight over it, but she didn't. When he next went into the room, the poster had been removed.

That evening, after she had been so shockingly ill-mannered with Dr King, there had been a scene at home. Kaveri had been sulky and defiant, arguing with their father. The next day he had cycled over to Dr King's clinic with his sister's note of apology. It had been brief again to the point of rudeness. Dear Dr King, I am sorry for my behaviour last evening. I did not mean to be rude to you. Your's sincerely, K.M. Kaveri.

'My sister is sorry for her behaviour. She did not mean to be rude to you,' he said.

'Have you read her letter, then?' Dr King said, even before she opened the envelope.

He bowed, flushing with shame and at her unfairness in showing *him* up. 'She has been behaving badly with me too.'

'You're very fond of your sister, aren't you? I remember, you used to be great friends, ganging up against your cousins.'

He looked up sharply to see her watching him.

'She's older than you. She's growing up. You'll still be friends, but not like before.'

'She does wrong things,' his voice was grave with judgement, 'She disobeys our father.'

'When you grow up and start thinking for yourself, you may often end up *disobeying* rules. . .'

He looked up, perplexed, wondering whose side she was on. Surely she did not support the boys who had attacked her?

'Will you take a note to your mother?'

From the parlour, where he waited, Setu could see Dr King's bedroom beyond, a very modest sized room—even the coconut room in his house was bigger—with a bed in the middle that seemed to be keeping the walls apart and a gloomy mosquito curtain suspended above the bed from the ceiling. A chest of drawers was squeezed to one side. There was a small verandah to the west of the parlour where he had left his slippers, and the door to the room on the other side, probably the kitchen, was shut. The small weather beaten suitcase under the bed, her doctor's bag on the chest of drawers, her sturdy shoes and her mud-encrusted bicycle in the verandah, these seemed to be all her worldly goods. Not counting the books and photographs on the mantelpiece. There was a picture of two fair haired girls, probably her nieces and a hand-drawn picture of a baby. He was wondering why Dr King would possibly have a crudely drawn picture of a baby on her mantelpiece when she came out of her room and handed him the note for his mother.

He would not have done it if she had not shamed him so, but she had so he stopped under a lamp post and read the note. After the usual salutations, which he skipped, Dr King had said 'Please thank your husband for sending those boys over to apologize to me. They came first thing in the morning and were quite abject, they did not know that I was the famous Dr King! But yesterday evening was an eye-opener. I must thank your daughter as much as the boys who tried to foist the national flag on me. I cannot but read the writing on the wall. It will not do to "tempt fate", something I learnt from your people. I say this not out of a sense of defeat — it would take more than a few boys to frighten me—but out of realization that my task is done and I must leave. In all my years here, I have faced daunting situations but I have never felt unwanted. If I continue here, I will always be dependent on the kindness of right-thinking people like your husband and yourself and that will not do. I have lain sleepless last night and thought it through. This morning I wrote to my brother. I will have to decide soon.'

'You have driven Dr King away,' Setu accused his sister.

'Don't be silly,' she returned, not stopping to talk to him or even ask how he knew.

'You. . .Hunterwali!' he threw bitterly after her and heard her mocking laughter.

That night, as Setu kept his lonely vigil in the hall, he felt a strange tingling—painful and pleasurable in equal parts, all along his body, as if a line of less-viciously-disposed ants was crawling under his skin. That shows that you are growing, his grandmother would have said. But what would she have made of his nightly sweats, the sheets that stuck to his skin, so much that he rolled over to the cool ground to sleep. Sometimes, when he caught a glimpse of boys in white walking together, banding at the bottom of the field in the afternoons, he felt forlorn. His own group of friends had all but disbanded. Only rarely did they play cricket or a nameless game of their own invention in his backyard. The old games, Prison Riot and Caning the Prisoners had been worn threadbare. The log that they whipped instead of the satyagrahis lay in the woodpile, deeply lacerated, soon to stoke the fire that would heat the morning's bath-water.

And then suddenly, there was a flutter of activity and it looked as if his gang would revive, thanks to the flag. The flag in question, the flag that was to drive Dr King away, was not the royal Mysore flag with its emblem of the twin-faced bird, the Ganda Bherunda, but the tricolour of the Congress— bands of saffron, white and green, with the charkha at its heart. Successively, in two places in the state, at Shivapura and Vidurashwatha, the Congress had hoisted its flag to mark its stake in the affections of the people. Despite the government's prohibitory orders, people flocked to public meetings addressed by the leaders of the Congress and processions were taken out. At Vidurashwatha, the police opened fire on the crowd. The newspapers said that thirty-five people were killed in the firing, though the 'official' figures quoted a much smaller number.

And in the excitement, the boys began to gather again in Setu's backyard. Benki Basappa, the police officer dubbed the 'butcher' of Vidurashwatha, had briefly revived their interest in their old games.

'The flag that was hoisted at Vidurashwatha, is right here,

in my house. My father brought it home,' Ramu confided to them.

Narayana Rao had returned from Vidurashwatha, bringing home the flag that had been hoisted there, fully intending to hoist it here in the Gandhi maidan, in the face of the district commissioner's prohibitory orders. The rumour had got around, and a raid on the Congress office proved fruitless for the authorities did not know what every schoolboy knew. That the tricolour lay neatly folded among Narayana Rao's wife's saris. But unlike in Vidurashwatha, there were no fireworks in their town. The authorities were forewarned. Narayana Rao was still in the process of delivering his 'seditious' speech when he was arrested, and the flag was removed before it could be hoisted.

'Rukmini, get the coconut room cleared, will you,' Mylaraiah said. 'We need plenty of space.'

This time Mylaraiah had said that he would not defend Narayana Rao—anyway Narayana Rao hadn't a leg to stand on—but he would help him all the same. Narayana Rao had refused to pay his penal fine and the district commissioner had ordered his office furniture and books to be seized and auctioned off. Mylaraiah planned to buy the whole lot and store it in his coconut room.

'What will we do with it?' Setu asked, when the desks and chairs started arriving.

'Return it to him when he comes back.'

In a reckless flush of patriotism Setu joined Chapdi Kal and his rag-tag-and-bobtail gang, game for anything bordering on the lawless, but the excitement of holding a tin of black paint while Chapdi Kal misspelt 'British—Go Home' and 'maharaja—Shame Shame' on the walls of disused buildings or throwing fire crackers into post boxes, which only turned cold in the womb of governmental authority, waned. We must do something truly earth-shaking, Chapdi Kal said. We must outdo the Youth Movement, Setu said, and that Shyam.

Then one evening, Chapdi Kal turned up with one of Mr O'Brien's kittens. Mr O'Brien who worked at the Mission's carpentry workshop, had a Siamese cat, admired for its beauty and its temperamental disposition. Mrs O'Brien had to take the cat in her lap and feed it with her own hands, no leaving milk in an enamel bowl for this cat. Mr O'Brien had also acquired a reputation for another reason. When his cat littered, he would give away as many kittens as he thought would be looked after, to deserving homes, and drown the rest in a tub in his backyard. Chapdi Kal had managed to fish one of the kittens out from the tub and it now lay supine in his arms, a dark wet furry rag, blinking wearily when they poked it. Chapdi Kal said that they were doing it for Bhagat Singh, just as the man in the maidan had said. A rope was found in the cow shed. The mango tree held out its branch invitingly. They were consumed by the attendant ritual, getting the equipment right. The rope in the cowshed turned out to be too thick, string would do for a kitten or better still, Setu suggested, the twine with which his mother hung her paintings. Finally, they got the right kind of rope, the kitten was given some warm milk and then it was strung up on the mango tree. They got it right the third time, when it jerked and struggled and swung and finally went limp. Then they ran round the tree and whooped and whistled and clapped, just as they did at the speeches in the maidan. Then they cut it down and buried it at the foot of the tree, hoisting a hastily contrived tricolour over the mound and decorating it with red flowers. But the dogs dug it up in no time at all and chased the carcass around till it was thrown away by one of the servants.

There was another game that the boys had played as long as they could remember, going round the house in a procession, singing a ditty to the accompaniment of a beat played out on an old tin. It was an old song and an old game but once again they had to abandon it.

The Mission in these parts was so well entrenched and its activities so much a part of the fabric of the place that its presence was scarcely noticed. In the villages of the district, on the days of the weekly shandy, sometimes a band of roving missionaries would organize a small show with songs and speeches, which soon came to be considered part of the entertainment of the bazaar. They also played a 'film' on a rudimentary bioscope, the sort that showed a series of stills when cranked and which had a keyhole on one end, from which one person at a time could watch the show. The 'film' usually included scenes from the Nativity, pictures of Queen Victoria, of shepherds with flocks of sheep or saintly men tending to the sick. The bioscope was very popular in the villages with people queuing up for their turn at the keyhole. A small band with a drum and a harmonium struck up a tune now and then. There was one rhyme that was the most often sung as it sat well to the beat of the drum. It told of a rat being chased by a cat.

There was a rat
That was chased
By a cat—
Dammar-dammaro-dum-
To save the rat—(the lead would take up)
Did your Rama come?
Dammar-dammaro-dum?
No, he didn't, no he didn't—(the chorus would reply)
Did your Krishna come?
Dammar-dammaro-dum?
No, he didn't, no he didn't—
Did your Allah come?
Dammar-dammaro-dum?
No, he didn't, no he didn't—
Did our Yesu come?
Dammar-dammaro-dum?
Yes he did, of course he did—
He killed the cat
And saved the rat
Dammar-dammaro-dum!

It was the beat of the drum and the gusto of the rhythm that made it popular. Every schoolboy sang it, without thinking of the words, though once, on reflection, Kaveri and Setu had wondered why Yesu had to kill the cat. Surely, the god of the

Methodists, more so of Miss Butler, would think of a way of saving the cat *and* the rat.

But now, almost a hundred years later, the ditty had sparked off a riot in the Thursday shandy in one of the villages and the reserve police had to be called in. It was a reflection of the mood of the time, of the uncertainty and the volatility around, but it did its damage.

The Mission had to do something to pour oil on troubled waters. Moreover, the one hundredth year anniversary of the Mission was approaching and they had to think of ways of smoothing ruffled official feathers, saving face with the people at large and re-establishing things on even keel. Mylaraiah, as legal counsel to the Mission, had long discussions with Reverend Spencer and the others on the Mission Council about the programme. Against his advice, Reverend Spencer agreed to be part of an elephant parade, which was expected subliminally to re-instill some of the awe and respect that the people had felt for the Mission and overwrite any memory of the riot.

'I can't believe it,' Mylaraiah remarked to Rukmini, 'he's such a sensible man. And now he insists on going more native than the native. I just can't convince him how silly he'd look. Imagines he is a prince going on a festive procession or on a royal hunt, I suppose!'

The elephant parade started off in chaos and ended in tragedy. The reverend's howdah got entangled in the celebratory arch put up to welcome him, he fell off and got underfoot the elephant. Amidst the noise of the drums and the conches and the crowd it took some time to attract the mahout's attention and ask him to stop. But by then it was too late. It was an accident, but the timing seemed to turn it into an act of fate, something pre-destined.

The reverend was buried in the local churchyard and there was a large turnout at the funeral. But they could not persuade Mrs Spencer to stay on. The Mission is over a hundred years old here, you are as much part of this place as I am, Rukmini told her. I have to think of my children, Mrs Spencer replied.

As soon as the war was over, she would leave. Rukmini dared not ask Dr King what she had decided for she was sure Dr King would leave too. She had remarked on her last visit that her brother in Calcutta was pressing her to wind up her affairs and join him as soon as she could.

Mylaraiah and Rukmini sat on the verandah in the mornings now, their coffee growing cold on the window sill as they watched the convoy of supply trucks on the road. One morning, an army truck hit a calf from the house that had wandered on to the highway. The calf tottered to the side of the road and collapsed. The trucks were stopped and people gathered round the calf but the police came quickly and dispersed the crowd. The authorities did not like crowds of any sort for there was no telling what incendiary purpose people gathered for these days. No, it was the events outside that were getting to her, Rukmini thought, her exhaustion was a reflection of the spirit of the times.

1941

'A boy is coming to see you,' Rukmini told Kaveri and waited for her reaction.

Kaveri said, 'I won't walk in with the coffee and I will not get my nose pierced.'

See, she's not averse to the idea, Mylaraiah said to his wife.

'You just have to serve the coffee, not make it,' Shivaswamy teased. 'By the way, can you make coffee? No? Rukmini, have you taught her how to cook? What? Sixteen and can't even make coffee!'

It was Shivaswamy who drew their attention to how ill Rukmini was looking. Her drawn face and her lack of appetite could no longer be attributed to her grief over her mother's death. After all, it was six years since Bhagiratamma died. Nor was it just the summer traffic of guests that was tiring her out. Why was she sleeping during the day, she who wouldn't even sit down in the afternoons, except to drink her tea on the verandah? Mylaraiah was too preoccupied with his work, he implied, this travelling to Bangalore almost every other day was too much. And Kaveri was no longer a child, she had to be made aware of her responsibilities. Immediately remorseful, Mylaraiah set up a meeting with Dr King and Rukmini replied calmly that Dr King knew about it and had been giving her medicines all along, which had helped at first but now seemed to have stopped working.

Kaveri sat on the swing in the courtyard, her hair flying behind her, lost to the world with Shivarama Karanth's *Marali Mallige*, hot off the press, on her lap. Mylaraiah watched her with the fond indulgence of a father who knows he is soon going to lose his daughter in the most appropriate way possible—to gain a son-in-law. Setu watched her, noting the disorder of her hair and the careless toss of her sari, with the confusion of an adolescent who is just discovering the potency of the feminine ankle and hence disapproves of it. Rukmini watched her daughter mooning away, losing time. It is not enough, she tried to tell her, to know what you do not want, you must know what you want. Most people discover what they want after they have already burnt their boats. You must not spend life regretting turns you did not take. Apply your mind to it, Kaveri.

It would be so easy to resolve the question by applying one's mind to it, thought Kaveri. What did she really want? Life to lap by like this, the sun in her hair and the wind in her face as she read in the afternoon, dreaming, giving to Shyam some of Rama Aithala's sensitivity, Sir Percy Blakeny's chivalry and the curl of David Copperfield's hair? Shyam had taken her out of her soft, literary ambit; he had made her think. For the first time she had seen herself in the context of larger things, a world beyond her home and her town and her books, beyond her father's circumscribing if comforting vision and her mother's, full of foggy longings. The newspaper had become more than the warm thing that smelt freshly of newsprint; it had become a gateway to the world. And he would not stop with opening her eyes and her mind, he would goad her into action if she let him. Once you find a purpose you have to act upon it, he said. But at the same time, knowing Shyam seemed to foreclose all other possibilities, the excitement and the adventure promised by the photographs and horoscopes of the hordes of unknown men who waited for her. That she could do without either had not occurred to her and even if it did, she would have dismissed the possibility;

the solitary life was for the likes of Kalyani, those whom fate had crossed. If anything Kaveri was flattered that so many men should seek her hand as she leafed idly through the horoscopes and photographs that Shivaswamy had collected—anyway, nothing would happen till she had finished her Intermediate, her father had promised and she still had a full year.

Reprieve came from yet another quarter, most unexpectedly. The first few proposals turned out to be duds. The most promising on Shivaswamy's list was the Bangalore Boy. A letter was sent off to the Bangalore Boy's parents. But the day they were to come and 'see' Kaveri, there was a freak storm of such intensity that it blew the tiles off the cowshed. The Bangalore Boy's people had to return halfway, and this was considered an inauspicious omen. They called the whole thing off and everybody, including Mylaraiah, was relieved. Another promising horoscope arrived, accompanied by a photograph, but it was summarily rejected by Kaveri as Setu pointed out that the boy had an 'overhanging lip'.

The next time round, the whole household talked of nothing but the Bayer and Company Boy from Calcutta. Kaveri liked the black silk top hat that he wore in the photograph, just like she imagined Professor Higgins would in *Pygmalion*. Mylaraiah met him in his parents' home in Shimoga and pronounced him a 'smart young lad'. The boy's parents came down to see Kaveri, and Rukmini, applying her yardstick of 'judge the son by the mother' was impressed by the mother who was the leading light of the Mahila Mandali in Shimoga. Such a family would put their daughter-in-law through college themselves. It was decided that they would make a formal proposal and exchange letters and Setu had even begun teasing his sister in 'Bengali'. On the day the letter making the formal proposal had to be sent, Achamma announced that the nanda deepa, the lamp under which the letter had been kept, had gone out. It was inexplicable. The lamp had been burning in one corner of the puja room where not the slightest breeze could reach it. It could only mean that the lamp had snuffed itself out. That very day, by coincidence, Rukmini's cousin's telegram arrived from Jamshedpur saying, 'Bayer Company Boy Immoral Drunkard'. Later, the cousin revealed in a leisurely letter that when he had paid the boy a surprise visit he had found him sitting in a dirty dhoti, surrounded by bottles.

'Finished, Kaveri,' Setu said, 'The only person left for you to marry is Rama Aithala from *Marali Mannige*.'

Over the year, Shivaswamy continued to bring news of 'boys' but few got beyond the horoscope-matching stage. In that the final year of college, Kaveri took to dropping in at Shanta's place after college, though it meant a detour from her normal route back home. I have to pick up a book, she'd tell the scowling Timrayee who was a most conscientious escort, or that she wanted a drink of water. Timrayee was scared of her sharp tongue; if not he'd have asked her why she didn't go straight home then.

Shyam was often away from home, on 'important work', Shanta would tell her. Kaveri waited for him to return with news of Bombay. One afternoon Shanta had a photograph and a new song for Kaveri. The rage right then in Bombay was actress Shanta Apte. Kaveri looked at the straight-featured, heroic profile, such a contrast to the masked Hunterwali, Fearless Nadia. She sang her own songs, just like K.L. Saigal, and so popular was she that when she ventured one night, late, to take a walk on the beach, she was mobbed. Shyam had attended one of her concerts when he was last in Bombay. She had sung Malkauns—'the same as our Hindola', and he had bought a 48 rpm record of it. They would borrow their neighbour's turntable to listen to it.

Shyam wished they could have seen Shanta Apte's film, *Duniya na Mane*. In fact, he would like the whole Samaja to see it. It was about an orphan girl who was forced to marry an old man, with children as old as herself, but who refused to accept him as her husband, encouraged by none other than the old man's daughter. Finally, he commited suicide and set her free.

'I feel sorry for the old man,' Kaveri said immediately.

'Trust you to take the most contrary position. The story doesn't interest you. . .' Shyam said.

Kaveri smiled and shrugged her shoulders. Marriage with an old man was the last thing on her mind. With widowhood, she was slightly acquainted, as her mother would keep giving her bulletins about Kalyani from time to time.

'There is a song the heroine sings in the film, in English, based on a poem. . .*in this world's broad field of battle. . .be not like dumb driven cattle. . .be a hero in the strife. . .*' he sang in a high, quavering voice.

The students who had gathered in the verandah suppressed their smiles as best as they could while Kaveri and Shanta laughed outright.

However, Shyam found out the name of the poet and Kaveri located Longfellow's *Psalm of Life* in the ever-dependable Palgrave. 'Tell me not in mournful numbers, Life is but empty dream!' his next article urged, in which an account of the film and an exhortation to act sat cheek-by-jowl. There was a short interview with the actress as well in which she had said that she would never countenance such a situation in real life. Why, she had horsewhipped a man who had written some rubbish about her. In such shackled times, we need heroines like this, Shyam had written. As the poet had said, lives of great men (and women too) all remind us, we can make our lives sublime.

'I like her puff-sleeve blouse,' Kaveri said, looking at the photograph. 'Shanta, do you think our Sayaji tailor can copy this style?'

You are not serious, Shyam said. The cut of Shanta Apte's clothes was the least important thing about her. What one must see is that she is a true heroine.

His heroes and heroines were impossible, Kaveri pointed out, piqued. A real-life Hunterwali. And Hitler. How could he admire Hitler?

Because he was their man of destiny. He would deliver the country from the British. Subhash Bose's broadcasts from Berlin, which he had listened to in Bombay, said it was any time now.

As usual, the conversation returned to the war. When he was at home, there would be groups of students gathered in the already-cramped verandah, waiting for the war broadcasts and to listen to what Shyam had to say about them. He was vehemently against the maharaja's support for the war—'the Imperial Mysore Lancers, more fodder for the Germans!' and lamented the capitulation of the Congress—'if at all we had joined the war, it should have been to support the enemy's enemy'.

He would walk up and down on the small verandah, taking narrow turns, ruminating over the way the war would go. 'Let's see now,' he'd declaim to the gathering of students who had started speaking knowledgeably about German submarines and U boats. 'Let's see how far blood and sweat and toil and tears will take them, let's see how far they will hold out!' when the German planes blitzed London. 'This is the time. The iron is hot. If Gandhi makes up his mind, we can *smash* the British!' he'd bang his fist on the table and send the coffee in the cups eddying dangerously. 'And all he can think of is writing pathetic letters to Hitler. As if it would make a difference to the Fuehrer!' Shyam's latest article had included a sarcastic rejoinder to the letter, which had caused Mylaraiah to call him a 'truly intemperate young man' and to wonder aloud how much longer he'd stay out of trouble. C.G.K. Sir had better get ready for another round of penal fines.

Kaveri could not but notice the different reactions the same radio broadcasts produced in the two sitting rooms. The Radio Berlin bulletins, which Mylaraiah dismissed as 'German propaganda!', were greeted as the authentic picture of the war by Shyam and his boys' club.

It needled Kaveri into echoing her father's views, his admiration of British valour and heroism. 'Britain will last it out, Hitler will not win the war.'

'That's wishful thinking.'

'How can you admire a man who has so little sympathy for us?'

'So you did read *Mein Kampf*?'

'No,' she blushed slightly, 'but my mother read out bits to me. I believe he says that the British will not give up their Indian empire.'

'Unless they are forced to by the sword. . .'

'. . .and that he would rather the British ruled India. He has little faith in Indian uprisings.'

'Nothing will ever be given to us, we must seize whatever we want.'

'My father says there is nothing more destructive than effort without direction. It will lead to anarchy. . .'

'Better our own anarchy than a foreign order and discipline. We will learn from our mistakes. It is touching, the implicit faith our people have in the goodness of the British, and so little in themselves. . .' he said it gently, his smile taking the sting out of his words, and knowing his opinion of her father she knew that his restraint had been for her sake.

'I only hope,' he added 'that you use my arguments as provocatively with your father. . .' He smiled and held her eyes and there was an unmistakable appeal in them, suggesting that in the competition between the two, he hoped he had the advantage, for if he had it in second-hand argument with her father, he could count on it in her affections as well.

If Kaveri came close to falling in love, it was at that moment.

For some strange reason she felt the tears welling up in her eyes. She turned away hastily and said something innocuous to cover her confusion. Thankfully somebody called from the door and the moment passed.

'My brother is staying longer than usual this time,' Shanta mused, 'usually, he should be up and away by now, he's so restless.'

College was soon done, the exams were over and the results were out. Kaveri's marks this time too did not inspire much confidence, but Rukmini asked her the mandatory question, whether she should ask her brother in Mysore to get forms from the university. Kaveri made no definite reply. She was restless now, and impatient. Impatient for the next horoscope to arrive, for something to happen. For once college was done, Kaveri found her activities severely circumscribed. Mylaraiah had decreed that Kaveri should not go out unnecessarily; she should stay at home and learn to manage the household. The only outings she was allowed was to the Samaja where she now managed the Bal Vadi, staging plays with the children and teaching them patriotic songs. There was no excuse for her to go to Shanta's house for they would meet at the Samaja. Occasionally, Kaveri gave spirited accounts of the proposals she received to Shanta and they found themselves laughing to tears over them. Shanta herself was safe for she was promised to her uncle, her mother's brother, when he acquired his law degree and returned from Bombay. One day after a particularly good imitation, Kaveri found her tears of laughter turning into something else. 'One of these days, I might just say yes, you know,' she said, not quite meeting Shanta's eye. But Shanta made no reply and brought no message even of the glancing, humorous sort, the one-liners and aphorisms that she usually did.

One evening, at a Samaja meeting, Kaveri found herself inadvertently in the limelight. Of late, the flavour of the proceedings of the Samaja had turned distinctly political and nationalistic, one of the reasons that Rukmini had dissociated herself from its offices. They usually began these days with a patriotic song. The Samaja would invite luminaries to speak on the burning issues of the day. People had spoken on khadi and spinning, on why it was necessary to learn Hindi; it was in one of these meetings that Shyam, in the days when he had still been Shanta's brother, had distinguished himself and become a local hero. That evening a literary heavyweight had been called to talk about the power of the written word in changing the world, in creating heroes and Kaveri had warmly championed not the usual Gandhi or Bhagat Singh, not a real-life hero but an imaginary creation in the real world. She had spoken on *Marali Mannige* and had been eloquent about the young Rama Aithala. His combination of sensitivity and idealism and vulnerability, his love of music and his land, his very humanness, made him her ideal, she declared. And never before had she read a book that presented a slice of life as it was lived. You could smell the sea and taste the salt in the pickle and hear the crunch of the sandige on the pages. Moreover, for a man to have written such a book in which the details of women's lives had been portrayed with such accuracy and sensitivity—why they should accord him honorary woman's status! In her flush of enthusiasm she had been extraordinarily eloquent and she had eclipsed the literary heavyweight completely.

At the end of the meeting she noticed that Shyam had been in the audience. She was surprised for Shanta was not there, having left for an extended tour of her relatives' houses whom she could not visit after she got married. As she was preparing to leave, he made his way to her side and whispered to her, 'You lifted him off the page and breathed life into him. He has become flesh and blood, a true hero.'

It was quite an admission coming from him and so heady was she with all the approval and applause that it led her into something foolish. She gave Timrayee the slip and agreed to go out with Shyam for coffee. As they settled down on the wooden bench of the Udipi hotel on Ashoka Road she sensed that she was doing something vaguely dishonourable but they were soon immersed in conversation and she forgot her earlier misgivings. They were joined by a group of Shyam's acolytes and a lively debate started over the merits of fictional heroes over real life ones.

That was the whole point, Kaveri said. People in fiction were the same as people in real life, only better. One dimensional, Shyam countered. No, the spotlight is only on one of their characteristics at a time, Kaveri said. Even if one were to admit they were the same, didn't she think, Shyam was asking her, that Rama lacked fire, that essential quality of heroism and hadn't she noticed that even the author Shivarama Karanth did not approve of Gandhi's methods. Shyam himself would have preferred a man of action, one who would go out and plunge into the fray and not turn tail and run. Was it necessary to be sensational to be heroic, Kaveri challenged. What about those who did their best in the station allotted to them? Why must it always be giant leaps and not small steps forward?

'Tell us,' one of Shyam's shishyas said, 'what your ideal hero would be like?'

Kaveri caught Shyam's eye for the briefest second and then answered. 'Someone tremendously brave and dashing and yet constant and gentle, someone whose strength you can feel and yet he makes you feel a little sad for him,' she said, stirring her coffee vigorously.

'No, no room for weakness in a hero,' Shyam cut in laughing. A hero or heroine must be spectacularly brave, he said, must reach for the sky and wrench a star out of it, do something which only the lion hearted would attempt. Wrenching a star out of the sky, Kaveri laughed, was ridiculous. A more down-to-earth, more believable courage was preferable. Then he would forever remain a domestic creature, forever plodding, not daring to run even, let alone fly, Shyam said.

At that Kaveri was reminded of her father and suddenly realized where she was. She glanced round the room and noticed that she was the only woman there and curious looks were being thrown in her direction. People had probably even recognized her as Advocate Mylaraiah's daughter. Going to a coffee house even with the family was exceptional; it was allowed perhaps once in all of the summer holidays when her cousins visited. But to come alone with a man, and that too one her father clearly disliked, the consequences were too drastic to imagine. Her father would stop her visits to the Samaja too. Moreover, these were uncertain times, any minute a rally may turn violent and there might be a lathi charge or a firing, and her father was particular that she should be home before dark and that she should not go about unescorted.

She left hastily, hurrying her tonga through the still-brightly-lit streets. It was only when she reached home that she realized that her father was away at Bangalore and her mother would most probably be resting and she need not have hurried, but it did not put her any more at ease.

Even as she hurried in, her brother came out from the shadows in the unlit porch. 'Where have you been?' he asked. 'There were no lights on outside. The house was in darkness when I came home. The night light in Amma's room had not been switched on.'

'You could have turned on the lights if you were so bothered,' she said, mustering up a casual air.

'Where is Timrayee?'

'How should I know where he is?'

'Wait! Don't walk off like that. Where have you been, I said. What have you been doing?'

'I was at the Samaja. Today was my talk, remember?'

'You didn't tell me. . .'

'Would you have been interested? Anyway, Amma was supposed to be there. . .'

'She has a headache again. . .'

Kaveri shrugged. '*I* haven't been torturing cats in the backyard, I can tell you that much.' That, she knew, would keep him quiet. He wouldn't dare tell on her when their father came home.

A few days later, after she returned from her extended tour of her relatives' houses, Shanta brought her a sealed letter from her brother. Handing it over she said, you needn't reply if you don't want to, not right away in any case.

She read the letter quickly once and then just sat with her eyes closed, blocking all thought, allowing the rising tide of warmth to spill over her. Then she read it again and again in rapid succession, thrilling each time to its unexpected delights. A jewel among women, he had called her. He said he admired her intelligence, her sensitivity and skill in argument. Her feminine radiance inspired him. He was sure her energy, if directed correctly could be used to purpose. She was the ideal helpmate for a man like him, a man of passionate ideals and avowed direction. Right then he had little to offer but his devotion; he could promise her they would never be rich and her life would not be as soft and coddled as it was now, it would be khadi, not silk, but he had a feeling that would not matter with her. Would she wait for him?

'My adamantine friend,' the letter began and was signed off just 'Yours—', with no name, not even a squiggle of a signature.

'Amma, what does "adamantine" mean?' she called out from the verandah.

'It could mean as brilliant as a diamond and as hard too. . .'

She sat back and felt the corners of her lips and her cheeks lift into a smile, and bit her lower lip to stop herself from laughing out loud. She saw him in the act of writing the letter, awkward, trying to snatch a private moment in his crowded house. He must have grabbed the first sheet of paper available—why it almost looked like blotting paper—and skimmed his mind off on it, hastily, in disjointed sentences and in ghastly purple ink. Of course he would have had no time to compose it or perhaps even go over it after he had finished; such a contrast to his sure, precisely worded, unambiguous, loudly declaiming articles. She saw the letter for what it was, the nervous proclamation of a man afraid to open his heart out completely for he was not sure of his ground, a man afraid of rejection, of being laughed at; a man who was confident when he had to commandeer the world at large but completely lost when it came to himself, to matters of the heart. She also saw his predicament. He was asking her to wait for him and in that event he could neither promise nor expect anything more affirmative.

She lingered over the details. She liked the play of meaning in 'adamantine', it was to tease her for he must have been sure she would not know what it meant. But still, he had called her a jewel among women. The next sentence brought her to her intelligence, her sensitivity and her skill in argument, how very like him to juxtapose two abstract qualities with a

A Girl and a River

concrete skill. Trust him to speak his mind and say that her life was soft and coddled (which it was), but at least he had paid her the compliment of saying that he knew she could do without the coddling. Finally, he had asked forgiveness for his lapses—by then he must have been quite prostrate with the effort of writing the letter. When she met him she would laugh at him, she would be quite merciless. She would throw phrases from his letter at him and watch him blush. So she was to be his helpmate and that was all? So, her energies were all used up for her own enjoyment, were they? Your tuft is my hand and my grasp is nimble, she would say to him. When she had read the letter for the hundredth time perhaps, she admitted to a slight stirring of disappointment. Even while he confessed he did not measure up to her fictional heroes, she would have liked more ardour; she had looked in vain for the word 'love'. 'My adamantine friend' he had called her, tantalizingly, but then again, he had not proposed marriage, he had asked her to wait for him.

Even as she carefully put away the letter so that her brother would not find it, she reflected upon the unfairness of life—that her real-life heroes should fall so short of the creatures of her imagination—a Rama Aithala or a Scarlet Pimpernel on paper were so much more substantial and comforting and well, less *messy* than a Shanta's brother or a Bayer and Company Boy in flesh.

'Amma,' Kaveri said when they were settling down for the night. 'I've decided. I want to go to college in Mysore. Will you send for the forms? And tell Anna. . .'

n i n e t e e n

---

quit india

Early in 1941, along with supplies for the army, the green Mann trucks brought the first lot of Italian prisoners-of-war from Sidi Barani in North Africa, to be housed in the camp on the outskirts of town. The maharaja of Mysore, genial host, had agreed to house more than twenty thousand prisoners in the state. The newspapers had reported off and on the fortunes of the legendary 4th Indian Division, the 'pebble in David (England)'s sling' which had been sent off to Egypt the year the war began and had fought the Italians heroically in Africa. When the trucks rolled into town, a crowd gathered to see the Goliaths whom the Indian David had felled, and leading the camp arrangements was Zafar Ali, formerly of the Imperial Service Corps, winner of the British Government's Military Cross, a first class medal of the maharaja's Ganda Bherunda Order and the White Eagle of Serbia for having distinguished himself against the Turks at Gaza, Jericho and Haifa in succession in the first World War. In a few weeks' time, Zafar Ali had put the camp to order. There was a furniture workshop in the POW camp and there were sounds of musical instruments being tuned—some of the prisoners were going to form an orchestra. But the reason the boys and the men in town gathered outside the high wired fences was to watch the Italians practising football. Soon, thanks to Zafar Ali, matches were fixed between the Italian POWs and the local clubs and for a few days the excitement of these matches eclipsed the World War and Gandhi Mahatma as far as the town was concerned. There were anxious moments in the coffee houses. How would the local hero Jayaram, who had played for clubs in Bangalore, fare? Should Morris's Eleven, led by Morris Jr the son of the Mangalore-tile factory owner, combine with the town club team and form a new team? There was much shaking of head over Muniraju, the games master from the high school who acted as referee in all the local matches. He had a perpetually stuffed nose which caused him to breathe through his mouth and he was known to blow the whistle at all the wrong times.

The debate got so heated that one day, the local newspaper shifted the fortunes of Rangoon, bombed in December that year by the Japanese, into the second column. Dr King brought news fresh from the front from Ella, who had volunteered with the Ladies General War Committee. Calcutta was next on the Japanese list, it was rumoured, then Vizag and next, Madras. She had heard that people were asking to be evacuated from Ooty! Ella had not got her dream post of Manager in the Army and Navy stores but had become a secretary in the same company as her sister. She was now being trained to be a cipher clerk to be posted in a camp on the Burma Road. It was all absolutely thrilling, she had said, having to sign the Official Secrets Act saying she could be shot if she gave anything away. They also had to be in readiness to burn the cipher books and smash the machines the minute they heard of the Japanese advance and one of the officers had advised her seriously to keep the last bullet for herself if things got really bad. Meanwhile the refugees were pouring in from Burma, Hong Kong and Singapore. 'You should see some of the things they are trying to sell off here in Calcutta,' she wrote, 'far classier than ours. They've been better up on fashions than we have.' While Ella trained in deciphering code, her actual duties appeared to be wrapping bandage rolls, preparing food packets and dancing with the soldiers of the defeated Fourteenth Army to keep up their morale, when they came on weekend leave. There was ice cream and hot chocolate sauce at Firpos and 'rinking'—where couples skated together on a large floor at the club but all strictly part of her 'duties'. Her kit bag was packed and ready to go in case she was needed on the Burma Road. The new 'bunnies' or sanitary towels that had arrived were a god send, she had written.

There were other, serious developments to follow. In August that year, the year of 1942, Gandhi asked the British to 'Quit India' and spun into immortality the phrase 'do or die'.

'We are on the verge of a precipice,' Mylaraiah read out from the newspaper, quoting Nehru, 'and we are in dead earnest.' Seldom, he thought as he rested his head on the frame of the chair, had the newspapers reflected his state of mind so cannily. A few days back Rukmini had left for Vellore with Shivaswamy on the first of successive trips, to see a specialist for her now undeniable 'condition' which no doctor seemed able to diagnose, let alone cure. And she could no longer hide the fact that she was in pain.

In the phlegmatic, neither summer-nor-winter air of the town, this new turn in the political wheel of the country caused but a ripple at first. There had been other make-or-break resolutions in the past which had gradually petered out. Narayana Rao and two others were among the several Congressmen from the state to be arrested at Guntakal railway station on their way back from Bombay, after attending the meeting where the Quit India resolution was passed. Early in the morning, as Mylaraiah paced his vast garden, distracted over Rukmini's condition, trying to compose his opening argument for the session in court later in the day at Bangalore, and wondering whether the train that was bringing the new housekeeper—a distant relative of Rukmini's whose name was either Raji or Vishalakshi, he couldn't remember, would arrive at all, he heard the faint singing of the khadi clad group of volunteers as they went past on the main road, on their morning round or prabhat pheri. Even from the distance, he had to admit, their singing had a rousing ring to it. The processions seemed to grow longer each morning and there were quite a

A Girl and a River

few women in it.

Mylaraiah summoned both Kaveri and Setu to the verandah one morning. He knew Kaveri and her friend Shanta were part of a patriotic chorus in the Samaja for Kaveri was forever singing about the time her chains would fall off—and not getting the bit right, and that Setu and his friends indulged in some slogan-shouting in the back yard.

'You will not,' he said firmly, looking at Kaveri, 'be part of any committee or public meeting that is involved in these protests against the government. I want you to promise me.'

For this time round, there was an urgency, an unpredictability in the air that was new, even for their town. Moreover, the authorities had very foolishly arrested all the leaders of any stature who were associated with the Congress and the students seemed to have taken over. Still, the crowds at the meetings were growing thicker, and the district commissioner and the police were becoming jumpy. During the very first week of the demonstrations, when the volunteers had tried to shut down the mandi, urging the traders to go home, the district commissioner had arrested many of them. Narayana Rao and the others, even the 'second line' of command of the Congress in town was behind bars, but still the processions continued and more people gathered. Other than asking the British to read the writing on the wall, undeniably the maharaja was being asked to recognize the democratic script as well.

Rumours were that a mammoth meeting was being planned. But the actual date and the venue were being kept secret. No one knew what would actually happen once the groups met. The authorities had been unsuccessful so far in unearthing the kingpin, the person or the group that was commanding the meeting. The students had sworn that every school in town and the lone Intermediate College would be represented. The ban on public meetings only seemed to provide a keener edge to the proceedings. Shyam and a few others had set off on a cycling tour of the villages, on a 'consciousness raising' campaign.

In the Government High School field, after school was

over, unknown to the authorities—or perhaps they pretended it was just another cricket group in the field—under the tutelage of the student volunteers, the boys 'rehearsed' their songs and slogans for the big day. 'Hindu–Muslim Ek Ho!' the volunteer would command from the head of the line, for the rank and file to chant after him. Only, the sheer unfamiliarity of the Hindi language in the deep south, and the reinforcement of set patterns led the boys to echo, 'Hindu–Muslim Ek Do!' completely in opposition to the sentiment being expressed. Sadly, no one caught the joke or corrected the boys. There were other such moments of inadvertent black humour. At the Samaja meetings, the women sang, in perfect melody, Mohammed Iqbal's, 'Saare jahan se achcha, Hindustan hamara', in praise of their Hindustan more beautiful than the whole world, but when they stretched out the 'Hindoo-sa-tan' there was some speculation whether the Hindus were slyly being called 'satans' or 'shaitans'. But such things notwithstanding, the practice sessions continued in preparation of the mother of all public meetings.

The demonstrators grew bolder. Led only by students, now that all the 'recognized' leaders had been arrested or gone into hiding, they did daring, spasmodic things. The government offices in town had braced themselves to face demonstrations of any sort and the district commissioner had strictly forbidden them from closing. A delegation of students forced their way into the courts one morning and physically unseated the judge, saying they'd conduct the case themselves in a 'people's court'; they walked into the land records office and scattered all the papers, 'in the interests of equitable justice' and forced the clerks to shout 'Bharat mata ki jai!' and 'Gandhiji ki jai!' after them. There had been no train to Shimoga this past week as a section of the tracks, close to the town, had been dug up.

Every time a slogan against the British or the maharaja appeared on the walls of government buildings, the district commissioner would assiduously have the wall white washed, but now he found that there were far too many walls in town to reclaim. One evening the district commissioner found the 'national' flag, the tricolour with the charkha in the centre, flying on the flag post above his office—someone had shinned up the drainpipe at night and hoisted it. The next day, he sent for the reserve police from Bangalore. Already, he had lost his patience as his men had not been able to catch the students who were allegedly behind the new spate of 'bold' acts.

Two days before the event, Timrayee brought Kaveri a note from Shanta. There were but two cryptic lines in the note but she understood perfectly. She must compliment him, she tucked away the aside into her mind, on how much his skills in composition had improved. Why, the two lines could qualify as poetry. In the margin of the note was a rough sketch of a masked face. Take heart from her, it said. The note, a bare slip of paper, was already crumpled when she received it from Timrayee's retreating hand. She read it twice and burnt it.

For two days she churned it in her mind. When she stood at the gate each morning, watching the student processions go past singing, she felt a surging restlessness, as if the world were going past her house and leaving her behind; it was only her father's admonishing breath, hot on her back, that kept her from opening the latch and slipping out. The more she thought of it, the more certain did she become, the more urgent Shyam's presence and words grew and the more unreasonable her father's diktat. Without the antidote of her mother's influence, her father seemed more prickly and overbearing—with Setu as his willing agent; readily she imagined herself a victim of his caprice. As she sat on the swing in the courtyard, pushing herself listlessly, a vacant look on her face, Setu watched her.

That morning, Kaveri waited for Setu to leave for school before ironing her white khadi sari with the green border. In the afternoon, after school, Setu hung around in the grounds to watch the contingent of boys marching round, chanting 'Hindu-Muslim Ek Do!', and wondered whether there would be a variation in their routine. He usually waited for them to finish marching, after which they would break up and play cricket before going home. Setu scrupulously stayed out of the marching but joined in the cricket. But four o'clock saw a sudden upward pitch in the excitement. Even as they were marching, rather listlessly, for the nth time round the field, one of the boys from the Intermediate College came running and the crowd of dust halted. The 'leaders' immediately went into a huddle and the rank and file started shuffling and pushing. One of the leaders turned round and called them to order, giving the nearest boy a smart rap on the head. They were to maintain perfect discipline, no shuffling or running or pushing, he said. Didn't they want independence? And how would they get it if they kept on talking in line? The leaders and the messenger from the Intermediate College consulted some more and then one of them turned round to announce that they would be marching to the church square and they would be taking the longer route. It would take them twenty minutes to march there if they were quick and in step and did not stop midway. So, Setu thought, today *was* the day. And no doubt they would be taking the longer route, for the volunteers were preparing to pour ragi batter on the cobblestones leading to the Square, so that the horses of the mounted police would slip when they rode in. The boys set off, led by a keen volunteer but were shouted back by another. There seemed to be some confusion about when to start marching.

Even as they were resolving the confusion, they heard a thundering in the distance and a large posse of mounted police rode past on the main road, the men more poised over their saddles than seated in them, and the boys stopped marching and gave up all pretence of composure and huddled together in the middle of the field, watching the dust kicked up by the horses. The leaders shouted out to the boys, trying to keep order but clearly they didn't know what was happening either. And then they heard the lightning rip, in quick sharp bursts, which was strange for there was not a streak in the clear blue sky. It was a sound, Setu was to recall later, that seemed to detonate his heart and tear through his bowels. And then a roar travelled through the air, from the direction of the church square, growing louder as it approached them.

The flags and buntings were abandoned. The boys ran pell mell and Setu made for the edge of the field, fell down even as he began running but picked himself up and with the taste of blood and dust fresh in his mouth, dashed past the small section of shops in Electric Colony, whose shutters were being downed hastily, past houses whose doors were being secured, found himself lost in an anonymous by lane but kept his head and finally managed to reach home before the bullets or the horses got him. He cleaned up at the tap in the backyard and when he sat down for his tiffin a little later in the coffee room, except for the pounding of his heart and the heat in his cheeks, which he alone could feel and his distracted appetite, there was no sign of his misadventures.

'Where is your sister?' Achamma asked.

Setu caught his breath. His right hand, poised to put a segment of dosa-chutney into his mouth, dismounted slowly. Surely she had not—

'She was there when your father returned from Bangalore in the afternoon. There were no trains, he said. He came in a government jeep.'

She would not have had the courage to disobey their father, he thought, pushing his plate aside. Even she would not have been so foolhardy.

'Where is Kaveri?' Mylaraiah had hurried home from his chambers. He still had his shoes and coat on.

Setu just stared at him, his mouth ringed with a milk moustache, and shook his head, preoccupied with excuses to defend himself if he were asked how he had let his sister go.

'Wipe your mouth, will you!' Mylaraiah said. 'Achamma! Where is Kaveri?'

Neither of them replied.

'And Timrayee? Where is he?'

'He is with her Ayya, wherever she is. And you know he takes good care of her.'

'The police have opened fire in the church square. I believe three people have been shot.'

'She was wearing her white sari. . .the white sari with the

green border.' Achamma clapped her hand across her mouth.

'That is where she must have gone. To the meeting in the church square. . .' Setu said, at last.

Mylaraiah drew his breath in sharply and father and son looked at each other, and looked away.

'Ranga!' he called, 'Go to the Samaja ... Balarama, come with me. Achamma, if she comes home, keep her with you. No one is to leave the house, Setu do you hear! And let all the dogs loose in the compound!'

The shadows lengthened on the compound wall as evening fell. The blue sky, softer now and cloudless, arched overhead unperturbed; the evening flight of birds winged across as usual. You could not tell that there had been shots fired in the square less than two miles away. Mylaraiah paced the verandah wordlessly. There was no sign of her anywhere. There was no one in the Samaja, the main door was locked. The road to the church square had been blocked by the police. He had left word at both the district commissioner's and the inspector general's office. Then, just as he was about to ask Achamma to go to Shanta's house to enquire about the girls, there was a noise at the gate. A green army jeep had driven up and was blocking the driveway. Even as Ranga set about restraining the dogs, several pairs of khaki-clad legs swung out from the jeep. A small procession made its way to the verandah, the inspector general leading, followed by Kaveri, with men in khaki bringing up the rear. Mylaraiah's eyes rested fleetingly on Kaveri and then he made his way to the inspector general. There was a brief, subdued conversation. The Inspector General shook hands with Mylaraiah, clasped him briefly above the elbow and left.

When Mylaraiah went in Kaveri was sitting at the table in the coffee room with Achamma and Setu standing on either side. He noted that her sari was dusty and her hair dishevelled and she looked a little dazed but other than that she seemed unharmed.

'You went to the meeting?' he said.

'All of us from the Samaja went, Anna. It was not just me alone.'

'Speak up! Don't mumble. You went even when I had expressly asked you not to?'

'All the women of the Samaja were there. Umadevi was with us.'

'Didn't you or anyone in the Samaja know that public meetings were banned, that you could get into serious trouble if you attended one?'

'We just sang a few songs, we did nothing wrong.'

'And that's what you thought it was all about. Going up on stage and singing songs?'

'I wanted to be part of the programme. It would have been cowardly of me not to have gone.'

'And where is your courage now? The district commissioner had told the organizers in no uncertain terms that the meeting should not be held. The inspector general says you were just next to the podium, closest to the organizing committee. I believe they were planning something big. Thankfully, the police arrived early, before all the groups had gathered. It is only because the inspector general recognized you that he brought you home and did not arrest you as a conspirator. He brought you home on trust that no daughter or son of mine would be involved in such activities. Do you understand the enormity of what you have done? I had to tell him that in all innocence you thought it part of a Samaja programme and not any thing bigger.'

'I did not ask to be brought home, I would have stayed with the rest of the women who were arrested. Shanta was still there.'

'You dare to talk back to me like that!' Mylaraiah sprang at her and made as if to strike her and she flinched. Achamma put her arms around Kaveri's head.

'And what would I have told your mother when she returns tomorrow? That her daughter is in jail. For singing a song? And *that* is her pitiful understanding of the movement into which she has flung herself? Because she thinks Freedom is all about singing on a podium and giving heroic speeches?'

'You will sleep in the morning room tonight. Achamma too

will sleep there. And you will not stir out of the house. Get the house in order for your mother. Go now.'

'Anna. . .'

Mylaraiah, who had turned to leave the room, stopped at what sounded like a mewl of pain. He turned round and looked Kaveri full in the face for the first time since she came home. He saw the unshed tears in her eyes, he heard her swallow and choke, he saw too her quivering, despairing mouth—it had turned downwards like that even when she had been a baby and he could not bear to see it droop and contort like that.

'Anna. . .' she said again, and her hand lifted a little towards him—in appeal, possibly in hopelessness. If Mylaraiah had been prescient or if he had just followed his first instinct, he would have crossed the room and taken his daughter's hand and perhaps reclaimed the future. But Mylaraiah saw that Setu was waiting and watching, and Achamma too, and he thought of his absent wife. He had to be all things—father, mother, husband and head of the household. And he made up his mind.

'Yes. . .' Mylaraiah said, allowing for nothing.

'Anna, they shot him. . .they just shot him like that . . .'

'Shot whom?'

'Shyam. . .'

'Who Shyam?'

'Shanta's brother, the Kole boy.'

'Good riddance.'

The next morning there were no newspapers and no trains either, but plenty of rumours. The meeting in the church square was a front for something bigger, more serious than just a public meeting. Someone had informed the inspector general that there was to be a bomb attack on the police chowki. It was the district commissioner's office that was to be targeted, somebody else said, and the district commissioner had been forewarned. At this the reserve police, on the orders of the district commissioner, had turned quite trigger happy. In this town, which had known no other mass punitive measure than a lathi charge, the police had fired simultaneously in two places, at the church square and on a procession of students headed for the Gandhi Maidan. Reports of the number killed varied from three to eight, including a nine-year old boy who had been in the act of closing his father's shop. It turned out that the rumours had been completely false. Other than speeches and songs, there was nothing else to the programme. While the maharaja's secretariat issued a statement of regret about the firing, the inspector general's office maintained that the police had fired to quell imminent rioting. Despite orders to the contrary the student organizers, many of whom were known to be armed with country-made bombs, had planned a massive meeting. Providentially, the district commissioner's office had got to know of it in advance, and that it had not just been a rumour.

But they had little time to discuss the firing or get any further details. The household was thrown into complete confusion when they heard that Rukmini's train had been stopped halfway from Bangalore and she was stuck in a small village en route. Mylaraiah had to find a car to bring her home and the prohibitory orders would make it difficult to hire one. Again, the inspector general was called upon and Rukmini arrived by afternoon in a police jeep, paler and thinner than she had been when she left, but happy to be home, and when Kaveri clung to her and wept, she assumed her daughter was just overwhelmed with relief to have her home.

'Kaveri,' Rukmini said, when a watered down version of her daughter's 'escapade' had been given to her, 'what is this I hear? You disobeyed your father?' She stroked her daughter's hand with her skeletal fingers and Kaveri shuddered at the caress, at how alien her mother's touch had become. 'You cannot get involved in things half-heartedly or impulsively, which you cannot follow through. And fighting for the freedom of the country isn't a thing done on impulse. You have to be like Kalyani's father. He gave up everything to get involved in something he believed in. And he is now paying the price for it. His family is too.'

'Amma, Shanta's brother. The police shot him. Right there, on the podium. For no reason.'

'I heard. I feel sorry for the family. I must go over and pay my condolences. He was a rash young man, but. . .'

I was standing next to him when he fell, Amma, she wanted to say. I touched him when he was lying on the floor, collapsed next to the flag post, when he was still warm. It was no use, Kaveri realized. Her mother would not understand. 'Amma,' she tried tentatively, 'about my BA. I want to go to Mysore. . .will you speak to Anna. He will not listen to me. . .'

But it was too late. She had lost her ally.

'You must do as your father says.'

'Tell her,' Mylaraiah said, for he wasn't speaking to Kaveri, 'tell her it is now between her and her husband.'

She had had two days to make up her mind after receiving his note and for two whole days she had churned it in her mind and sieved it through. The weeks of isolation after she had stopped going to college, this estrangement from the routine and the familiar, her mother's illness and her father's preoccupation had led to days of desultory uncertainty. And underscoring everything was her brother's hostility. She had lost herself. Even as she unfolded the note—a hasty purple scrawl on a bit of ruled exercise note book paper—she admonished herself. She had become lazy and slothful. When she read his note, she resurrected him from the hazy memory he was becoming. She heard him speaking to her, she heard his voice, the inflections in his tone, the gentle chiding, the appeal and the persuasion. She heard the half-hinted accusation of pusillanimity, the gesturing towards her father. She smiled at the blotchy sketch at the bottom of the note—Fearless Nadia. Take heart, he had urged. And the blood rose in her. Of course she was not made of straw. She would not stand aside and watch when the entire Samaja chorus, including Shanta, was ready to be part of the programme. All she had to do was sing the invocation along with them. There was nothing unlawful in what she was doing. Surely she could sing a new anthem in celebration of a free nation. How could she stay away from the moment that history was to be made?

Her mother would know how she felt, her mother would understand. She was the one who had said that it was important to know what you want and not just what you don't want, and now things had fallen into place with such a flash that she reeled from it. Shyam's note, tossed off hastily no doubt—he hadn't even waited to find a whole sheet of writing paper—had irradiated so many connections, so many streams of thoughts had started flowing. It was not just about the meeting, about singing a song, not even just about the precious tremulous thing that was stirring between them, it was much more; what she had heard as a faint monotonous buzz had grown into a thunderclap, the nebulous shades had yielded a burst of colour. The men in the photographs, whose proposals had come to nothing, were mere phantoms. Here, close at hand, lay her life, her future for her to decide. She would go to Mysore, to college. She would write to him from Mysore; they weren't truly friends yet, they had to get to know each other. There were many dimensions to Shyam that lay dormant, waiting to be quickened—the life of the imagination, a certain softness, a breadth of mind. In knowing each other, they would unfurl; she would realize her own blueprint in the light and warmth of his tutelage.

When they had walked from the Samaja to the square, she and Shanta arm in arm, with the other women, she had been giddy with excitement. She quite believed that they were marching towards a new future, which was theirs to fashion as they liked. She had turned to Shanta many times to speak to her, but at the very last moment she had held back; she would write to him herself. On the podium, when they had tuned their instruments, just as they had done for College Day, and she had seen the different groups, each with its own banner, gather in the square she had exulted in her own nobility. The delegation of students had arrived and taken its place right in front. He had come at the last minute, but had been too preoccupied with the failed microphone to catch her eye and she wondered if he had noticed her at all. When they sang the invocation, never before had the notes rung out so clear and pure and high. Then he had started speaking.

'Brothers and sisters of a free nation!' he had begun and she had felt the rush of adrenalin in her veins.

And then before they knew it, the place had been swarming with an assortment of uniformed men—some on horse back—the crowd had begun to break up and run and shots had rung out, three in quick succession. She had looked around wildly, seen the people scattering across the podium and even as she tried to concentrate on the orders that Umadevi was shouting out, she saw him fallen on the floor. At first she could not recognize him, so small and stumpy did he look, his eyes closed with the whites showing, his hand still clutching the disabled microphone. It was when she saw Shanta distraught beside him trying to staunch the blood that she realized who it was. She remembered sitting next to Shanta and holding his hand, she saw his spectacles fallen nearby and even as she reached out for them they were crunched under a fleeing pair of feet.

She had felt no fear when they had herded all of them to one side and pushed them into the church to wait. They had waited in silence behind the solid wooden doors, listening to the sounds of horse hooves and people running, of stray screams and shouts. Sitting in the pew, watching the icons that looked silently upon them, the leather bound hymn books mute, the high stained glass windows letting in an eerie light, she realized the incongruity of the situation. She had sat in this pew before, with Dr King and Ella, and the icons had beamed as kindly upon her even then. And later, when she came face to face with the inspector general, she had felt again the start of displacement, and the first flush of shame had stolen upon her. She could tell that he recognized her vaguely, but could not place her as she was out of context. She usually met him when he was not in uniform, at the club where he and his wife played tennis with her parents, at home in one of her mother's garden parties or with his daughters on a picnic, where he smiled indulgently at her and told her mother how unrecognizably tall she had become.

Once she came home—the inspector general had politely ushered her into the jeep when she had told him who she was—there had been no time to think, no space to ruminate, let alone grieve. For grief to swell and grow and then abate, it needs solitude; solitude for the cycle of memories, recrimination and wishful thinking to play itself out; an empty stretch of time to unburden your heart bit by bit and lighten the load. It could also do with a sympathetic ear and a closed mouth but that was not to be. The hectic routine intervened relentlessly. Thankfully, it had absorbed her father's burning anger as well and prevented a further confrontation. Kaveri was not left alone even for a moment. Her mother's health, which seemed to be improving, had taken a turn for the worse. The house was full of people. Her father spoke to her only to give orders.

Days later, on the train to Bangalore, en route to Madras to see another doctor, the whole incident seemed like a mirage, or the memory of a tragedy she had heard about, that had happened to someone else. At one time she had thought that in their brief conversations, they had exchanged wax imprints of each others' hearts. But now, watching the fleeting landscape from the train, tending to her mother, measuring out her medicines and draughts, trying to listen to what her uncle Shivaswamy was saying, she realized that they had barely spoken to each other four times and never alone at that. The only letter he had written to her she had lost in her haste to keep safe. There had been just six lines in it and as for the nuances of the letter, she must have imagined them all. When she tried to think of him, to summon him to life, he evaded her, she could not remember his face or his voice, she only saw him lying on the floor, his eyes, sightless white crescents, his mouth twisted to one side. What remained was the sadness, an ache of complete disorientation and dull stupidity, but no memory of the man whom she had touched for the first time only after he was dead.

It was at this juncture that the proposal and the photograph came. This must be pre-destined, Mylaraiah breathed in disbelief when he opened the letter. It was from the district judge Vishwanath Rao himself, tipped to be chief justice, the man who had moved heaven and earth to get him the post of government advocate, and was holding out tantalizing prospects of future collaboration and mutual benefit. And now their official relationship was to be cemented by bonds of matrimony! It was his humble request. Would Mylaraiah consider his son as a possible groom for Kaveri? He did not believe in the matching of horoscopes and would not ask for the girl's. However, if Mylaraiah was particular. . .

Mylaraiah stormed through the verandah into the house, holding the letter aloft like a flag, calling out, 'Do you hear!' to Rukmini in such excitement that she got out of bed and came into the courtyard.

'He has written to me himself, Rukmini. Do you know what this means! I would not have imagined it. Two destinies being made with one letter! And his son is a rising star in the education department! What humility! He's sent his son's photograph—which should satisfy even our finicky daughter.'

The boy, it turned out, was the very same 'young, dynamic, charismatic' director of public instruction with whom Rukmini had corresponded when she had suggested a lowering in the age for girls to take the middle school exam, a suggestion that he had put through. They were a fine old family, not orthodox, which was such a blessing. They had a huge house in Bangalore near Lalbagh, and countless properties and ran some worthwhile charities, including a school. They were in a hurry as the judge's father, the boy's grandfather was ill.

And then Rukmini put forward the first note of dissent. The

'boy' was thirty-two years old, double Kaveri's age.

Mylaraiah checked his anger with difficulty. 'God has opened his eyes and thought it fit to be merciful, but you don't seem to see it,' he said. 'Have you forgotten your daughter's misadventure? Be glad that word of it has not spread. A man like Judge Vishwanath Rao has come to our door unbidden . . .we must clasp his feet with both hands. . .'

Moreover, he continued more temperately, if you wanted someone with an established career and who could afford all the trappings of a household, he would have to be that old. It would be ridiculous if Kaveri married a stripling and continued living with them while he completed his education and then went on to search for a job. This 'boy' would steady her, he was a mature person. Kaveri's opinions were forming without the backing of knowledge, experience or intellect, he replied. He was afraid she would turn out to be a shallow creature, with all the waywardness of one who wouldn't ever be put to the test. Really, he thought, Rukmini's health and intransigence seemed to be returning hand-in-hand. He wanted to be rid of the responsibility, Rukmini's health was his main concern now and Setu's education. They would be moving to Bangalore at a good time, he was looking forward to it. The Rao family was very progressive. Kaveri could study further if she wanted to or get involved in one of their family charities. And Rukmini should have no complaints, he added as the clincher. Even her Gandhi's son had married a sixteen year old when he was thirty.

When Mylaraiah went next to Bangalore he met the boy in his office and pronounced him an 'honest, sober *man*' adding that it was a such a relief to meet someone who knew the art of keeping his opinions to himself in these squawking times.

The boy and his father paid a brief visit to 'see' Kaveri, and her loud refusal to be 'seen' while handing out the coffee came to no avail. She was not required to hand out anything, not even water, for the summons to 'bring the girl' did not come at all. She was Mylaraiah's daughter and that was enough, Judge Vishwanath Rao declared. Finally, it was

Rukmini who led Kaveri quietly into the room and made her sit in an unobtrusive corner. The judge filled the room quite effortlessly with his gold turban and his conversation. He was truly a splendid man and for once, Kaveri saw her own father dwarfed. He held forth on the political situation and other matters with the surety of one who was not used to being contradicted and Mylaraiah agreed with him that they were in for an uncertain future. We were not yet ready for dominion status and as for representative government, were we fit for it? Neither the boy nor his father stared embarrassingly at her, in fact she wondered if they even took a good look at her, not that she noticed, which, she convinced herself, was better than being stared at from beginning to end. The boy spoke little, possibly out of deference to his father and hers. He sat still, with his back straight and his feet under the seat of his chair, without fidgeting even once—splendid posture, especially for one with a desk job, did you notice, Mylaraiah said. And Kaveri, who was loathe to agree with her father on anything, had to admit that they seemed like decent people.

'Rukmini,' Mylaraiah said after they had left, 'I want no fuss on this. They have given us a week's time, but I'd like to go as soon as possible with flowers and fruits to their house. And then start preparations for the wedding. . .'

'Well Kaveri,' Rukmini said later in the evening, 'Your father and I are both for the match. The boy is intelligent, educated and is doing well in his job. He would be a worthwhile partner for you. As your father says, you can even study further once you go to their house. Shivaswamy cannot stop praising the family and our luck.'

Some hope, it seemed to Kaveri, still remained. Safe passage could still be had perhaps. Ever since the photograph arrived, Kaveri had been looking at it often, slipping it out of its envelope every now and then. A young handsome man looked into her eyes and smiled. He sat on a rattan easy chair, in a tree-filled sun-dappled courtyard, looking up from his book, one hand resting on his dog's head. Everything in the photograph conspired to make the man—the chair he was sitting on, the book, his posture, the dog. Especially the dog, for what can humanize a man more than a dog at his feet? Rarely, it appeared, had a photograph captured a person's spirit as this one had. She had the advantage of comparing his arrested likeness in the photograph with what she had seen animated in the flesh. He was dark complexioned like she was. His round, gold-framed glasses glinted in the sun, and she knew that the eyes behind them were slightly myopic; they had met hers briefly across the room. The hands that held a book whose title she could not read, which had been alternately folded across his chest and steepled on his knees when he had sat in this very wicker chair she was sitting on, were well formed, the fingers long and slightly flattened at the knuckles. She recalled the prominent half moons of his finger nails arching into perfect ovals and his slightly curly hair, which suggested a certain fragility. The cut of his lips was deep and thoughtful; she gave him idealism and fire, with gentility, with restraint. The angle of his shoulders revealed both vulnerability and resolve. The gold edging of his kurta reflected in his face a certain regal splendour—it brought to her mind a faraway snatch of conversation, she imagined the governor of Bengal.

A certain young man's shoulders winked and dazzled like gold in the sun, the muscles colliding in one smooth movement as he plunged into the waters. She heard a chorus of women singing softly in the background. She thought of the Scarlet Pimpernel kissing the spot on the parapet wall where his wife's hand had rested. It had brought tears to her eyes to think that Marguerite would never know how much her husband loved her. She thought of Shyam, one moment standing next to her, pulsating with the promise of her whole future— on that podium she had felt that he was immortal—and the next, an ungainly heap in the dust. And the tears, which she had held back for so long, would not stop flowing.

When Setu came home late that evening he found the whole house in a stir. He had missed the boy as the 'seeing' had coincided with the football game that the whole town had been waiting for, the Italian POWs had beaten the local club 14-0, despite their hero Jayaram's cavalry-like dashes across the field.

'Kaveri,' he said in sudden panic, 'you're not getting married!'

And while everybody else started laughing, his sister burst into a fresh flood of tears.

Much later, much much after the wedding, when Rukmini was almost completely eaten away with cancer, it emerged that Shivaswamy whom she had entrusted with the task of making 'discreet' enquiries about the boy—he may be quite a catch but she had to satisfy herself on certain vital counts—had met an old friend on his way and stopped off at a coffee house to talk to him. He had sent his son Chamu, all of twenty-four and newly turned father, and Setu, brother of the bride-to-be, to make the necessary enquiries. The two boys had in turn encountered a shendi cart on their way, the covering of palmyra leaves still fresh upon the barrels of liquor. What do you say, Setu, Chamu had said, do you still want to go further? For a moment Setu had hesitated, for he was not used to disobeying his mother. But even he knew that the liquor cart was the ultimate sign of auspiciousness, a sign that the gods themselves had blessed this union. Moreover, as Shivaswamy said, his father had set his heart on the match. It would be a propitious new beginning for the family. A proposal from Vishwanath Rao was not to be treated lightly, or turned down because of some vague cock-and-bull stories that were floating around. A man in his position was bound to attract envy. Jealous people might say all sorts of things. We have seen the shendi cart. That is enough. Let us return, Setu said. As you wish, Chamu replied, and they turned back without meeting the people who knew the boy well.

Moreover, with all the confidence of a fourteen-year-old who had just accomplished a task of fateful intervention, Setu felt that he was in the astral know. How else would he have intercepted Timrayee and read the note from Shanta to his sister, in two seconds flat, the time it took to walk from the gate to the porch, even as she sat in the porch, reading a book? And did they think they could fool him with that poetic twaddle? His sister must have forgotten how well he could read her mind and that any puzzle that she was able to solve, he was always able to unravel before she could. Did she think she could barter her heart away, so. . .so cheaply, when the unspoken rule was that her heart was not hers to give as she pleased, neither was his. The rule he would apply to himself, he had applied to her.

The note contained just two lines. Two lines boxed into a rectangle with a cross on top. *Tomorrow, before the sun sets, the birds will sing*, it said. *Tomorrow we will lift the lid off the sky, the fireworks with sound into the future.* The big meeting is tomorrow in the evening in the church square, he had told his father. Shyam, C.G.K. Sir's son, is the one who is leading it and they are planning something serious. He is an expert at making bombs, he had added for good measure. The district commissioner knows about C.G.K. Sir. Tell him to ask his son Mukunda. His father had done the rest. In such panicky times, people were extremely suggestible, particularly those in high office. And on that cocky high he had said to Chamu, I fixed Shyam, I fixed him for good.

The shendi cart was just the thing, Mylaraiah assured him. They had done right in not pursuing the matter. Besides, if Vishwanath Rao found out that they had been making 'enquiries' about him, he might get offended. They had reported to Rukmini that all was fine. As for the boy's mother, about whom Rukmini had been so particular, Shivaswamy had written that she was a good cook, a woman who ran the large household of dependents very capably, so Kaveri would live like a queen—she'd have no work to do.

In her last few days, as she drifted in and out of consciousness, Rukmini called her husband close. She had two questions to ask. Why, she asked him, was his coat looking so shabby, he who was always impeccably dressed and why had he stopped wearing his white trousers. He seemed always to be in a dhoti of late. And then she swallowed painfully and closed her eyes and whispered, 'Is it true, tell me the truth now. . .' But she could not bring herself to say it. Or perhaps she was too tired. Was it true, she wanted to ask him, that he had made over their best-yielding paddy lands to Vishwanath Rao? And about the boy? Was it true? Had he known?

Then she called Setu, scrabbled for the collar of his shirt to pull herself up to his ear and whispered, 'Keep an eye on your sister. Take care of her.'

1987

*M*y *adamantine friend. . .*

You are a jewel among women—I admire your intelligence, your sensitivity and your skill in argument. Permit me to say that I find your feminine radiance inspiring. I am sure that your energy, if guided correctly, could be used to the right purpose. You would be the ideal helpmate for a certain kind of man—a man of passionate ideals and avowed direction. I cannot measure up to your fictional heroes and I have nothing to offer but my complete devotion. I can never provide a soft and coddling life, the kind that you are used to. Life with me will be khadi, not silk. That would not matter to you, I am sure. Will you wait for me?

Yours. . .

P.S. Forgive me my lapses in letter writing. This is the first time I have written a letter like this.

I know this letter by heart now, I can rattle it off in my sleep. And still every time I read it it prods me afresh. I am saddened by its cowardice—the letter is not addressed to her nor has he put his name down to it, in case he was asked to make good, I presume. I still flinch at the colour of the ink. The paper is so coarse-grained that the purple ink has mapped its way across in tiny rivulets and blotted several words out;

the handwriting is small and cramped, just like its writer, I imagine. It is such a scrap of a letter—it was just by chance that I found it among the soap wrappers in the Finlay's tea tin. I could easily have missed it. And now the letter lies in four pieces, which I piece together, like the origami game I used to play as a child, when I want to read it. 'Adamantine'—a flashy word, ungenerous, a double edged sword. A letter full of conditions and disclaimers—ready to take back even before it gave. She was a jewel among women but as hard as a diamond, she could inspire a man he granted but her energy needed his guidance. While he was full of passionate ideals and avowed direction, she would have to stand behind him, the rock-solid helpmate. He sounded pompous and self-important and presumptuous and censorious too. For a man who offered little other than his devotion he asked for too much. Even if I were a queen I wouldn't care to be told that my life was soft and coddled. A girl as spirited as she had been, deserved better.

But, the letter improved on acquaintance, that I must admit. The last two lines redeemed him for me. Despite his worldly stand, he was an innocent, just like her. Here was an awkward man, but a man undoubtedly smitten, a man a little afraid.

The torn fragment of the picture I found along with the letter—the masked woman with the whip and the white thigh— I have identified as the remains of a film poster, the film is *Hunterwali* and the actress Fearless Nadia, a circus girl-turned-actress who played the swashbuckling rescuer—Phantom, Zorro and Spiderman rolled into one; newly reclaimed feminist icon for she did her own stunts and was known to have thrown a man across her shoulder and walked the length of a moving train; ironically, the daughter of an English soldier, who was turned into a symbol of the freedom movement by her adoring fans. It pleases me to think that Kaveri thought it worthwhile to save half of her.

Sometimes I sense her so strongly that I can almost see her. I know her well, an intense, imaginative little girl growing up playful, confident and passionate too I should think, for she had induced an unbending kind to blubber. I believe I look a lot like her, the glint in the eye and the chin that lifts a little too high.

For a long time I puzzled over why a girl like this gave up, why she ended up hostage to destiny. I eventually found out what actually happened—my father's cousin Chamu was only too happy to supply the 'facts'. But 'facts' never add up to the whole. But this I know and cannot forgive; my father had a hand in it. He could have helped his sister from slipping away. But again, for that perhaps he would have had to be a different person.

Part IV
Deliverance

Part IV

Deliverance

1947

Many a morning Kaveri had lain in her bed watching the creatures that chased across the ceiling, till she realized that they were cobwebs, a whole ceilingful of them, rippling in colourless waves, like a goosebumped shiver down the spine, in the morning breeze. It was only the westerly sun that reached her room, so her mornings were dark and the same morning breeze that sent the cobwebs a-shiver, brought in the smells from the garden, most overpoweringly of the drain outside her window, a narrow mossy channel that ran right up to the servants' and women's gate. She knew she ought to get up and close the window but she felt too tired to move—in any case it was pointless. Moreover, the sharp metal edges of the bolts and channels on the window hurt her fingers —the tower bolt on her door was cruel on her knuckles every night. It had rained the previous night, the sky was still a bulging grey, so even if she got past the scummy drain to drink her morning's coffee in the garden, everything would be wet. Scum and slippery wetness, she saw it and felt it and smelt it everywhere in the house—even the kitchen was full of large open vessels with a thick soft sedimented crust of yellow cream on the sides, from being boiled over and over again— every morning she shuddered when she saw it. What would Rukmini say, was her first thought, or as she corrected herself, what would Rukmini have said, for Rukmini was dead now.

The cancer had been insidiously eating away at her insides, when all along she had been accusing Achamma of putting too many Guntur chillies in the food.

She could lie like this behind the closed door the whole day, she knew, and no one would bother her or bother about her. She was expected to do nothing in the house—nothing, except rest and amuse herself; if the servant came to sweep the room she could dismiss her—sometimes, the only thing she recognised of herself was her skill at being sharp with servants. If her daughter cried—this sniffling, restless creature who would wake up soon—one of the women would come in and take her away, which was such a relief. She wondered at the sundry collection of women in the house. Of course they had been there in her house as well, the collection of poor relatives, mostly women, who had stayed with them for years at a stretch, the procession of cousins and aunts in the summer. But they had been gentle creatures and had kept to the periphery of her life, the grey background against which she had shown off her colour—including the mad aunt who had gone berserk one evening and then died in the night, like a star that burns itself out in a spectacular blaze.

Here, of the sharp, watchful women, she had come to recognize two of her father-in-law's sisters—harpies, shaven widows whose self-appointed task it was to keep a jealous eye on what they imagined to be their brother's interests, and two younger women of indeterminate status, probably her mother-in-law's relatives, whom she had offended by presuming they were servants. They thrived on discord and strummed its strings every morning, experimentally, just to keep their hand in. After all, no servant was beyond rebuking. They were afraid of her, Kaveri could tell, for they couldn't go very far with her, but they believed in testing the waters and if they failed in riling her they could always be hostile. The moment she stepped out of her room they would fix their eyes on her— *Why beast, why have you come out of your lair*? Earlier, they used to ask her what she wanted, but now they ignored her— *No new tricks to show us*? She too, in turn, did not speak to them unless she wanted something or had an order to issue, 'I want the tonga to be brought round at three in the afternoon, I'm going out.'

She had learnt through her mistakes. She remembered the look on her father-in-law's face the first morning when she had walked into the verandah and reached out for the newspaper—his newspaper. Later one of the harpies had told her that the English newspaper and the verandah—the only part of the house where the sun came in the mornings—were the preserve of the men of the house. The women had the back of the house with its separate entrance, and the Kannada newspaper, all to themselves. Her insistence that an English newspaper be brought to her at the back of the house had been met with disbelief, till her mother-in-law had granted it with a shrug, as if to say these were tiny, impervious flailing fists against an implacable wall that destiny had erected.

When had she first sensed it? When her mother-in-law had sat down at the banana leaf her father-in-law had got up from, the very same one that he had eaten out of, pushed the pile of leftover curry leaves and red chillies to one side, and begun her meal on it. She had exclaimed involuntarily that she hoped she was not expected to do the same thing and her mother-in-law had paused, hand in mid-air between leaf and mouth, and said no, *this* they did not expect of her. And she had caught the women exchanging happy glances.

There were many things that made the harpies smirk—that she put her mouth to the rim of the tumbler she drank water out of, instead of pouring it from above, that she bit into a banana or a kodbale instead of breaking it off with her fingers, thus contaminating the whole object to be eaten with her spittle *before* it entered her mouth, but what made them hiss with disapproval was that she would not sit 'out' when she had her periods. How were they to tell then, when she got pregnant?

Her daughter sniffled on the bed next to her and flung one thin leg out of the blanket. She averted her eyes from her, this the fruit of her love-making, when her husband still remained a stranger. Other than the three days they had spent together in Mysore after they had just got married, part of the large gaggle of relatives, she could count the number of times he had been with her on her fingers. He would disappear for days together, 'on tour' as her mother-in-law tersely explained, and then suddenly appear one evening. Finally, she had fallen back on the ultimate tragic feminine gesture of protest, she had bolted her door on him. In the early days of her marriage, sometimes at night she would hear his voice in the front of the house, talking to her father-in-law, and she would rush to secure her door, the stiff, sharp-edged conical tower bolts notwithstanding. Then she realized that it was not necessary, for he never tried to come in. His gold-rimmed glasses were still grave, the half-moons on his onion-pink nails still promisingly delicate, and she knew in her treacherous heart that all she needed was to hear the knock. She would unbolt the doors immediately, no matter what. But he did not knock, and she came to realize that he was a visitor to the house.

She had confronted her mother-in-law one morning and all the women had come scurrying into the kitchen, their eyes bright with anticipation. But her mother-in-law had led her by the elbow into her room and shut the door behind her.

'He is busy,' she said, 'I told you he tours a lot. His is a very responsible job. Sometimes he stays over in his office.' And then, catching the look on Kaveri's face, she stopped. 'Men, by nature,' she said, feeling her way about, 'are very different, not house-bound like us. . .Is there anything you need? Are you not comfortable? Are we not doing enough for you? Are we stinting on anything?'

But Kaveri was not listening to her. 'Does he have any . . .habits,' she asked, thinking of her uncle Shivaswamy and his hip flask.

'Of course not!' Her mother-in-law was shocked at her crudeness. 'My son neither smokes nor drinks.'

'Look. . .' her mother-in-law said shortly and then searched for the right words, 'We have only one son and you are our chosen daughter-in-law. You know what our standing in the community is, you couldn't have even dreamt of better. This house, everything we have is yours. . .of course, it is up to us to keep our men in hand. You must do your bit. . .behave . . .' she broke off impatiently for she was getting no help from her daughter-in-law. 'You cannot be so obtuse, so adamant . . .you must be more amenable. . .you must understand. . .'

'Understand what?'

'Why can't you be more. . .more. . .*womanly*? Did nobody teach you? A woman's lot. . .'

'I was not taught that her lot is different from a man's.'

'You speak very well, you have an answer for everything, but what's the use of it? I don't see how that is going to help you. Rukminiamma always was. . .well, that's what comes out of being too refined. . .' She stood at the window, her back to Kaveri. And then she turned round and looked keenly at Kaveri.

'Do you know what our scriptures say about the qualities of an ideal wife, the kula dharmapatni?' she said. 'I'm sure you don't though it is the duty of every mother to tell her daughter this—*karyeshu daasi*, be his hand maiden. . .*karneshu mantri*, a sage minister giving him good advice. . .*rupecha Lakshmi,* as beautiful as Lakshmi, the goddess of wealth and well being, with all her graces, of course. We wanted an educated girl from a good family, so we compromised on the colour, but you have very neat features. . .*kshamaya Dharitri*, as forgiving as Mother Earth herself. . .*bhojeshu mata,* to feed him like a mother. . .' She had hesitated before elaborating on the last quality but she came out with it, '*shayaneshu veshya,* to please him. . .like. . .' she couldn't bring herself to say the word 'whore', 'like the apsara Rambha. . .you will see, things will be different when you give him a son. . .'

She broke off for her daughter-in-law had begun to laugh, and laugh hysterically.

'You mean it's my fault? You're asking me to use my feminine wiles on him?'

'No, my dear girl, what I meant was you'll have to be as patient and as forgiving as Dharitri herself, to be a true kula dharmapatni. The future of this household is in your hands. I will not be around forever. . .'

'I don't want to be a kula dharmapatni! I want to go home, right now!'

Her mother-in-law had let her cry her heart out, there on the bed, her face to the wall. And then Kaveri had felt her gentle touch upon her shoulder and heard the infinite pity in her voice. 'Of course you can go. I'll order the tonga round right now if you like and send for your train ticket. You will even have a servant to escort you. But how long will you stay? This is your home now. You will be cared for. You may not believe it but I am your friend, I wish you well. . .Be patient. . .all will work out for the best.'

Cry as bitterly as she may, there was no denying the truth of it—this was her home now. She had no money. Her mother was dead. She would have to ask them for her ticket and the tonga to go back home, to go anywhere at all. Besides, her father would not countenance a married daughter returning home except on specific occasions and that too with the full formal panoply of clothes and gifts and an entourage to drop her home and pick her up.

Her father visited—with tired newspaper bags of fruit, his turban limp, his black coat bulging open at the stomach where a button was missing, his eyes elsewhere. She joined in her mother-in-law's show of hospitality, urging him to stay for lunch, reaching out for this jar of pickle and frying that special sandige and when it was time for him to leave and he turned to ask her how she was, she said, 'Fine, I'm fine. All is well.'

There were certain things that her mother-in-law was particular about, that they appear at weddings and family occasions together, where he came in his gold-edged silk kurta— that false friend from the photograph (as for the dog, there was no sign of it)—and she wore a selection of her now vast jewellery. But that too was fast becoming rare. She remembered their last outing together, to her home, to visit her mother when she was dying, where with all piety he had touched

Rukmini's feet, reaffirming in gesture that he would cherish her daughter. Kaveri had been big, enormous actually, with child then and her mother had been happy to see her. 'Good, a child will bind the two of you together,' she had said and Kaveri had just smiled.

At her mother's suggestion she had visited her old friend Kalyani, who now taught at the Mahila Vikas Samsthan, a girls' school of repute. The school was part of the samsthan's larger social rehabilitation activities and Rukmini was keen that Kaveri should be part of the samsthan. Kalyani was assistant head mistress of the school and warden of the hostel, despite her young age, she was just twenty-two. But in that sparse room with its grid-iron windows and bare board of a table, Kaveri had confronted a woman to whom all approaches were closed. She could not strike a match on their remembered childhood and watch the sulphur-head of memories flare; even the fatigue of relentless experience had not weakened the hinges, Kaveri could not get her foot in the door. She had met a stranger, her hair pulled back, her forehead and neck and wrists bare, her sari pinned on the *outside* to her blouse with a large, uncompromising safety pin; twice widowed but still childless—relieved once of a young husband on the day she had got married and the second time of a middle-aged man with grown children. Education, Kalyani's demeanour seemed to suggest, was for women who could not do better.

And as she sat there on the hard visitor's chair, she had seen herself as Kalyani must have seen her, with her eight-diamond earrings and her sixteen tola gold necklace, the vermilion brand of marriage ablaze upon her forehead. She had felt the silken folds of her sari carelessly between her fingers a willing accomplice in her self-deception, and realized how clever her mother-in-law was. She had not said, don't go to the Mahila Vikas Samsthan, that splendid organization, refuge of abandoned and unfortunate women, you who are married into one of the richest families in the community, you who carry the mark of your male protector on your forehead and round your neck, despite your raw bitten lips. Kaveri's mother-in-law had got the measure of her daughter-in-law, to know not to forbid her from anything, for then Kaveri would surely do it; she only had to wait for Kaveri's initial flail of protest and then for her sensibilities to recognize the truth of the situation. And so they faced each other, the two of them, Kaveri and Kalyani, old friends, newly striated and differently lacerated, the protective moult of their childhood buried behind them. There was nothing for her here, Kaveri had realized; like elsewhere she would become an object of curiosity.

Sometimes she wished she had her mother-in-law's habit of prayer, but she only read the newspaper. Her brother's letters came to her, disembodied voices from the outside world. But of what use was it all, Kaveri wondered, for nothing was certain, even the newspapers contradicted themselves. For one day they said that Bose's Indian National Army and the Japanese were coming to free the country from the British and the next that Subhash Bose had disappeared. *Disappeared*? One day that India was free, the British were gone and the next that Gandhi was dead, *shot*. Had he fallen in the dust, she wondered, the whites of his eyes showing, his spectacles smashed, lying at arm's length from him.

She had thought that if there was one thing that even babies knew instinctively, it was the certainty of being loved, of being wanted. And here as she lay on her bed in the narrow room where even the sunshine was uncertain, in this house of cadaverous, watchful, banana-breaking women, the only certainty she knew she could depend upon was the secret voice in which she spoke to herself. Sometimes, she found herself floating, high above in a distant space, dissociated from everything. Was this the state of equanimity that the saints craved, where all was one; hot and cold, sweet and sour, day and night, good and bad, kith and kin and strangers, your left foot and your right so that slippers were interchangeable, and your head the same as your feet, so that you could walk on your head?

twenty-two

1955

Illness, an astrologer Setu's grandmother had once taken
him to see against his mother's wishes, had told him, would
change his life. Illness would change everybody's life, his
grandmother had said dryly. They didn't need an astrologer
to tell them that they would all die one day. Illness and death
had always been there, if anything they had been more in
evidence when he had been a boy. He himself had been lost
almost, to typhoid, he remembered his sister alternating
between tears that he would die and gory descriptions of the
carbuncle on his head. But what the astrologer had not specified
was that it would be the illness of others that would intrude
so dramatically and so completely upon him.

He tried to recall when they had last been 'normal', his
sister still the teasing companion, his father still the man he
knew and his mother healthy, and he, still the boy who thought
a public demonstration the extension of a backyard game.
The year the war broke out, the Ganesh Chaturti celebration
in his house had been really grand. The house had been full
of people, he had hidden his sister's book—*The Three
Musketeers* it was—under the parijata bush and had clean
forgotten about it and it was reduced to pulp in the rain, there
had been so many kargadabus frying in the kitchen that they
had thrown them up in the air and aimed slingshots at them.
In the evening, a procession had left the house, Timrayee

carrying the idol of Ganesha and he, Setu, ringing the bell and shouting himself hoarse as they danced all the way to the pond. That year Ganesha had been immersed and he never came back, not the clay idol at least. The next year onwards, his mother had said that the silver idol would do; they would worship him and keep him at home, she hadn't the energy for the festivities that a clay Ganesha involved.

Then Kaveri was gone and he was in Intermediate College with only Ramu still left among his friends, Chapdi Kal having joined his mandi merchant father in the family business. During his two years in the Intermediate College Setu had learnt of necessity to spin fast, furiously and simultaneously in different orbits. To college, where he had begun to enjoy his maths classes and back home to the smell of disinfectant and bulletins of hopelessness. He made trips to Vellore with his mother and he had watched her waste away and become thinner and thinner, till on her deathbed she had become so thin that he could carry her like a baby. And it was he who had kept a grip on reality then—it had become his sole virtue in those days, the ability to just keep track of things—a virtue he did not want to lay claim to. He had become his mother, the mistress of the household. The servants had started coming to him for instructions, and gradually, money as well. Shall it be pumpkin curry today? Achamma would ask in a whisper and Ranga would touch his forelock and say apologetically that the cattle shed door had rotted clean away or that the calf was surely sickening for something and the vet had to be called immediately. When he walked in the cornfield at the back, it brought back no memories of the games he had played, not even the cat he and his friends had hanged, he was intent only on inspecting the crop for termites.

His father, his implicit touchstone in everything, the master of the house, had alternated between pacing the corridor outside Rukmini's room and travelling to Bangalore and meeting people in anticipation of being confirmed as the government's advocate—when it was clear to the meanest of wits' that he had lost the race. He had been pipped at the post, the job going to a man whose caste was on the ascendant and Judge Vishwanath Rao had smoothly changed horses mid-stream, abandoning one protégé for another. At one time the term 'government advocate' had been bandied about so much in their house that it had become their favourite game. Kaveri would drape her mother's sari round her shoulders and march up and down issuing severe pronouncements to 'clerks' and harsh punishments on 'criminals', with him cowering on the floor, as both 'clerk' and 'criminal'. His sister, well, she was married and did not count now. She had come to visit once, with her silent, grave, handsome husband, and kept a vigil by their mother's bedside.

'If your leg aches, Setu,' she had told him, 'don't fold it backwards from the knee. Try folding it forwards. It helps.'

He would see her again only three years later and to his long letters from Calcutta, he received only monosyllabic replies on a post card and sometimes not even that. Write to me, she said, your letters and *The Hindu* are all I have.

Calcutta, the city he had always wanted to live in, claimed him for the next five years. One of the last decisions his parents had taken together, apart from Kaveri's marriage, was that he should go to Calcutta to specialize in statistics. Your uncle, whose aptitude you have inherited, went there and he says you must go nowhere else, his mother said. He knew she had dreams for him. A Ph.D. from Cambridge like that fabled uncle, and like the famous Ramanujan himself!

But as always his timing seemed to be wrong. Between the pre-Independence riots and the post-Independence influx of refugees, and his father at home, he managed to graduate with a high first but had to abandon his post-graduation. Out Cambridge, goodbye Ramanujan.

'Today, classes at the university were disrupted,' he wrote to his sister. 'We joined a protest march against the trial of the INA officers.' As the procession had made its slogan-shouting way from Dharamtala to Dalhousie Square, at Lalbazar, the police had attacked them with lathis and opened fire. 'This is the real thing,' he wrote to his sister. 'You see fervour in the raw on the streets here.' Later in the evening, a military truck, along with its black American driver, had been burnt close to the students' hostel and he had heard it burst into flames. From the terrace of the hostel they could see smouldering fires in several places. And then in August of 1946, the city burnt again when the call for 'Direct Action' to carve out their portion of the country was given by Jinnah and the Muslim League. 'There are bodies on the tram tracks on Rash Behari Road, close to where I live, and I have seen people searching the pockets of the dead, for their ration cards.' He had actually gone past the ill-fated Kamalalaya Stores, recently burnt and resurrected, as it was being looted and burnt again, but like the Phoenix it was sure to rise on its ashes as it did after every communal riot. But she need not worry about him, he reassured her. The arrangements in the Keyotalla Lane flat where he now roomed with a Mysore family were pukka, he said. They were prepared for any attacks. The men waited on the first floor with revolvers—why, he could fire a .38 himself—the women on the second floor, while the spill of oil on the ground floor made sure that any intruders would slip. Of course, there was the incident when poor Ghosh babu, unable to bear the 'tension' had let off his revolver. What a commotion that had caused. And all the wrong people had slipped on the oil. He had been on two rescue missions already, going in a truck with the Sikhs of Bhowanipore from their gurudwara, armed with knives and swords, to places where they received SOS messages from. Every workshop in Calcutta, Setu wrote, was busy hammering swords and spears into shape, and the women had turned their skill at blowing conches, usually exhibited at weddings, into sending riot-alert messages.

The Setu of old surfaced in the letters home, the show of boyish bravado to conceal his anxiety. To one of his letters assuring his father that he was safe and classes would resume soon, his father wrote back saying that Setu's fish in the cement totti were safe too and that it was a myth that frogs ate fish, for there were frogs and fish swimming side by side in the tank. But the lotuses were withering away, he was sad to say.

At first he was bewildered by the enormity of change in his father, then the thought of him made Setu impatient, driving him at times to a white hot rage. Rukmini's death had been hard on all of them; often, Setu woke to the sound of her footfall and heard her call his name in the dark, and stayed awake the rest of the night. Mylaraiah may have lost the government advocate's post, but he still had his practice in town. But he seemed to make no effort to resist the tide, to reassert his mettle. Setu had a good mind to throw in his father's face his lectures about duty above everything else and iron in the spine, the staple diet of Setu's childhood, ideas that he had grown up on and had come to believe were as natural as the air he breathed. In those early days after her death, Setu would tell the unfamiliar grizzled man who sat at the table in the coffee room, his shirt front stained with food, 'Anna, you must shave before you leave for the courts in the morning.' After that, his father had taken to sitting in the verandah and reading out the newspaper and expounding his 'death of the nation with the departure of the British' thesis to the semi-circle of attentive servants at his feet.

Each visit home brought new evidence of the rot that was setting in—white ants in the book cases, tiles missing from the roof and snakes in the garden. No servants, no one to light the evening lamp, and no dogs. For the first time, the house was without dogs. His father seemed to be managing, but barely. His eyes still stared a little vacantly, but his black coat was not shabby and his shoes were polished. A distant relative had been installed as housekeeper and she seemed to be taking care of him, only she had quarrelled with the servants and sent them away.

'I am talking to Darcy Riley, about that post,' Mylaraiah nodded assuringly at his son.

'Anna, why don't you talk to Narayana Rao, after all he's a minister now.'

'Narayana Rao! That upstart! There was a time when I did him favours. And I doubt whether he can do anything at all. No, I'm talking to Judge Riley, don't worry.'

'Who,' Setu asked Balarama, the only one of his father's clerks who was still around, 'is Judge Riley?'

'Darcy Riley, an old-time British judge,' Balarama smiled wanly, 'long retired, gone back home. Must be dead by now.'

'And does my father still go to his chambers?'

Balarama looked out of the window and cleared his throat. 'His partner manages the practice,' he said at last.

A scholarship to do his post graduation bought him a further reprieve from home. He had lost time; his graduation had dragged on and so would his post graduation, but he was glad to get away. His father seemed to be managing in his own way. In fact, the scholarship had made him happy. In a brief moment of complete lucidity, his father had become his father again and had patted him on the head, as he used to, when Setu had been a boy and had managed to please him by doing a simple thing like running to the corner shop and buying him a nib. But Setu was back home within two years, without taking his degree, summoned by his uncles and the widowed aunt who had been installed in his home to look after his father. His father, it appeared, needed to be taken firmly in hand.

The summer that Setu came back for good was particularly beautiful; every tree in town must have been abloom. The copper pod and the rain tree in his own compound greeted him as if he were a hero returned from the war. Each government office in town sported the flag of the newly independent nation—bands of white, green and saffron with Ashoka's chakra of peace in blue in the middle, a variation of the flag that Narayana Rao had been arrested while attempting to hoist and Shyam Kole had given his life for. It seemed to matter little, what they had done; it had passed like everything else, whisked into a void. Men of greater stature had met more bizarre ends in pursuit of their flags. Subhash Bose was lost, quite literally, somewhere in China or Central Asia, no one knew where for sure, in pursuit of his tricolour with the springing tiger in the centre. Gandhi had not attended the ceremony when the new flag was first hoisted; he saw little sense in the celebrations when the bloodbath of Partition was barely over. Moreover, he had wanted the original flag with the charkha in the middle, which he had considered the symbol of the struggle for freedom. But his displeasure was to no avail. His job was done and he was out of the reckoning and soon enough an assasin's bullet would save him from further disillusionment.

The house was in shambles. The tiled roofs of the cowsheds at the back and the store rooms had fallen in and there was nothing left of the coconuts and the grain. The gate hung indecisively on its hinges, tempting those who had not originally intended to come in. The garden had become a thoroughfare between the main road in front and the cross road at the back, and all kinds of people loitered in it, helping themselves to whatever was handy. Once he found his father deep in conversation with a stranger in his office room; it was only after the man had left that Setu realized that he had managed to take the coat off his father's back and the slippers off his feet. There were government officials on the prowl too, jealously guarding the rights of the new nation, eyeing the house, convinced that it would be better off as the new irrigation or land records office. Then too the slew of litigation started, from people claiming their right to Mylaraiah's various lands, for despite being meticulous about the cases he handled, Mylaraiah had been careless about his own records, often leaving things entirely to his clerks.

Balarama had left and Achamma had retired, too old to cook. All the servants were gone and what had precipitated the crisis was that the last one, a young woman, newly inducted into the household, had thrown herself into the well at the back. His father, who had now given up his practice completely, had refused to see the police, for he still believed that it was his clerk's duty to attend to such things. He would meet the inspector general and no one else, he said, and there was no convincing him that he had no clerks left. All Mylaraiah did now was to set off promptly in the morning in the direction of the courts and hang around in the Udipi coffee house all day, sitting majestically at one of its tables and holding forth on his pet themes to whoever would care to listen. Very shamefacedly, the proprietor came to Setu with the bills that his father had run up and not paid. And yes, he was acquiring quite a reputation as a coffee house sage.

At the end of a day's stock taking and sorting out, Setu would sit in the sagging, eternal wicker chair on the verandah, in the discouraging shadows of twilight, telling himself that this too would pass and he had only to concentrate on the tasks on hand and things would come back to normal. If he was sometimes besieged by a strong rush of feeling, he allowed himself to shed a few tears and then he found that he was ready to confront the next crisis. Had he been less prosaic, he could well have seen his misfortune as part of a grand tragedy; if he could have articulated that strong rush of feeling he could have said that the claims of his family and the destiny of a nation had conspired against him. All he knew was that he should guard against the lead settling in his soul.

'Your father needs a proper doctor. Take him to Bangalore,' his uncle told him. 'You could get a teaching job in a school, it won't be too bad. Or you could run the factory my friend has. He's looking for someone he can trust. The money will be a lot better than the teaching job.'

Of course; in action lay the answer. There was no point getting sentimental or fatalistic about things. That was not his normal bent of mind, not his naturally sunny, solution-seeking disposition.

'Excellent idea,' his father said when he was told they were shutting the house down and moving to Bangalore. 'It has been my life's ambition to breakfast on the *dumrote* in Modern Hindu Hotel every morning. There is nothing to beat it. Make sure you take up a house nearby. Let us move to Bangalore at once.'

Even in those early days when he had just moved to Bangalore with his father, he still had the feeling that there was hope. It was more than ten years since his mother had died and he had had to close down their home. He must be the only factory accountant, he often thought wryly, with an aborted post graduation in mathematics, a course that he had had a scholarship to pursue. There was a time when he had thought he could follow in Ramanujan's footsteps! But destiny deals with an uneven hand. You have to make the most of what you have been given, that Setu had come to accept. When his tonga trotted through the broad, tree-lined roads and the air was cool against his face, he felt his senses quicken; he was young enough for that. There was his father, yes. But there was also the boulevard of South Parade, the city lights and the cinemas. The Tommies still cruised the cantonment area with pretty Eurasian girls hanging on their arms. He liked the girls in their short dresses, their pomaded hair and bright red mouths. All is not lost, they said to him, where's your spirit?

Ah well, Setu told himself, so long as you did not allow your mind to dwell on what might have been. His father he had now learnt to cope with. But there was also his sister. And there he stumbled. He wished his father had been more of a help there but he drew the line at a cheery, 'How is Kaveri doing?' To which Setu could make no other reply than 'Fine, she's fine. I had been to see her just the other day.' Until it became an unvarying routine. So much so that his father soon had to just raise his eyebrows and his hands and Setu would supply, 'She's fine,' and there the matter would end.

Every visit was the same. Things did not get easier. On those days, circled in red on the calendar, the circles growing fewer in number with successive calendars, he would start telling himself all would be just fine, right from the morning. But at the mere thought of it, even as he saw himself walking down the pathway through those ornate gates, a feeling of helplessness overcame him.

This was the house of the man who had been the chief justice of the state, a prominent pillar of the community, a man whose reach was long and who had the ear of those in power. Within those ornate gates, the very air seemed to grow columnar, standing at attention in the presence of such compelling majesty. After it grudgingly gave of itself for him to breathe, and Setu proceeded, a little short of breath, there was the watchman's salute, the deference of his gesture belied by the flash of curiosity in his eyes. The next step in his disarmament was the library, draughty, dusty, with uncomfortable chairs in which he was sure no one sat, the shelves lined with intimidating law tomes, where his sister's father-in-law, the retired chief justice, would make him wait. That was a calculated move on the old man's part and Setu never failed to rise to his expectations, for when the judge made his entry, he would find the young man sitting hunched up in the worst chair in the room—the wicker chair with the protruding nail, which could be depended upon to send away any one who sat in it with a right-angled tear in his coat tails—too intimidated even to look around the room or study the titles on the spines of the books. Resplendent in his starched, gold thread-edged turban, the judge would slip into his role of potentate and Setu, despite himself, into that of grateful, humble retainer.

The opening comments were always about the state of the nation. 'What is Nehru doing to this country?' the old man would ask and proceed to answer it himself. Setu was expected to do nothing but nod. Then there would come the parade of names. 'I was lunching with Nijalingappa the other day . . .Your Narayana Rao's days are numbered. . .useless man, can't get anything done. . .people can't be expected to remember your freedom struggle sacrifices forever, you know. . .' And once the way was smoothened, would come the solicitous enquiry about his father, the cue for Setu to ask about his sister. At that, with a sigh and a heave and a change in tone, the judge would say, What can I say, we are doing our best. And the awkward silence that followed would be broken by his sister's mother-in-law, rolling in the trolley with the refreshments. It had always struck him as incongruous that this household should have a trolley but he had also paused to wonder why in a house full of servants, it was the woman of the house who had to bring it in. Right through the plate, spoon, tumbler and napkin-giving ceremony, (he had to admit, her badam milk was unbeatable, he had never drunk anything like it), she would creak and sigh around him, making it very clear that whatever hospitality she was extending to him came at great physical cost to herself; she had had plenty of buffetting on the high seas in her days and it was time someone else, like a daughter-in-law for instance, took over these duties of hers.

He had already been outwitted, he knew; he was going through the motions of a game where the fall of the dice and the fate of the pawns had already been decided. But there was so much ceremony to the charade, such an intricate web of etiquette through which he had to pick his way. One (false) solicitous enquiry about his father was exchanged for one (false) solicitous enquiry about his sister—your rook for my castle, and in the process he would have forgotten about his inert and circumscribed king, till the wretch toppled over. Every time it was the same. He could never bring himself to mention the unmentionable, the real thing, for every time he looked into the judge's eyes he could read the warning there; beware, it said, don't go too far, you are the dandelion in my hand and it is so easy to snap your head off.

And by the time his hostess had finished with him, plying him with exquisite food and drink, and managing to convey her immense tact and her suffering, he was almost convinced that they were in the right. They were good, noble souls and perhaps he should go home right then.

But of course, he would not be allowed to go. For after that he would be conducted through the dark maze of rooms to the back of the house, escorted by a retinue of women. As he stood in his sister's doorway and tried to talk to her the women would peer over his shoulder and make encouraging clucking noises at him. Sometimes, she would talk to him but that was very rare, as most of the time she would just lie on the bed with her face turned to the wall.

And amidst all those women was his niece, a thin girl with

scabby knees who scratched her head all the time, whose eye chased him with the nakedness of a raw nerve, only to look away when he caught it. When he looked at the girl, he felt the fervour of his mother's fingers as they had scrabbled at the collar of his shirt and he smelt her failing, sour-scented breath as she had entreated him, 'Take care of your sister', and with a sinking heart he knew—and this he knew very clearly— what it was that he must bring himself to do eventually. And that, if the truth be told, was what finally got him.

In time he came not only to depend upon his desires being thwarted but even perhaps to do what he could to thwart them himself, well at least to side-step them. Forearmed, he told himself, is forewarned. He wished for things in a lukewarm way, so that he need not work to make them come true. Soon the kindling of a wish and its dousing became simultaneous and from that it was but a matter of time to think that desire was meant to be extinguished—that was the way to equanimity, the state of mind in which all things appeared to be the same.

Part V

Post Script

1987

It is a tradition in my family to name its girls after rivers. My mother is named after a lost river, of which no traces can be found now. A Himalayan river—ice-fed, perennial, with no fear of going dry, lends her name to me; my great-grandmother too had the same name. But Kaveri is a straightforward commonplace name. Every family in the state of Mysore at one time had a daughter named after the river, the goddess whose life-giving waters were being harnessed to provide for a future writ large in letters of gold. While driving to the city of Mysore once, when I was a still a child, the car rattled over a bridge and looking below all I could see were rocky outcrops, some with full grown trees, separated from each other by streams of sand marking the course of a river. Of the river itself, if a river means water, there was no sign. A few buffaloes drank from pools, which had formed in the shallows of the rocks in the river bed. So when my father proudly said, '*This* is the Kaveri,' I could only stare.

Those brought up in apparently quiet families where nothing happens on the surface, but a river of disquiet runs underneath, have a curious ability. While they learn early to limit their world, to shut out things that don't concern them, their antennae lie dormant, to pick up the slightest adverse signal, like a virus in the blood stream that leaps to life the moment the body seems preoccupied. My parents did their best all right, by keeping quiet and lying low, hoping that a semblance of normalcy would be the thing itself, that a placid surface would be proof from tremors.

I remember a meeting with one of my professors in the college campus. Those were my desperate days, I was desperate to get out of home, and she, the professor, was advising me on the universities I could apply to and the courses I could choose from. There was a clump of trees on one end of the grounds and we made our way to it and chose a sprawling ficus, and sat on the cement platform built around it. We commanded a view of the landscaped grounds, framed by a stone pavilion roofed with a pergola. The sky that morning was blue and the air, vitaminously healthy. A creeper trailed through the ribs of the pergola. My professor was happy with me, my performance and my manner; I suppose I embodied the promise of youth, of confident new womanhood and she possibly saw in me what she would have been had she been born a generation later. I had done quite brilliantly in my exams, so bending a proud gaze, now proprietorial, now maternal over me, she was telling me that I could get into a good American university and was discussing the relative merits of the various universities, their aid packages and their programmes. And there, as I thanked her for having first introduced me to Stephen Hawking and she spoke about the advances in particle physics, I saw a squirrel lying fast asleep. It was sleeping on the mud just behind where my professor was sitting. She was sitting with her back to the tree and I was standing in front of her and all through our conversation, I was aware of it and was absurdly pleased—it added the right touch to the conversation—and was about to remark on how trusting the animals on the campus had grown of humans, when I realized that it was dead. It was so close behind her that if my professor leaned back to make herself more comfortable or stretched her hand, she would touch it. It was lying in perfect repose, its tail curled round its body, only the spot of blood at the bottom of one closed eye, catching the sunlight like a bubble of blown glass, suggestive of an unnatural, violent end.

My days were like that then, with an undertow beneath the placid surface that threatened to pull me in; only I could see the ruby-red eye.

It took me some time to figure out that the woman I had caught a glimpse of when I had accidentally visited the hotel-hostel with my mother those years back, of whom the only memory I clearly carry is of calloused soles and cracked heels against a blue bedsheet, was the same as the girl who had underscored the lines that had moved her in the book; the girl who had thought that her fervid pleas in the margin could change the pre-ordained course of the characters' lives, that she could will differently the course of a pre-scripted world. She was not the kind to buckle down tamely—she had had the spirit to pin up the picture of a daredevil stunt woman, and it had meant enough for her to preserve a fragment of it but when she had been given a half chance to change the script of her own life, if the testimony of a blotchy purple scrawl were to be believed, she had refused it. But then my memory plays tricks on me for I also think of her as the girl in a white tunic, with whom I had played awhile on a red cement slide, whose unusual face I remember clearly. This, then, the gentle creature whom my mother had not wanted to bring home, and who had died in the front room leaving it permanently smelling of floorwash, was my grandmother—my mother's mother, and my aunt—my father's sister. I must have been around fifteen by the time I figured it all out and it explained some of the whispered confabulations of my childhood. My parents had been perfect conspirators; I had not known a thing, except that sometimes, just sometimes, I felt I had a film of prickles over my skin, and I had a faint suspicion that the eye that watched over us was a red-flecked bubble of spittle.

'Why didn't you tell me?' I demanded of my mother with all the indignation of a teenager who believes that everything of consequence that will happen to you is encoded in your childhood. Freud was popular in the 1970s.

'Tell you?' she seemed truly bewildered. 'What is there to

tell, and that too to a child. . .' These are things to be hidden, she seemed to imply. Tragedies must be played out and suffered softly and quietly.

'What happened?'

'What happened! Even if I did tell you what happened, it wouldn't be what actually happened,' my father said, getting up to go out of the room.

'Surely I have a right to know what has happened in my family. . .'

'No, you do not. You have not lived through it.'

'Don't,' my mother begged, dropping her stitches, 'don't do this to him.' As if she had nothing to do with it.

The house with its dark-red stained floor and its small closed windows trapped me in; when I came home for the vacations I took to hiring a bicycle and cycling round and round our area—I was not allowed to venture too far. Perhaps it was then that the seed of flight was resolutely planted in my mind, how long could I keep on pedalling around known streets, where neighbours looked at me strangely and asked my mother why I talked to myself as I went past their houses. I was reading Simone de Beauvoir then, in my fifteenth year and the irony of reading *The Second Sex* with my newly discovered circumstances cutting so close to the bone was not lost on me. And yet I also listened to Neil Diamond telling me in a seductive baritone that I'd be a woman soon, soon I'd need a man. That was also the time I read whatever I could lay my hands on on mental illness and the human mind. When I was not pedalling around or reading or listening to music, I would churn things in my mind, thinking up of things to bait them both with, these two who had thrust me by their silence into a theatrical melodrama of the worst sort, the sort you watch on screen and cry about even while telling yourself that such things can't be true, that these are only devices to help you live out your worst fears vicariously.

When I went back to school that final year, I brooded over it. I dropped a round-bottomed flask full of concentrated acid in the chemistry lab one day and watched the black leather

A Girl and a River

toes of my right shoe melt away before my eyes and the floor at my feet smoke, hiss and crater. The teacher was so alarmed that she forgot to fine me.

Finally, overcoming my distaste for him, I wrote to my father's cousin Chamu and asked him about Kaveri, and no, not that same old weak nerves and habitual Mysore inertia story again, I said. Weak nerves and vapours were the preserve of old ladies and maidens in English fiction. I wrote to my mother's Brahma Kumari cousin as well. She took a long time to reply but when she did, she asked me to concentrate on God and my studies. People tended to talk too much, she said. She herself had been on a long mauna vrata and since she had forsworn speech, she had not been able to write earlier.

Chamu wrote back amazingly quick. Shadenfreude was a word I had not yet come across but when I read the letter I understood the emotion perfectly. He did not know if it was the truth, he said, he was only telling me what people said and what he had heard. He also added that he had not told my father he was writing to me. Your father's family had everything, he said, but then Mylaraiah got too greedy and Rukmini, too complacent. They had reached above themselves and got Kaveri married off into the best family in the community—the only hitch was that the boy was already married. You couldn't discount the nerves, he said, because people said that the shock of discovering that her husband was already married must have sent her off. The man was married to a Japanese beauty, employed by the maharaja as a translator in the cultural department. People called them Beauty and the Beast—she so fair and exotic-looking and he so dark and well. . .They had met when he was asked to teach her Kannada. He had three children by this woman, three girls, and had got married again at his mother's insistence. He was not to blame. He was a good man and his family was renowned for its acts of charity to distressed women. Everyone, *everyone* had known about that business with the Japanese woman except your people, he said. Of course, Kaveri had always been acknowledged as the daughter-in-law of the house and people said she could have been happy if she wanted to. Such arrangements were not unknown. Even later, she was very well taken care of. And yes, Chamu had added, he had converted in order to marry that woman. So Rukmini's romance with the Methodists had come a full circle. Only, she hadn't been alive to see it. And one more thing. It may not have been just this Japanese woman thing that could have sent Kaveri over the edge. You could not blame her husband entirely. There was some talk of Kaveri and a freedom fighter type. The man had got killed in a demonstration. Mylaraiah had seen to it. Ask your father, Chamu had written. He was complicit in everything, a mere boy though he had been, in getting rid of his sister's suitor and in arranging her marriage to a married man. Of course, none of this would have happened if Kaveri had married him, Chamu, as his father had suggested to Rukmini for his was the very first proposal she had received. But Rukmini had been too proud. Of course he didn't believe what some people said that my parents—her brother and her daughter—had abandoned her. Made off with her money and consigned her to an asylum. There was no denying it, Chamu said. There is something in your family. The slightest untoward thing unhinges you people. Mylaraiah too. . .Why don't you ask your father. . .

The relish with which the letter had been written was unmistakable, especially that bit about Rukmini. He seemed to have bided his time to say it, and he probably would not have had the courage to say it to my father. I felt a mild regret at my transgression, I remembered my father calling him a 'bounder', but he was no help, my father. There was no other way I could have found out.

So, he had been the writer of the purple letter—the 'freedom fighter type'. I thought of the lukewarm declaration the letter contained, a half-measure from a reluctant man who would always put his 'cause' first. However, even the half chance to subvert her future had been lost to her. The man had gone and died.

In the showcase in our house, a bejewelled Ganda

Bherunda—the crest of the royal family of Mysore, has pride of place. It is plated in gold with real rubies for the eyes of the two birds (the rubied eye seems to be the letimotif of my script). The Ganda Bherunda, a shawl and a scroll are evidence of my paternal grandfather's loyalty to the Wodeyars. My father is very proud of those mementos—it is strange how he can be simultaneously reverential about Churchill, Gandhi and 'His Highness!'. My mother's grandfather too, I believe, was a high-profile judge, chief justice of the state. I thought of how unevenly they were matched, a cabal of hefty men and women in blue who could carry anyone away kicking and screaming and a serious little girl, her funny face frowning, her large mouth a moue of concentration as she looped her l's and curled her c's, quaking self-righteously at fictional injustices—'Murderer-stone', 'Don't marry Dora!'—little aware of the invidiousness of real life. I know the book by heart, each smudged pencil line, each childishly scribbled comment, the crackle of the onion paper when I turn the pages especially those that have turned stiff with, I imagine, her tears. And as for the purple letter, it now lies in four parts. Whenever I want to read it, I fit the pieces together.

'You could have brought her home. That was what that Brahma Kumari cousin of yours used to hint at all the time, isn't it?'

'We had a child at home to bring up.'

'You sent me to boarding school.' Dumped me there quite unceremoniously too.

'She left you a lot of money, didn't she, and property . . .'

My mother would say nothing to me but look strangely baffled as one would if a stranger had suddenly started throwing stones at your house.

Those were the days when my tongue was a whiplash. 'And you,' I would ask my father from time to time in different ways, 'what did you do for her?' Other than making sure she was safely out of sight. Don't scoff at the Mysore predilection for prevarication, Chamu had written, cowardice runs in our blood in many different guises. Did you know, I would tell my father, that there was a time when 'fools' were shipped across the seas to other places, far away from their own, and some were known to have made their way back, like intelligent, faithful dogs. Towns in Europe made money by exhibiting their insane and inviting people to throw stones at them.

'Don't you dare speak to your father like that!' This from my mother, to whom my father speaks as he likes.

They are in it together, this incestuous pair, part of the grand conspiracy of silence. They say nothing in explanation or in defence of themselves. All that my father would do, undoubtedly, was recommend coffee, for coffee is known to calm the nerves, cleanse the bowels of wind, to absorb excess water without heating the body. I would also recommend to him soap, eaten plain, and cold water baths.

After school, our ways practically parted. My father wanted me to do maths, but I chose to pursue physics, despite dire warnings that it was very difficult and all that I could hope with the results I'd get was a job as a schoolteacher. But then I like explanations, figuring things out and here was a subject where the simplest of physical systems were analysed and understood, where the world could be reduced to an experimental problem in a lab or expanded to study the cosmos. Moreover, I am gifted with brains and also the ability to apply my mind relentlessly to something when I want it badly. And I wanted right then to get away from home. Not just go to any old place but somewhere where I could go in a blaze of glory. I topped the university in the subject and got the gold medal—you've inherited your father's brains, an old timer told me, and your family talent for maths and science, much to my annoyance, adding, I hope you have better luck than he had. In my years at college, I made a systematic study of all the universities in the US, which offered the courses in theoretical physics I wanted, the scholarships they offered, and worked out the details about the work I'd have to put in, the sort of testimonials, the proofs I'd have to offer of my mettle. Father protested mildly that I could do research 'right here in the Institute of Science', but shrugged and gave up in the face of my resolution. You are like my mother, he said, as determined. So, I got my brains from him and my determination from his mother. What, I wondered, would I inherit from my grandmother, his sister?

It was at its height then, the dull discord of our daily life, and by implicit understanding we stuck to those transactions that were absolutely necessary, speaking to each other only when it was unavoidable. That was the time when I spoke to my parents only when I wanted money.

twenty-four

1987

Even as I longed to get away, on the reverse was the need to see things in black and white, to establish cause and effect, to which I also attribute my love of whodunits, those with a clear plot and structure and characters whose motives are unambiguous. As meticulously as I planned my career and groomed my plans for the future, I launched on the search, the unravelling, which didn't get very far. I stumbled on most things by chance.

I discovered the house she had lived in, the house my mother grew up in. It was quite funny, the way it happened. Right through my college years, I had been following various slender threads—Chamu, as usual and his distant leads, trying to locate the house when my mother pointed it out casually to me when we were driving in that part of town. As usual she would say little else, except that she did not remember.

'I just grew up,' she said, 'there were a lot of women in the house and it is easy for a child in a houseful of women.'

What women, I ask. Oh an assortment of relatives, she says. In some houses you have them around, widowed sisters and aunts. I am grateful to them, she adds, they took care of me. I can almost read in parentheses, they kept me safe from her. And what became of them, I ask. If I ask, what became of your father, my grandfather, I know the conversation will end immediately. I don't know, she says. I never went back after I got married.

It was a large shabby property, which had obviously been partitioned and sold off in bits. It was now part house and part office, two multistoreyed offices in fact. One part of it had come to her, my mother says blandly, when the property was eventually partitioned. That is her way of pointing out that her father had done the right thing by her. One of those office buildings has paid for my American degree, the part not covered by the scholarship, for my airfare to and fro, off and on. So I too am pinned into the heart of the conspiracy. I get a share of the spoils. I want to ask her, was this what it was all about, all those undercurrents, but I know she will say, what undercurrents, you must have been imagining things. Always, her loyalty to my father and to hers too, I could say, has been absolute. And to her mother too. Perhaps, as she says, she really didn't give it too much thought, she just went through it day by day, event by event, seeking the comfort of things that would bloom gratefully under the toil of her fingers, things like applique work pillow covers and cross-stitched table cloths or even a garden. I have belatedly tried to understand how it must have been to be brought up by a houseful of indifferent women, to go to a school round the corner—I don't think she went beyond high school, my mother—and then everlasting gratitude and loyalty (and perhaps even love!) to the man who married you but who does not bother to mask his indifference to you. But I find it difficult to sympathize with those who have almost willed themselves into their circumstances and shift drearily through; it is like going through each day of you life with a low grade fever.

I took to walking in Lal Bagh, reconnoitring, looking for signs of human habitation in that bombed-out shelter, speculating on the family I might have had—I imagine meeting girls in kimonos and white pancake make-up, like the women I saw in 'The Last Geisha'. I had asked my mother, fresh from Chamu's letter, whether she had kept track of her sisters. What sisters, she had shrugged, I was an only child.

In my third year of college, I visited the house. I just

walked in one afternoon.

The gate creaks as I open it. The office buildings are cut off from this still-residential bit by a high wall. There is a name on the stone plaque on the wall outside, too worn away for me to read. There are no dogs. I walk unassaulted to the door on the side of the house, past a narrow, scummy channel with a thin stream of putrid water flowing through it. It really smells. I have chosen to come in the afternoon, when the men will be away. They cannot possibly know that I have walked on the uneven pavement opposite this house several times, waiting for time to ripen.

A young girl in school uniform opens the door and I tentatively explain my mission to her. Behind her I can see a large black stone-paved hall, empty except for the odd bits of furniture on the fringes.

'A girl has come,' she announces, with no preamble, 'asking about the Number Four who used to live here.'

A few more heads appear in the darkness, a household of women. They ask questions. Who am I? I stick to my explanation. I am making enquiries on behalf of a friend whose grandmother used to live here. We are studying together, this friend and I. As the girl looks me up and down, eyeing my trousers, the others speculate on Kaveri's identity. I am lucky that the women are artless and they like to gossip. People with a little more self-awareness would have asked me to leave or at least have been more guarded. But I suppose it doesn't matter to them. It makes for a welcome diversion before they resume their evening's chores. An elderly woman, whom the rest call Doddakka, says that her father-in-law's brother's family used to live here at one time, and they had a daughter-in-law whom they used to keep confined to the room at the side. She had heard a lot of stories, of course she hadn't seen her herself, she only knew what people said at that time. The poor creature, 'it' she says, used to wander all over the garden—the garden used to be huge before it was partitioned—even in the pouring rain, completely unmindful of it. But such people are like that, she adds. They do not feel the cold or the heat, hunger or thirst, they do not know if it is night or day.

'I believe she used to lie in her bed and read English novels, all day long; and do no work at all. . .'

What do you expect, she means, when you live in an imaginary world, your emotions being wrung by second-hand sensibilities, your nerves being subjected to make-believe destinies, when you withdraw more and more from the real world.

She had heard that it began when her child was born. The sight of her daughter used to drive her into a rage. 'A woman's womb is a funny thing,' Doddakka says gravely. 'It isn't fixed firmly to the body. It keeps moving and that drives women mad.'

She apparently grew so bad that they had to shut her up. She started running away—twice they brought her home from somewhere in the city. 'As long as her mother-in-law was alive, they kept her here in that room, but as soon as the old lady died, they sent her off. . .'

'Who sent her off?'

'Her husband. But he could not have managed it without her brother's consent. Together they put her away, her husband and her brother. . .'

No, she knows nothing of his 'other' family. There were rumours about that too, but no one spoke openly about it. Not that she had heard.

As I come out of the house, the setting sun in the trees hits my eyes directly and I am blinded. I rest my head on the gate for a moment and breathe in the strange mix of the fragrance of champak flowers and the sour smell of sewage. My feet are leaden, I do not want to leave. I wish they had not told me that my father had signed the certificate, condemning her forever to Number Four. *Number Four?* Now I get it. It is a reference to the bus route that used to go to the mental asylum in Byrasandra. This will not do. I cannot go around hunting like this and ending up feeling dizzy and sick—it cannot just be the large tumbler of boiled tea that they gave me.

Unreal problems demand surreal solutions. I had to find other ways of cracking this. I had tried going back to the asylum—the hotel-hostel of my childhood—armed with a name but found no records, no histories, no leads of any sort; any that had been there had most probably been deleted with the inmate's death. (I couldn't imagine my parents keeping them as mementos, to remember her by.) Moreover, it is no longer an asylum but an institute of mental health. The buildings have multiplied but the old stone building, colonially solemn is still there as also the rain trees and the garden with the lover's lane, but the people in white are no longer in evidence. It was then that it occurred to me, vaguely, that I should get someone to find out for me, someone neutral and to a person hooked on whodunits, the first thing that would come to mind would be a detective agency. Of course, we did not have a Pinkertons or even a Hercule Poirot, but we had the Globe Detective Agency which advertised its services for 'surveillance' and 'information gathering' with a discreet gun as its logo.

1987

I am late, unforgivably late and I cannot curse myself enough. I took the wrong train and had to retrace my path by *taxi*. I can't understand how I could have made a mistake when everything was so clearly laid out in the map before me. I had to travel from section 94 in the grid to section 67, from Heathrow Airport to the British Museum where we had agreed to meet. I had checked my instructions several times, Terminal Four and then the tube from the station. This was the first time I was venturing into London, but I knew them all—King's Cross, Marylebone and Regent's Park—I had bought them all up at Monopoly, I couldn't get lost in a place I knew so well.

I wonder if she will still be waiting for me. I had picked the British Museum as it doesn't charge for entry. By the tantrik Ganesha, in the Indian section of the museum, we had agreed. I have fine-tuned this meeting for months, having anticipated it for years. On my way home from Chicago, I would stop by at London and meet her. It would be ridiculous, after having broken my journey, after all the trouble with the visa to accommodate this detour into the city, if I were to miss her. This is my only chance for on my way back I plan to take the Pacific route. I was already beginning to regret this. There was nothing that she could tell me, nothing more than what she had written to me about.

'Ella King?' I put out my hand. 'I'm sorry, I caught the wrong train.' I launched into a long explanation about routes and my general stupidity in reading maps, giving us the time to size each other up.

She had brown hair and a red mouth and was wearing a dress of some dark green stuff with matching low-heeled shoes. A brooch of distinctly Indian design, green stones, emeralds perhaps, of the familiar mango pattern, was pinned on to her dress, above her left breast. Her eyes behind her black framed spectacles waited for me. Now I know why I wanted to meet her so desperately. I have always imagined that if I see someone who has known Kaveri unawares, untainted by the future, I will know what Kaveri would have been like.

'So you are the author of *Sailing on the Hoogly*,' I said, as I searched for something to say, 'At last!'

'*Tales by the Hooghly*,' she corrected me, '*Sailing on the Ganges in a Rubber Boat* is another collection. It came later.' She had a soft accent and a low pitched voice.

'Yes, yes of course.' I had read the book so many years back that I barely remembered it now.

'My books have been out of print for so long, it's nice to meet someone who still reads me.'

I stared at her. Of course, there had been more books than the one with the ghastly cover. Clearly she was expecting a reader, a *fan*. She had probably been a moderate success as a novelist at some time and had now sunk (deservedly, if her one book was anything to go by) into oblivion. I remember the list of publications her publisher had sent me had other titles and I racked my brains trying to remember the names of her other books, at least of one more, correctly.

'They are trying to reissue my *Brave Hearts of Rambaug*.'

'Yes of course, *Brave Hearts of Rambaug*. I loved that one,' I said, unwisely.

'Really! Where. . .how. . .?'

'Shall we go outside? We needn't talk in whispers then. We can stroll on the grounds or sit in the park opposite.' And even as I said it I realized I had no money to take her anywhere, not even to buy her the pancakes that I had seen a man selling outside. All my precious pounds had gone on the taxi.

'Ella King,' my father, blessed man, had said turning the brittle pages of the book with the lurid cover when I had pestered him with it. 'Must be Dr King's niece. I remember she had come down a couple of times. My mother and Dr King used to be quite thick—a lady with light hair riding on a bicycle. She used to smoke in the dining room and that used to really annoy the cook.'

It is such incidental salvos that I have always locked away for future reference. I must say, my father is replete with memories of the cook.

'Miss King. . .Ella,' I took a deep breath. I had to be out of there in fifteen minutes. 'Do you remember, in the town where your aunt lived, she went on to be the Chief Medical Officer of the general hospital there—you must have gone there for your holidays. . .'

'Once. I just went once. I told you that in my letter. My aunt died a long time back, almost as soon as we returned from India, which was in 1953, I think. I had to wait to publish the Hoogly stories because one of them is based on her life—the one about the English girl and the maharaja's secretary. It happened when she was in Baroda. Of course, they never married and the child she had was stillborn. All my stories. . .'

'Yes, but do you recall. . .' I am not interested in her aunt. I jog her memory, I toss names and places at her. Did you keep in touch with her, I want to ask. Who were her friends? What sort of a girl was she? Was she as sharp as I imagine she was? What was her life like? Do you know who wrote her that purple letter?

But she can remember nothing.

It is too slim a thread to go by, I know and have known all along, but it is all I have. Given my father's refusal to remember, my mother's intransigence and Chamu's lip-smacking judgements, all I can depend upon are the tangential observations of acquaintances.

She cannot recall the town or the people she met there. Her aunt obviously was peripheral to her life. All she can remember is going to a wedding and seeing the groom getting washed away—but that too she remembers because she wrote about it. The woman you are looking for, was she the bride?

No, I say, she was not the bride. I am certain of that.

'People ask me, or they used to, whether I'd made up my stories, they can't. . .couldn't believe such things could actually happen, but every one of them is true. You know the one about the soldier and the brain fever bird, that was Captain Milcher of the Fifth Dragoons. . .'

I hear her out. It's only fair. I cannot tell her that this is my last trip home and that I am counting on her to tell me things about myself and make me whole. I cannot tell her that I have tried all these years and am now tired of it all. I want to set it at rest and wash my hands of it and never see them again. So I ask the right questions in the fifteen minutes that remain. Her one regret is coming back she says. So was it her aunt's. They had no idea it would be so cold and rainy and so tough, no servants and what with heat being so dear. The only thing she could do was write about the life she had left behind. She had not married, presumably. There was no ring in evidence and her name had remained the same, which had helped me find her.

I thank her and bid her goodbye and can see that she is disappointed. She probably expected me to ask her about herself, the avid fan trying to delve into the depths of her writerly imagination. But still, she has had an airing after thirty years and she might not get a chance to talk about her books again, ever.

It struck me then that I might never find what I was looking for, that I would be dogged forever with those niggling feelings of uncertainty. I had my future ahead of me, and I couldn't go into it with that frame of mind. I had a life to build, a change of citizenship to effect and three men dangling after me—a Japanese American (it must be sixth sense I think, my prefiguring the Japanese connection); an Italian (it's true, all that they say about the Latin lover) and an Indian (whom I will definitely dump). It was there in the unreal and vastly removed environs of my university, gluttoning on gangster films and detective fiction that I made up my mind about the Globe Detective Agency, an address in that most official of roads in Bangalore—J.C. Road, named after the last maharaja of Mysore, and wrote to them. It had such a melodramatic feel to it that I began to enjoy my correspondence with them— piecing together the discrete bits of information I had about my family. The first thing I would do on reaching home was to go to J.C. Road and meet the man behind the discreet gun. Once the case was closed I would move on and never look back. I would cut myself loose from the baggage of the past. As for my parents, I was going home to bid them goodbye.

closure

The first thing you learn about stories is that they must have a beginning and an end. When I was a child, all stories began, 'Once upon a time' and they ended 'they all lived happily ever after'. As a child too, I remember refusing to get up from my warm cinema seat till 'The End' flashed with dramatic reassurance on the screen. People, I now know, are untrustworthy narrators. They are either indifferent or forgetful or they spin things the way it suits them. I have gathered a clutch of stories, about the same person, but each with its own beginning and ending. To the women in the old house, Kaveri was an interesting footnote, a woman who had willed her own end; to Chamu she was the whipping boy in his story of the family that had somehow managed to breast the tape at the finishing line ahead of his own and had got the comeuppance it deserved; she was the ghost who hovered in the background of Ella's story, never to come to life. To my mother and father she is no story but a life they have endured. To the Brahma Kumari cousin, she was irrelevant—perhaps I should have listened to her and concentrated on God and my studies. But I too have a Kaveri story that deserves an ending. Few stories end happily I know but each deserves closure, for ends to be tied, for the connections to be complete. All I needed now was to lay to rest the aborted narrative so that I could go in peace.

I have lasted almost three months in my parents' home without a single quarrel, nothing major that is. My parents too are kinder to each other, I notice. I am none the wiser, no closer to clearing up the debris of the past. I feel more charitably towards them though, especially my father. In these three months I find that familiarity has crept upon me unawares. Possibly it is because their routine is so unchanging, they are so settled in their hole, a square peg and a shapeless pebble abraded to fit the angles of the peg. The associations are most unexpected—waking up to a certain slant of light in the morning, the smell of freshly ground coffee and in the afternoon, asafoetida seasoning in ghee—I must be careful of becoming a child again. Even as I unbend towards them, I cannot stray from my course. My future is elsewhere, I don't quite have iron in my soul but I can taste the rust on my teeth.

I have been hard at work. By now T.P. Muralidhar, my local Sam Spade, and I have had several meetings and he assures me that he is making 'good progress' and well before I leave he will 'produce results'. But by now I have given up hope. There is just a month left for me to go back and he has unearthed nothing, though I have been paying regularly for all his false alarms.

I have not yet told them that this is my last visit home and that I will not be coming back, at least not for a long time, several years perhaps. Every time I begin to tell them, I stop. I cannot bring myself to say it. Perhaps I will not tell them at all but go back and write to them. They are beginning to be openly proud of me, I see that. No, not for another two weeks, my mother was telling someone from her bhajan group the other day. My daughter, you know she is a research associate at Chicago, she's also had offers from Wall Street as a financial consultant, well she is here for two more weeks and I want to be with her. But being with me meant sitting silently in the same room with me and looking up anxiously every time I got up to go out of it. My parents still have very little to say to each other or to me. Mother has turned religious of late. She has started visiting a nearby ashram with her friends and is part of their bhajan group. My father, of course, has an instinctive suspicion of anything that smacks of the religious. Every morning since I've been here, my mother has asked me what I want to eat, so that she can ask the cook to make it. She and the cook spend long hours in the kitchen drying, roasting, grinding and mixing spices for me to take back. The dining room is full of little heaps of ground spices set out to cool before being packed into plastic bags. My mother loves to hold a candle to the mouth of those spice bags and watch the edges melt and blacken and curl. Then she will label each one so that I can distinguish one packet of red-brown powder from another. My father and I have exhausted all conversation in the first few minutes of my visit, all civil conversation that is. I have told him all about my courses—nothing that I haven't already written about in my letters, but it is a safe topic as he can understand the work I am doing and that sees us through the minimum required conversation. But our long drive to his ancestral house—the house that had disappeared into thin air—has almost wrecked our fragile peace. I have begun to be tart with him again. Domesticity—those little bags of curry powder and shopping, has saved us, my mother and I.

And then, unexpectedly my Sam Spade—T.P. Muralidhar of the Globe Detective Agency—calls me. He has unearthed the remains of my grandfather's 'other' family. He calls me at home, excitedly, telling me he has located a 'survivor'. I avoid my mother's questioning look and go to his office, for much as I disregard my parents, I cannot let them know this. I haven't been able to convince them that the only way of laying things to rest is by digging them up by the root; or that I am doing it as much for them as for myself.

The 'other' woman, it turns out, returned to her native Japan a long time before my grandfather's death—I was happy to note that she deserted him. She also left him their three girls. Of my mother's half sisters, the eldest was untraceable—probably dead and the second one lived abroad and never visited. Muralidhar has located the third one. Her name is

Lucky Milton. *Lucky Milton*! For one moment I almost agreed with my mother that it was best not to know more—she has always maintained that she did not want to know and did not care what happened to her father's 'other' family. She, Lucky, was divorced from this Mr Milton, had no children and lived alone in a flat in one of the by lanes off Double Road and ran a travel agency.

I had found myself a new travel agent now.

For the return ticket, I would go to the Milton Travel Agency and deal only with the proprietor. Madam came only on Thursday and Saturday evenings, the girls at the counter informed me. One Thursday went by and there was no sign of Madam. I drove past the crowded lanes parallel to Double Road, where balconies of flats overlooked an open drain, but I could not locate the flat. On two days, a Friday and a Saturday, I found I had 'work' in that direction and just dropped in at the agency and though my ticket was ready, I would not take it. Madam would definitely be there on Saturday evening, the girls assured me.

And once I meet Madam, I decide, I will play it by the ear.

Come with me when I go to collect my ticket, I tell them. You rarely get out of the house. We will get the ticket, stroll in Cubbon Park, have an early dinner—there is a newly opened Chinese restaurant—and come back home. I don't know if they like Chinese food and I am sure my mother will want to know why they charge us so much for strange smelling rice, and that the cook could have fixed better at home for one hundredth the price but I won't let that bother us. Over the soup and the noodles, I will tell them that I have no definite plans to come back, so why don't they come and visit me instead. Maybe I would add, you could book through this new travel agency; after all it is run by a relative—your sister, I would tell my mother.

When we enter the office on Saturday evening, she is there. I look in her direction and look away quickly. I don't want to see her yet, I want to push the moment as long as I can. I go instead to one of the assistants. I fill up a form and she checks all my documents. Then she asks me to see Madam.

Madam is wearing a nylon sari and in her sleeveless blouse her arms are plump and fair. Her short hair stands stiffly black on her shoulders and her mouth glistens.

'Yes,' she says and I look into her grey-green eyes.

She looks at the sheet of paper in front of her and I wait for her eyes to settle on the column that has my address and my mother's maiden name. I anticipate her reaction. I hope she will start, catch her breath and look up in confusion. Of all the scenarios I have run in my head, this one is my most favoured one—dinner in a setting of Hollywoodian sentimentality, a casual announcement, surprise, disbelief, initial denial and then curiosity, a tearful reunion of sisters. I will have to take them by surprise. All will end well. They will talk about their father, and who knows, perhaps about their mothers.

She runs a manicured forefinger down the form, not pausing at the column where I have filled out my mother's maiden name. Her father's name, including the characteristic family middle name, juxtaposed with another, does not cause her finger to falter. For the first time it strikes me that she too might not know about my mother, or care.

I feel a rush of anger. Wait a minute, I want to say. That there, the name you so casually ran over, belongs to the woman sitting across the room on your sofa, glancing at your travel brochures, your sister. I am furious to be trapped like this between them—my mother, whose tired, trusting smile I catch across the room, this fat woman across the desk, with spreading hips and cellulite specked arms, and my father, who as usual has refused to come in and is pacing the corridor outside. I feel so helpless, so tightly wound up that my hands and feet tingle; I would so like to be whipped off a string and spun on the ground like a top and whirl my anger away, coming eventually to rest on my side.

Outside the long glass-fronted windows, I can see the darkening sky and the sudden breeze whipping up the dust into spirals. My father is standing in the driveway leading to the main road, empty today of the usual office traffic, as it is a Saturday. The wind sends his trousers flapping and blows his hair askew and even as I watch, he bends and strikes an instantly recognizable pose. He looks up, squares his shoulders and pats the ground with his bat as he waits for the ball to come down the cement driveway. He watches the ball spin through the air, and as it comes up to him he looks ahead and drives it straight past the bowler, freezing into position with the blade of his bat held in front of him, looking down to see whether his feet are placed correctly; and I watch his eyes as they follow the ball all the way as it goes across the ground for a four.

As I follow the ball to the boundary I see the crowd leap to its feet and roar, I see the boy in the sixty-year old man, I see a life lost and reclaimed, a life given him in dribbles. I sense the shadows of other worlds, worlds I have not known and have no inkling of, except that I feel their chill and shiver in their gloom, out of their sun.

Then I see my mother. She is poking in the ditch outside and has come up with a plant, something she will plant in our garden no doubt. She catches my father's eye just as he strikes the ball and smiles.

I remember once, in the days when I had swilled freshly with self-righteous anger, I had asked him what he had done for his sister, and he had replied—I did the only thing I could, I married her daughter. And I had had the grace to feel ashamed.

How audacious one gets, I thought, when assured of love— love unchanging and unconditional.

When you have lived through things, he has tried to tell me, you cannot sum them up, for then you would be reducing your life to nothing and there would be no hope.

How can I think that it is all a matter of air space and road lengths, of airports and bus terminals, of distances in the sky and kilometres on land? Wherever I go I will carry them all with me, a book with underlined sentences and pleas in the margin, my lost schoolboy of a father, my ostrich-with-its-head-in-the-sand mother, even this raddled woman across the table, and of course, their taint of madness.

When I had first arrived at Chicago, I had been terribly homesick but loathe to admit it in my letters. I had written about the weather, my courses, the food and the friends I never had. In the first package my mother sent me from home, among the pickles and the pudis, there were four rolls of incense sticks, the ones that were always lit at home, morning and evening. I have been lighting one every day in my room over the years and each day, as their mild fragrance spreads through the air, I bless the manufacturers of that brand of incense sticks for their constant hearts or their lack of enterprise, whichever it is, for the perfume has remained unchanged in the past twenty years. And each day I breathe deep the fragrance of my childhood, the subtly invading perfume which has now become the odour of my body.

Lucky Milton is holding my ticket out to me. I thank her with a smile and put it into my bag. I pat the sleeping dogs and bid them lie. Outside, it has grown dark. My father has stopped playing cricket and come home. My mother has started to look anxious again, and is reminding me to check whether something or the other is in order.

'No time for a walk,' I say and see them staring at me because my voice is trembling. I clear my throat. 'Let's go straight for dinner.'

acknowledgements

This book is a work of fiction that owes much to family reminiscences and lore. I thank all the members of my family—immediate and extended—for making the effort to remember and answering my questions patiently.

Of my many readings, I owe a special debt to *Swatantra Senani Talakere Subramanya (jivana mattu sadhanegalu)*, by T S Visweswaria; *Modern Mysore: From the Coronation of Chamaraja Wodeyar X to the Present Time*, by M Shama Rao; *Mother India*, by Katherine Mayo; *The Dust in the Balance: British Women in India, 1905-1945*, by Pat Barr; *Netaji: The Man, Reminiscences*, by Dilip Kumar Roy; and the collected letters and articles that appeared in *Young India*, 1927–1929.

READ MORE IN PENGUIN

The Chosen
Usha K.R.

Her familiar existence disrupted after her father's death, Nagaratna is forced to move from her village to the semi-squalid environs of Vitthala Colony in the city of Bangalore, where her brother lives. A former village that has been engulfed by the expanding metropolis, Vitthala Colony retains some of the 'primitive' characteristics of a south Indian village. It is the bastion of the lesser tradition, for here live Plague-amma, the goddess who was created when an epidemic of plague swept the land, and Nallikai Swami, a no-nonsense swami named after the four gooseberry trees in his compound.

Trapped in this world with people whom she sees as leading truncated lives, people with thickened sensibilities and no hope, Nagaratna yearns for 'something uncluttered and noble and fulfilling'. And then a job in an exclusive ashram school allows her to glimpse a world where the human state of grace has been restored, a school emblematic of the restraint and good taste inculcated by a more sophisticated awareness . . . Nagaratna is transfigured by the life it offers and the people she meets, and most importantly, by the love she believes she has found.

Set in southern India, shifting between Bangalore and a fictional French protectorate on the western coast where the ashram is located, *The Chosen* tells the compelling story of a young woman torn between who she is and who she wants to be.

Fiction
India Rs 295